MASTER OF HER DESIRE

Garnet couldn't bear Drew's being so close, couldn't bear the wicked, delicious thoughts he inspired.

Drew stepped within an arm's reach of her. "What you really want is for me to do this," he growled. He grasped her shoulders and pulled her forward, his face angling down, his lips brushing against hers.

Garnet pulled back, breathless. "You attempt to take advantage of my confusion, sir."

"You've already taken advantage of my generosity," he shot back. "Seems a fair trade to me." His hands moved decisively, capturing her slim waist.

Then he kissed her with no hesitation, kissed her, touched her, teased her. And soon Garnet was soft and pliant, molding to Drew's desires and demands. . . .

HEARTFIRE ROMANCES

SWEET TEXAS NIGHTS
(2610, $3.75)
by Vivian Vaughan

Meg Britton grew up on the railroads, working proudly at her father's side. Nothing was going to stop them from setting the rails clear to Silver Creek, Texas—certainly not some crazy prospector. As Meg set out to confront the old coot, she planned her strategy with cool precision. But soon she was speechless with shock. For instead of a harmless geezer, she found a boldly handsome stranger whose determination matched her own.

CAPTIVE DESIRE
(2612, $3.75)
by Jane Archer

Victoria Malone fancied herself a great adventuress, but being kidnapped was too much excitement for even Victoria! Especially when her arrogant kidnapper thought she was part of Red Duke's outlaw gang. Trying to convince the overbearing, handsome stranger that she had been an innocent bystander when the stagecoach was robbed, proved futile. But when he thought he could maker her confess by crushing her to his warm, broad chest, by caressing her with his strong, capable hands, Victoria was willing to admit to anything. . . .

LAWLESS ECSTASY
(2613, $3.75)
by Susan Sackett

Abra Beaumont could spot a thief a mile away. After all, her father was once one of the best. But he'd been on the right side of the law for years now, and she wasn't about to let a man like Dash Thorne lead him astray with some wild plan for stealing the Tear of Allah, the world's most fabulous ruby. Dash was just the sort of man she most distrusted—sophisticated, handsome, and altogether too sure of his considerable charm. Abra shivered at the devilish gleam in his blue eyes and swore he would need more than smooth kisses and skilled caresses to rob her of her virtue . . . and much more than sweet promises to steal her heart!

MASTER OF HER HEART

TERRI VALENTINE

ZEBRA BOOKS
KENSINGTON PUBLISHING CORP.

ZEBRA BOOKS

are published by

Kensington Publishing Corp.
475 Park Avenue South
New York, NY 10016

First printing: June, 1990

Printed in the United States of America

DEDICATION

To Heather and Miranda,
my daughters,
for all of the sacrifices you have willingly made
so Mother could write.

A special thanks to you, the reader, for without you there would be no reason for me to write my books. I hope you enjoy reading this one as much as I did writing it. I would love to hear from you. Write me c/o Zebra Books.

Prologue

Monterey, California
September 1870

The ghosts of his past came round about to haunt him. Bain Carson snatched the note from the Chinaman's outstretched hand and read the familiar scrawl with darting gray eyes.

"Mr. Drew, he velly sick. He say you come right away."

"Where is he, Ling Chow?" Bain's strong, square jaw tightened with apprehension and—yes—dread as he read the single sentence. "If you don't come, brother, I'll tell Nattie the truth."

"At the wharfs. His ship dock only few moments ago."

Bain nodded, turned to gather up a lightweight jacket from the hall seat, and followed Ling Chow out the front door, across the wide porch on the front of the house, and down the steps into the street.

Damn him. His brother always was the one to stir up trouble at the most inopportune times. Thank God Nattie had returned to the ranch earlier that morning and wouldn't know Drew's ship had arrived in port. She would have wanted to fly down to the wharves to greet him. Instead, he would have a few days to assess the situation and hopefully send Drew on his way before she demanded to come back to town.

Pushing his fingers through his dark hair, bleached on the tips from many hours in the California sun, he hurried after his Chinese escort. Chances were he'd find his brother as healthy as ever. Drew had used similar ruses in the past to force Bain to meet him on his own turf. Usually his needs were unvarying—money.

At the wharves, he followed Ling Chow to the pier where Carson Shipping leased several berths on a yearly basis. The *China Jewel* was anchored, the gangplank already extended, and its proud lines looked weatherworn, the long voyage from the Orient apparently having taken its toll.

"This way, Mr. Bain," the Chinaman directed, pointing toward the gangplank.

What was Drew up to this time? Usually these meetings took place in a wharfside tavern, upstairs in one of the private rooms. There he'd find his brother sprawled on a bed with a serving girl and more drunk than sober, declaring he'd been out to sea much too long and his desires needed tending to. The fact that he was still aboard ship left Bain to wonder. He frowned. Perhaps this time, Drew really was ill.

He followed Ling Chow across the deck and down the companionway into the long corridor connecting the half-dozen cabins. A stench rose up to greet him, the smell of rotting seaweed and tar that always seemed a part of ships, a part he'd just as soon forget. To Bain the smell of freshly cut hay or newly turned soil was much more intoxicating—a scent that was power and fulfillment all wrapped up together.

"Where the hell is that damn Chinese?" The indignant roar issued from the cabin at the end of the corridor—the captain's quarters.

"Mr. Drew velly angry at Ling Chow." The little

8

Chinaman began to tremble.

Bain touched his shoulder and squeezed, trying to convey assurance. "It's all right. Go on home. I can handle him from here."

Ling Chow nodded gratefully, and dashed toward the stairway leading to the upper deck. Bain watched him go, then turning with a sigh of resignation, he approached the portal prepared to deal with his drunken brother—God help him—his twin, identical at least in appearance. They looked so much alike, even close family friends had trouble telling them apart.

When he opened the door the putrid odor of decay slapped him in the face. Drew lay upon his bed, the stump of what had once been a perfectly healthy leg wrapped in soiled bandages.

"Dear God, Drew. What has happened to you?" Stunned, Bain stood in the doorway with his mouth unhinged, unable to believe the change in the other man.

His brother swung his head around. His eyes, the exact shade of gray as his own, were sunken in, the skin of his face and neck sallow and loose as if it were no longer attached to his body. "Bain," he groaned. The pain in his voice ended in a gurgle, and taking a labored breath, he squeezed his eyes closed.

Bain leveled his gaze to the only other occupant he could see in the darkened cabin, an old sailor they had nicknamed Doc a decade ago. Not that the man was a qualified physician, but he knew more than a layman about medicine. He was good for removing an ailing tooth, or an ingrown toenail, but whatever had happened to Drew was beyond his capabilities.

"Doc, what's going on here?" Bain pushed toward the bedstead and knelt beside his only brother, taking up his limp, skeletal hand. They had their differences, but the closeness of their relationship made it impossible for him not to feel every pain Drew felt.

9

"It were bad, Cap'n."

Bain avoided looking at the old sailor. No one had called him captain for a long time.

"There was this woman in Foochow. Cap'n Drew went after her, and the next thing we knowed we found him crawlin' along the docks, the girl taggin' after'm. There was a bullet in his leg, done blowed the bone clean into. We had to get out of port 'cause them Chinee were comin' after us."

"Damn you, Drew," Bain cursed. "Can't you just leave the Oriental women alone? I told you I didn't want you sneaking in any more girls for illicit profit. I forbade you."

Drew opened his eyes and stared up at his twin for several minutes. His mouth worked as if he were trying to gather the energy to speak. "It's not what you think, Bain. I swear to God."

Angered and unwilling to listen to his brother's lies, Bain whipped about, facing Doc. "Hurry. Go get Dr. Hancock from town. Tell him it's an emergency. Tell him it's for me. And Doc. Send down a couple of the men with fresh bandages and a bucket of clean water. I can't let him lay in his own filth like this."

"Yes, sir, Cap'n," the old man muttered, his tone suggesting he was more than relieved to allow someone else to take charge. He turned to do Bain's bidding. At the doorway he glanced back. "Cap'n, I did the best I could. When the wound began to fester and turn black, I knew he'd lose his life if I didn't take the leg."

"I know, Doc. I don't blame you. Now go on and hurry." He tried to smile, but he knew he hadn't succeeded.

Alone with his brother, Bain turned his attention to the horrifying remains of Drew's leg. Images of it being himself lying there seemed all too real. Slowly unwinding the soiled bandage, he felt the bile rise in

10

his throat.

"It's bad, ain't it, brother?"

Glancing at the other man's concerned face, so like his own, he tried to make light of the situation. "You did it up right this time."

Drew let out a groan and dropped his head back against the mattress. "I swear, Bain, it's all different than before."

"Just shut up, Drew." The injured flesh was swollen and black around the stump.

"No, you gotta listen. You gotta take care of this for me."

"Just because you've lost a leg doesn't mean you can't handle things for yourself."

"I'm gonna die, Bain. I can feel it in here." Drew clutched his chest with one trembling hand.

Their gazes met, and at that moment Bain realized the truth in his brother's words. Drew *was* going to die, and a little bit of himself would die with him.

"You gotta find her for me. Please, promise."

"Drew, I don't want to get mixed up—"

"No. You don't understand. I love Suey Wah." With a shaking hand he reached out, took a photograph from the table beside the berth, and shoved it at Bain. "I didn't know she'd had my baby. And when I discovered the fact and traced her down, her father had sold her and the child into slavery. You gotta find her when she reaches San Francisco."

"Drew," Bain protested. Staring down at the water-scarred picture, he couldn't tear his eyes away from the young woman peering back at him. She was beautiful, and from a wealthy family if her clothing was any indication. Probably the sheltered daughter of a rich merchant.

"And you gotta take care of Mae Ching for me."

"Mae Ching?" Bain's head shot up.

From the corner of the room he heard a shuffling as soft as a field mouse would make. He turned, his face

11

highlighted in the lantern glow, and there on the edge of the circle of light poised a little girl no more than five or six, her mouth opened, her eyes widened in fear as she scrutinized his face. By her looks she was half Chinese, half white. He studied the picture and then his brother's gaunt face. There was no doubt in his mind exactly who this tiny creature was.

"You had no right to bring this child. . . ." As he swung about to criticize his brother's foolishness, his protest abruptly ended. Drew stared at him, but there was no life in his once-sparkling eyes. "Drew," he cried, grabbing up the limp body and shaking it, trying to draw the spirit back into the still-warm flesh. A crumpled piece of paper dropped from one lifeless hand.

"*Fahn Quai! Fahn Quai!*" Mae Ching backed up pointing an accusing finger at Bain, her thin voice quivering with emotion.

"What are you saying, child?" Releasing the body, he turned to the frightened girl and tried to take her in his arms to reassure her. "I know he's dead."

"*Fahn Quai!*" she screeched, struggling to escape. Slippery as a wet seal, she wiggled free and rushed to the doorway, and right into one of the sailors toting the pail of water Bain had requested.

The man dropped his burden and scooped her up.

"*Fahn Quai!*" she wailed.

"What's she saying, mister?" Bain demanded, grabbing her up and holding her tightly to his chest although she kicked and scratched like a cornered alley cat.

"Hell, Cap'n, how would I know? I don't speak Chinee any better than you do."

Bain turned, the struggling child still clutched under his arm, hoping beyond reason to find Drew watching his predicament with his usual amusement. Instead, he spied the piece of paper that had fallen from the dead man's fingers, and he stretched

12

out his arm to retrieve it from his brother's side. Spreading it open, he read what it said: "Li Fung, procurer of young women, Jackson Street, San Francisco."

San Francisco. He turned, his jaw set in frustrated anger. What choice did he have except to go?

Chapter One

Fukien Province, Eastern China
September 1870

Garnet Sinclair carefully inspected the row of small, upturned palms presented to her.

"Kum Yong, your fingernails are still dirty," she declared in soft, fluent Mandarin, reaching out to gently take the little girl's hand in hers. "Go back and try again."

"Yes, *Sse Mo*," the child responded in her native tongue, dipping in a curtsy before rushing out of the schoolroom.

Garnet's lips lifted in a smile as she touched the next set of hands in approval and moved on down the line. How she adored the name her children had bestowed upon her. *Sse Mo*. A title somewhere between mother and teacher. But most of all, how much she loved the nine girls entrusted to her care each day. She instructed them about life, about the paths opened to them even here in China, and prided herself in helping each of them grow into a woman worthy of notice by the world about her. And though she taught them the songs from her father's hymnals, she was satisfied if they learned to believe that God— under any name they wished to give Him—was the loving, gentle deity that was a part of her life.

Continuing her inspection, she paused in front of the last girl, the oldest and probably the dearest to her. Choie Seem, her tiny feet bound and deformed by the mandates of her society, had been the first to come to her—the one she hoped to turn the school over to when the time came for her and her father to return home to England.

"See the children seated at the table, and I'll find out what's taking Father so long to bring tea." She smiled, one hand moving up unconsciously to check that her ash-blonde hair, drawn back in a stylish twist at the back of her neck, was still in place.

"Of course, *Sse Mo*," Choie Seem replied. In that pitiful, little shuffle of hers, she ushered the freshly scrubbed children toward the plank table set up under an ancient banyan tree near the river.

Garnet turned and, lifting the green and blue poplin of her skirt, started toward the rectory. If a storybook jinni were to give her one wish, she decided, she would use it to restore Choie Seem's deformed feet. She frowned, her perfectly arched brows coming together between her jade green eyes. Her father would say such thoughts were a sacrilege. She should simply pray to God for a miracle. Very well then. If God were to grant her one miracle, she thought, correcting herself.

Approaching the building that served as home and church—its scrolled, tiled roof reminding her more of the gingerbread houses her mother used to bake when she was a child than a temple of God—she allowed her dress hem to fall back into place and waved her hand in greeting when her father emerged with the tray of tea and biscuits. She rushed forward to assist him, knowing only too well he might drop the food, for as usual he'd tried to carry too much in one trip. Taking the tray from his hands, she gently chided him. "Father, when will you learn? Don't try to do so much at one time."

"God praises the efficient and scorns the wastrel, daughter," he lectured. "I would never want to be counted as one of the latter."

She smiled with tolerant love. "No one would ever accuse you of being wasteful." *A bit absentminded, perhaps*, she thought with affection. Watching her step, she carefully balanced the tray with both hands and started toward the waiting children. Her father trailed in her wake, humming the fragments of a hymn.

"I heard the children singing this morning. What a glorious sound, the voices of angels, a proclamation to those who passed that God resides here in our village."

"Those who passed?" she inquired, her head swiveling in curiosity. Visitors were rare coming into their tiny community. "Did you see someone?"

"Someone of importance, daughter." He dipped his chin in earnestness. "Earlier this morning. The ornate sedan chair was carried by two fine horses instead of men. The bodyguards wore silk of the finest quality."

Something inside Garnet registered quiet alarm. A sedan chair and bodyguards? Who were the travelers and what did they want here so far from the coast? There were rumors that slave traders were on the prowl, looking for young girls to smuggle into that most uncivilized American town of San Francisco. She shivered with dread and fear. Surely such people would not bother with a village as small as theirs.

Reaching the terraced steps that led to the riverbank, she concentrated on her footing, careful not to trip over her gown. There was nothing to worry about, she assured herself. Even if the strangers were there on the pretense of seeking young girls to enter into marriage contracts, she was confident most of the parents in the community would never agree.

17

For the last year and a half she had repeatedly lectured the villagers to be wary of such offers. But she frowned at the pessimistic turn her thoughts took when she considered one particular family. Regardless of how hard she tried to stop them, her fears only multiplied.

"What is it, Garnet, dear?" her father asked.

"Nothing, Father," she replied, setting the tray on the rough-hewn table before the girls, who chattered and giggled with the lightheartedness of the innocent. Her lips curved upwards to assure him. "Nothing to worry yourself about."

The gaiety of the afternoon gathering washed away Garnet's concerns. By the time the students had finished up their refreshments, and had turned to play in the long grasses along the bank, she was confident that if the travelers were posing as matchmakers, she would have heard something by now if any of her students were involved. As she was apt to do quite often, she'd allowed her imagination to override her common sense. Glancing at her father dozing beneath the gnarled aerial roots of the ancient banyan tree, she smiled. She must learn to be more like him, not so suspicious of everyone and everything.

Joining her wards by the swirling waters, she sat down beside Choie Seem, giving the younger students a chance to expend some of their pent-up energy before taking them back into the schoolroom for their final lesson of the day. Garnet watched in sympathy as the crippled girl unconsciously tucked the flowing soft silk of her sahm about her to cover her tiny slippered feet.

"Oh, *Sse Mo*, how does it feel to run?"

Garnet's heart contracted with pain. How to explain the exhilaration of a feat she'd taken for granted as long as she could remember? "It's not much different than riding in a cart, the wind

18

whipping at your hair, only your legs tire, your heart races, and"—Garnet wrinkled her nose—"you have a tendency to perspire. Most unladylike." She rolled her eyes.

Choie Seem laughed, the sound soft and tinkling. "Then I guess I've not missed that much."

"The burdens God ladens us with, He bestows by special design, child."

Both young women looked up at Reverend Sinclair, who stood over them, polishing his spectacles on one corner of his frock. If there was truth in her father's statement, Garnet declared inwardly, there was no fairness in this world.

But somehow, she doubted that. She thought of herself as strong of mind and will. God rarely tested her, and when He did, she found the challenges easily met. She was whole of body, quick-witted, and most of all happy. Glancing about her, she realized there was nothing she wanted, except to ease the pain of those around her, and to teach them to believe in their own abilities.

And teach them she would. She rose to her feet and clapped her hands. "Children," she called out in their native tongue, "line up. We've another hour of class work to complete."

Unlike the students she had taught back home in Gloucester, who complained at every turn, the nine girls were a delight in every way. They were eager to learn, anxious to please, and most important to her, they loved her dearly.

As they returned their cups and plates to the serving tray, Garnet counted herself most lucky. Her father would say God had blessed her. She eyed that most loveable of men. Perhaps he was right.

Turning, she placed her arms about her father's waist and hugged him. He reared his head back to stare down at her. "What brought that on, daughter?"

"Nothing much. Just wanted to thank you for bringing me along. I know when we first arrived here in China, you thought my being here a mistake, but I'm so happy." She dropped her head against his chest, her hands unclenching and settling in the big pockets of his jacket, something she'd done since she was a small child when she had groped their depths searching for pennies and taffy he had planted there for her to discover.

"There, there, Garnet, what an outburst for such a proper young lady," he chided gently, taking her by the shoulders and holding her away from his large body. "Besides, I still think you should have accepted the Squire Trevelyan's offer of marriage rather than come with me. But I must admit I am glad you're here." He chucked her lovingly under the chin. "I would forget my head each morning if you didn't remind me."

As she eased her hands from his pockets, her fingers brushed against a piece of paper. She sighed, taking the folded note from its lodging. "What have you forgotten now?" she asked in mock dismay. He was notorious for writing reminders of things he must tend to and just as quickly forgetting them.

"Ah, yes," he said, slapping his forehead with the palm of his hand, "the messenger."

Her earlier suspicions resurfaced. "What messenger?"

"From the Ch'ens, calling for their daughters to return home immediately."

Kum Yong and her sister were two of her youngest students. It was well known among the village that the Ch'ens were in need of money to pay for the funeral of their grandfather, who had died less than a month ago, but after Garnet's warnings, surely they wouldn't resort to selling their daughters.

"Choie Seem," she called, stuffing the note into her own pocket, her mind made up. She wouldn't

20

allow anything to happen to any of her girls. "Take the little ones up to the rectory. If you see strangers coming this way, hide them in the secret passage, especially Kum Yong and her sister."

"What is it, Garnet? What do you fear?" her father demanded.

"Slavers."

"But these people are our converts." He frowned. "They would never do something so heathen as to sell their children into slavery."

"If it were anyone but the Ch'ens, I would agree. Sometimes I think they are little more than rice Christians, nodding and agreeing only for what they can get out of the Church."

"I think that a bit unfair. Be not a Doubting Thomas."

She shook her head, then turned, starting up the pathway that led back to the rectory.

Dogging her footsteps, he demanded, "What do you plan to do?"

"Confront them. I will not turn over two of my girls until I'm sure of their fate."

He grabbed her by the arm. "We must be careful, daughter," he warned. "The Tientsin Massacre was not so long ago."

How could she forget the horror of that ill-fated event? The people of Tientsin had wrongly accused a convent orphanage of killing young children in sacrificial rites. The villagers had rioted, murdering nuns and foreign officials alike. Less than a month later there was still unrest across China because of it, but the situation here was not the same. She was only trying to protect the innocent.

"Besides," he continued, "if it's God's will . . ."

"Is it God's will that young girls be treated like chattel, to be bartered and sold into a life worse than death?" she demanded. "God is not so cruel."

"The sins of the fathers are visited upon the

children," he said, justifying his passiveness.

She threw her hands up in frustration. It was impossible to argue with her father and his theological beliefs. "I see no harm in talking to the parents before sending the two girls home."

He paused and held out his hand. "I see no harm in talk either. It's just that I fear what you'll do once the dialogue is over. You've always been such a righteous child—the avenging angel from heaven."

"Oh, Father, I can't just send them home without knowing their fate." She closed her eyes and sighed.

"I'm well aware of how you feel." Putting his arm about her shoulder, he gently patted her ash-blonde hair, and clucked his tongue with understanding. "Come, child, I will not allow you to go alone. We'll face the adversaries together."

"Oh, thank you, Father, I knew I could depend on you." She blessed him with her most brilliant smile of victory.

"Don't be so presumptuous, young lady. Just because I've agreed to accompany you, doesn't mean I go along with what you're planning to do."

"Of course, Father." But she knew him better than he knew himself. Once he was caught up in a cause, he would see it through to the bitter end.

"Whoa."

The reins wrapped around her leather driving gloves, Garnet jerked back hard, forcing the little mare they used to pull the dogcart to a skittering halt.

"We've got to hurry, Father," she cried. "We must get the children hidden before they get here." Garnet's breath came in short gasps as she scrambled from the driver's seat to the ground to race toward the rectory.

The situation was just as she had feared. Parked in front of the Ch'en house had been the sedan chair her father had seen earlier. The anxieties she had managed to explain away on the short trip to the village had returned full force upon discovering the old woman sitting in the Ch'ens' front room. Producing signed contracts, the marriage broker had demanded the brides she had purchased for a few measly tael. In angry indignation Garnet had refused. Her girls were in trouble, and only she could—or would—help them.

"Garnet, Garnet." Her father jumped down from the vehicle and skirted the heaving horse to catch up with her. "Do you realize what you're doing? Those men aren't going to politely accept your refusal and just go away."

"I know, Father," she pleaded. "But if we can convince them the children are no longer here, what can they do? There's room to conceal all of them in the priest's hidey-hole under the pulpit in the church. No one knows of its existence except you and me and Choie Seem."

He stared at her for one brief minute, and her eyes pleaded for his assistance. The moment of decision. If he agreed to help her, nothing could stop them. "Very well then, girl. Hurry. I'll do what I can to delay them."

Flashing a quick smile, Garnet gathered up her skirts and rushed to the church, where Choie Seem had herded the students upon her departure. She found the eight youngsters clustered about the crippled girl calmly finishing up their lessons. Bless Choie Seem. She knew she had chosen her future successor well.

"Quickly, children," she said with a sharp clap of her hands and an even voice. "We must hurry." Moving behind the pulpit and using the toe of her shoe, she released the spring lock hidden in the baseboard. It had been by pure accident that she had discovered the secret entryway. She and her father had been in China just a few weeks and Choie Seem had been her only student at the time. While scrubbing the floors of the ancient church that had stood vacant for several decades, they had sprung the latch, revealing the hiding place the priests had used during raids in the early days of the missionaries. Until now, Garnet had never thought she would find a use for the hidey-hole.

Peering down into its dark depths, she worried that the children would be frightened huddled in its confines. Turning, she gathered up the tapers from the candelabrums that lined the altar.

"God forgive me," she mumbled, snatching up the silver matchbox as well. Lighting a wick, she bent, illuminating the underground room. Signaling to the children, she took the first one by the arm and helped her maneuver on the rickety wooden ladder. "Don't worry, Kum Yong, there's nothing to be afraid of."

"I'm not afraid, *Sse Mo*." The girl's almond-shaped eyes looked up at her with trust as she inched her way into the tiny underground room.

Moving as quickly as she could, Garnet helped each of the children down the ladder. With the last one, a girl of twelve, she handed her the candles and the matches, knowing Choie Seem would need both of her hands to join them. "Use them sparingly, and be very careful not to allow them to tip over." The girl nodded and descended with the stalwart grace of Joan of Arc.

At last there was only she and Choie Seem remaining. "Hurry, we haven't much time," Garnet whispered, urging the older girl to join the other students.

"I'm staying here with you, *Sse Mo*," Choie Seem announced in a quiet voice.

From the front of the building the thunder of approaching horses pounded closer.

"Don't argue," Garnet insisted. "The children would feel much more secure with you among them."

"I know, but I can't climb down the ladder." The Oriental girl pointedly stared at her deformed feet. "It will take much too long."

Garnet saw the wisdom of the girl's words. The slavers had no reason to touch the older girl. Their contract called for two children ages nine and ten.

"Very well, Choie Seem." Moving behind the pulpit, she placed her shoulder against it, pushing it back into place. As the platform slid into position, eight upturned faces watched, fear shining in their dark eyes. "I'll come back for you," she whispered, then she allowed the latch to snap into place.

"Halt," she heard her father cry. "This is a house of God. How dare you desecrate its sanctity."

"Where is my property?" the high-pitched voice of the old woman demanded.

"The children were gone when we got back." Garnet knew how much strength it took for her father to lie. He prided himself on always having told the truth for as long as she could remember.

"Out of my way, you white heathen." She heard the sound of flesh slamming into flesh.

"Father," she gasped, taking a step backwards in surprise, her hand flying to her open mouth. She hadn't anticipated the situation turning violent.

Choie Seem moved closer; their arms interlocked. Garnet glanced about the church. She must do something to appear calm. With nervous fingers she grabbed up a prayer book and, leading the other girl to a pew, sat down. Then she opened the book and began to read aloud.

When the ruffians she had seen with the marriage broker burst into the church, she raised her head and frowned. Her very insides quaked with fear, but she refused to show it. "Have you no respect for a temple of God?" she demanded, and for a moment she thought they might back away in superstitious fear.

"My property. My property," the old woman shrieked as she pushed her way into the church. Her yellow face was wrinkled and painted with so much makeup she looked like the circus clown Garnet had once seen as a child.

Garnet licked her lips and straightened, closing the volume with quiet fortitude. "I sent them away," she lied, hoping the old woman would accept her words. "You'll never find them," she added.

The prunelike face turned red with anger and seemed to bloat like an air-filled balloon. "No one steals from Yoke Wan." The slanted eyes skimmed over Garnet's trim figure, assessing. Then she smiled, a wicked, unpleasant expression. "I contracted for two females." She puffed up like an adder, her tiny hands straddling her hips. "And two females is what I will take back to Foochow with me." Turning to her bullyboys, she tossed her head in the girls' direction.

The old witch didn't mean to take her and Choie Seem—or did she? The men advanced as if controlled by a single lever. Garnet rose, forcing the stumbling Choie Seem behind her back. "You can't do this."

Her protest was like a dribble of water tossed upon a blazing building. The men fanned out, circling them. Garnet took a quick glance behind her, saw the open door leading into the rectory, and on impulse spun about, racing toward the archway and pulling Choie Seem along behind her. If they could reach the living quarters, perhaps she could lock the intruders out.

The children, she prayed, reluctant to leave them behind, but she had no other choice. *Please make them keep quiet.*

On the threshold the crippled girl stumbled, tumbling to her knees. "Run, *Sse Mo,*" she cried.

Garnet stood poised in the rectory. No. She could

never leave Choie Seem behind to face alone a fate worse than death.

The hands that grabbed her were not gentle. They pinched and pulled, forcing her to kneel beside the other girl. The old woman strutted forward. First, she inspected the Oriental girl, assessing her dark hair and smooth cheeks with a critical eye. Without a word she turned to Garnet, fingering her silky ash-blonde curls. "A white woman." She opened her mouth, revealing her nearly toothless gums, and cackled. "I think we've got much more than we bargained for." Her lips clamped shut. "Bind them and put them in the vehicle."

"No," Garnet cried. "We are protected by the British consulate. You have no right."

Silenced by the bitter-tasting rag stuffed into her mouth, Garnet found her hands secured behind her back with a piece of biting twine. She glanced over at Choie Seem, saw the tears of fright coursing down the girl's smooth cheeks. She felt so helpless, so angry that she could do nothing to stop the terrible nightmare that had them in its grasp.

Picked up and tossed over a broad shoulder of one of the ruffians, she refused to submit without protesting. She kicked, hoping to strike a most vulnerable part of her kidnapper's anatomy.

He growled a warning and shook her until she thought she would lose consciousness, but still she refused to concede. Twisting her neck, she grabbed his queue in her lips and pulled with all of her strength. Yelping, he swung about, her head cracking against the door frame through which they were emerging.

Her upside-down world spun crazily, and her body dropped limply against the man who held her.

"The white one, she will cause much trouble," the old woman snarled. "Place her in the sedan chair and bind her tightly. That way no one will see her and question her presence among us. These Engleesh," she continued, spitting at the ground. "They know not their lowly place."

Through her haze Garnet watched the ground over which they carried her. She caught a glimpse of a dark-clad figure lying in the dirt of the front yard.

"Father," she groaned against her gag, but the downed figure didn't move or respond. From her vantage point, she couldn't tell if he even breathed. He couldn't be dead. He just couldn't be.

Tossed in the sedan chair, her skirts bunched about her waist, she tried to squirm away when her slant-eyed captor grabbed at her ankles. But wise to her ways, he managed to bind them together, leaving her helplessly, hopelessly at the mercy of these demons from hell.

The old woman stepped into her view, one gnarled hand reaching out to comb through the strands of hair that fell in disarray about Garnet's face. "Relax, my beauty. We have a long ride to the harbor ahead of us."

Garnet jerked her head away from the repulsive feel of the woman's rough flesh on hers. She glared her refusal to cooperate, but the words of warning set her heart to pounding. The harbor? That must mean they were being taken to a ship. From there she could only imagine what lay ahead for them.

The woman cackled in delight, then turned and pointed toward the dogcart still standing in front of the rectory. "Put the other girl in there. She'll give you no problems." Looking at Garnet one last time, she dropped the concealing curtain.

The last thing Garnet saw was her father, lying unnaturally still on the ground. *I'm so sorry, Father,* she sobbed inwardly, closing her eyes and dropping her head against the silk lining of the sedan chair. *I did not mean to bring such tribulation upon us all.* The fleeting glimpse of eight little faces looking up at her from the hidey-hole in the church tore at her conscience. Who would let the children out? No one remained who knew they were there, yet if she confessed to the old woman, wouldn't their fates be worse than death?

Faced with a dilemma that had no easy solution, Garnet squeezed her eyelids closed. *Oh, God,* she cried in her first earnest supplication to a stern, unyielding deity. *Why have you done this to me? I was only trying to save them.*

Lying in the dark stench of the ship's hold, Garnet placed the back of her hand against her lips and swallowed. Her stomach roiled and seemed to leap into her throat each time the craft pitched in rhythm to the violence of the sea. Until now she had doubted the existence of Hell, but listening to the women and children around her moan in their own agony, she knew that the nether world was not just the rantings of some ancient, Biblical fanatic.

Her body sore and stiff from inactivity, she tried to turn on her side, but the chain about her left ankle clanked its defiance and held her in place.

"Choie Seem," she whispered, reaching out into the darkness for the person next to her.

The Oriental girl groaned incoherently.

Garnet groped for her hand, and to her dismay found it clammy and limp. She closed her eyes, clutching the one thing familiar to her, kneading the soft flesh, willing life back into the gentle soul of her student who had looked to her for protection. In the distance she heard the metal grinding of the ship's engines, a sound most commonplace to her now, then somewhat closer she honed in on another noise, one that sent chills of fear slithering down her spine.

"Squeak, squeak. Scratch, scratch." She shivered. Rats, she'd concluded days ago. She sat up, straining to hear better. Each time she heard the hairy little beasts they seemed closer, braver, and she waited in dread for them to run over her exposed legs and arms. Would they bite? Oh, God, she hoped she never found out the answer to that question.

Overhead she heard the rattle of chains. Feeding time. She maneuvered about so she could reach Choie Seem, and shaking the girl by the arm, she demanded, "You must get up."

As hard as it was to eat the awful swill the sailor served them twice a day, Garnet knew they would die unless they consumed their share. She must maintain her strength at all costs in order to keep not only herself but Choie Seem alive.

The rats scurried, the skitter of their feet as they ran harmonizing with the gruff voices of the men who carried down the malodorous buckets of food. A stream of sunlight poured through the open hatchway, blinding to her eyes, warming to her skin, alive with hope, a reminder that a world outside her hellhole did exist. She twisted and snatched up the two wooden bowls she'd kept hidden in a niche in the wall beside her.

"Here," she said, shoving one into her companion's hands, forcing the girl to sit up in spite of her weak protests. All around them the other prisoners stirred, crying out their pain, their hunger, their fear of dying. At first the cries had torn Garnet asunder. But over the days she had learned to ignore them. There were only she and Choie Seem. She no longer had the strength to care for more.

The sailors stepped down the iron grillwork, ladling the thin, soupy mixture into empty bowls. They didn't bother to count or note those who didn't receive their daily ration. No bowl, no food, no exceptions.

Helping Choie Seem lift her weakened arms with one hand, Garnet held out her own with the other, forcing the hatred from her eyes.

The men laughed, made crude remarks as they worked down the two lines of captives chained to either side of the ship's hull.

"Till I signed on with the *Jaded Lady* I never thought I'd want to puke from the smell of women." The man cleared his throat and spat only inches from Garnet's foot.

She ignored it. She had to. Lifting her bowl as high as the others, she stared down at her filthy shoe. How had she sunk so low?

"I knowed what you mean, Hal. You cain't pay me to sleep with one of these Chinese sluts." He slopped swill into Choie Seem's trencher, spilling more on what had once been a lovely sahm than went into the container. "All I can think of is the awful smell we have to put up with down here day in and day out."

"Looksee, touchee, doee," Hal mocked, kicking out at the crippled girl's foot that pressed against the grill on which they stood. "Hell, you can hear them all over town, callin' their filthy wares. Like dogs, they'll lie down in the streets and spread'm for a dollar."

Garnet scrambled to save the teetering bowl in Choie Seem's shaking hand, and pushed her own forward to be filled.

"Ain't you ever been curious to look and see if what they say is true, that their parts run east to west, not north to south like a white woman's?" the other man asked.

Hal laughed. "Hell, I did look once. A dead girl I had to bring up from the hold. I didn't see no difference."

Something inside of Garnet broke over the dam of mere survival. "You swine," she choked in indignation, lifting her brimming bowl and tossing it up into the faces of her captors. "You filthy swine."

Hal paused and wiped the smelly gruel from his

face. "Not hungry, are ya?" He laughed, and kicked the trencher from her outstretched fingers. "We'll see if you're so feisty in a day or two." Turning away, he continued down the line.

With a sinking heart, Garnet watched greedy hands snatch up her bowl. She had no doubt it wouldn't be returned to her. Sobbing with bitter resentment, she turned, placing the remaining food to Choie Seem's lips. "Please, drink."

Unaware of what had just taken place, the girl complied, slurping the liquid. Her own stomach growling in hunger because of her inability to keep her mouth shut and her head lowered, Garnet poured the last of the gruel into the crippled girl's mouth and gently wiped her cracked lips with the sleeve of her plaid dress. A dress she had once been very proud of.

"Pride goeth before destruction, and a haughty spirit before a fall." How many times had she heard her father quote those words?

Garnet lifted her chin in defiance. "We'll make it, Choie Seem," she vowed to the sleeping girl, the image of her loving God crumbling about her. "By damn, I'll see to it, if it's the last thing I do, but we'll make it."

Chapter Two

San Francisco, California
October 1870

"Captain Carson, I'm velly honored by your presence." The Chinaman bowed from the waist, and welcomed Bain into his plushly furnished office with the sweep of his arm enveloped in the long sleeve of his san, a jacket the Chinese all seemed to wear with pride.

Bain imitated the bow—a bit stiffly perhaps—and stepped forward, adjusting the lapel of the heavy black coat he wore. Drew's coat. "Li Fung. It's damn good to be back," he replied in his brother's devil-may-care manner of speaking. It was important this man think he was Drew in order to assure the success of his plan. He smiled, cockily tilting one side of his mouth the way his brother had always done.

"Sue Ling will be velly pleased you returned," the man said, indicating a seat in front of his desk. "Where you staying? I will send her around to your rooms this evening if it is your wish."

How like Drew. A whore in every port of call. Bain sighed inwardly, accepting the proffered chair but wanting no part of the woman. "The Palace," he replied. He doubted the prostitute was that eager to

33

be with him either. Drew had a reputation for being a little over-enthusiastic with his paramours.

"Ah, of course, Captain Drew. I should have known. The Palace is your velly favorite."

Bain allowed his shoulders to relax. Apparently Li Fung, a businessman who had dealt regularly with Drew for several years, did not detect the deception. And if Fung didn't suspect, chances were no one else would either. Except possibly for one of the women who knew his brother intimately. He would have to be careful around them.

The idea of this masquerade didn't set well with Bain, but he could think of no other way to accomplish the task at hand. As much as he abhorred the thought of tracking down a woman in San Francisco's Chinatown, he had made the deathbed promise to his brother, and he would keep it.

Besides, there was Mae Ching. The child's frightened face haunted his dreams. He had carried her kicking and screaming from her father's ship to the family residence in Monterey. There he'd managed to quiet her down with the help of Doctor Hancock, who spoke a smattering of Chinese.

"Fahn Quai," she had called him over and over, until her little voice, cracked and raw, quivered with exhaustion. White Devil. Apparently she had never seen twins, and had assumed he had stolen the spirit of her father—the only person she knew in this strange, new world he had brought her to. She had then turned to crying, *"Yun Mo"*—Mother. Bain's heart had gone out to her, remembering only too well how it felt to be without maternal guidance at so young an age.

"Yun Mo," he had assured her, communicating through the doctor that he would find her missing mother.

And he would. He refused to give up his search until he did, even if he had to lie about his identity.

"Captain Carson?" The Chinaman cleared his

throat in uncertainty.

Bain looked up, embarrassed, realizing that wasn't the first time Li Fung had spoken his name.

The Oriental smiled, attempting to mask his shrewd perception that everything wasn't right with his guest.

Bain grinned in the inane way he's seen his brother do whenever caught unaware. He knew only too well how the Eastern mind worked. Never let the enemy— or a friend for that matter—know what you're thinking. The lack of discipline could be detrimental in future negotiations. Let Fung think him a bit deranged.

"You have not said why you come to Chinatown. Usually you have cargo to sell to me, but I am told your ship's holds are empty."

Cargo could mean only one thing—women. Inwardly Bain cursed his brother's name, though he was careful to reveal nothing of his anger and surprise at discovering the extent of Drew's involvement with the slave traders. Instead, he shrugged his wide shoulders, his gray eyes narrowing as he fingered the leather lapel of his coat. "I didn't come to sell, I came to buy."

For a fleeting moment Bain saw the daggers of danger reflected in the other man's sloping gaze. "I would think, Captain, it would be much cheaper to gather your own merchandise from the source if your plans are to go into business for yourself. It would be most shameful if we were to become competitors."

"I do not wish to rival you, Mr. Fung. I am only looking for one particular girl."

Li Fung relaxed visibly. "Ah, yes. The Foochow incident. Rumors reached me of your attempt to steal this Suey Wah from the hands of her owners."

Bain tensed. Was the man simply toying with him? How much of that sordid incident did he know about?

"I heard you suffered velly terrible injuries at the

hands of Chinese tong." His gaze flicked casually over Bain's undeniable health. "My information must have been wrong."

"It looked worse than it was," Bain answered, his gaze steady.

"And so, you come seeking this woman."

Bain nodded.

"And you think I have her." The Chinaman's hands eased under the desk.

"Not at all," Bain quickly assured him, certain the man reached for a weapon. "But I know she must go through the barracoon. I thought to find her there."

"You know as well as I foreigners not allowed entry into the auctions."

"I had hoped you would be able to see me clear of the restriction."

"You are velly bold, Drew Carson." Fung's eyes narrowed with resentment, but his hand returned to rest on the desktop. "Only you would ask so impossible a thing."

"Perhaps," Bain countered, gambling the man had many secrets he wished to keep hidden from the outside world. "But it's nothing more than I've done for you in the past—and will do in the future."

Their gazes locked in mortal combat, each struggling to gain control of the moment.

"Velly well, Captain Carson." Li Fung looked away. Apparently Drew knew something most important about this man. "Meet me this evening at the gambling parlor near St. Louis Alley and Grant Street. I will see that you gain entrance to the barracoon below and have a moment to look over the list of names that have passed through over the last few weeks. But I warn you." He raised one long-nailed, tapered finger and pointed it at Bain. "Do not attempt to bid on any of the girls. If you see this woman or discover who is her master, come to me. Only I can help you get her back."

Bain nodded his agreement, and studied the

Chinaman, wondering if he himself would live to see the morning light.

Blinking like an owl in the bright sunlight, Garnet hugged Choie Seem to her heart and followed the line of women and children in front of them to the far deck of the ship. Glancing down at the ragged dress that had once fit her to a tee, she couldn't help noticing how it now hung on her thin frame. Concern twisted the emptiness of her belly, but at least she was alive and so was Choie Seem.

Her eyes at last adjusting, she stopped with the other women and surveyed her new surroundings. They were in a harbor, the city before them a hodgepodge of rundown wharfs and warehouses, the streets teeming with an assortment of humanity and conveyances, the smells most obnoxious. But nothing could be more foul than what she had suffered the last few weeks confined in the hold of the slavers' ship.

She shivered in the slight chill of the October air, hugging Choie Seem's thin body closer to her for mutual warmth. Turning, she stared back out to sea—the endless ocean—to where China should be. Would they ever get back to where they belonged? Deep inside she knew they probably wouldn't.

For a fleeting instant, she wished the hand of God would end her misery by swooping down and knocking her from the deck into the watery depths of the ocean.

The wet stream hit her backside with the force of flying glass, the roar it made like some demon from Hell released upon them.

"Oh, no, I take it back. I didn't mean it," she cried in protest amidst the din of female screams all around her. She twisted, hunching her shoulder to protect the wobbly girl in her arms from injury. Someone next to her crashed into her side knocking all three of

37

them to the decking. Gasping, she tried to catch her breath, and only managed to gulp a mouthful of icy, foul-tasting water.

Had God answered her foolish prayer? Was the ship sinking here in the harbor? Why else would a wall of water wash over them? Her heart thundering with denial that death was so near, she peered out from beneath her arm and saw the giant waterspout coming toward them again. Hugging the wooden planks beneath her, she feared for her very life.

"Get up, you filthy sows," a voice barked.

The wall of water flattened her where she lay, and even if she wanted to obey the command she couldn't. Choie Seem, who was still beneath her, groaned in pain as Garnet's weight crashed against her fragile form.

Then the pressure let up like a receding tidal wave, and Garnet rolled, dragging the crippled girl with her. Again she looked up, trying to understand what was happening. The jet of water washed down the line of screaming women toward the far end.

That was when she spied the horse-drawn fire engine parked on the wharf, the long hose attached squirting water like an arc toward the group of prisoners.

The wave rolled back in her direction, but this time she was prepared, and took the brunt of the stinging jet with her back and shoulder. Just as quickly as the assault began, it stopped, the loud roar softening to a fizzling hiss.

"At least you don't smell like the bowels of Satan anymore," the sailor, Hal, announced, sniffing the air as if it were the finest bottle of French wine.

Garnet stood, pushing the wet mass that was her hair from her eyes, water dripping from the ends of her lashes, the tip of her nose, her chin. Shivering violently from the cold, she glared at him.

His eyes met hers, and he smiled and stepped toward her. "Ah, yes, our fair-haired beauty."

38

Grasping her by the arm, he dragged her away from the other soaked women.

"Choie Seem," she cried, unsuccessfully reaching out to grab her friend, knowing in the pit of her soul they were about to be separated.

"Don't worry, she ain't goin' nowhere." Forcing her around a corner, Hal laughed as Garnet began to struggle in earnest fright. "Don't worry, honey. I don't plan to hump ya." He stopped before a large barrel and pointed. "Get in," he demanded.

Garnet's jade-green eyes widened in disbelief. She shook her head in unwillingness, clawing at his restraining fingers. If he planned to toss her in the sea, she refused to go sealed up in a keg like a helpless pup.

Clasping her wrist tighter until she thought the bones would surely snap, Hal jerked her closer to the container. Then he scooped her up and dumped her unceremoniously into its depths.

Forced into a most uncomfortable squat, she tried to push her way out, but he held her down firmly on the top of her head. "If you want to see that Chinee girl again, you keep quiet, no matter what you hear."

She tilted her chin ever so slightly and her eyes rolled to the tops of their sockets in order to see the sailor. He meant what he said. She nodded once and caught her breath, not sure what to expect. But for Choie Seem's sake she ceased her resistance.

He dropped the lid into place over her head, and she heard the pounding of the hammer sinking nails to secure the top in place. Like a coffin closing in around her, the barrel was suddenly quite small. Her chest grew tight as if her lungs refused to work. Was his plan to suffocate her?

She wanted to scream, to pound on the staves and beg for release, but she remembered his warning. If she wished to see Choie Seem again . . .

Spying the tiny air hole in the lid, she tilted her head so her nose pressed against it. She forced her

39

lungs to breathe in, breathe out, and then she snapped her eyes closed. There behind the security of her eyelids, the darkness held no meaning. No matter what, she would be brave.

Then the barrel tipped over, and she was rolling, rolling. And though she tried to brace herself with her hands, elbows, and knees, the breath was soon knocked out of her, leaving her half dazed and more nauseated than she'd ever been before. When the rotations stopped, the barrel gyrated like a top. Garnet placed her hand over her trembling mouth. If she started gagging, she would be heard. She must keep still to protect Choie Seem. The barrel was righted—thank God she wasn't on her head—and something tapped the top.

"Dishware," she heard Hal say gruffly.

A mumble of distant voices reached her, but she could only catch a word here and there.

"No need to inspect . . ."

"Move along . . . inspector sees us . . . trouble . . . hurry."

Then the container was hoisted up, and she could feel the motion beneath her as a wagon, no doubt, began to move creakily down the street.

Taking a deep breath, she pressed her aching head against the thin padding on the inside of her tiny prison. What further horrors did the day hold for her? she wondered, vowing that no matter what was forced upon her she would do what she must to protect the girl whose life she felt deeply responsible for.

Standing outside the mah-jongg gambling parlor, Bain watched the street for signs of Li Fung. One of San Francisco's heavy fogs enveloped him, swirling in the erratic breeze like wind specters looking for a means to escape. With the sleeve of his coat, he wiped the gathering moisture from his face, then pulled the collar up about his neck to ward off the penetrating chill. The thought crossed his mind that the Chinaman might have had a change of heart and decided not to help him after all.

Then he heard the sound of a carriage approaching in the darkness. Straightening, he stepped into the street and waited for Li Fung to emerge from the interior of the vehicle, surrounded by his bodyguards.

"Ah, Captain Carson," the Chinaman said, smiling in his deceptive way. "Have you waited velly long?"

Bain had been there nearly an hour, but he shrugged his shoulders. "Just got here myself," he replied, knowing the dampness of his hair and clothing belied his words.

Li Fung's eyes flicked over him, his dark eyes slitting in amusement. "Velly well, Captain. Did you bring money with you in order to make your purchase?"

Bain could feel the thick square of banded hundred-dollar bills concealed in the inside pocket of his jacket. A small fortune, money he had found in the ship's safe upon Drew's death. He nodded.

Fung stuck out his open palm. "You best to turn it over to me, Captain. I will be the one to bid if we find this Suey Wah of yours."

Bain stared at the beringed hand and hesitated. He didn't trust the Oriental, especially with a lot of money. Then he eyed the group of bodyguards, wondering if this meeting was no more than a plan to steal his cash. If that were the case, he decided, he would go down fighting.

"No, Mr. Fung, I will give it to you when the time is proper, not before."

"You no trust Li Fung?" The man's plastered smile widened, showing yellow teeth that reminded Bain of the fangs of a wolf.

"I trust you as much as you trust me."

41

The guards tensed, and Bain was sure they were about to attack him. His muscles gathered for action.

The Chinaman laughed, easing the tension. "Velly good, Captain Drew. I like your way of thinking, I always have, but if you wish to enter the barracoon it will cost a hundred dollars to bribe the guards." He waited, his arm still extended.

Reaching into his breast pocket, Bain took out one bill and placed it in the other man's hand.

"Velly good." Fung tucked the money into the flowing sleeve of his san. "Remember. Say nothing, and stay next to me."

Silently Bain followed his escort into the gambling parlor. The large, open room was crowded on both sides with black lacquered tables and chairs filled to capacity even at that early hour. Beneath a wall decorated with scrolls bearing Chinese characters stood a cluster of young Oriental girls—prostitutes—no more than thirteen or fourteen years old, dressed in flowing robes that concealed little of their budding breasts. Bain's mouth screwed tight with disgust at the way these people treated mere children.

Li Fung and his men never paused, but continued to the back of the room to a narrow staircase that wound into the bowels of the earth. Taking a deep breath, wondering what was in store for him, Bain followed uneasily.

At the bottom, Fung paused and, speaking softly in Chinese to a huge bear of a man, placed the bribe into his beefy hand. The doorman smiled at Bain, bowed from the waist, and stepped aside.

Bain frowned. That had been easy. Too easy, he thought as he brushed by the guard. Had Fung duped him all along? Perhaps he didn't need the Chinaman's assistance.

"Do not think unworthy thoughts about Li Fung," the man whispered, as if he'd read Bain's mind. "Without me, the doorman would have simply slit your throat and tossed you out into the alley."

As he entered the underground room, the acrid odor of burning opium filled Bain's nostrils. The auction was already in progress. A young girl stood upon a platform, her skeletal body completely exposed. Bain reeled. He'd not expected such barbarism to exist in this day and age. Li Fung touched his shoulder and pointed toward an ancient man standing in a distant doorway. "We check the ledgers." He smiled. "Cost three hundred dollars."

Narrowing his eyes in distrust, Bain forked over the bribe, his anger growing with each breath he took.

But true to the Chinaman's word, a few moments later Bain was thumbing through a large accounting book of names. In that same amount of time the poor slave girl on the block had been sold for a mere fifty dollars and dragged away in tears by her new owner, only to be replaced by another.

Bain looked away, concentrating on the ledger. The list of names was endless, but none even remotely resembled Suey Wah. Perhaps Drew had been wrong, the woman had never come to San Francisco. Frustrated, Bain continued his searching, flipping further and further back into the book.

Then he saw it. Suey Wah from Foochow. His heart raced as his finger traced across the ledger to discover her fate. Written in the final column: "Died." Nothing more to tell him what had happened to the woman who had given the world a child as sweet as Mae Ching.

"Damn," he mumbled under his breath, and slammed the book closed.

"You find her, Captain?" Li Fung asked.

"Yes. She died."

"So solly," the Chinaman replied matter-of-factly. "That is not unusual." He took Bain by the arm and

43

led him toward the middle of the room, and stopped in a strategic point near the auction block.

"I'm ready to leave, Mr. Fung."

"So soon?" the man asked. "But there is much yet to see."

As much as he knew Drew would have found the auction a source of entertainment, Bain had no desire to continue the masquerade. All he wanted to do was go home to Monterey and forget such things as slavery existed. He glanced at the Chinaman, saw the doubt clouding his dark eyes, and realized that if the man discovered the duplicity, he might very well have him murdered on the spot. Bain relaxed his shoulders and prepared himself to stay. "Very well," he said, forcing his eyes to show interest. "I've paid for the evening, I might as well stay."

"You will not be disappointed. There's a velly special offering tonight, one I am sure will make the wait worthwhile. That is why so many attend the auction this evening. This is one purchase I want to make at any cost."

Bain eyed the Chinaman with curiosity. What kind of woman could cause such a stir? He couldn't imagine.

The bamboo stave struck the back of Garnet's bare calves, the stinging pain shooting up her legs. She gasped, pulling at the hands that held her pressed belly-down against the table, but she still shook her head in refusal. "I will not do it. Nothing you can do to me will make me willingly degrade myself so."

The flexible rod struck her again, this time on the tender flesh of her upper thighs. "No," she cried, biting down until she tasted the saltiness of her own blood.

She heard the whoosh of the whip rise once more, and she tensed, prepared for the onslaught, but it never came.

"Perhaps something a little stronger." The sing-songy voice of the whoremonger rose to a high pitch. "Turn her about so she can see what I have in store for her."

Forced to her back, a sharp corner digging into the base of her spine, she struggled against the hands that held her spread-eagle on the table. Her eyes followed her tormentor as he moved across the room to a pot of glowing coals in one corner. He stooped and lifted a red-hot poker. Pointing its smoldering tip at her, he circled the air, spiraling closer to her with each revolution until she could feel the intense heat. "Perhaps this will make you more agreeable."

Garnet's knees began to knock. She wouldn't give in. She wouldn't. The thought of standing before a room of masculine eyes and taking off her clothes was more horrible than any physical pain these people might inflict on her. Her chin notched, and she bit down on her tongue, praying she wouldn't cry out.

The poker moved closer. She squeezed her eyes shut and tensed, turning her face away. *I will not give in. I will not give in,* she chanted in her mind.

"Halt."

Garnet's eyes snapped open. Standing in the doorway was the auctioneer, whom she recognized from his periodical visits to the holding pens. His rotund figure filled up the entrance, the fury on his face undeniable. The whoremonger turned, dropped to his knees before his master, and began to snivel.

"Why is she not prepared?" the heavyset man demanded.

"She refuses to cooperate, master," the cowering man, who had only moments before frightened her beyond belief, whined. "I was only trying to subdue her as is customary."

"By damaging her? This one must be flawless.

45

Much promise rides on what she will bring to me this night." He stepped forward, grasped her face in his large hand, and squeezed until she thought her jaws would shatter. "Your resistance is useless, my beauty."

"Do what you want," she spat. "I will never agree to flaunt myself for your benefit."

"What a shame that such loveliness possesses so biting a tongue." He picked up a pair of tongs from the table beside her and snapped them at her like jaws of a mad dog. "Perhaps I should simply rip it out. From the block no one could detect its absence."

Garnet's soul quaked with fear as his hand pressed tighter, forcing her mouth to open.

"Master," the whoremonger hissed, "there is a better way. She asks for another named Choie Seem. Perhaps she would yield if you threaten to punish this girl," he chortled with self-congratulations.

The auctioneer's eyes lit up as he dropped the pincers back on the table. "Most brilliant. Bring me this Choie Seem."

Garnet's heart hammered against her rib cage. She couldn't allow them to harm the crippled girl no matter what she was forced to do, but to strip off her clothing and stand meekly by as she was sold to the highest bidder was the worst nightmare she could imagine.

The moment Choie Seem was brought in and thrown at the feet of the slaver traders, her gentle, dark eyes looked to Garnet for protection. Picking up the bamboo rod, the whoremonger turned and raised it high above the young girl's head.

"Stop," Garnet cried, her eyes glistening with unshed tears of frustration and humiliation. "If you promise not to harm her, I will agree."

The auctioneer smiled in triumph. "You are wise, my beauty. Her death would have meant nothing to me."

Her arms released, Garnet rose from the table, rubbing at the bruised flesh of her wrists. The whoremonger presented her with one of the long, flowing robes held together in the front only by a sash she'd seen the other girls wearing.

"Put it on," he demanded, and stood there waiting for her to obey.

Looking down at the frightened Choie Seem, Garnet knew she had no choice. She reached up to unbutton the bodice of what was left of her blue and green plaid gown. Ignoring the probing eyes to the best of her ability, she removed her dress, her shift, and finally her chemise—her corset having been discarded long ago aboard the ship—and slipped into the silky black robe, drawing it to the base of her throat before she secured the sash in a double knot.

The whoremonger's eyes glinted with what she knew instinctively was lust, but he was not what she feared. The crowd in the auction room, the stranger who would buy her and use her for whatever purpose he decided suited his needs—those were the unknowns that left her trembling deep inside. She glanced down at Choie Seem, knowing the girl's fate would be the same as her own, and a spear of guilt coursed through her.

"I'm sorry, *Sse Mo*," Choie Seem whimpered, clutching at the hem of her robe.

"No," she replied, kneeling beside the prone girl and patting her soft, dark hair, "it is all my fault. It is for you to forgive me."

As she was jerked to her feet by the auctioneer, her eyes clung to the other girl's until she was forced out the door and down the long corridor that she knew led to the auction room.

"I will thump my pole twice, and you are to allow the robe to slip slowly down your arms," he instructed.

Her head lowered to rest on her chin, Garnet didn't

acknowledge what he was telling her. The heavyset man stopped, twisted her arm until she crumpled to her knees before him in order to avoid the pain. "Do you understand?" he demanded.

She nodded, swallowing hard the lump of fear and dread clogging her throat.

"Good." He allowed her to rise and continued down the hallway. "And when I tap it again, I want you to turn slowly around, so the bidders can see all of what you have to offer them."

She bobbed her head once more. But, oh, when it came time, would she be able to do something so wanton?

As they reached the auction room, she could hear the impatient crowd demanding a new offering to bid on. Her heart pounded, her mouth went dry, her ears began to ring.

The auctioneer forced her to look at him one last time. "Do not disappoint me, my beauty. One mistake, one moment of hesitation, and the girl will die a slow and painful death." Then he stepped forward, leaving her in the protection of the guards.

Glancing out on the sea of eager male faces, Garnet wanted to shrivel up and die before parading herself before them, but she could see no way out of her predicament. The auctioneer approached his box, and then with a nod, when he had the attention of his customers, he called her forward. "White Lotus," he announced.

Garnet moved forward as if in a dream—a nightmare from which there was no escape. Mounting the auction block, she stopped on the cross marked on the floor, her head held high, her long ashen hair mantling her shoulders like a waist-length cape, her eyes focusing on a lantern above the crowd.

A gasp of admiration rippled through the audience, but she couldn't look—she didn't dare or she

48

would be tempted to turn and run.

"Two hundred," cried an enraptured voice.

The bidding was underway.

"Five hundred."

The auctioneer began to list her attributes, her age, her ability to speak fluent Mandarin—her virginity.

"A thousand."

Tears of humiliation crested her lashes, but she held them in check, and she turned her head to swipe them away. That's when she saw the smoky gray eyes amidst the sea of dark, almond-shaped ones.

Try as she might, she couldn't pull her gaze away from the tall, attractive American who stood out among the shorter Orientals like a diamond amidst glass baubles. Something in his gaze fascinated her, something more than the lust focused on her like pinpricks from all the others in the room.

Thump. Thump.

Garnet jumped at the sound of the auctioneer's stick pounding on the floor. The command that she remove her robe. Her heart stilled and she couldn't swallow. The gray eyes watched her as if they couldn't believe she was real.

She glanced at the auctioneer, saw the anger molding his features, and knew Choie Seem's fate was in her hands. Reaching up, she untied the sash, allowing it to drop to the floor. The robe parted, revealing the curve of her breasts, her navel, the long line of one bare leg.

Her gaze jumped back to the gray-eyed American. Then in morbid fascination, she shook the garment from her shoulders and allowed it to trickle down her arms to fall like a cloud of silk at her feet.

"Fifteen hundred."

Her eyes darted to the Oriental man standing next to the American who had just made a bid, then back to the American again. The play of emotions running across the strong features of Gray Eyes held her

49

spellbound. And though she knew he studied her with the gaze of an aroused man, she wasn't ashamed. In fact, she felt a thrill of pride course through her. Dear God, what was wrong with her? How could she possibly take enjoyment from what was happening to her?

"Two thousand," came a call from the back of the room.

Lifting her eyes, she stared at the ceiling, and found herself suddenly floundering in a sea of humiliation as the lustful stares about her penetrated the mental defenses she'd thrown up to protect herself.

Thump. Thump.

The signal to turn.

She pivoted slowly, her eyes following the wall, grateful that she could no longer see the audience. As she presented her back, a strange need to know what the gray-eyed American was doing brought her head around to look over her shoulder. Her hair dripped like wheat-colored silk to her waist. She found him. He was frowning. He glanced at the Oriental man standing beside him as the man upped his bid.

"Two thousand, five hundred."

Gray Eyes glanced back at her, their gazes uniting with an electricity she had no way of comprehending. As his lips parted, his hand raised in a clenched fist of defiance.

"Five thousand," he said in a voice as rich as molasses.

The crowd gasped. The Oriental man beside him turned in anger and began shouting.

Her world began to spin like a child's top; her knees sagged. Just before she hit the ground, the full impact of what had just happened struck her. The handsome gray-eyed American was now her owner and master.

Chapter Three

The tiny, jeweled dagger plunged toward Bain's middle, and he sidestepped, dodging the razor-sharp blade held in Li Fung's long-nailed hand. He glanced down. The knife glistened dangerously.

"I have ignored your double-dealing in the past, Captain Carson, but this time you go too far," the Chinaman hissed, slashing out at Bain once more. "This time you die."

The auction forgotten for the moment, the crowd parted as Bain again jumped back to avoid being cut. "What's the matter, Fung," he replied with a belying laziness. "The stakes too rich for your blood?" Bain retreated a step further, knowing his taunt had served only to incite the Chinaman's anger further. But he'd had enough of Oriental games. He would do things his way now. His outstretched hands curled, beckoning, daring his adversary to follow. He glanced up, saw Fung's bodyguards pushing their way through the crowd to assist their employer. He didn't have long. A few moments at best, if the throng didn't turn against him as well.

"No one makes a fool of Li Fung." The Chinaman lunged once more.

Bain edged backwards again, his goal the sale block where the auctioneer stood, the fallen woman at his feet. Deep inside he sensed the rotund man wouldn't have a qualm about accepting a white man's money, if Bain could reach him before Fung had a chance to carve him into mincemeat.

The spectators apparently felt no loyalty to their fellow countryman. They gave Bain space, their singsongy chatter all around him. As they spoke a universal gambler's language he had no trouble deciphering, their quick glances and eager faces were easy to read. They wasted no sympathy on him either. They merely placed their wagers among themselves as to how far he would get before Li Fung and his men killed him.

Fung followed with the stealth of a stalking alley cat, switching the knife into his other hand. His slanted eyes narrowed, and his mouth widened in a deadly smile. No longer bothering to conceal his true feelings, he would strike without mercy.

Reaching the base of the auction block, Bain never took his eyes off his adversary. "My bid was five thousand dollars," he reiterated in a low, even voice. He waited for the auctioneer to acknowledge his claim.

"Five thousand," the slavemonger repeated. "Do I hear a higher bid?"

A sweat-sheened tension filled the crowded room. Bain sent Li Fung a silent challenge. Then he smiled, his hands curling again in that taunting beckoning motion that drove the Chinaman wild. "Well, does he? If you want the woman so bad, Fung, all you have to do is top my bid."

He waited, a bluffer's fear coursing through him. Would Li Fung meet his affront and outbid him? Quickly calculating the roll of money in his breast pocket, he knew he had only an additional two hundred dollars beyond the five thousand he had bid so far. If Fung raised the bid he would have no choice except to concede. He seriously doubted he would have much of a chance to snatch up the woman and bulldoze his way out of the underground auction room. The crowd would never give him that much leeway.

Fung held his ground, the knife still hanging suspended in the air in his deceptively relaxed hand. The moment his bully-boys reached his side, he straightened. "Take him."

Bunching his muscle, Bain prepared to leap up on the auction block to avoid capture.

"Stop." The auctioneer's voice raised to a high pitch with his demand, his beady eyes pinning his fellow countrymen with a glare. "This is *my* territory, Li Fung. Here we do things *my* way."

Fung stepped back, but Bain could see he visibly shook. His eyes slit with calculated anger, his mouth thinned. Then he dipped a respectful bow to the slavemonger.

With a silent sigh of relief, Bain relaxed, his arms falling to his sides.

"Do not think, Drew Carson, that this matter is settled between us," Fung stated in a voice stiff with frustrated infuriation. "The woman may be yours— for now, but I know of your perverted way. My girls have told me of the things you make them do for you."

Bain frowned and cocked his head in perplexity. Just what was it his brother did to women?

"Did you think they would not tell me of your sadistic demands? Or that I would not see the burns and scars you left on their bodies?"

Bain's frown deepened. *Oh, Drew, what terrible things have you done that I know nothing about?*

"I will have this woman, one way or another," the Chinaman's threat continued. "I will not have her damaged by the likes of you." Fung's hand reached out to caress one of the woman's long ashen curls that cascaded over the side of the auction block.

Bain turned his head to watch, his own hand darting out, knocking the Chinaman's fingers away. The woman stared up at him from her prostration, her frightened green eyes meeting his gaze with horror and disbelief. He bent to reassure her that he meant her no harm.

"No," she cried. "Don't touch me." She recoiled, her stare daring him to defy her demand. She had apparently heard every accusation Li Fung had made.

Her crisp, foreign speech pattern surprised him. She was English. What in the hell was she doing here in San Francisco? Appraising her nudity, he found it not what he expected. English women were supposed to be dried-up old prunes. Her lush curves suggested more of a ripe plum aching to be picked, its sweet juices begging to be tasted.

"Captain Carson," the auctioneer said.

Bain snapped his attention up at the rotund man.

"Pay the cashier, then take your property and leave."

Ignoring the woman's glare, he reached across her bare midriff and gathered up the black silk wrapper. "Put it on."

Without a word, she obeyed, drawing the fabric tightly against her beautiful throat as she tied the sash at her waist.

Taking her by the hand, he dragged her from the platform, forcing her to follow him through the crowd though she tried unsuccessfully to wiggle from his grasp.

What the hell had gotten into him? He had just bought a woman. Bought one! No, he had to be fair with himself. That wasn't the complete truth. He had rescued her—saved her from the degradation Li Fung had planned for her. Yet her obvious lack of gratitude for his generous gesture didn't make him feel heroic.

But then, just how heroic were his plans for her? Remembering the lush globes of her bared breasts, her tiny waist, the womanly flare of her hips, he wallowed down the desire that was having a field day with his emotions.

That wasn't why he had done what he had. It was strictly his chivalrous nature that had made him speak up and spend a fortune to buy her. Five thousand dollars would have gone a long way at the ranch.

He was back to that again. He *had* purchased her. Frantically he searched his mind for a more logical reason for his illogical actions. Of course. The auctioneer had stated that she spoke fluent Chinese. He had need of someone to help him communicate with Mae Ching. Yes, that was it. He had bought her for Mae Ching. A substitute to take the place of the mother the little girl would never see again.

Satisfied with his justification, he tightened his grip on the woman's arm. More than willing to follow the auctioneer's advice, he threaded his way through the crowd. He would feel a hell of a lot better as soon as they were out of Chinatown.

Garnet assessed the back of Drew Carson's head as he dragged her through the all-male crowd. Torn between the relief that this man had snatched her from a life of certain degradation had one of the Chinese bidders been successful and the fear that he might demand much worse from her, her mind was in a quandary. Should she fight him or go willingly? There had been such strength in his gaze the first time she'd noticed him, and she had taken it as a sign of benevolence, but there was power to be found in evil as well. The things the Oriental man had said about him—how could a kind man treat a woman, any woman, with such gross disregard? She shuddered, remembering only too well the way he had looked at her time and again. Just what did he have planned for her?

She glanced about, seeking a compassionate face where she knew there couldn't possibly be one. No one at this auction cared one fig about what happened to her. Her eyes traveled the length of the dark, cavernous room and focused on the auction block. Standing on the marked spot where she had stood only moments before was Choie Seem, her head meekly bowed in shame as she was forced to disrobe.

The maternal need to protect the innocent girl brought Garnet to an abrupt decision, and she stiffened in her determination. The fingers about her wrist tightened, painfully so, but she dug her heels into the floor. She wouldn't forsake Choie Seem.

"No," she cried.

Drew Carson turned, and for a moment she swore she saw that gentle soul she'd witnessed earlier residing in his gray eyes, but then his gaze hardened. "What do you mean, no?"

Glancing at the auction block where the bidding had begun, she knew she only had seconds to plan her strategy and convince this gray-eyed American to help her.

"Choie Seem. I can't leave her behind." She pleaded with her eyes, not caring what he thought of her.

He glanced up. "The girl on the block?"

Her head bobbed. *Please, let him have enough heart to help me.* Her pulse fluttered with anxiety.

After a moment of hesitation, he shook his head. "As much as I'd like to, I can't buy every girl here that is in trouble."

Her choices flashed before her eyes. She could accept his refusal—she had tried and no one would ever condemn her for her failure—or go against all she'd been taught about propriety and throw herself

56

at his feet, a martyr willing to offer up herself for the sake of another. There was no clear choice here of right or wrong; whatever path of solution she picked lay in an undefined gray area of morals. But for Choie Seem, God help her, she knew she would do whatever was necessary.

"Please," she whispered, swallowing down the lump of dread and pride clogging her windpipe. "I'll do anything you want—anything. I won't fight you. . . . No matter what you demand of me."

Resentment sparked in his eyes, turning the gray into a violent storm. "I find your willingness to sacrifice yourself for your friend most intriguing. Should I believe you?" He seemed genuinely astounded, but then perhaps he was already planning some ungodly perversion she couldn't even begin to imagine.

She nodded, her heart thumping fearfully against the hollow at her throat.

His mouth curled in what she interpreted as a sardonic smile. "One hundred," he shouted, lifting his turbulent gaze from hers to watch the auctioneer. Seconds later he returned his attention to Garnet. "I fully expect you to keep your bargain."

Their gazes met, his eyes granite hard as if trying to penetrate her conscience. Without a doubt he meant what he said, but when the time came to pay the piper she wasn't sure what she intended to do. If his demands were anything like what she'd overheard the Chinese man describe . . .

Praying he wasn't clairvoyant, she swallowed so hard she knew he must have heard the sound.

No one challenged the bid and, with relief, Garnet saw Choie Seem gather up her robe and step down from the block.

"Thank you," she squeaked, covering up the betrayal oozing through her veins.

"We aren't out of here, so don't thank me yet." He

gave her a dark look and jerked on her wrist.

Jarred into motion, she followed him to a table set up in the far corner of the room. Her eyes widened when he whipped out a fat roll of bills from the inside pocket of his black leather coat and placed the wad on the table. She had never seen so much money at one time, and Drew Carson tossed it around as if it were nothing.

With a calculated slowness the cashier counted the money, then he jotted down the amounts in a ledger book. Garnet's stomach tightened into a knot of turmoil. She had just been bought and paid for by a stranger, a man of unsavory character if what she'd heard was true. Maybe she'd made a mistake by entrusting Choie Seem to his care as well.

A moment later the crippled girl was brought forward. *"Sse Mo,"* she wailed, and Garnet gathered the dark head to her heart, allowing the childish tears to wash over the silk of her robe.

"It's all right, Choie Seem," she cooed in Chinese, patting the girl's sleek black hair, receiving as much comfort as she gave. Glancing at Drew Carson over the bowed head, she saw him frown and heard his whispered curse.

She winced at the foul words and squeezed her companion tighter, her doubts about what she'd done vanquished. Her decision to beg for Choie Seem's deliverance—right or wrong—had at least kept them together. And together they could face the demons of Hell if need be. She had a sinking feeling they would be confronted by nothing less.

Moving through the deserted corridor that led to the stairway exiting out of the underground barracoon, Bain clamped the slender wrist tighter. All he could think of were dragonfly wings, delicate gossamer, yet strong enough to support the ferocious

58

insect to which they belonged. The woman was like those translucent bits of webbing. She accepted as truth the terrible things Li Fung had said, believed he was his brother Drew, thought she had offered herself up to sacrificial rites in order to save her friend, but when it came to the virtue she had so willingly used to bargain with the Devil, Bain had no doubt she would fight like a tigress to protect it. Fragile yet stalwart enough to survive, a woman different from the others he had known.

There were gentle women like his mother—like Nattie's mother—who had been unable to prevail against the hardships. That's why he chose to remain a bachelor rather than subject the kind of woman he would marry to the rigors of the life he preferred to lead. And then there were the other kind—hard women who managed to survive the obstacles but lost their femininity along the way. The West had plenty of that type of women. Bain found them a poor substitute. But this woman whose fate was now in his hands was a special breed all her own.

He paused on the winding steps and did an about-face. "Your name," he demanded. "I don't know your name." He hoped it wasn't something common like Sal or something old-maidish like Gerty.

"What?" Her jade-green eyes glistened up at him in surprise. "Garnet. Garnet Sinclair," she replied in a voice husky with confusion.

The crispness of her accent made him smile. Yes, this woman was definitely different, and her name suited her well, strong yet beautiful, a jewel to admire. "Well, Miss Garnet Sinclair, I'm . . ."

"I know precisely who you are, Captain Carson," she snapped, holding her head at a stiff, proud angle.

He tightened his grip and felt her cringe beneath the pressure. "I suppose you think you do." He grinned, but he couldn't help himself as he found her ambivalence delightful. Sensing she had misinterpreted his smile—again, he twisted back around and continued up the stairs, forcing her to follow, confident the Oriental girl would be close behind.

A glower crossed his face as he led the way through the crowded gambling parlor. The Oriental girl. Choie Seem. She was young, much younger than Garnet, not much more than sixteen. He had no need for a crippled Chinese girl. What was he going to do with her? Perhaps it would be best if he turned her over to one of the church organizations here in San Francisco that would see her returned to her home and family. He glanced back at the girl, saw the way she clutched at Garnet, and knew in his heart it would mean releasing the Englishwoman as well.

Something he wasn't ready to do yet. He had a need of Miss Garnet Sinclair and her ability to speak Chinese. He had a strong desire to get to know her better.

He frowned, aware he had yet to hear her say anything in Chinese. He whipped back around, concerned. "You do speak Chinese, don't you?"

She looked at him as if she expected him to say something crassly suggestive in that most confusing of languages. "I am multilingual, Captain," she replied, her chin lifting with pride. "Quite adequate in Chinese, French, Spanish, and Italian, as well as tolerable in German and Greek. And if it should prove necessary, I can make myself understood in Russian and Arabic."

"I'm impressed, Miss Sinclair."

"As well you should be, sir," she replied, her nose inching higher.

Contrary to his words, his eyes sparkled with amusement at the haughty way she'd declared what she thought of as her superiority over him.

She buttoned her lips with the air of a prudish old maid. He ignored her, wheeling about and continuing across the room. She was not a woman to mince

60

words, and she had plenty more to say. He had no doubt he would hear more of her opinions before the night was over.

Reaching the front door, he issued a sigh—a mixture of relief and frustration at his predicament. It was hard to believe they had made it this far without incident, but thank God they had. Now all they had to face were the dangers and uncertainties of the San Francisco streets.

He released his grip on Garnet's arm and pulled his coat closed to button it. Then he turned to suggest the women bundle up as well since the damp October fog could chill one to the bones in a few seconds.

"Damn," he muttered, eyeing their thin wrappers and silk-shod feet. They were not dressed to face the cool of the night. In fact, they weren't sufficiently clad to go anywhere except perhaps a whorehouse. He couldn't trust them to be alone without his protection, not even long enough to round up a public carriage to take them to the ship.

Shrugging off his coat, he dropped it about Garnet's shoulders. She clutched it gratefully, and he noted with satisfaction how it swallowed her petite form. Then his eyes slid to her companion. What was he going to do about Choie Seem?

Glancing about the small foyer separated from the main room by a mother-of-pearl screen, he spied the row of jackets hanging on the far wall. Pressing his lips together, he reached out and snagged one. So far this day he had lied, participated in slavery trafficking, and made an enemy out of one of the most powerful men in Chinatown. Now he could add stealing to his list of crimes. He dropped the stolen jacket over the Oriental girl's shoulders and signaled for the women to precede him into the night.

As they stepped into the street, he heard the soft singsong of Choie Seem's voice, though he couldn't understand her words. Garnet shook her head, answered in the same language, and glanced once over her shoulder at him, then looked back at the younger girl and repeated her words.

It annoyed him that he couldn't follow what they were saying. "Speak English," he growled, grabbing Garnet by the upper arm a little rougher than he meant to. But they were still in danger, and there was no time for childish secrets.

Her mouth angled down in what he could only describe as a schoolmarmish frown. "You wouldn't know proper English, Captain Carson, if you heard it," she declared, struggling to escape his painful grip.

"Perhaps not, Miss Sinclair," he replied, releasing her, "but at least I don't sound like I have cotton stuffed up my nose." His gaze slid over her slender form, concealed for the most part by his jacket. "Nor do I walk as if I have sandpaper stuck in my behind."

She flinched at his crudeness, and he was instantly sorry he had said it, but it *had* shut her up.

"I had better damn well understand what the two of you are saying from now on, or I'll have you both keelhauled when we get to the ship. Is my English clear enough?"

"More than enough, sir," she bit back, pulling the jacket tighter about her shoulders.

For a few moments they walked in silence, and he could tell she was self-consciously trying to walk relaxed. He found the stiff little swing of her hips most tantalizing.

"To the ship?" she questioned, at last breaking the uneasy silence between them. "Just where are you planning on taking us?"

"Home."

She whirled to face him, her eyes widening, and she gushed with gratitude. "Captain Carson, your generosity is overwhelming. I never expected so much. China is a long way from here."

62

Bain cocked his head and laughed out loud at her naiveté. "You're right, Miss Sinclair, China is far away, but we're only going down the coast to Monterey. *My* home."

"Then you have no intention of being a gentleman and seeing to Choie Seem's and my safe return." Her countenance changed like quicksilver, confirming her disillusionment and disgust.

"Did you really expect me to be a gentleman?" He could clearly remember the horror on her face at Li Fung's accusations.

"No, but I could hope."

Her truthful confession stung, but then what had he expected? Staring at her rigidly held shoulders, he could well imagine the stuff martyrs were made of. "It's a free country, Miss Sinclair," he replied with a shrug that covered up the crazy disappointment coursing through him. "I can't stop you from hoping."

Her small hand reached out and touched his shoulder with a gentleness that sent a lightning bolt zigzagging to the center of his conscience. "You have no intention of letting us go, do you?" Her plea came from her innocent heart as if she sensed the good in him in spite of what she'd heard.

What was wrong with him? He should reassure her that he had no desire to harm her, would treat her with the upmost respect, only had need of her talent as a teacher. That was what Bain Carson would do without hesitation. He had always been the good twin, the gentle twin, making up for Drew's impetuous nature and tendency to be cruel.

But this women did something to him. Perhaps Mae Ching had been right all along. White devil she had called him, claiming he had stolen Drew's soul upon his death. No, that was pure nonsense. A bit of the adventurer had always been there. He'd just suppressed it, because it had been necessary. But this woman, her touch, her smell, her very essence made him feel more alive than he had felt in a long time. He couldn't let the opportunity to experience this new sensation escape—not yet.

"No, I don't. We have a bargain to settle between us. I expect my money's worth."

She jerked her hand away as if she'd touched slime, and wiped it on his jacket draped about her shoulders. "I'm a Christian woman, Captain. I would rather die than do some things."

"Well, I'm a man of my word, Miss Sinclair. I don't take lightly to someone going back on theirs." He angled his chin at the Oriental girl standing in the protection of her shadow. "I could always send your friend back to the barracoon."

He read the disbelief and horror in her eyes, and it pained him. His hand lifted to touch her, to take back his threat, an empty one he had no intention of following through with even if she refused to cooperate—but she didn't know that. Then he stopped himself. It would be so easy to be snared by the vibrant charms of Garnet Sinclair—so easy. Before he allowed that to happen he had to know. Would she crack or harden when confronted with the cold reality of life? Any woman he considered allowing into his life could do neither. He'd do her a favor, do them both a favor, by putting her through such a test.

His hand curled into a fist at his side. Oh, God, how he yearned for her to pass the stringent test.

Gathering the black leather coat—his coat— closer, Garnet felt more than heard the rustle of paper against her bosom. Following Drew Carson as he wound his way through the unfamiliar streets of San Francisco, she had no idea at first of the importance of her discovery. Curious about what he would have in his pocket, though feeling somewhat like a thief in the night, she slipped her hand inside the lapel, dipping her fingertips into the depths of the material. The single sheaf was crisp, rectangular, the size of . . .

Money. Her heart began to hammer with a surge of renewed hope. The captain had left cash in his coat pocket. Was he aware of what he'd done?

Her fingers curled about the lone bill, her mind whispering a silent prayer of thanks as well as one of forgiveness for her trespass. She had no idea how much money she held, but it must be a lot. She had seen the roll of one hundreds he had used to pay the cashier. Hopefully that was how much she had. One hundred . . . American . . . dollars. Her head spun, calculating. How much would that be in English pounds?

Enough. More than enough to get her and Choie Seem to a safe haven. The thought that she would use the money for more than herself eased her conscience. She darted her gaze to the other girl and smiled reassuringly. "Follow me," she whispered in Chinese.

The girl nodded unquestioningly.

Then she glanced up at her captor, Drew Carson, his thick, dark hair lighter on the tips suggesting he spent a lot of time out-of-doors, his broad shoulders evidence he was more than familiar with manual labor. She sighed with relief when he didn't look back or acknowledge she had spoken. Only too well she remembered his threat to keelhaul them both if they didn't converse in English. Though she didn't know exact what keelhauling was, the way he had said the word suggested it was a most ghastly punishment, and she shivered with fear. She didn't want him to understand what she'd said to Choie Seem. Surprise would be her only advantage.

Curling her palm about the money, she could only

pray they could escape into the darkness before he had a chance to react to their sudden movement. Hopefully, Choie Seem's handicap wouldn't slow them down too much. Remembering their long-ago conversation about how it felt to run, Garnet wished now more than ever for a miracle. But she really didn't expect one. If God had planned to help her out of this predicament, He would have long before now.

Then as if to defy her cynical reasoning, the peal of a church bell echoed in the night. The thick fog about them served only to enhance the chiming. Her heart soared. Of course. They could find solace in a house of God. No matter how uncivil San Francisco might be, there still had to be plenty of churches.

Clutching the money to fortify her bravery and determination, she gave Drew Carson a final assessment, then quick as a blue streak, she spun about, grabbed Choie Seem by the hand, and raced toward the shadows of the buildings across the street.

"What the hell?" she heard her tormentor demand in surprise and confusion, but she didn't stop. In fact, his words spurred her to move even faster.

"*Sse Mo*," Choie Seem gasped, "slow down. Please, I cannot keep up."

"Only a little farther, around this corner, and we'll be safe," she urged the other girl, but in truth she feared she asked the impossible and Choie Seem would lose her footing and fall.

By some miracle—she realized it was exactly that—they reached the other side of the thoroughfare. They weren't far from the wharves, of that fact she was sure, as now and then the blast of a foghorn rent the air. She paused, her heart hammering, her lungs whipping in and out with a grating harshness harmonized by the sound of Choie Seem's ragged breathing. The church? Which way was the church?

"Damn it, Garnet, where are you?" Carson called, the sound of crates and garbage cans being overturned clearly audible as he searched for them not far away.

She shrank back against the side of the building that was deep in shadows, dragging the other girl with her. The captain was close, too close for comfort.

"We have to keep going," she whispered.

The girl shook her head. "I can't," she replied, and Garnet knew she spoke the truth.

It had been foolish to think they could run away. Their only chance was to conceal themselves and hope Drew Carson didn't find them. Then when he moved on, they could take their time locating the church.

Touching the money in the pocket of the jacket to reassure herself it was still there, she settled for this change of plans. Perhaps she would be able to find a carriage for hire on the streets to take them to their desired destination once she was sure they were safe from Captain Carson. All was not lost. At least, not yet.

Spying a sagging stoop a few feet away on the side of the building, Garnet grasped her friend's hand. "We'll hide." She bent low, moving cautiously as she felt her way along the rough, brick wall. Her feet made contact with something sharp and piercing on the ground, and she stumbled, trying to avoid the pain.

The noise her misplaced feet made seemed loud enough to her to wake the dead. Gripping Choie Seem's tiny hand in hers, she slipped beneath the platform, breath held, her blood roaring with fear in her ears. Had Drew Carson heard the sounds as well?

The mist swirled, thick and wet. A foghorn blasted, once, then twice. Then silence, so ominous; the sound of her swallowing down her anxieties was much too loud.

The seconds skipped by and still nothing. Her

heart slowed, her throat unlocked, and she sagged in relief against the wall against which she pressed. If Carson was out there surely she would have heard some evidence by now.

Releasing Choie Seem's hand, she turned, situating herself on her hands and knees to peek out from their hiding place. Not that she thought she could see much, but perhaps she could hear better what was happening.

Her head bumped against something that hadn't been there before. She reached out to push the object aside, and discovered a boot, tall and hard. A man's boot.

"What the hell?" The boot and its mate shuffled against the hard-packed dirt.

She shrieked in response. It was him. It had to be. Reaching up, she balled her fists and slugged with all of her strength where she estimated the backs of his knees should be. She felt the muscled legs buckle from the onslaught, but she didn't wait to see if he toppled. Grabbing Choie Seem's wrist, she jerked the girl out from beneath the stoop and started running blindly, into the circle of yellow light emitted by an overhead street lamp.

Then he was upon her. His arms were like vises, curled about her midriff, crushing her ribs, but she refused to give up. Kicking backwards, she heard the smack of her foot as it made contact with his shin. She wished she wore riding boots instead of the thin Oriental slippers she had on.

"Why you little piece of baggage," he grunted with pain, his arms squeezing tighter, constricting her diaphragm and forcing the air from her lungs.

Then without any regard for her femininity, he whipped out his foot and wrapped it about one of her exposed legs. Thinking the bone would surely snap from the unrelenting pressure, she couldn't keep her balance, and down they went in a heap, him on top.

The side of her face pressed painfully against the rough ground beneath her. Her legs, completely exposed in the melee, were scratched and throbbing where bits of stone and broken glass had cut them. The palms of her hands were scraped raw as well. The only parts of her body uninjured, ironically, were her upper torso, protected by the thickness of his leather jacket, and the curve of her rump where his groin pressed intimately, enough so that she could feel the manly bulge in his pants.

"Get off of me, you bloody blighter," she demanded between her gritted teeth, raising her hips in a frantic attempt to throw him off. She didn't care that she sounded like some guttersnipe from the streets of London. But the movement was a mistake as he only pressed against her harder—more intimately—to keep her from escaping.

For some crazy reason all she could think of was standing on the auction block removing her clothing and the feel of his burning gaze caressing her. The same thrill that had shuddered through her then did so now with a full-blown power as he lay atop her pressing his groin into the soft valley of her buttocks.

This was disgusting! This man was practically mauling her, and all she could think of was how good it felt.

"Get off of me," she choked, striking out blindly with her arms and legs, needing above all else to get away from the feel of his muscle-hard body.

As if sensing she'd reached the end of her mental tether, he pushed up on his knees, releasing her. She twisted, trying to squirm away, but he caught her by one shoulder and forced her over so they faced each other. Her legs were still trapped between his knees, and his hand rested heavily on her upper arm, the back of his fingers mashed against the soft, flattened mound of one breast where the coat had fallen open. His breath was ragged, but she knew it wasn't from exertion any more than her own inability to breathe. Their gazes locked, everything forgotten except the undeniable sparks of desire sizzling between them.

Then she knew. He was going to kiss her. Sucking in a lungful of mist-thick air, she held it, unable to move, barely able to think.

At first his lips merely brushed her tight-lipped mouth, his warm breath as soft as duckling down against the sensitive corners. Then he turned his face at an angle, the very length of his body aligning itself to hers beneath him. His mouth opened, tender, exploring, and through the haze of shock and wonderment that settled like a fog over every nerve in her body, she felt his tongue skirt along her sealed lips.

They parted on their own volition. Before she could clamp them shut again, his tongue slipped into her mouth. At first she lay there, unable to believe a man could do something so vile to a woman. Then from some unknown source deep inside her, she felt a rush of excitement course through her, and as if her own tongue had a mind of its own, it began to move, to intertwine about his.

What kind of jezebel was she that she permitted such liberties to a man—especially this man? She turned her face, ripping her mouth from his, shame and confusion clogging the back of her throat.

"Get off of me," she pleaded, reaching up to wipe off the feel of him from her lips, the words barely audible even to her own ears.

Clutching her chin, he forced her head back around. His mouth that had moments before given such pleasure flattened in what she could only interpret as bewildered anger with himself as much as with her.

"Don't you ever try to escape me again," he demanded. "By damn, I won't allow it." He waited for her reply.

I must escape, her conscience screamed, *or I will surely be pulled down into a whirlpool of forbidden sin.*

His fingers squeezed her chin, commanding compliance and an answer.

She nodded, her eyes wide with fear as she focused on his mouth. His damnable mouth that now held such fascination for her. She bit down hard on her bottom lip to stop the forbidden thoughts.

Though she had agreed to his demand, in her heart she knew if the opportunity to run away presented itself again, she wouldn't dare hesitate to take advantage of it.

Chapter Four

Garnet Sinclair. Her name was every bit as beautiful and intriguing as she was. Bain watched the unconscious swing of her womanly hips outlined by the light of the shipboard lanterns left burning on his orders. She walked in front of him up the gangplank of the *China Jewel* clutching the hand of her crippled companion. When she paused, he stiffened. If she tried to turn back or run away again he would stop her. He was not about to let her make a fool of him once more.

The thought appalled his sense of right and wrong, but he didn't try to deny the feeling existed within him. She was no different than the wild ponies he captured and gentled each spring in the valleys beyond the ranch, no different than the virgin soils he cultivated and planted quite often with his own hands to yield the fruits of his patient labor. He watched her nose wrinkle in what he assumed was disapproval, then he latched onto the key word. Patience. In time she would be his as much as the land and the livestock were.

His gaze returned to the rhythm of her hips until she crossed out of the ring of light. Who was he fooling? Here he was comparing the honorable way he made a living—he, Bain Carson—to the calculated seduction of a woman. That was something his brother, Drew, would have done with such compulsion. Drew the scoundrel, not Bain the redeemer.

For one unfettered moment he could understand and sympathize with what had made his brother the way he had been. His perception cloaked him with an unsettling feeling, and he brushed at one shoulder in an effort to rid himself of it. Perhaps once he shed his pretense of being Drew, he would return to normal.

Damn. He couldn't wait to get home, couldn't wait to return to those things he loved best: his ranch, his lifestyle, Nattie his little sister, and Mae Ching. Which reminded him of his reason for bringing Garnet with him in the first place, to teach his little niece English.

Aboard ship, he hurried forward and took Garnet by the arm. "This way," he indicated with a jerk of his head.

Without comment or protest she allowed him to guide them toward the companionway, past the gape-mouthed sailor on guard duty who had known the purpose of his trip to San Francisco.

"Cap'n," the man acknowledged with a nod and halfhearted salute.

Bain gave the seaman a stern, silent glare as he brushed by him, squelching anything the old sea dog might have been about to say. Down the stairway they moved, and he brought the two women to a halt before the door of the captain's cabin. Drew's cabin. The place in which his brother had taken his last labored breath. The room had been tidied, the soiled bedding destroyed and replaced with a new down-filled mattress, but Bain still had trouble thinking of it as anything but Drew's domain.

He leveled a glance at Garnet. How would she feel knowing she stayed in a dead man's quarters? Would it bother her? In her mind's eyes Drew Carson was alive and well and holding her against her will. Deciding that what she didn't know about the room wouldn't hurt her, he opened the door and entered first to light the lantern by the door, then made a gesture to indicate she should enter.

Garnet strolled forward, that inquisitive nose of hers again lifting to take a sniff. She shot him a frown, as if to say, "If this is the best you can do," and reached for the other girl. "Come, Choie Seem," she said guardedly.

"No," Bain stated in a flat, even voice, capturing the Oriental girl's arm. "She'll come with me."

Choie Seem's almond-shaped eyes widened with abject terror, and she shrank back from his outstretched hand.

"Surely you can't mean to separate us," Garnet choked, the pain and fear—not for herself but for her friend—evident in her jade-green gaze.

"That's exactly what I mean to do. I think such a move will deter any notion you might harbor of trying to escape before we weigh anchor in a few hours." There. He could see the guilty flash in her eyes. That was precisely what she'd considered doing. He felt no qualms about separating the two women. In truth it was for their own good. Alone in San Francisco, especially at night, two scantily clad females would be in trouble before they could figure out which way to go. "You'll stay here until I deem it's safe to let you out." He turned to go, and then as an afterthought swung back around, pointing toward the far wall. "Should you get bored or find you can't sleep, there's a trunk of women's clothing in the corner left by my br—"

He bit down on his tongue as he had nearly given himself away and said "brother." "You're welcome to go through it. If anything should suffice for either of you, you can have it."

75

When he had discovered the trunk he had been truly surprised at its contents, knowing Drew as well as he did. His brother had not been one to bestow gifts upon women, at least not anything they would value. No doubt the trunk of dresses had been meant for Mae Ching's mother. Had Drew in truth loved the woman the way he'd claimed he had on his deathbed? Bain sighed inwardly. A mystery he would never have an answer to—not now.

Before he grew sentimental and changed his mind about separating the women, he pulled Choie Seem out of the doorway and shoved the barrier closed. As a final precaution he took a ring of keys from his pocket and locked it.

He heard Garnet rush forward, felt her shake the door handle in protest before he released it. It was better this way. At least he would know she was safe.

"You brute." Her muffled dressing-down filtered through the walls as her fists pounded a staccato on the door.

Bain ignored her as well as the painful twist in his heart at the sound of her desperation. Taking Choie Seem in hand, he led the shuffling girl down the passageway to the tiny chart room he had been using as his quarters on the trip to San Francisco. He opened the door to the cubicle and, finding the light already lit, he signaled for the girl to enter.

"I have no intention of locking you in unless I hear that you've tried to leave your quarters or are in any way attempting to communicate with Miss Sinclair. If you know what's best for both of you, you'll obey my orders."

The Oriental girl's head bobbed like a corked bottle in a surf. Bain felt confident she would give him no trouble. He was just as sure Garnet Sinclair would, if given half a chance.

*　　*　　*

Garnet lifted her fists and pounded again on the locked door. What nerve that insufferable, vile . . . American had. She made a snort of pure disgust and and attacked the unyielding barrier with renewed strength. Nothing but silence greeted her from the other side.

Drew Carson had dared to treat her like a prized brood mare at an auction, had forced her to follow him through the dark streets of his barbaric city, then had had the audacity to throw her on the ground as if she were no more than some chippy of the night seeking his tasteless advances. But if that wasn't bad enough, he had locked her in a strange cabin on a foul-smelling ship and offered her the cast-off clothing—and probably the bed—of some other woman, most likely his current mistress, as if he expected her to be eternally grateful. He had gall, unbelievable gall, to think she would be even remotely appreciative of his gesture.

In angry frustration she whipped around, slamming her back against the unyielding door. Jerking off the leather coat—his coat—that she still wore, she vented her anger by balling it up and pitching it against the wall, its brass buttons smacking against the dark, walnut paneling with a metallic clack dangerously close to the sputtering whale oil lantern. Air hissing between her clenched teeth, she closed her eyes and pressed her shoulders against the door, desperately wishing the jacket was Drew Carson's head instead.

Taking several deep, cleansing breaths, she began to see the futility and ineffectuality of her reaction. If she wanted to get out of this situation, then she must be the one to do something about it. For too long, since that ill-fated day at her father's mission, she had been like a bit of flotsam in a raging sea, battered back and forth between the wills and wants of others.

It would not be that way anymore.

But what could she do locked in a cabin of a ship sailing to some unfamiliar locale? She dropped her head into her hands, almost ready to accept defeat, but then she spied the despicable condition of the black, silk robe she wore.

Her jaws tightened with determination. She wasn't sleepy, and she had no intention of lying down on that bed unprotected. So the first thing she would do was see she had something decent and proper to wear. If *that* meant accepting Drew Carson's offer, then by all means *that* was what she would do. Her gaze drifted reluctantly to the trunk in the corner.

Pushing away from the door, she marched across the room. After only a moment's hesitation, she knelt before the plain, brassbound chest and pushed up the heavy lid. The odor of camphor rose to meet her, but the chest was in shadows, and she couldn't make much of its contents. She stood, retrieved the lantern from the holder on the wall, and set it on the floor beside her as she returned to her knees.

Just as he had said, the coffer was full of women's clothing, amazingly stylish by her standards, More amazing was their perfect order. Somehow she'd expected to find a jumble, the results of a pirate's looting, but instead each gown was lovingly wrapped in a sheet of tissue paper, pressed and folded with minute detail to see that it was as wrinkle-free as possible.

Sitting back on her haunches, she blinked, feeling as if she'd invaded a private sanctuary. Then clenching her teeth together, she moved forward again and reached out to touch the top dress, one of lilac silk poplin with an abundance of lace and bows. It was beautiful, too much so. Carefully she set it aside.

She riffled through the first pile, one gown after another, until she came upon a cuir-colored silk with

78

a simple cut, the only attempts at design thin bands of darker brown ribbon near the skirt hem and a touch of fringe at the shoulders. She lifted it out, shook off the tissue, held it up for inspection, and decided she liked it, especially the fringe. To her surprise the dress looked as if it had been cut to fit her. Setting it aside, she continued her search until she located everything she needed: camisole, drawers, corset, and even a pannier to attach at her waist to puff out the back of the dress in the latest style. Lifting out the contraption, she stared at it it in amazement. This one was different from the horse-hair bustles she was familiar with, obviously the latest style as it collapsed when she pushed on it. What would they think of next?

At the very bottom of the trunk were shoes and stockings to match. Finally, in a small pocket in the satin lining of the trunk she found a brush, gold hairpins, and ribbons to compliment the ensemble. Whoever had purchased the clothing had thought of everything. Had that person been Drew Carson? If so, it gave her new insight into his personality.

Straightening out the contents of the chest, she closed the lid and rose to her feet, scooping up the lantern to set it on the table near the bed in a holder that was obviously made for just that purpose.

She glanced at the polished surface of the table, then down at the clothing in her hands. What kind of man was Drew Carson? He had treated her with such insensitivity, yet she could distinctly remember the flashes of compassion in his gray eyes the first time she'd seen him in the crowd at the barracoon. He had seemed so gallant, so brave at that time, not at all the brute who had manhandled her in the streets.

Perplexed by his swing of personality, she began to get dressed. Then she remembered what he had said when he'd shown her the chest. *There's a trunk of women's clothing left by my br—*

79

His what?

"Br-r-r." She rolled the phonetic sound on her tongue and racked her brain to come up with an answer as she put the final touches on her toilette. The only word she could find to fill in the blank was "bride." She paused, staring into the oval shaving mirror she'd found attached to one wall. Did these clothes belong to Drew Carson's wife?

The thought startled her—upset her more than it should have. If he was married, or about to be, how could he have kissed her the way he had earlier? Some emotion she couldn't name, or refused to name, twisted her insides with a sharp pain. Now, more than ever, she knew she had to escape this man and the potential of sin that dangled before her like a forbidden carrot.

Bain drew the key from his pocket and slipped it into the lock. Then he paused, his hand on the latch listening, wondering what he would discover when he opened the door. The unbroken silence baffled him. When he had left Garnet she had been mad as hell and screeching like a nor'easter. That had been only a couple of hours ago, and he found it hard to believe the storm raging inside the cabin had quieted so easily. If she was up to something—and he wouldn't put the possibility past her—he was prepared.

Working the key, he turned the latch and pushed the door open. What he found unhinged his jaw, and he stood staring like a jackass, he realized, but he couldn't help himself. The last thing he expected was to find her asleep.

Garnet was beautiful, highlighted in the glow of the lamp she'd left burning, more so that he could have ever imagined. She sat on the edge of the bed, her back straight, her hand folded primly in her lap,

80

her head resting against the wall against which the bunk was affixed. Her gown, the color of freshly tanned leather, fit her to a tee. The ribbon streamers framing her face, from where she'd pinned them in the back of her upswept hair, gave her a feminine softness that literally took his breath away.

"Miss Sinclair?" he whispered, his voice breaking like a boy entering puberty, almost unable to believe this was the disheveled woman he had rescued only hours before. He glanced down at the discarded silk robe at her feet confirming that she was indeed one and the same.

She stirred, her eyes fluttering open, somewhat disoriented. Then her eyes flashed with fire.

"Captain Carson," she murmured, her voice still gravelly with sleep, the knob of her chin jutting forward, her mouth pursing unconsciously, accenting its inviting velvetiness.

Bain cleared his throat, wet his lips with the tip of his tongue, and remembered how that mouth had felt against his own. The urge to take what he wanted was so strong he strolled forward, but she tensed, the wariness in her green eyes stopping him halfway across the cabin.

Thrusting his hands into the pockets of his tight, charcoal gray pants, he lifted a brow, attempting to appear unperturbed by her presence. "I came to tell you we're out of the harbor now and will soon leave the bay and reach open waters. You are free to move about the ship as long as you don't stir up trouble."

"Thank you, Captain Carson," she replied, her voice crackling with emotion just as his had earlier, her gaze never leaving his.

Then it struck him. She was thinking about their shared kiss just as he was. She might even have been dreaming of it before he had disturbed her. Shifting his position from one foot to the other, he straightened.

What would Drew have done in this situation? He eyed her with speculation and immediately knew the answer. His brother would have ignored the tug of conscience—if he'd ever had one—and taken advantage of the moment and the woman.

And was that so wrong? She wanted him to kiss her as much as he wanted to.

As if possessed, he stepped back toward the door, and closed it. Her gaze followed, her body jerking when the latch clicked shut. Then he approached her—more like stalking her—her head notching higher and higher with each stride he took. Soon he stood directly in front of her, staring down at the long, silken column of her neck strained with the angle of her head.

The impulse to ask permission stuck like grit in his craw. The real him—Bain—always asked, even a whore, before he would proceed. How would it feel just to take?

He reached out and placed his hands on her shoulders and rubbed lightly up and down once. Gripping her flesh, he brought her to her feet. The pulse in her throat jumped like a jackrabbit trapped in the jaws of a coyote, and his thumb eased out to soothe it. She swallowed, her gaze pleading for release.

That he couldn't grant, not until he'd assuaged his own fantasy and desire. All he wanted was a kiss, just one little kiss, he assured himself, nothing more, and he would be satisfied.

Swift and hard, before he changed his mind, he pressed his mouth to hers. She didn't move; in fact, she barely breathed, but she didn't resist him either. Encouraged, he opened his mouth over hers, urging her to do the same. Instead she stiffened.

"No," she murmured, attempting to turn her face, her arms moving up to clamp the hard muscles of his forearms.

82

The challenge became full-blown in his mind. She wanted this as much as he did, he reminded himself.

"Yes," he insisted refusing to accept defeat. With his tongue he reamed her sealed lips until at last she relented to his demand.

She sighed, the rush of sweet, warm air making his blood boil with heated desire. Her fingers released their clutch on his arms and drifted downwards. Plunging into her open crevice, he savored the texture, the taste of her mouth.

He should stop, but, oh, God, he needed it to last just a little longer, and he deepened the kiss, taking his time exploring the untouched recesses he discovered, instincts telling him he was the first. The heady rush of knowledge served only to heighten his desire. This was new to her, but then the act of taking without permission was just as novel to him.

God knows, giving was a way of life with him. The women he had known had told him that and quite readily—not that he prided himself in his sexual prowess; it was just his way. He was a tender lover, even with women who most men considered unworthy.

Now, for the first time in his life, he held a woman who deserved tender loving, and he found himself battling with some inner rebellion in order to give it.

Swallowing down the lack of control, he pulled away, his breath as ragged as a set of leaking bellows. Her lips were parted and swollen, still moist from his kiss. Her eyes were closed, the lashes pale and thick where they lay against her passion-rouged cheeks. When at last they fluttered opened, the jade green of her orbs reminded him of the planted fields of home.

Sanity and chagrin crashed in on him. He should let her go.

Reluctantly, he relaxed his arms, one finger lifting to curl a brown hair ribbon about its length.

He should tell her the truth. Who he really was.

"Garnet," he began in a voice still husky with unsatisfied desire.

The floor beneath them lurched once, pulling them apart. Then it bucked again, throwing them back together, their bodies meshing from knees to chests. His arm shot out to steady her, knowing the reason for the sudden change in rhythm in the ship's movement was nothing to be concerned about. It happened whenever a vessel left the protection of the bay and hit the open sea, which was always rougher.

Something Garnet apparently didn't know. She screamed, pushing him away with all of her strength as she pitched herself toward the closed cabin door.

"No. Wait." Bain reached out to stop her, to comfort her, to explain to her what was happening. His questing fingers caught her shoulder and tangled in the strip of decorative fringe.

The ripping sound it made as she spun from his grip was ominous. He stood there staring stupidly at the bit of material left in his hand. Then he looked up and saw the disastrous rent in the arm and bodice of her gown, and the look of pure terror in her eyes. My God, she thought he had torn her clothing on purpose.

Their gazes held only a moment, and before he could utter an explanation, she darted to the door and snatched it open, one hand holding together the shredded pieces of her dress.

"Garnet, wait, damn it," he called, but he could hear her tread already on the companionway as she headed toward the upper deck. Still clutching the piece of fringe, Bain followed, a feeling of impending doom gathering in his mind like a band of black thunderclouds.

She should have known better than to trust him, to let her guard down even for a moment. Drew

Carson's intentions had been quite plain—the circumstantial evidence against him, her destroyed dress.

Garnet pressed the ruined bodice to her chest and felt the uneven pounding of her heart. He had forced her twice to kiss him, and now he wanted more—he wanted his payment for rescuing her from the barracoon—and his choice of compensation was not something she was willing to sacrifice.

She reached the top of the stairway and poised balanced on the balls of her feet, trying to decide which way to go. What she saw wasn't encouraging. Even at this early hour, the deck was crowded with sailors, many of whom turned to stare at her as they paused in their labor.

Was this how a mouse felt, trapped in a room with everyone chasing it? Frightened? Doomed? Nowhere to run? Behind her she heard the approaching gait of Drew Carson. She couldn't allow him to catch her, to do what it was he wanted to do. God forgive her, but she couldn't sell her soul to the devil without first putting up a fight.

Glancing out over the ship's rail, she saw the streak of sunrise painting the eastern sky, outlining the strip of white sandy beach in the distance. The shore wasn't that far away. If she were to jump, would it be that difficult to reach?

But what of Choie Seem? She looked behind her. Could she desert her friend? It wasn't the Oriental girl Drew Carson wanted. Choie Seem would be safe enough, so her mind reasoned.

The ship lurched beneath her, and she reassessed the choppy seas. Did she have the strength to reach the distant shore?

The sound of Carson's feet on the steps below her grew steadily closer. So little time to make up her mind.

"Garnet, come back here," he ordered as if he knew

she had nowhere to run.

Her heart hammered with indecision. What choice did she have except to trust her fate to the mercy of the ocean and God? Surely He would not forsake her now. Glancing at the sailors all around her who eyed her with curiosity, she realized mercy would be nonexistent on this ship.

She started running. The wooden heels of the new shoes she wore clicked against the decking. It seemed a shame for them to be ruined, but there was no helping it. Reaching the railing, she clutched the smooth, polished brass and threw herself over it without hesitation, without thinking about where she was headed.

Falling. Falling. Endlessly.

"Gar-r-r-net!"

She heard the faraway cry and recognized the distress in Drew Carson's voice, and she giggled, almost hysterically, at the fact there was nothing he could do now to stop her.

The water gripped her like stinging palms, slapping at her legs, her buttocks, her stomach, her face. It was so much colder than she'd expected. Her mouth opened in a giant gasp, and to her shock her mouth and nose filled with briny water, burning and bitter. Kicking her feet, she found them imprisoned in the weight of her skirts and useless. Using her arms, she reached upwards, fighting the downward motion that didn't seem to want to stop. Down. Down. Surely she would hit the bottom soon. Her lungs ached, her head pounded. Her mind accepted that death was only seconds away, but surely this was better than what Drew Carson had in store for her.

Then the motion reversed itself, and she was speeding upwards toward the surface. Pulling with her arms, she shot like a bullet through the water, bits and pieces of seaweed and trash moving with her.

From the corner of her eyes she caught the swish of a tiny fish scurrying out of her way. The fact that something alive in the ocean would dare swim so close left her in shock.

Her lungs passed the point of bursting and surprisingly no longer hurt as her eyes blurred, her head spun, her mind became disoriented. She couldn't possibly reach the surface in time, but death no longer seemed so frightening. For the life of her she couldn't understand why, and found herself smiling there in that watery grave.

The top of her head cleaved the surface, the frigid air enveloping her not at all inviting, even as her nose and mouth broke free, and she sucked a breath of oxygen into her empty lungs.

Surprised at her own survival, she treaded water, turning to note her surroundings, gasping as the cold fingers of air wrapped about her. To one side the dark wall of the ship blocked her view, but just ahead she could see the horizon streaked yellow and white against the beach.

The beach. She turned and began to swim as best she could, but her progress was slow due to the weight of her wet skirts. Behind her she heard a loud splash, and remembering the tiny fish she'd seen earlier, all she could think of was of some giant sea predator coming after her, crushing her body between its mighty jaws, ripping the flesh from her bones. She cried out and continued her struggle, aiming for the faraway shore that seemed to grow farther away as the sun rose higher.

Something clamped her skirts and pulled.

"No," she screamed, kicking with her feet, envisioning the toothy beast that had her in its clutches. Then she went under, the water cutting off her protest and making it nothing but useless bubbles. Her foot touched something solid, and she struck out again, hoping beyond reason to do damage to the sea monster determined to make her its morning meal.

Something hard and strong clamped her arm, and she shrieked, the sound surfacing the same moment as her head. Anticipating the feel of sharp teeth ripping at her flesh, she rolled, her free hand balled and ready to do battle, David against Goliath, her fist as lethal as a slingshot. Expecting the beady, bloodthirsty gaze of a shark, she instead was confronted with something worse—the angry gray eyes of Drew Carson.

"You," she gurgled, seawater rushing into her open mouth. She spit it out and swung her fist, aiming for the side of his face.

He dodged her blow by merely ducking under-water and taking her unprepared with him. Their gazes met beneath the surface, and she tried to swing again, but the water made her arm ineffectual. His hair stood on end, encircling his face, making him appear more frightening than ever. Then her own hair floated between them, blocking her view.

Only when she thought her lungs would burst, and she ceased her struggle, did he allow them to come up for air. But she was not bested, not yet. Taking a deep breath, she curled her fingers into claws, striking out at his dripping cheek. His eyes narrowed, and he went down again, dragging her with him.

This time she had plenty of air, and be damned if she couldn't outlast him. Pressing her lips tightly together, she prepared to wait, allowing her breath to trickle out a bubble at a time. Slowly her lungs emptied, yet he seemed in no hurry to go up. Even underwater she could read his challenge, and realized she'd misjudged his determination and his lung capacity.

Her reasons for jumping overboard had not been

suicidal, only to escape, but die she would if she didn't get air soon. She reached out and gripped his arm, a signal of her momentary relenting. Momentary, she assured herself as he pushed upwards to the surface.

The second their heads crested, his hand tightened on her arm. His hair lay plastered to his skull, and she knew hers must be as well.

"What in the hell do you think you're doing?" he demanded, attempting to shake her but doing nothing more than hurting her arm.

"I will not be subjected to your ghastly treatment," she sputtered. Yet in truth, she was only too glad that he held her up, as she was tired, bone tired, and didn't think she could fight the fury of the sea another minute.

"Ghastly treatment?" he mocked. "Hell, I just saved your wretched life."

"I would have made it, if you would have simply left me alone," she retorted, angry that he resorted to foul language, angrier still that he was right.

"About all you would have made, Miss Sinclair, was fine driftwood. Good, Christ, woman. _I_ couldn't have swum that far, and I'm a damn good swimmer."

She wanted to shout at him, to call him vile names. Instead she said in a voice that would have pleased her father to no end, "There's no need to use the Lord's name in vain, Captain Carson. You could have just as easily made your point without doing so. Now, turn loose of me this instant."

For a moment she thought he intended to oblige her and let her go, so obvious was his ire. Instead he began moving toward the ship, dragging her behind him.

"Miss Sinclair, I have no doubt one day I'll regret saving you, not once but twice."

"And I suspect, Captain Carson," she retaliated,

aware that he was careful to keep her head above the water as they moved, "I'll regret it too." The moment she returned to his ship there would be no escape, not from him nor the uncontrollable desire urging her to succumb to his demands of compensation.

Oh, why? Why did he have to display this undercurrent of concern for her? And why did she have to be so acutely aware of it?

Chapter Five

Once they reached the side of the ship Garnet had no will or strength to fight him anymore. At Drew's command, a rope was tossed over the side. She didn't protest when he told her to put her foot into the loop at the end and to hang on; no matter what, she was to not turn loose of the rope. Then she was being pulled aboard, the motion slow and jerky.

She swung against the side of the ship, hitting her shoulder, which nearly knocked her from her precarious perch.

"Use your foot, Garnet. Push off from the freeboard each time you get too close."

Freeboard? Having no idea what he was talking about, she glared down at him. He grinned encouragement at her. She pursed her lips in response, trying to ignore how vulnerable he looked treading water below her. But the next time she swung too close to the side of the ship, she put out her foot to keep from banging against it.

Soon she was gripping a stanchion and pulling herself over the rail with the help of several sailors.

"Ma'am," one of them said with courtesy, touching the edge of his hat with a fingertip. He sat her to the side and dismissed her, his attention returning to the sea below where his captain waited.

She stood there, the frigid October air seeping into her pores causing her to shiver. Soon her teeth joined in chattering, clicking, and clattering, until she thought her jaws would lock and cramp. She had been cold in the water, but nothing had prepared her for the bitterness of standing in the freezing wind dripping wet. Curling her arms about her shoulders, she closed her eyes trying to conjure up body warmth.

"Damn it, where's another blanket?"

Garnet's eyes snapped open to see Drew striding toward her, ripping off the heavy coverlet someone had draped about his shoulders. Without a word, he came forward, wrapped her cocoon-style in the scratchy wool—it was warm, oh, God, so warm—and swept her up into his arms. Her cheek—so cold— pressed against his bare chest where his shirt had come unbuttoned. His flesh radiated heat although it was still wet, a hard plane matted with soft down, a pillow for her throbbing head, the sound of his racing heart a comfort.

She nestled close, couldn't help herself, and was rewarded as his heartbeat picked up tempo against her ear.

"You little fool, you could have well been the death of both of us. And you still might if we don't get out of these wet clothes." He tore his gaze from hers long enough to look at someone to the side she couldn't see. "The bath and warm water," he ordered. "Hurry. And wake up Doc. Tell him to make up one of his famous tonics to ward off the chills."

Down the companionway and back into the room from which they'd come. In the corridor a few doors away stood Choie Seem, her eyes bright with worry.

"*Sse Mo*," she called, shuffling forward with as much speed as her crippled feet could muster.

Garnet hadn't meant to frighten the girl, but in truth she had to admit she'd been only thinking of herself when she'd jumped overboard. Ashamed at her selfishness, she reached out a conciliatory hand and squeezed the girl's smaller one.

"It's all right, Choie Seem. I'm fine. Really, I'm fine."

Shaking with fear, the Chinese girl looked up at Captain Carson. "Please allow me to take care of her," she pleaded.

He frowned and shook his head. "No. I can take care of her myself."

The girl didn't argue, and unbelievably neither did Garnet, as he spun about, angling so he could fit them both into the doorway, leaving Choie Seem standing in the hallway.

Garnet's heart buffeted her rib cage like a set of tidal waves smashing the shore. When he set her on her feet in the middle of the room, she remained motionless, waiting, shivering as much from anticipation as cold.

He paused, looked around, and seemed to mentally shake himself as if this cabin held memories and images he'd much rather forget. She wanted to ask him about them but didn't dare, certain his answer, if he gave one, would not be to her liking. Her eyes darted to the chest packed with feminine clothing. Had it something to do with the woman to whom they belonged?

She found herself breaking one of God's explicit commandments—thou shall not covet—unable to stop the rush of desire bubbling up from the core of her being to seep into every nerve of her body. How could she, who prided herself in her abilities to effortlessly choose between right and wrong, be feeling what she did for this stranger she knew so little about?

How could she not? The way he stood there, absorbing every nuance of her—this man who could be arrogantly cocky one minute, as unsure of what he should do next as she was.

"Oh, Drew," she whispered, closing her eyes and lowering her head, an emotion she'd never felt before blotting out the morals that had been a part of her life for as long as she could remember.

She heard his deep intake of air as if the sound of his given name on her lips distressed him.

"Garnet, I . . ."

The knock on the door cut off the rest of what he was about to say. Two men lugged in a tin bathtub, and returned a few minutes later with buckets of steaming water. As the bath was prepared he and she stared at each other from across the room, eyeing, assessing, caressing.

She blushed, even in her innocence understanding what was taking place between them, and to her amazement he reddened also. It was as if she saw a totally different side of him—a chameleon who could change from brown to green, arrogant to retiring, experienced to untried, as she watched him.

In reality, what kind of man was Drew Carson? Her insuppressible curiosity sealed the cracks through which her conscience tried to reenter her being.

At the very last, one of the men set a coffee pot and two mugs on the table. "Doc says to drink it all. He says this stuff will take the chill out of an iceberg."

"Doc must have the eyes of a clairvoyant. He has no idea how rightly he's assessed the situation," Drew mumbled, tearing his eyes from hers and nodded his dismissal to his men. Yet even when the door closed leaving the two of them completely alone, he didn't move, not until she shivered beneath the wool blanket that was beginning to smell like a wet mongrel.

He took it from her shoulders and made a face. "I don't know who this belongs to, but I swear, sailors are no better than stray dogs; they won't bathe unless you threaten to throw them overboard.'' He wadded up the blanket, stepped to the door, and tossed it out into the corridor. Turning back, he narrowed his eyes, his fists planting on his hips, a little of the arrogance returning. Then he moved to the table and picked up a mug, filling it with the aromatic brew and presenting it to her with a deceptive laziness. "Why don't you go first," he offered, indicating the tub with a jerk of his head.

The enticing smell of peppermint curled about her. Taking the drink, she swallowed a mouthful, the warmth like lava flowing down her throat. She watched him fill a second mug for himself. He eyed her over the rim as he drank, and she knew he awaited—no, anticipated—her response to his suggestion.

She shook her head, refusing to comply, denying the feelings swelling like waterlogged debris pulling her down, down against her will, against her better judgment.

"Very well, then.'' He set his empty cup on the table. "I'll go first." He reached up to release the bottom two buttons of his damp shirt.

"No." She clutched the mug in one hand and the fasteners at her own throat with the other, attempting to trap her floundering strength of will.

"No? Then would you have the water turn cold?" One brow lifted, the corner of his mouth following as if attached. "Don't be foolish, get in that bath."

"I will if you leave.''

"I don't want to, and you don't really want me to either.''

"That's not true.''

"Isn't it?" He stepped forward, took the mug from her fingers, and settled it beside his own discarded one.

The muscles in her stomach rebelled against his brazenness as well as the warmth of his hand so close to hers. Pressing her palm to her fluttering middle, she held her ground, knowing he was right. She did wish he would stay.

"What you really want is for me to do this." His next step brought him within arm's reach. He grasped her shoulders and pulled her forward, his face angling downward, his lips brushing against hers.

"You're arrogant," she stated, slanting her face away, as if that would stop him.

His tongue touched the corner of her mouth. "You smell and taste of peppermint."

She pulled back, her mouth open. She panted, her tongue darting out to swipe at her lips. "You attempt to take advantage of my confusion, sir."

"You've already taken advantage of my generosity. Seems a fair trade to me." His hands moved down decisively, capturing her slim waist.

This time, when he kissed her there was no hesitation. His lips covered hers, his tongue probed, and it shocked her to discover she found its presence most natural, most agreeable. She couldn't say the same for his arrogant assessment of the situation. Wedging her hands between their bodies, she pulled her face to the side and pushed against his chest. His heart hammered against her open palm.

"I think, sir, you're mistaken. I'll strike no bargain with you."

His fingers clamped about her jaw and brought her face back around to confront his. "I think, Garnet, I tire of your games. You're the one who offered anything."

"And like Satan himself, you've come round to collect your errant soul." She tried to lift her chin, but his grasp wouldn't allow movement.

"Keep your soul, Garnet. I have no use for it."

His words were harsh, and she expected the same from his touch. To her surprise, his hands were gentle upon her flesh. Chill bumps followed in the wake of his caresses, leaving her breathless and wanting more. At that moment she would have gladly exchanged her soul for the strength of mind to do other than melt like so much paraffin beneath the heat of his questing fingers, but no devil came to bargain. Soon she was soft and pliant, molding to his desires and demands.

His hands, at first, remained within the bounds of propriety, fondling her arms, her shoulders, the curve of her back. His mouth, however, grew much bolder. His kiss was deep and thorough, a mixture of tongue, teeth, and wetness that not only plundered her lips, but her cheek, finally settling on her ear. The feel of his hot breath against the sensitive shell sent her mind spiraling deep into a vortex from which there was no escape.

She knew what it was that possessed her, had heard her father devote many a sermon to the evils of lust. She was being tested and failing miserably, and at the moment didn't care. Her hands moved up to clutch his broad shoulders, clinging in order to stay on her feet.

"Garnet," he whispered, his hands finally moving into forbidden territory. One cupped the roundness of her backside, pressing her pelvis against the hardness of his thigh and leg, which lifted slightly to mold against her femininity. The other found her breast, and even with the layer of clothing between them, the peak hardened, straining against the fabric as if begging for release.

Without giving her a chance to realize what was happening, he unbuttoned her bodice, his hand slipping inside her camisole. His palm was warm, shockingly so, and calloused, rough as a cat's tongue, the hand of a man not afraid to work. Arching her spine to press closer, she moaned, her head lolling back in surrender.

97

A strange tightness gathered in the pit of her stomach, an ache almost, a sensation that tautened with each stroke of his hand. His knee pressed harder against that forbidden area between her thighs, the place where she had never been touched, the place that she had never even dared to acknowledge existed. Opening to his insistent pressure, she felt his leg moving against her. Like flint against steel, a shower of sparks ignited the kindling of desire within her. Her knees buckled, and she slid down his leg, which served only to stoke the flame brighter. His hands on her waist, he guided her up and down, a slow, deliberate torture. Her heart raced, slammed to a halt, then raced again, threatening to burst from the confines of her chest.

She heard his throaty chuckle. "You like that, Garnet, don't you?"

Her only response was to move against his leg on her own accord. Try as she might, she couldn't stop herself.

His arm curled against her small of her back, and he lifted her high, bringing the exposed flesh of her bosom to his mouth. Warm and wet, his lips encircled the aureola, tugging and licking, the suckling sounds he made serving to stimulate her further.

Never in her life had she experienced such bliss. Never in her twenty-one years had she thought such uncontrollable delight could exist. Her father had preached that temptation would rear its ugly head, but nothing had prepared her for how impossible a task it would be to resist it. Temptation, sin, lust, her mind screamed in protest. Her body moved quicker against his leg, her fingers reaching up to entwine in his soft hair to make sure he didn't stop the tender assault on her breast.

"Drew," she gasped, the huskiness in her voice sounding foreign—wanton—to her own ears.

He scooped her up, one arm behind her knees, the other about her rib cage, his palm laying claim to his newly acquired domain, her breast. The ache between her thighs intensified now that his body no longer touched her there. She flung her arms around his neck, pressing her face against the soft matting of his chest. He smelled of the sea: warm, alive, and very masculine.

At the edge of the bathtub, he hesitated for only a moment, then, as if he shrugged away demons of his own, he took a deep breath. He stood her on her feet and, without a word, he reached down to finish unbuttoning the front of her dress. "No more foolishness, Garnet. I want you in that bath."

Her eyes followed his movement, gloried in the way his fingers deftly slipped each satin-covered fastener from its loop. Raising her eyes to meet his, she could find no reason to stop him. He had seen her before divested of clothing; what would it matter if he did so again?

Moments later he had the wet, ruined gown stripped from her body. Pulling at the string at her waist, he untied the bustle and dropped it on the floor. Picking at the water-swollen knot of the ties of her corset, he mumbled a curse when it refused to succumb to his demands. He reached into his pocket, took out a spring knife, sliced the cords on each side of the knot, flipped the blade closed, and returned it to his pocket before she could utter a protest. Without the ties the corset was useless.

The severed strings unlaced on their own accord, freeing her upper torso from the restricting confinement. Unconsciously she took a deep breath, her breasts rising proudly with her actions. His hands captured them, pulling down the tiny cap sleeves of her camisole and liberating the feminine globes. As he lifted their heaviness in his palms, his thumbs stroked over the nipples, circling, eliciting a response, a tightening that ricocheted through every nerve and fiber of her body.

With a deep sigh, he let go of her, and finished the task he'd begun, even kneeling to strip the stockings from her long, shapely legs.

"Now," he said, standing, one hand propped on his hip in studied disregard, though she noticed his Adam's apple bobbed with regret. "Get into that water."

She complied, stepping into the tin tub and sinking into the warm water. The liquid soothed, smelling of an assortment of herbs, some of which she recognized, some of which she didn't.

Taking up a square of cloth that had been draped over the rim of the tub, he squatted beside her and lathered the rag with a bar of sweet-smelling soap. Then he began to wash her, his hand gliding over every inch of her flesh, lingering in sensitive places, leaving a tingling wherever he touched her. She closed her eyes and laid her head back, more than willing to allow him to do what he wanted.

"Garnet?"

From far away she heard his call, and she opened her eyes to find him smiling down at her.

"You can get out now."

"Oh," she cried, aware how she lay in the water, her knees relaxed, the tips of her breasts peeking from the water like islands of flesh in a sea of soap foam. Clamping her thighs together, she sat up, hunching over in a tardy attempt to cover herself.

His face crinkled and he laughed. "A bit late for modesty, isn't it?" His countenance grew serious as he reached under her arms and forced her to her feet. "Much too late for either of us." Then he picked her up, mindless of the dripping water, and carried her across the room, where he deposited her on the bed.

Systematically he stripped off his own clothing, his gaze never lifting even for a moment from her.

100

And she watched him just as intently, aware of the ripple of muscles in his arms and shoulders, his chest, across his stomach, and lower. Her heart missed several beats. Nothing in her past had prepared her for the sight of his awakened manhood.

"Drew," she stammered, desperate to say anything that would forestall his intent. "What about the bath? Shouldn't you warm up?"

"If I was any warmer, honey, I'd break out in a sweat."

Before she could object further, he was upon her. With the knee now intimately familiar to her, he forced her legs apart, and soon her inner thighs enveloped his muscular hips. His rigidness met her softness, and the excitement his leg had stirred earlier there was nothing compared to the sensation of him pressing against the folds of her womanhood.

He held back nothing, his mouth hot and fevered on her still-damp flesh. He took from her, gave back threefold, lifting her to planes of sensation she thought couldn't be surpassed, then took her higher. His tongue was everywhere, exploring the hollows and peaks of her body, lapping at the beads of moisture remaining from the bath.

She knew in her heart what she did was sinful, but, oh, God, how could something that created such wondrousness be wrong? His mouth drew a line of caresses up the hollow between her ribs, scaling to the peak of one breast. Her head thrown back, her spine arched, she felt his hips return to the cradle between her thighs.

"Garnet," he whispered, his mouth moving up to fondle her neck, her ear. "If you want me to stop, I will." His words were labored, and she knew it took extreme effort for him to make such an offer.

Their eyes met, their bodies perfectly still, yet pressed closely together. She read the mixture of dread and anticipation in the gray depths of his gaze.

To her surprise his words were not a hollow attempt at chivalry. He was prepared to honor her desire to maintain her virtue if she so demanded.

Oddly enough, she was no longer sure that was what she wanted. Virginity seemed such an incidental thing at this moment of awakening. Would losing it change her so much? She'd been taught to believe that a woman deflowered out of wedlock would find her life tumbling about her like the walls of Jericho. Somehow she found that hard to believe, but she found it just as difficult to deny her upbringing—at least verbally.

Closing her eyes, she shook her head.

His sigh of relief encompassed her. His mouth covered hers, his kiss reserved, waiting for her passionate response, but she held back just long enough for him to notice. His face lifted, his breath fanning across her cheeks.

"Garnet, look at me."

Her lashes fluttered open to find him staring down at her, a concentrated frown between his eyes.

"Are you sure?"

"Oh, Drew, no, I'm not sure." She lowered her gaze in confusion. "But then I never thought I would ever be faced with this decision. Please, don't ask me again, just—"

He understood; he took charge, his kiss cutting off the rest of what she was about to say. His hand moved between their bodies, his fingers finding her secret place and dipping into its untried depths, stroking, circling, making the aching emptiness inside her that instinctively she knew only he could fill grow to monumental proportions.

And then he was filling her, fulfilling the craving that left her open to his foray. For a brief moment her body rebelled, the barrier of her innocence refusing to surrender. He paused, took her face between his hands, his eyes mesmerizing, soothing her. "Easy,

Garnet. I promise the pleasure that will follow the pain will be well worth it."

Then his hips plunged, shattering the last vestiges of her resistance. His kiss absorbed her cry and again he halted. Beneath her fingers she could feel him tremble with the need to continue, yet he held himself in check until she grew accustomed to his presence deep inside of her.

She relaxed beneath his knowing mouth, which kissed away the tensions and fears. Then as if he sensed her readiness, he lifted his hips and plunged again.

Biting down on his lip, she prepared herself for another sharp stab of pain. Instead she was rocketed with an electrical bolt that sent her mind soaring beyond the realm of her known existence.

He moved once more, his rhythm building, pushing her senses up a steep cliff that seemed to have no apex. Soon she was meeting him halfway, climbing, clawing, reaching out for whatever it was that was just out of her grasp.

And when she reached it, she thought her heart had surely ceased beating, her lungs had stopped breathing as she hung suspended at that crest of oblivion. Plummeting, she experienced an uninhibited joy that was new to her. Tears of release gathered on her lashes.

The narrowness of her world split wide, bringing reality back into focus. Drew was there still, moving against her, a drip of perspiration beading on his chin and dropping to her cheek, wet and warm and alive with what he'd worked so hard to give her. Lowering his head, he buried his face against her neck, tenderly nuzzling, asking only that she give him back the same. At his moment of climax, she hugged him to her, much as he had held her, her lips against his temple as he shuddered his release, so vulnerable, trusting. Her heart opened, allowing

103

him entrance, as he'd left his mark upon her soul as well as within her body.

When finally he raised his head, there was a softness in his eyes. Gray eyes. The eyes that had first seen her over the crowd of the barracoon, then had spent a fortune to rescue her from the depths of hell.

"Drew," she said, wide-eyed with wonder. She reached up to run her fingers through his hair, darker now with the dampness of their lovemaking.

His hand snapped up and encircled her wrist, pushing her arms away. "No, Garnet. Don't praise me." He rolled to the side, leaving her exposed and feeling naked without the cover of his body. "This was a bargain you made with Drew Carson. A bargain made and kept. And that's the end of it."

He stood, staring down at her. His gray eyes raked her, cold and arrogant, not even a glimmer of regret for what he'd done.

Snatching at one corner of the coverlet still beneath her, she bit back a sob. Temptation. Now she fully understood. The mighty walls of her world that had once been so confident at last came tumbling down around her.

Chapter Six

Bracing himself against the rail, Bain stared out over the side of the ship, watching the turbulent waters crash against the bow and reluctantly part. The ocean, a siren that could bring the good or the bad out in a man, was for him the enemy. It brought out the very worst. He needed solid ground beneath his feet. Otherwise the undesirable facets of his nature took control, making him into someone he didn't wish to be—a scoundrel of the lowest kind, a cad willing to seduce an innocent woman just to sate his own desires.

He should have known something terrible would happen; it always did whenever he returned to the sea. This time, he swore silently, when he reached home he would never again challenge this briny nemesis.

Dragging his fingers through his hair, he dropped his head into his left hand, the heel pressing into the bridge of his nose. His pledge wouldn't change what had already happened. It was bad enough he had callously seduced Garnet Sinclair, but then he had treated her so miserably. But when she had called him Drew in the aftermath of their lovemaking, her eyes wide with commitment, he could no longer make excuses for his deception. Wrongly he had lashed out at her in an attempt to place the blame on someone other than himself, where it rightly belonged.

To blame Garnet, or his brother's spirit or the sirens of the sea, was merely an easy way to evade the truth. The facts were simple and unavoidable. He was not as good as he thought he was—more than capable of committing unsavory deeds that even Drew might have questioned. At least his brother had been honest about who and what he was. Bain couldn't say the same for himself.

Now, there was no going back, at least not in regard to Garnet Sinclair. How did a man tell a lady he had just seduced he was not who he claimed to be? If he could be sure of nothing else, he could be positive Garnet was a lady of the highest standards.

He groaned, bringing his right hand up to join the other. Lies. Perpetrating more lies. He had not meant for the charade to go so far. Now the irreversible damage was done. He'd deflowered an innocent girl—he shook his head with the irony of it all—he had managed to lose his heart in the process, the gentle heart of Bain she had no idea even existed.

He lifted his head, returning his gaze to the untamed ocean. If he was experiencing such remorse, how must Garnet feel at this moment? She needed comfort, he realized, but not from him. He had taken everything from her, her virginity, her freedom, her companion. Her innocence could not be restored. Her freedom he wasn't ready to give back, not yet, if ever. But Choie Seem—he could reunite Garnet with her friend.

Pushing away, he caught the eye of the closest sailor. The man snapped to attention and dropped the rope he was in the process of coiling.

"Go below, mister, and escort the Chinese girl in the chart room to her mistress in the captain's quarters."

106

If the man wondered about Bain's change of heart, he showed no indication. "Aye, sir," he replied, and turned to do his master's bidding.

Bain watched the sailor move away, and he clamped his jaws in determination. Once they reached Monterey, he would put his brother, Drew, to final rest and never allow his personality to resurrect again. Never, by damn. His twin had stirred up enough trouble while he'd been alive; be damned if Bain would allow him to continue his antics in death.

Garnet dipped the washcloth in the tepid water of the bath that no one had bothered to remove from the cabin. Dabbing at the red stains on her thighs, she washed away the last vestiges of her lost innocence, sacrificed for nothing to a man who cared less for it. She paused, swaying, and placed the back of her hand against one throbbing temple, her headache no doubt a form of punishment for her earlier misdeed. It was as if the shame was a living, breathing entity pounding against the inside of her head.

Brushing back a solitary tear with the knuckles of one hand, she returned the washrag to the bath and rinsed it out, watching the water turn a shade of pink from the blood of her foolishness.

She wrung the cloth out and scrubbed her skin until it chafed with the roughness of her ministrations, her lips a slit of grim determination. Just what had she expected? the pounding in her head mocked. For Drew Carson to fall madly in love with her simply because she'd allowed him use of her body? Only a ninny would expect such fairy tales to come true.

And she was through believing in fairy tales, jinnis, and miracles. If her experience with Drew

Carson had taught her nothing else, it had taught her the cruelties of mankind.

Images of eight tiny faces staring up at her trustingly from the hidey-hole in her father's church in China reinforced her newfound beliefs. Had her children survived, or had they died a slow, horrible death waiting for her to return? And her father, what of him? The single tear of self-pity burgeoned into a flood of remorse for the many who must have suffered because she had been so sure that what she did was right.

At the sound of the door latch turning, Garnet whipped closed the panels of the black silk robe, securing them with the tie, and spun to face the intruder. If Drew Carson dared to return, she would send him packing.

Choie Seem's pale face peeked around the doorway, her almond-shaped eyes wide with apprehension. *"Sse Mo?"* she called.

Garnet tossed down the washcloth and raced to greet her friend. "Oh, Choie Seem," she cried, her arms opening in welcome.

Their hug was furious, thankful, relieved. They were together again, even if it was only for a few moments. Then at arm's length, they stared at each other.

"Are you all right?" they asked in unison.

As she nodded, the Oriental girl's eyes spanned the room, pausing at the sight of the pink-tinged water in the bath. "You're hurt." She frowned, her gaze skimming over Garnet's concealed form.

"No, not really," Garnet replied, though the pain of Drew Carson's deception stung deeply. "Nothing I won't survive, and nothing for you to be concerned about."

Confusion clouded the girl's innocent face, then realization dawned. "The captain forced himself upon you." A look of shock crossed her youthful features. "Oh, *Sse Mo*, how terrible. I didn't think he would do something so . . . so . . ."

Guilt pierced Garnet to the deepest depths of her soul. No matter how she looked at the situation, she had not been forced. She molded her mouth in the semblance of a courageous smile. "You're too young to know of such things," she chided the younger woman.

"And you are too good, *Sse Mo*, to have such a thing happen to you," the girl replied, her gaze filling with adoration.

Six months ago Garnet would have accepted what Choie Seem said without self-doubt or incrimination, but not anymore. Her fall from grace could be blamed on no one but herself.

Her fall from grace. Her fingertips returned to her throbbing headache, which grew worse with each moment. God help her. She bit back the shame clogging her raw, aching throat. Suddenly, swallowing took every bit of strength she had to accomplish. Standing seemed even more impossible.

Angling toward the bed, now devoid of the stained coverlet, she dropped down on the mattress. She was tired, extraordinarily so, and freezing cold. But most of all she wanted to escape the nightmare truth. That was surely why she couldn't pry her eyelids open.

"*Sse Mo?*" She heard Choie Seem's concerned voice. "What is wrong with you?"

She hadn't the strength or desire to answer.

"*Sse Mo!*"

Then the blessed oblivion took over, and she was free of the guilt and of the man who had the power to make her turn her back on everything she'd been taught to believe.

Bain glanced up at the sound of running feet outside the chart room. The door crashed open without the usual ceremony.

"Come quick, Captain. That slant-eyed gal is rantin' and ravin' that the lady in your cabin is dyin'." The intruder's chest rose and fell with excitement.

"She's what?" Bain roared, scattering the maps of China he'd been staring at, his chair falling backwards as he rose. Pushing the sailor out of his way, he charged from the room and down the corridor. What foolishness did Garnet Sinclair plot now?

He burst into the room, where he found Choie Seem hunched over Garnet's prone figure.

"What's wrong with her?" he demanded, confident she was merely pulling another reckless stunt like throwing herself overboard.

The Oriental girl turned tearful, accusing eyes on him. "She just collapsed. She's burning up with fever."

Bain stepped closer, reached out a hand toward Garnet's face, still wary she was up to something. When he touched her hot cheek, he jerked his hand back. She was not faking.

"Get Doc down here immediately," he ordered the sailor who had followed him into the quarters.

When the man left, Bain glanced down at Choie Seem. She held Garnet's hand, squeezing it, massaging the knuckles, murmuring softly in Chinese. He wanted to push her away, wanted to take her place at Garnet's bedside. Instead he stood there uselessly, feeling an intruder on his own ship.

Garnet mumbled something back, in Chinese. His inability to understand what was being said frustrated him. "What did she say?"

Choie Seem glared up at him. "Nothing that has anything to do with you, Captain Carson," she said with a bravado he hadn't thought the girl possessed, her gaze unwavering.

She knew what had taken place here on this bed

110

less than an hour ago; the look in her dark eyes told him that much.

"That's where you're wrong, girl. Everything about her is my business."

They stared, an impasse.

"Why should you care?" Choie Seem asked, the gentleness returning to her voice.

"I don't know why, but I do," he answered in all honesty.

His reply seemed to satisfy her. She took his hand in her small one and placed it on top of Garnet's. "In my country, Captain, there is a story about a two-headed dragon. One head was ruled by the demons of Wind, a fire-breathing monster who destroy everything in its path. The other head was ruled by the Earth gods, kind and gentle, the tears it shed for its counterpart the rain that restored the land to its green and healthy lushness.

"A mighty warrior of the Emperor came, Captain, with the purpose of chopping off the evil head, but as he watched the giant dragon, he came to realize that if he did cut off the one head, the good would die with the bad. So this warrior set a trap to capture the dragon, and when he had him secured in a thousand ropes, he carefully cut away the left side of the Wind's head and the right side of Earth's head, and, just as he had hoped, the two remaining halves merged into one, making a strong ally for his people's northern border. You are very much like that two-headed dragon, Captain Carson."

She slipped out of her seat beside Garnet, offering it to him. "I think you are the one to comfort her. I will be in the small cabin you gave me." She bowed, her hands templed in respectful submission, and she shuffled out of the door.

Bain stared after her, the story she'd told him leaving an uncanny uneasiness in his heart. Choie Seem's wisdom and perception beyond her years

111

unnerved him. How had she so easily seen through his deception?

Garnet groaned, and he focused his attention on her. He lifted his hand and gently placed it on her forehead, smoothing away the blonde waves from her face, so hot and dry.

"Don't worry, *pequeña joya,* I'll take care of you always." He bent from the waist and placed a chaste kiss on her brow.

Garnet stirred and issued a deep, mournful sigh. *Pequeña joya,* his little jewel. How appropriate the endearment was.

He twisted to stare out the open door. What was taking Doc so long to get here?

The wizened little man appeared, an old black ditty bag tucked under one arm. Bain moved out of his way, yet he refused to relinquish Garnet's hand.

Doc dropped his satchel on the floor beside the bed and placed a palm on her dry brow. "A fever," he announced, "a high one at that."

"Little fool," Bain mumbled under his breath more for his own benefit than for Doc's. "If she'd not thrown herself overboard."

"Maybe, Cap'n, but I'd say this here girl's been through a lot more than just an icy dousin' in the ocean."

Bain frowned. Doc was venturing into dangerous territory. What had occurred between the two of them was none of the old charlatan's business.

"She's been abused in the worst ways," the man continued, either ignoring or oblivious to Bain's growing impatience with his interference.

Bain tensed, his mouth opening to order the other man out.

"Look at them bruises on her arms." Doc pushed aside the black silk from Garnet's knees with a professional air. "And them legs." He dropped the robe and shook his head. "I done seed how tired and

112

thin she were the moment you brought her aboard. Just what alley did you scrape her outta, Cap'n?" The old man cocked his head, giving Bain an innocent, questioning look.

"I bought her from the barracoon," Bain informed him matter-of-factly.

Doc nodded his head as if the explanation was an everyday event. "Bamboo staves. That accounts for the bruises." He turned, taking up his bag and delving into its depths. He pulled out what Bain thought of as weeds and roots, lifting several to his nose to sniff. Some the old man put aside, others he returned to the satchel. "These should help her cool down a bit." He rose and moved toward the door. "I'll send the brew round as soon as it's steeped. Get her to drink as much of it as you can."

"Doc?"

The old sailor faced him, the grimness of his features not encouraging.

"Is she going to make it?"

"I'll do my best, Cap'n Bain," Doc answered evasively.

Bain nodded, dreading the worst. The old man's best had not been good enough to save Drew. It might not be sufficient now to heal Garnet.

Hours later Garnet went from bad to worse. At first, she had lain quietly, accepting the bitter tea Bain had forced her to drink, cup after cup until the nauseating smell of mint, wormwood, and hyssop had compelled him to shove the mug away. Now she cried out in her delirium, sometimes speaking in English, as often as not ranting in Chinese. If only he understood the language, maybe he could make sense of what she said and give her comfort, but the bits of information he received were just enough to drive him to distraction. That she had suffered and still did

113

was all he could derive from her ramblings. What miseries and injustices had she weathered before he had intervened in her destiny?

She spoke of a father and children, many of them, their names repeated so often he recognized them even when she slipped into Chinese. Then there were the biblical quotes, ominous warnings that left no doubt in his mind Garnet Sinclair was a woman of strong religious convictions. Remorse for his callous treatment of her expanded into full-blown self-flagellation.

What could he do, besides honor her unthinkable request for freedom, to ease her anguish and relieve his own guilt?

Garnet began her maundering again.

"No, Father, don't do it. Stand back." Her body stiffened, and her head lashed from side to side.

"Easy, *pequeña joya*," Bain soothed, brushing back the tangle of soft blonde waves from her face. For the first time he noticed a thin sheen on her skin. His heart quickened. The beads of moisture were a good sign. Leaning over her, he poured another cup of the potent brew Doc had given him, then forced the rim to Garnet's lips. "Drink," he ordered.

Apparently the command registered, as she opened her mouth and swallowed the bitter tea without protest. Then her lashes parted, and the jade green of her eyes pleaded up at him, though he could tell she didn't recognize him.

"Please," she begged in a voice rough with fever and pain. "Help the children. We cannot let them die."

Her eyelids snapped shut as quickly as they had opened, and again her head began tossing back and forth on the pillow, which was slowly becoming soaked with the perspiration of her labor.

"I will, *pequeña joya*," Bain promised, aware his words were an empty assurance. "I will." Then he

114

lifted his face and smiled, a plan formulating, solidifying in his mind.

Floating. Floating. God help her, so hot.

Garnet knew she must be dying, her errant feet already implanted deep in the fiery bowels of Hell.

But that didn't surprise her. Though she couldn't recall exactly why, she knew she deserved her fate as surely as any sinner did. Biting her lip, she swallowed the desire to cry out. She would face her punishment with the strength of Job.

But why? Why must the children suffer so? Softly she murmured the eight names of her students, dearer to her than life itself. "Save them."

Then a voice answered. "I will, *pequeña joya*. God help me, I'll do whatever I can."

The endearment whispered in Spanish seemed so familiar, so appropriate. This was not the first time she'd heard it, this caring, masculine timbre calling her "little jewel," but for the life of her she couldn't put a face to the voice.

Not her father. The pitch was much too deep, too full of life. Then who? She should know, but something forbade her to remember, as if doing so would cause her considerable pain.

Then the liquid fire consumed her, washing away all remnants of sanity. The eight upturned, little-girl faces became mere plaster-of-Paris images crumbling to powder in her fevered visions. Ashes to ashes. Dust to dust.

She sobbed. "No. No. Please let them still be alive."

Then a coolness swept over her like an ocean breeze, and she burrowed deep into the safety of sleep. Blessed sleep. If only she could stay there forever.

*   *   *

Bain tucked the fresh sheet under Garnet's chin marveling at the thick tangle of lashes resting against her pale cheeks. Aware he was being watched by the other occupants in the room, he dragged his gaze from her face and regarded them.

Doc grinned back as he packed his ditty bag and snapped it shut. "The lady's gonna make it, Cap'n. I'd stake my life on it."

Solace flooded through Bain. If Doc said so, he was satisfied that Garnet would recover. He turned to study Choie Seem kneeling beside the bed, her tear-streaked cheek resting against Garnet's slightly curved palm, surrounded by a profusion of Belgian lace on the cuff of the nightgown the girl had dressed her in earlier.

"Oh, *Sse Mo,*" the girl whispered, her relief as evident as his own. "What would I have done without you?"

Whatever Garnet had suffered the Oriental girl had experienced as well. His eyes narrowed in contemplation. Choie Seem had the answers to all of his questions.

Bain squatted beside her and angled her reed-thin body so she had no choice but to return his gaze. She was so young, so tiny, no more than a child by his standards, but in her own country she was considered a woman in every way.

"Choie Seem."

She looked up at him, reluctantly, as if she realized he was going to ask questions, very personal questions, that she might not wish to answer.

"I have to know."

Her eyes, dark and frightened, darted to the sleeping woman on the bed, then back to him.

"These children Garnet has spoken of, who are they? Where would I find them?"

"They are her students, in China, at her father's mission."

His brows knitted in consternation. "A teacher?" The revelation shouldn't have surprised him, but it did. "Where exactly?"

"A small village in Fukien Province." She swallowed, her lips sealing as if she'd said all she intended to tell him.

"What happened?"

The girl tried to twist away.

Bain tightened his grip on her arms, which were as fragile as butterfly wings. "Tell me," he insisted, with a gentle firmness that betrayed his true feelings.

"No. I don't dare. You are one of them," she cried.

He knew whom she spoke of. Them. People who preyed on young girls, forcing them from their homes and families all for the turn of a profit. "Listen to me, Choie Seem." He shook her for emphasis. "I am not one of them. You know that."

"Aren't you, Drew Carson? You paid your money and made your purchases and received your goods in exchange."

"That's not the whole truth."

"Isn't it? I know what you did to her." She notched her chin at Garnet.

"I know what I did too. But you were the one who entrusted her care to me only hours ago. Have you forgotten?" He struck a chord and knew it.

"The two-headed dragon." Her mouth bowed into a wistful smile. "I speak to the life-giving Earth spirits now, don't I?"

He nodded.

Her shoulders relaxed, and she told him everything. The old woman selling false marriage contracts, the children, the hidey-hole, Reverend Sinclair's attempt to stall the marriage broker, the horrors of the ship. By the time she was through, she was weeping softly, the tears unchecked.

Bain rose and cast a gentle look upon Garnet, the

117

woman who had tried so hard to make life better for others, and his heart expanded with a feeling he had never experienced before, and couldn't put a name to. He whirled in confusion and pushed his way out of the cabin.

He would get Garnet her answers regarding her family and students, and he only prayed that what he found out would be less painful than never finding out the truth at all.

Bain hunched over the unscrolled map and tapped the linen with his finger. "Start in Foochow."

"But, Captain, there has to be a thousand nameless villages in that province. It could be any one of them." Enoch Sharp confronted his superior, his face a mask of wrinkles and lines sharpened by the many years he'd spent in the sun.

"How many could have a Christian mission run by the Reverend Sinclair?" Bain demanded in exasperation. "You'll find the answers, Mr. Sharp, or you won't come back." His ultimatum hung heavily in the small chart room.

The first mate, easily ten years Bain's senior, scratched his thinning hairline and chewed his bottom lip.

"Besides, Enoch," Bain continued, trying to ease the tension, "you know that part of China better than any American alive, probably as well as Drew knew it." Enoch Sharp had been his brother's first officer for as long as he could remember. "The girl mentioned the river. You might start with the Min." He traced a curving line on the map. "Chances are the village is somewhere along its banks."

The sailor sighed and offered a half-hearted salute of concession. "Aye, Captain. As soon as we reach Monterey tomorrow, I'll lay in supplies and hire on extra crew for the long voyage."

Satisfied his will had prevailed, Bain straightened, allowing the chart to reroll itself. "You're a good man, Mr. Sharp. I don't know how you managed with my brother all those years."

"Captain Drew wasn't that bad, at least not to his men." He shrugged. "However, I can't speak for the women he knew."

Bain stared at the other man for a moment. It seemed odd to hear someone say something remotely generous about his brother. He had never stopped to think that perhaps there had been a good-natured side of Drew. Apparently his men had respected him, even liked him. He remembered Drew's final words. They had been concern for a Chinese woman and the child she had borne him in disgrace. Until now he had simply dismissed Drew's insistence that he had loved the woman as the rantings of a dying man. Bain could no longer be so sure his opinion was accurate. Had Drew loved her?

"Thank you, Enoch. I'll anticipate your return to Monterey. Send a message to the town house, and the servants will notify me even if I'm out at the ranch."

Sharp nodded his understanding. The two men rose and shook hands, and Bain watched his first officer saunter out of the door.

Garnet would have her answers. He would see to that. In the meantime, he would keep her with him, use her talents as a teacher with Mae Ching. But most important, he would introduce her to the real Bain, the kind and giving twin, and do everything in his power to make her forget that Drew—with all of his dash and arrogance—had ever existed, at least as far as Garnet Sinclair was concerned. She had to be made to see just how wrong for her such a scoundrel would be.

She couldn't fall in love with the image of Drew

119

Carson. That would never do. His lips curved downwards with determination. He would see to it that she learned to hate him instead. The thought of hurting her further left a bitterness in his mouth, but doing so might be the only way to eliminate the false illusions he had created so unintentionally.

Chapter Seven

Monterey, California

"This is ridiculous, Captain Carson. Put me down." Garnet's protest was laced with a prim gaiety. "I'll have you know I am quite capable of walking."

Up the companionway steps he carried her, one arm beneath the back of her knees, the other cradling her shoulder. He shook his head in denial. "You're only beginning to recover. I won't have a relapse of your condition on my conscience."

The parrot-green skirt of her gown—another pilfered from the trunk in her cabin—spilt downwards from his supporting arm, nearly touching the deck, and radiated as brightly as the morning sun that splashed across the horizon with streaks of gold and orange. The collapsible bustle, which had never been right since she'd gotten it wet during her escapade in the ocean, squeaked in rhythm to his jaunty step, harmonizing with the squeal of the ship's booms and tackle. If Drew noticed the peculiar sound, he said nothing. She was more than grateful for his show of decorum.

Garnet's hand pressed against the cream in-set lace on the bodice of her dress. The bay before her was extraordinary. In all of her travels she had never seen anything to rival its beauty, except perhaps the Bay of Naples. "Oh, Drew," she exclaimed, lapsing into familiarity without realizing it. "Monterey is a visual delight."

"It's home." His mouth lifted on one side in studied jadedness, but she noticed from the corner of her eyes he stopped nonetheless, staring out over the water as fascinated as she was.

Home. The word brought to the surface a gush of memories for her, both pleasant and painful. The children. Her father. She glanced up at Drew's square, handsome face, softened with his own thoughts of home and family. Surely he could understand her need to return to hers.

Once they reached the dock Garnet expected him to put her down. Instead he turned and ordered, "See that Miss Sinclair's trunk is brought up to the town house right away."

The trunk. He was calling it hers. But what of its previous owner? Who was this unidentified woman, and how did she figure into Drew's life? Garnet wanted desperately to ask, but wasn't so sure she was willing to hear his explanation. Desperate to escape the burning questions, she turned her mind to other things. "What about Choie Seem?" she inquired, angry with herself that she hadn't thought of the Oriental girl's fate until this moment.

"She can come ashore with the luggage." The look on his face told her he would have it no other way as he continued down the pier into the street past an adobe-walled plaza where several unoccupied benches lined the tidy public square.

"Drew," she protested, struggling against the unrelenting strength of his arms. "You can't mean to carry me all the way to your house. What will your family say?" she asked in alarm that someone would think the worst of her. What of the unknown woman? What would she think? she didn't ask aloud.

His mouth quirked, and his brows arched in amusement at her discomfort. "The house will be empty. Besides, what would it matter what they'd say? If I were you," he warned in a derisive voice, bringing his mouth down close to her ear in a show of melodramatics, "I would be more concerned about what *Señora* Martino, the old widow who lives in that adobe house across the street, is thinking. She sits every morning beside that front window watching whose husbands are leaving the taverns, and whose lovers are sneaking out the back doors." He laughed. "Then she spends her day gossiping to anyone who'll listen about what she's witnessed."

Garnet's head snapped about to stare at the indicated dwelling. She could see no one behind the screen of the lace curtain waving in the gentle ocean breeze. "Oh, Drew, you aren't serious." She giggled nervously and turned her face, attempting to hide it from curious eyes, realizing that if he was telling the truth, her actions came too late.

"Very serious. I can't count the number of times she tattled on me," he bragged.

She whipped up her face and glared at him, unable to believe he would so willingly discredit himself in front of her. It was almost as if he were proud of what he'd done or as if he wanted her to think less of him. But that was silly. He was only trying to amuse her and make her feel more at ease.

"Oh, Drew," she responded in a kidding tone of her own, tapping him on one broad shoulder with a fingernail. "Don't tease, will you?"

They reached the front steps of a large house of a most unusual design. Its walls were made of adobe like so many of the Spanish *haciendas* they had passed, but instead of a one-story sprawl, this one was two-story, with a wide veranda on the ground floor and a matching balustrade balcony on the upper one, both of which skirted the entire structure. The large windows all around promised an airiness on the inside that would be most pleasant.

As he crossed the veranda, he swung open the door and strolled inside, past an open-mouthed serving woman who was sweeping the breezeway.

"Put me down, Drew," Garnet pleaded with a halfhearted staidness accompanied by a giggle.

"*Señor* Drew?" the servant said with a shriek as if she'd seen a ghost. The Spanish woman backed out of his way, throwing her broom to the floor.

"No," he replied, denying Garnet's request as he swung about to move toward the stairway leading to the second story. He completely ignored the maid except to shoot her a warning glare.

"Blessed Mother of God," the woman muttered in Spanish and scurried away, her hand fervently crossing herself over and over.

"Drew, let me go," Garnet demanded in all seriousness, more than a bit leary of his intentions. The bedrooms would be on the second floor, and it wasn't proper for him to escort her, much less carry her up, to one of them.

He paused on the first landing, his face darkening. "Never, Garnet. I'll never let you go, not until I'm good and ready."

The intensity of his decree rocked her to the core of her being, as she remembered how desperate she was to return to her own life. "Drew, please. Can't you understand? I must go home. I have a family who needs me too."

"What of my needs, Garnet? Aren't they important?"

"Drew," she choked, struggling with the raw emotions ripping her apart, remembering only too well how willing she'd been before to assuage his needs. "This is wrong. We can't—"

His mouth came down brutal and hard against

hers. "I don't care if it's wrong," he murmured against her parted lips. "It's what I want."

Resentment ignited like a fireball in her heart. How could he be so callous? "Even if it is not what I want?" she ground out, ripping her mouth away.

He laughed, the sound harsh and grating against her ears and insulted sensitivities. "Oh, don't worry, my dear. I'm confident I can convince you to want it in no time at all."

She began to fight him in earnest, and the more she struggled the more he seemed to enjoy it. He frightened her, this man of such a turbulent nature, yet at the same time she was appalled to realize she found his arrogant dominance exciting.

These most improper feelings wouldn't do. They simply would not do!

"Let me go, Drew, or I swear to God I will scream." Her fingernails dug into the flesh of his arm. If she hurt him, she didn't care. He was hurting her in ways much worse than physically.

He paused in the central hallway on the second floor, shaking off her biting fingers as if they were no more than irritating flies. His gray eyes danced with unruffled defiance. "Then scream, my love, for soon your protests will turn into shrieks of delight. And if you're worried about what the servants will think, don't be. They're used to my ways. They know better than to disturb me no matter what they might hear— or see."

Tramping into one of the rooms, he slammed the door closed with one booted foot. Dark and smelling of disuse, the heavily curtained bedroom was a gloomy place, more like a shrine to the dead instead of a room to comfort the living. It was Drew's room, of that she was sure, but she couldn't understand why a man so vibrantly alive would want to live in such a tomb.

Unceremoniously he deposited her on the bed,

then turned and lit the gas lamp above her head. A strong smell of burning dust issued from the hissing fixture. When was the last time he had been in this room? And, dear God, what had he done to make the maid so afraid of him?

Garnet couldn't believe that a house full of servants would simply ignore the cries of a helpless woman. No one was that cowardly or devoted. Her eyes narrowed as she studied Drew in the yellowish light. He was bluffing, and she would call him on it. She sat up, opened her mouth, and emitted a loud, uninterrupted scream. Only when her throat felt raw and damaged did she cease.

"Are you finished?" he asked the moment her jaws snapped shut. He turned and locked the door, sliding the key into the pocket of his jacket with total unconcern.

She gathered her breath and screamed again.

His only response was a chuckle as he moved closer to where she poised on the bed, balanced on knees pressed tightly together. "Very amusing, Garnet. Keep that up, and you'll have no voice left at all."

"Damn you, Drew Carson," she sobbed hoarsely. "I despise everything about you."

His mouth quirked on one side, and he shrugged out of his jacket. "It really doesn't matter, my dear, what you think of me. It doesn't change what's going to happen."

"You would take me against my will?"

"Like I told you. I don't think that will be necessary."

"You arrogant bastard," she hissed.

"I am, aren't I? Drew Carson is the lowest form of life, and I don't want you to ever forget it." With confident fingers he stripped the shirt from his torso and tossed it on the growing heap on the floor.

How could he be saying such cold, calculated things to her? Garnet's chest rose and fell with

126

disbelief. He wouldn't go through with his threat. He just couldn't mean it.

"Drew," she choked, her innocence and belief in the goodness of all mankind clawing at her battered throat, demanding to be confirmed.

Then he was upon her, his fingers tangling in her long, ash-blonde tresses that had tumbled from their pins. His hand was almost cruel as he jerked her head back, but his mouth was a tender caress upon the convulsing column of her bared throat. She willed herself to concentrate on the pain, not the pleasure he gave her.

He balanced on his knees, his spread thighs pressing hard and muscled against her legs making her only too aware of his arousal straining against the thin material of his trousers. He towered over her, bending her willowy body like a reed as his mouth moved over her chin to claim her trembling lips, muffling her quiet sob of defeat.

His tongue invaded her mouth, plundered the private recess, stripping her of her last ounce of resistance. With a sigh, she closed her eyes. His head angled, changing his course of attack, a lock of his dark, gold-tipped hair dropping rakishly over his brow. She found it impossible to stop herself from adjusting to the sensual curvature of his mouth. Then his face lifted, the mingled moisture of their kiss stamped upon her lips, sweet and intoxicating.

"I cannot believe you would force me," she reiterated in a whispered plea, her hands moving up to clutch the thickly corded muscles of his arms.

"Believe it, Garnet." He sucked her bottom lip between his teeth and nibbled ever so gently, a physical contradiction that she wanted to trust in more than his callous words. "I am capable of that and worse. Much worse. The fact that I desire you makes me anything but a saint."

"And if I should tell you I desire you as well? What

does that make me?"

He paused, his mouth lifting from hers for a moment. Then he groaned as if her confession had struck a sensitive cord he was trying desperately to conceal. "That makes you a woman. Foolish perhaps. But a flesh-and-blood woman, no more, no less." He drew her hard against his heart, which pounded furiously against her ear. "Aw, damn it, Garnet, you should know better than to get mixed up with a man like me."

She clung to him as his hands moved to her back, dislodging the tiny pearl buttons of her gown. Drew was right. She should know better. God knows, her lack of will was a sign of weakness. Burying her face against the man-smell of his thickly matted chest, she inhaled deeply and pushed away her nagging conscience, which warned that on the morrow she would regret her compliancy.

Warned her that Drew would not be a changed man merely because of her generosity. No man went from black to white, bad to good because of a woman's submission—her love.

She leaned back to study his face, intense with the desire that racked him. Surely it wasn't love she felt for Drew Carson.

She closed her eyes as a pain so sharp she sucked in her breath pierced her confused heart. Fate wouldn't be so cruel. She'd grown up to believe she would fall in love with a man of the same nature as her father, a giving man, a man of God. Drew was exactly the opposite of what she'd expected.

"Garnet."

Her name upon his lips brought her gaze back up. Their eyes met, and she saw the struggle taking place behind the smoky windows of his soul. Regardless of what he said aloud, he cared for her, but fought as hard as she did to deny it. Why? The reason was only too clear in her mind. There was no room in his life

128

for a woman like her.

She pushed up on her knees and pressed her mouth against his, her kiss as ardent and demanding as his had been only moments before. Vaguely she recalled his arrogant boast. He could easily make her want him, and, oh, God, she did. She wanted him in the worse way.

Her parrot-green dress puddled around her knees, she said nothing as Drew reached in front of her body to unbuckle her bustle. "Are you aware this damn thing squeaks worse than bed springs in a whorehouse?"

"I wouldn't know, Drew. I've never been in a house of assignation."

A deep spurt of amusement erupted from his throat. "You're amazing, Garnet Sinclair. You can make even prostitution sound respectable." He threw the contraption aside. Then pushing down her petticoats, he began working on her stays with nimble fingers. Soon she wore only her chemise, the thin linen hiding nothing from his seeking gaze.

Lowering her lashes, she lifted her mouth, willing—no eager—to accept what little he offered to give, anticipating the kiss that would surely come.

But it didn't. Confused, she glanced up in askance.

His brows were knitted, his mouth tightened with deadly determination. He reached out, grabbed the ribbon neatly bowed at the top of her cleavage, and gave it a vicious tug. Ripping out of the tatted eyelets, the satin strip hung uselessly about her neck, the garment gaping open revealing the round globes of her breasts.

"Drew," she gasped, her hands flying up to cover her nudity. Surprised and baffled by his sudden brutality in the wake of her nonresistance—her wanton expectation—she tried to fathom what had made him change so abruptly.

He slowly twisted his hand in the ribbon, coiling it

about her throat until she could feel her pulse jumping in protest against the mounting pressure. Was his intention to strangle her?

"No matter what you call it, honey, exchanging sexual favors for compensation, whether monetary or not, is still whoring. So show me, Garnet, how willing you are to whore for me," he growled.

Garnet swallowed hard against his knuckles pressing threateningly against her windpipe as he forced her to her back on the mattress. Tears pooled in the base of her throat, promising to spill if she said anything, even uttered a monotone of protest. *Oh, Drew, Drew, why are you doing this to me?* she cried inwardly.

His hand moved to cover one of her naked breasts, kneading, flicking the nipple until it puckered proud and aroused against his palm. She sobbed, unable to believe she had so little self-control over her body, but, oh, God, his touch was warm and loving, nothing like the steely contempt of his gaze. She closed her eyes, trying to escape the nightmare truth of the sensations he could evoke in her with so little effort on his part. As if he read her thoughts, his hand continued toying with her flesh, traveling to capture her other womanly peak, rubbing, circling until the tight bud blossomed with unbidden desire.

"Please. Please don't, Drew," she pleaded huskily, feeling a little part of herself die beneath his blatant assault on her self-esteem. She hated herself for not resisting, but she hated him more for the calculated degradation he forced upon her.

His response was to laugh and slide his hand downwards across her rib cage, and beneath the waistband of her underwear to dip his fingers into the moist, silky depths of her womanhood, stroking, swirling, sending tiny shock waves skittering to every nerve-ending in her body. The tension—building, building—took control of her every thought, and mindlessly she obeyed when he urged her knees to part, to give him better access to her femininity.

His hand that had tangled in the ribbon at her throat fell away, then the warmth of those same fingers that had moments before been life-threatening cupped her breast, molding it upwards. His lips covered the hard, aching tip, tugging it deep into his mouth, his tongue like a hot maelstrom of lava branding her traitorous flesh. She arched her back, thrusting her breasts closer, and her hips ground into the mattress below her, yet he never missed a stroke as he pushed her closer and closer to the pinnacle of pleasure.

"Sex becomes you, Garnet. You're never more beautiful than when you're in the throes of passion."

His heated words whispered in her ear sent her tumbling over the top. Her lips parted as release gushed through her, and his mouth captured her whimpers of delight, sharing her ecstasy as completely as if it had been his own. When at last she lay spent, he paused, giving her a moment to catch her breath.

But only a moment. Before regrets and modesty could tumble down around her, he began again. Stretching out beside her, he hooked his leg over hers, forcing her to remain open to his caresses. And soon she was there once more, straining to attain the heights he so skillfully drove her toward.

She felt him shift, expected to feel the weight of his hard, muscled body covering hers, but instead he seemed to pull away, even his hand lifting from the cradle between her thighs. Disappointment rocketed through her, and she cried out her frustration of being so abruptly deserted.

Then he was back, touching her there, but not with his hand nor with his manhood. The warm wetness of his caress was more maddening than ever before, almost as if his tongue were . . .

Her eyes snapped open in utter disbelief. No one did such a thing to another person. Dear God, it was unnatural.

But there he was, his head cradled between her thighs, his arms wrapped beneath her buttocks, his hands meeting on the flat plain of her stomach, the soft waves of his hair brushing her legs, and his mouth . . . Oh, God, his mouth.

Her knees clamped against his shoulders, her palms wedging along his cheeks in an attempt to push him away.

Ignoring her show of modesty, he slid his hand around her body cupping her buttocks, angling her body so he could better reach her.

"No, Drew," she gasped, wiggling to twist her pinioned hips away. "This is wrong."

He looked up. "Why?" he demanded. His half-hooded eyes told her he found nothing at all wrong with his actions; in fact, he found loving her in this matter most intoxicating.

"W-why?" she echoed. She caught her breath, unable to find an answer. Why indeed? she asked herself. Because she had heard her father insist to his flocks as long as she could recall that other than for procreation sex was sinful? But then none of what she did with Drew could be justified by procreation. She gave herself to him willingly, eagerly—most sinfully.

Her hands fell away. Sin was sin. There were no degrees of judgment.

As if sensing her resistance melt away, he returned to his sensual foray, loving her with his mouth and tongue until the walls of her defenses lay scattered about her. Her fingers that had only moments before tried to push him away soon tangled in his hair demanding he never stop.

He gave her what she asked for, his worshipping mouth and tongue nudging her to the top of the tidal wave, where she rode the crest for what seemed like eternity. Spinning down into the trough of fulfillment, she cried out, uncaring who might hear her and rightly decipher what was taking place behind the closed door.

Spent, her breath ragged, her heart pounding in her ears, she opened her arms as Drew inched up her body to at last cover her slenderness with his much larger frame. When he entered her, swift and strong, it was as if an empty space within her had at last been filled, the floodgates of desire that she thought were surely drained and dry again springing to life in the wake of his driving need within her.

His rhythm restrained until she joined him, their bodies met and pulled away as if magnetized. His eyes were closed, yet he placed precise kisses on her throat, her jawline, the lobe of her ear as he strove to bury himself as deep within her as he could.

Striving to match him stroke for stroke, she could feel the knot of tension in her own belly drawing tighter with renewed vigor, but she ignored it, unconcerned for her own satisfaction, instead concentrating on gifting him with what he had given her. To her surprise the yielding washed over her with a gentle unhurriedness that was wonderment in itself.

With the unconscious tightening of her body, his release came with a gut-wrenching groan, his spill of seed leaving him momentarily weak and vulnerable, his face pressed into her collarbone, his hands gently squeezing her shoulders as he shuddered. His breathing sawed in and out against her neck, warm and alive with fulfillment.

At that moment she realized she loved and hated this man simultaneously. She lay quietly listening to his breathing, loving the sound yet knowing it would soon lessen, and that the man she despised with all of her heart who battled and bullied her would return, in control, no longer the giving lover who had taken her to heights she'd never even dreamed about before now. He had said she was beautiful in the throes of passion, and she blushed imagining how she must have looked sprawled wantonly before him. In the same way his most sacred defenses broke down beneath her caresses and revealed glimpses of the gentle, caring man he must have been before life had made him hard and caustic. Yes, loving made him beautiful too. But it was fleeting—short-lived—and no doubt gone by now.

His face lifted, and she was surprised to see a sadness—almost regret—in his smoke-gray eyes. Before she could question him, he rolled to his back, reached up, and extinguished the light, his hand guiding her head to rest on his sweat-sheened shoulder, which was beginning to grow cooler to her touch.

"Sleep," was all he said, his arm possessively cradling her bare hip, and he adjusted the pillow beneath his head and relaxed except for the grip about her naked body.

Exhausted, drained of every ounce of resistance by his expert lovemaking, Garnet acquiesced, her mind drifting down, down into a sated slumber of no worries, no dreams, just a peace she'd never experienced before.

Just before she lost consciousness her last thoughts were of Drew. Foolish musing of an even more foolish woman. Black to white. Bad to good. Wishful thinking, that was all it was or could possibly be. No man, especially a proud, arrogant one like Drew Carson, changed his nature overnight.

Bain lay in the darkened room listening until Garnet's shallow, even breathing told him she was asleep. An untroubled repose. Of that he'd made sure, taking her again and again to climactic heights until her sated body had sagged wearily against him.

It was best this way, he assured himself, gently stroking the satin curve of her hip, yet the calculated cruelty of his words and actions hunkered like molten lead against his heart. It was best she think the worst of Drew Carson, so when the bastard left her without forewarning, without good-byes, then he, Bain, could be there to soothe her wounded esteem.

He knew in his heart it was wrong the way he'd misled her, but deception had never been his intention. It had just happened that way. And once it was done, he could never allow her to find out that it was Bain who had treated her so callously. Let her go on believing it was Drew.

He turned his face and placed a tender kiss upon her brow. Garnet sighed, nestled into the crook of his arm, her hand feathering across his bared chest to come to final rest upon his stomach. His body lurched and tightened in response to her innocent caress, and he knew he had to disengage himself now, or he would find himself making love to her once more.

He took her hand and moved it away, tucking it against her naked breasts. Sweet Jesus, even in the darkness her warm flesh beckoned to him. He snatched his fingers away as if burned. Then with slow deliberation, he inched his arm from beneath her, his hand that had cupped her hip feeling empty as he pulled away—but separate himself from her he must.

As he eased up from the mattress, she rolled as if seeking his warmth, and he poised beside the bed waiting to see if she would awaken. His body yearned for her to do just that, awaken and reach out for him;

his mind prayed she would sleep on oblivious to the fact he was leaving her.

"It's best this way, *pequeña joya*," he whispered when she curled into a deep sleep. Pulling on his trousers, he bent, gathering up the remainder of his clothing, and quietly crossed the room. At the door, he looked back at the woman on the bed, a dim silhouette in the darkness.

"*Pequeña joya*," he mouthed again, then he slipped through the door into the hallway, where streams of bright morning sunlight poured in through the window at the end of the corridor.

Without hesitation he moved further down the hallway and entered another bedroom. His. Bain's. Where Drew's had been dark and sinister, this one was bright and airy, the curtains thrown back to allow the morning sun to splash over the contents. Going directly to the highboy, he took out a pair of worn Levi's, a checkered shirt, and a red bandana to knot at his throat.

As soon as he was dressed, he gathered up Drew's soiled clothing and returned to the hallway to descend to the main floor. There he found the maid, busy in a back parlor as far from the central stairway and the noises above as she could get, dusting furniture that was already immaculate.

"Constanza."

The little woman turned, spied him, and shrieked, dropping her feather duster, her face white with fear. "*Señor* Drew?"

"Don't be silly. You know as well as I my brother is dead."

Her breath rushing out of her thick body with gale-wind force, she mumbled, "*Gracias a Dios*. Then it was you, *señor*, I saw earlier with the *señorita?*" Her black eyes widened as if she still doubted her own words.

136

"Of course, Constanza, but you must never say anything to the *señorita*, nor mention Drew's death to her. She wouldn't understand. *Comprende?*" Now the servants were a party to his lies, but there was no helping it.

She nodded her dark head obediently.

"Good. Now take these," he said, shoving the bundle of clothing at the woman, "and get rid of them."

"Get rid of them, *señor?* Are you sure you won't need them for—?"

"I don't care what you do with them," he said, cutting her off. "I just don't want to see them again."

"*Sí, señor.* I will take care of it for you." She wadded the clothing under her arm and started toward the doorway.

As Bain watched her she turned about, another question on her lips. "And what of the *señorita?* Shall I see to her as well?"

He narrowed his eyes, suddenly feeling as if he couldn't trust the little woman who had been with his family as long as he could remember. "Not to concern yourself, Constanza. I will take care of the *señorita.*"

She nodded. "Of course, *señor.* Of that I have no doubt." Her gaze filled with a knowledge that set his teeth on edge.

"Constanza, you must trust me. I have only the *señorita*'s welfare in mind. There's more to this than meets the eye."

"Ah, *sí, Señor* Bain. If anyone but you would have told me that, I would not believe them, but you are pure of heart." She patted her ample bosom with meaning and flashed him a trusting smile.

Pure of heart? He nearly burst out in laughter as the maid shuffled from the room. His motives were about as pure as gutter water. His brows met over the

137

bridge of his nose. Lies perpetrating more lies, just as he had predicted. He was in so deep now, he wasn't sure he could ever wade out of the mire that was like a quicksand sucking him down, down in the bowels of a deception that seemed to grow worse with every step he took.

Chapter Eight

Garnet's eyes popped opened and focused on the empty pillow beside her. She was momentarily disoriented, and the only fact that registered in her confused mind was that she was alone. A thin thread of sadness as fragile as a spider's web drifted across her consciousness. Then memories of what had taken place in this bed a short while ago rushed in, clearing away the cobwebs, bringing back the push-pull of conflicting emotions—love, hate—black, white.

"Drew?"

She knew he wasn't there and didn't expect an answer, though she listened hard for any sound to contradict her pessimism. None came.

Sitting up, she clutched the sheet to her throat, and her fingers brushed against the chemise ribbon still dangling around her neck, a vivid reminder of how cruelly Drew had treated her. She glanced about and spied the pool of parrot green that was her gown on the floor where he had carelessly tossed it. His clothing was gone, as well as every indication he had been there at all, and he had not even bothered to shake the wrinkles out of her gown. Tears ballooned in the back of her throat. He'd not even bothered to bid her farewell.

Somehow she sensed he wouldn't return.

But that was foolish. She couldn't possibly know what his intentions were. Pushing the tangle of ash-blonde tresses from her eyes, she disguised the swipe she took at the tears spilling over her lower lashes. She sniffed back the welling weakness, forcing herself to face the inevitable facts. Drew Carson had used her like a whore. Her fingers knotted in the chemise ribbon as she remembered his callous words to her. *Exchanging sexual favors for compensation, whether monetary or not, is still whoring,* he'd warned her, and she had done nothing to turn aside his accusation. In fact, she recalled, her face heating with self-disgust, she had encouraged him to use her in the most debasing ways.

Did this mean she'd now earned her freedom? Was that what he'd meant by compensation? Untying the ribbon about her neck, she notched her chin in an effort to redeem her pride. If so, she would be only to glad to see the last of his insolent smile and his arrogant ways. She tossed the ribbon on the pillow behind her wanting only to forget.

Rising, she snatched up her clothing and donned them, shaking out the wrinkles as best as she could and managing to tie together the bits of shredded lace on her chemise to hold it in place.

If her hunch was right and Drew in truth had deserted her, there was nothing to stop her from seeking a means to return to China. Yes, that was what she would focus on—the positive; she was free.

First, she would locate Choie Seem, then head to the docks to try and hunt down a ship willing to take them home. How hard could transportation be to find? Drew's ship sailed to China from Monterey. Why not others? As far as money to pay their fare . . . ?

Well, she would think of something. God would provide. She paused in her attempt to restore order to her hair. If He thought her worthy to provide for.

As she whirled through the door deep in thought and decision-making, the toe of her shoe caught on something in her path, and she stumbled. She stared down into the drowsy, dark gaze of a Spanish child.

"*Lo siento, niña,*" she muttered in apology without thinking about it.

The girl's broad face broke into a gape-toothed smile at the sound of her native language. "You're awake," she responded in kind, her voice a Spanish warble. "The *señor* told me to wait here and show you to your room." Elflike, she scrambled to her feet, which were bare and broad as her countenance—and brown as morning toast.

"The *señor?* Where is he now?" Garnet asked, glancing down the empty hallway, wondering yet worried if she had been wrong about Drew.

"Oh, he is in the *comedor* having the noonday meal."

"He's still here?" Garnet's heart thundered with a combination of joy and apprehension. She gathered up her skirts and moved toward the stairway, deciding that it would be best to face him immediately and demand to know if he planned to release her, now that the debt was surely squared between them. The first time she'd succumbed to his skillful touch had been for Choie Seem's freedom, she justified to herself, the second for her own. He had said as much with his words of whore and compensation, hadn't he?

"Wait, *señorita.* What about your room?"

"That can wait, *muchacha.* What I have to say to the *señor* is much more important."

"But *señorita.*"

Garnet rushed by, ignoring the child's protest.

At the bottom of the stairway, she whirled about, seeking the dining room where the little girl had said Drew would be found. From behind her she heard a deep masculine voice speaking in monosyllables.

She turned and marched toward the sound, determined to demand her release from Drew. Nothing would stop her.

From the doorway she saw him, the serving woman ladling a rich red soup into his bowl. His back was to her, broad and familiar, pressed against the wheelback Windsor armchair in which he sat.

"Drew," she called in a determined voice.

The servant looked up, her Castilian features registering confusion. Why did everyone in this house look so strange when she said Drew's name?

"*Gracias*, Rosita," he said, dismissing the woman with a wave of his hand.

Garnet cocked her head. The inflection of his tone sounded wrong. Perhaps because he spoke in Spanish.

The moment the cook left the room, he rose from his chair and turned to take a look at her. He offered a courtly bow, his gaze registering a blankness as he gave her an assessing survey. It was as if he didn't know her.

How could he be so ruthless, this man who had made love to her only hours ago?

And then in a fluster it dawned on her it was not Drew she addressed—yet this man looked exactly like him. But there were differences—subtle ones now that she took the time to notice. Most obvious was his dress. Worn dungarees, a checkered shirt, a kerchief knotted at his throat. A personified image of an American cowboy that she'd marveled over in picture books as a child, and in direct contrast with the ornate furnishings of the room.

"Drew?" she queried, fingers clutching into a fist at her sides with confusion.

"I'm sorry, ma'am. My brother's gone. Can I be of help to you?" he drawled in a lazy voice, crossing his arms over his chest, one knee cocking, his foot balancing on the toe of his pointed boot.

Her hand drifted to her throat in shock. What did one say to a man who looked as if he'd been lifted from the pages of a Wild West dime novel and was the spitting image of one's . . . lover? She brushed away the despicable word, the only one to come to mind, a word that cleaved like a worrisome burr to her very proper social consciousness. *Hypocrite,* she chided herself. There was no denying Drew Carson had been her lover. Her lips were still swollen and bruised from his passionate kisses.

"Who are you?" How ludicrous the question sounded even to her own ears.

He smiled, the expression lazy and sunny and openly honest. Nothing like Drew, who was arrogant and cruel. "Excuse my bad manners, ma'am." He hooked his tumbs in his wide leather belt, his legs spread wide. "Bain Carson." His gaze dipped taking in all of her—wrinkled gown, thrown-together hair. "My brother promised you were beautiful, but he didn't do you justice." His gray eyes sparkled with a merriment that made his statement inoffensive.

If only Drew could smile like this man.

"Drew never told me you existed. You're twins." Her announcement expressed her incredulity. How could two men with such different personalities have originated from the same seed?

He laughed, and the sound was as easy and friendly as his smile. "Yes, ma'am, you could say that. But where are my manners? Please." He stepped forward and politely pulled out the chair at his right hand. "Join me. You must be starving. I know I am after . . ."

She shot him a leery look, but he had the manners to glance away. Why would he assume she was starving? It was almost as if he knew what she'd been doing, had been there, been listening. She blushed. Perhaps he had. The sounds. Plus knowing his brother as well as he must surely know him.

143

"Something light, perhaps, Mr. Carson," she conceded a bit stiffly, settling into the seat he offered her and draping the snow-white linen napkin across her lap.

"Something light," he repeated. "Of course." He angled toward another door leading from the room. "Rosita," he called, "Some of your *gazpacho* for Miss . . ." He turned expectantly for Garnet to supply her name.

"Sinclair."

He tilted his head, waiting for the rest of her name.

"Garnet Sinclair," she added. How strange it felt telling this man her name, but why she thought he should know it was just as odd.

"Miss Sinclair." He flashed that charming, lazy smile of his.

Yes, she thought, adjusting her bottom to her chair. If only Drew were more of a gentleman like his brother. Then she focused on the thoughts she'd had earlier. Black to white. Evil to good. It was as if a miracle *had* occurred. Bain Carson was more like what she looked for and expected in a man. Much more civil. Would he be just as polite in bed?

Dear God, where had that wanton thought come from? She blushed and looked up guiltily to find Bain staring at her, a knowing, yet cautious look in his eyes. He dipped his head ever so politely.

Then the door to the kitchens swung open and Rosita entered. Their gazes parted, Garnet glancing down at her hands, Bain directing his attention to the cook as she served them both.

"Rosita's an excellent cook," he declared as if trying to fill up the empty, embarrassing silence.

The cook chuckled. "*You* are easy to please, *Señor* Bain," she replied with obvious affection as if there were those in the household who were not. Drew perhaps?

As the woman set the bowl of chilled soup made of

144

chopped raw vegetables before her, Garnet inhaled deeply, appreciatively. She was starving, even if she wasn't willing to admit that aloud. In moments she'd devoured the spicy fare.

"Was that light enough, ma'am?"

She glanced at Bain to find to her relief he was finished as well.

"Or perhaps too light. Something else maybe." Without giving her a chance to protest, he waved Rosita through the door. The cook hurried forward, gathering up the empty bowls and replacing them with a dish that smelled divinely. The food before her was fit for royalty, and some of it she had not tasted or smelled since her days at home in England.

"Amazing!"

"How so, Miss Sinclair?"

She shot her host a suspicious look. The way he said her name—did she detect a hint of contempt? It was as if Drew had spoken. But no, this man's face was honest and open, no hint of deception there. The fact that they were twins would make for certain similarities, she thought, explaining away her apprehension about this stranger whose face she knew as well as her own. She smiled hoping he would return the gesture. To her pleasure, he did.

"Well, Mr. Carson." How funny it felt to say Mister instead of Captain. "In all of my travels I have tasted much of what is on my plate, but never all at the same time and place. I imagine having a brother in shipping makes many things possible."

"Not at all, ma'am." He laughed and shook his head. "Drew's abilities on the sea have never been directed toward the finer things in life."

With that she couldn't disagree.

"Everything we eat here and at Rancho Carmelo is grown, caught, or made locally."

"Really? How amazing." She lifted her fork, tasting the thinly pounded abalone steak, considered

145

a delicacy even in China, and beneath a layer of a most unusual-tasting cheese sauce she discovered fresh asparagus shoots, which she'd not had since the days she'd gathered them wild along the sandy shores near her ancestral home on the southern shore of England. Her fork delved deeper. The hearts of artichokes—they were rarely found except in diets along the Mediterranean. "Do all Americans eat so well?"

"Only if you have connections with Rancho Carmelo. We have orchards and gardens that the old mission padres would have envied. And our cheeses and wines"—he lifted his glass appreciatively—"rival any to be found." He took a sip, then returned the delicate stemware to the table.

"This Rancho Carmelo must be a virtual Eden," she ventured, bringing her own drink to her lips, somewhat surprised to find he was right in his comparison. The body and full bouquet were delightful.

"A good description, ma'am. I like to think of it as my Eden." He stabbed his fork into his food and began to eat.

By the tone of his voice she surmised that Rancho Carmelo was Bain Carson's pride and joy—as important to him as the sea was to Drew.

Ah, yes, Drew. Her purpose for coming downstairs had not been to feast, but to demand her immediate release. As kind as Bain Carson appeared to be, surely he would understand her dilemma and offer his help to her.

"How was your *siesta*, Miss Sinclair?"

Her gaze darted up to find Bain giving her a pointed look. Oh, God, he knew.

"It was restful," she replied evasively.

"And did little Ana show you to your permanent quarters?"

Ah, an opening. He was making this simpler than

146

she'd dared hoped. "That, sir, is what I would like to talk to you about."

"The room doesn't suit you?"

"The room is fine. Well, actually I don't know that for sure. I haven't really seen it."

He gave her a complacent look. "Then Ana was derelict in her duties. I must see that the child—"

"No. No, it's not Ana," she protested. "It is just that I have no desire to see my permanent quarters, as I have no desire to stay here permanently."

"I see." As hard as she tried, she couldn't make heads or tails out of his expression—eyes narrowed, mouth a mere slash across his handsome face. "Tell me, ma'am, just what *are* your plans?"

"I wish to return to China and my family as soon as possible. My father is a missionary in Fukien Province."

"And what of your Chinese companion? Do you plan to take her with you?"

"Of course, Mr. Carson. We were both kidnapped against our will and brought to this country." She leaped right in and began to relate the story of her abduction, but he cut her off.

"And so, Miss Sinclair. Just how do you plan to *pay* for your passage? You know, ma'am, fares are expensive."

His callous statement took her by surprise. Somehow she'd expected him to extend his sympathy, not a lecture.

"I had hoped, Mr. Carson, you might be willing to help."

His gaze never wavered, and he made no move to offer assistance.

"Perhaps I could earn it," she blurted out. "I have teaching skills."

"According to Drew you are already in debt to him for a considerable amount of money. I believe he mentioned five thousand one hundred dollars."

"That debt has been settled," she declared, lifting up out of her seat.

"Not according to what my brother told me. He did mention, however, the amount had been reduced by one hundred dollars for unspecified services rendered."

The amount he had paid for Choie Seem. "The circumstances were most unusual, sir. A gentleman would never hold a lady to such a debt."

He smiled. "Drew never claimed to be a gentleman."

"And you, sir? What of you?"

Their gazes met and held for a potent moment. Then he shrugged his wide shoulders, a gesture so like Drew would make that it boded ill in her mind. "To be honest, ma'am, my character is not what's in question here, but your own. I am not the one trying to wiggle out of a debt."

Bain Carson, in direct contrast to his brother, was so damn polite she wanted to claw his eyes out. Instead, she angled her chin, her mouth flattening into a thin line. "And I, sir, feel that the debt was honored with those same unspecified services rendered." She rose, determined to leave the room having had the final word if not a resolution to her problem.

"I think, ma'am," he said, standing with her and taking her by the arm, "you need to reassess your motives. Monterey doesn't take lightly to loose women."

She jerked her arm away. Yes, she decided, Bain Carson dripped with a politeness as irritating as his brother's rudeness, but at least she knew what to expect from Drew's insolence. He gave her the satisfaction of a good fight. She tossed her head and marched toward the exit.

"Miss Sinclair."

She spun back around, seething with the desire to

tell him just what she thought of his irksome mannerliness.

"I will be most disappointed in you if you don't stand by your debt." He dipped his head in dismissal, turned away as if he were confident she was going nowhere, and settled back down in his chair and to his meal.

Her eyes narrowing, she glowered at his broad shoulders. Damn his courtesy and words of honor. Then she smiled wickedly and tossed her head. *We'll see, Mr. Polite-even-in-bed, what your reaction will be when you discover I don't care one iota if you're disappointed. I'm going home and nothing, not you or your damnable brother, will stop me.*

Bain listened without turning to the sound of her determined, undefeated retreat up the stairs. It was important to get Garnet to the ranch before she had a chance to figure out a way to escape. She didn't feel bound by his claim of debts and honor, but he really couldn't blame her. He *was* holding her against her will and without a valid reason. But he needed her, Nattie needed her, his six-year-old niece, Mae Ching, needed her.

He pushed away his unfinished meal and sighed. How he had hoped the intimate ties that they had shared would compel her to relent to his desires. What a fool he had been. He should have known Garnet Sinclair was not a woman to be bound by carnal needs.

Perhaps he should just tell her all he wanted from her was her skill as a teacher so that he and Mae Ching could learn to communicate with each other. His mouth flattened. Knowing Garnet Sinclair as well as he did, he realized she might refuse to help him and continue to demand her release in spite of the valid debt between them. No matter what, he

149

must keep her here, at least until his man, Enoch Sharp, returned from his mission to China with information on her father's welfare. Here with him she was safe from harm, even if she didn't see it that way. Now that Drew was out of both of their lives, he wouldn't touch her, he vowed vehemently. He had better control over his own body than that. Bain Carson was not a person to force himself on any woman, and especially not a woman who was carving a special place in his heart.

He stood. The ride to Rancho Carmelo was at least an eight-hour trip if everything went smoothly, and there was no way to begin the journey now, this late in the day. But at first light tomorrow morning he would load the two women into the wagon. Once at the ranch, so far from town or even neighbors, Garnet would settle in. And when she set eyes on sweet little Mae Ching, her teacher's instinct would take over. Given the right situation and circumstances, she would grow to love the land as he did. Wouldn't she? How could she not? She had said it herself—a virtual Garden of Eden. She would never be able to resist its beauty.

All he needed was time. Soon she would forget her other life just as the image of Drew Carson would fade and be replaced by the kindness and care he and his family of orphans would show her.

Their relationship had begun on the wrong foot, but that was all changed now. They were two of a kind, gentle and fair, perfect for each other.

Bain smiled. Yes, Garnet Sinclair was exactly the woman he desired in his life. A good woman, yet a strong woman. By damn, he would restrain himself until she came to realize he only had both of their best interests in mind.

Ana skipped into the room, her long braids flying like kite tails, and she whirled as if presenting royal quarters to a queen. Garnet glanced about the bright, sunny bedroom. First she spied her trunk—she began to think of it as hers now—in one corner. Beside it, curled on a comfortable mahogany chaise longue, was Choie Seem, her dark lashes spread over her cheeks in exhaustion.

Garnet rushed to the girl's side. Her first goal was accomplished. Now all she had to do was figure out a way for them to escape and get back to China.

"Choie Seem," she said, shaking the girl gently by the shoulders.

The Oriental girl stirred, her lashes fluttering. *"Sse Mo,"* she responded sleepily. "I was so afraid you would not come back," she cried in Chinese, and threw her arms about Garnet's neck.

Garnet hugged her in return, tears of relief squeezing between her lashes. She had feared separation too. "We're together. Nothing and no one will divide us again. Nothing," she vowed in the same language.

Ana watched, her eyes darting back and forth between the two women speaking in a tongue she obviously couldn't understand. "You sound like the other girl," she declared.

Garnet turned, a surprised frown on her face. "What other girl?" she demanded, her heart thundering with wild imaginings.

"The one the *señor* brought back scratching and screaming from the ship."

"There were others besides us?" Garnet asked, her voice strained with misgiving. It seemed the Carson brothers were in the habit of collecting females from the Orient. That didn't surprise her, at least when it came to Drew. Was this another woman who owed him an unwilling debt of gratitude just as she did?

Now more than ever she and Choie Seem must escape. She whirled about to question Ana further. "What did the *señor* do with this other girl?"

"Took her to Rancho Carmelo."

"To do what?"

The girl shrugged. "I wouldn't know. I stay here at the town house with my mother, Constanza. But I can tell you this much." She leaned forward and glanced once over her shoulder as if she feared someone might hear her. "She has never come back from the *rancho,*" she replied in a hushed whisper. Garnet's eyes narrowed. A Garden of Eden was it? And Drew—probably Bain as well—were the serpents to be found there to spoil its beauty. She should have guessed as much. Drew had seemed too familiar with the workings of the barracoon, and Bain—well, he hadn't been disturbed by her unannounced presence in his house, not even the least little bit.

"And then there's *Señorita* Nattie," the little girl continued, "but everyone knows about her." She rolled her eyes. "It's just a matter of time before she goes *loco.*" She drew a circle in the air near her temple with one stubby finger. "Just like the old *Señora* Carson."

Señora Carson? Garnet's gaze shot to the steamer trunk full of clothing in the corner. Drew's wife, or perhaps Bain's. Were all of these women being held against their will at some faraway ranch? What kind of sinister plans did the Carson brothers have in mind for her and Choie Seem? She didn't wish to stay around long enough to find out.

They had to get away. Now. Not another moment could be wasted. Bain Carson could appear at any time to force them to go with him to this . . . Rancho Carmelo.

Standing, she spun about to face the Spanish child. There was no way to tell if Ana could be trusted, so the need to get rid of her was foremost. "Ana, please go to the kitchens and ask Rosita for a tray of food for Choie Seem. She hasn't eaten."

"But *Sse Mo,* I'm—"

Garnet squeezed Choie Seem's hand to silence her protest.

Ana squinted in consternation at the sudden change of topics, but with the trusting nature of a child, nodded and headed toward the door to do Garnet's bidding.

The moment the little girl's braids cleared the door, Garnet closed it, and spinning, she pressed her back to the barrier as if to ward off any possible intrusion.

"Tell me, Choie Seem, when you left the docks did you notice any other ships in the harbor?"

The Oriental girl stared at her in confusion. "Ships? You means besides Captain Carson's?"

Garnet nodded vehemently.

The girl thought for a moment, frowned as if trying to remember, then shook her head. "I don't think so."

Damn it. She couldn't blame the girl for her lack of attention. She herself had not done much better. If only she'd been more observant when she'd left the ship with Drew. But no. Instead, she'd been caught up in the unique beauty of the town and the feel of his arms about her as he carried her away from the docks. "There has to be a ship somewhere willing to take us back to China," she exclaimed under her breath in exasperation. Pivoting, she began pacing the room.

Choie Seem's dark, almond-shaped eyes followed her movement back and forth. Back and forth. "Oh, that's easy, *Sse Mo*. Captain Carson's ship is headed for China as soon as they take on provisions," she announced, as if their problems could be solved that simply.

Garnet paused and stared at her friend. Perhaps it could be just that easy. If they could sneak aboard the ship, there would be no need to figure out a way to pay for their fare. And once they were underway, Drew would never turn back, even when he discovered his stowaways. It was an unwritten code of the sea, wasn't it? Captains just didn't turn back if they were far enough into a voyage.

And once they were in China . . .

She would think of a way to escape. God would provide. Yes, she thought, giggling aloud at how simple the solution was, God would surely provide.

"Oh, Choie Seem, you're wonderful," she cried, taking the girl into her arms. "Tell me, did you see Captain Carson return to the ship?" Was it perverse curiosity that made her ask such a question? No. She honestly needed to know Drew's whereabouts.

The girl blinked as if unable to follow Garnet's line of thinking. "No. But I'm sure he must have. A ship doesn't sail without its captain, does it?"

Of course it didn't. Garnet paused in her madcap scheming. But what would that captain do when he discovered the woman he'd thought he'd left behind aboard his ship? What could he do? Except maybe strangle her with his bare hands. She was confident she had the feminine wiles to talk him out of that course of action.

She glanced about the room, looking for a means to escape the house, as she seriously doubted they could just waltz out the front door. Her eyes lighting on the mauve-covered poster bed, she snapped her fingers. Of course.

Hurrying to the window, she threw up the sash, a wash of cool, crisp October air rushing over her. Staring at the railing, she noted the distance between the balustrade posts. She pulled up her skirts to climb out the window and bent over the railing, judging the distance to the ground below. It would take at least a half-dozen bed sheets to pull off her plan. Spinning about, she hurried back into the room.

"Look, Choie Seem. Here is what we're going to do," she said conspiratorially, shutting the window against the chill.

The girl leaned forward in anticipation at the excitement and authority in Garnet's voice.

"As soon as it's dark, we can make a rope from the

154

bed sheets and climb down to the ground."

The girl swallowed in fear and shook her head. "Oh, no, *Sse Mo*. I cannot do that. My feet . . ."

"I've already thought of a solution to that problem. With enough sheets I can wrap the rope around a couple of the posts to gain leverage. I can lower you down."

The girl looked at her as if she wasn't so sure of the idea. If the truth be known, Garnet wasn't too confident of her plan herself. "Don't worry, Choie Seem, it will work. I know it will," she said, as much to assure herself as her companion. "We don't have much time and need more sheets before Ana returns. The only place I can think to get them is from the other bedrooms."

"No, *Sse Mo*, it's too dangerous." Choie Seem reached out and placed a restraining hand on her arm.

"Not if I'm careful." Garnet patted the girl's fingers. "Drew will be on the ship. I can take the two from his bed and I'll find two more. How difficult can that be? It will take only a few moments."

She rushed toward the door and cracked it open, craning to look through the small opening up one end of the central hallway and down the other. It was clear for the moment. She pushed the door wider and stepped out.

"But *Sse Mo*," the girl protested in a concerned whisper.

"Shhh. Don't worry. And if Ana returns before I do," Garnet added, "just tell her I'm in the water closet. A bit of indigestion." She smiled brightly and closed the door in Choie Seem's face before the girl could protest.

Slinking down the hallway, she slipped into the bedroom next to hers. Drew's. Dark and dreary. The curtains drawn tight. She must remember that this room would be empty later and to use the posts in front of its window so no one would see their

155

clandestine maneuvers. The bed was rumpled, just as she had left it. Without dwelling on the events that had taken place between the wrinkled sheets, she stripped them from the mattress and balled them up under her arm.

Back at the door, she peered through a slit. The hallway was still empty. Hurrying, she slipped into the room across the corridor. This one was bright where the one she'd just left had been gloomy, but she didn't stop to take note of its furnishings. As quick as she could she tossed off the chocolate-brown coverlet and jerked the neatly made sheets from their tucks to stuff them under her arm with the others. Then as an afterthought, she quickly threw the spread back over the stripped bed.

She moved forward, stumbling over a trailing tail, and mumbling under her breath, she rolled the sheets tighter and hurried to the door. She sighed in relief to discover the corridor still empty.

Back at the entrance of her own room, she placed her ear against the door listening. Silence. Good. That meant Ana hadn't returned yet. Blustering in, she rushed to the bed and fell to her knees. Shoving the stolen sheets under the bedstead, she rose. And just in time for Ana's knock.

"Come in," she said, her voice rippling with calmness. Smiling serenely when the child entered the room ladened down with a tray of food, she ignored the way her stomach fluttered and danced with nervousness.

Her plan would work, even if it did mean dropping right back into the lion's jaw by returning to Drew's ship. Gnawing at her bottom lip, she lifted her chin with determination and optmism. She had to believe that with all of her heart and soul. If they weren't successful, she could think of no other way for her and Choie Seem to return to China.

Chapter Nine

Hours later she and Choie Seem sat side by side in a warm puddle of afternoon sunlight patiently knotting the ends of the pilfered sheets together until they made one long rope, which reminded Garnet of the gaily tied scarves in a magician's trick. She reached out and rolled the entire mass into her lap, and methodically tested each knot to make sure it would hold. They couldn't afford a mishap because the sheets weren't tied together properly.

Finally satisfied with their efforts, she looped the linen rope from hand to bent elbow until it was in a nice, neat coil about her forearm.

"Now, all we can do is wait," she said, taking the roll and returning it to the hiding place underneath the bed.

She sat back on her haunches, ignoring the look of abject fear in Choie Seem's gaze as well as the unsettled pounding of her own heart. The waiting only made the situation worse. It gave them both time to doubt their line of reasoning and their ability to pull off what was beginning to sound more and more like a harebrained scheme even to Garnet.

Refusing to give in to the manifesting fears, Garnet stood, ignoring the urge to throw open the window and reassess her plan. *No. It will work. By*

God, it will work.

"Maybe we should both try to get some rest," she suggested, unable to stand for another moment the way her companion's eyes followed her every movement. "We've a long night ahead of us." She was relieved to see the girl nod her agreement.

They lay down side by side on the mauve coverlet, both acutely aware of the bareness of the mattress beneath it.

"What if I should fall?" Choie Seem asked.

Garnet understood her question. She too had been going over in her mind the details of their escape plan with a fine-toothed comb, and wondering if she had the strength to lower the crippled girl to the ground without dropping her. She reached over and patted Choie Seem's fingers, which were laced over her stomach. "You won't fall," she assured the girl. "You see, it's a matter of leverage. The posts will be doing all of the work, not me."

"But what if someone should catch us?"

"They won't," Garnet replied, fervently needing to believe her own words.

After several more what-if's the Oriental girl grew silent. Her hand still clasping Choie Seem's, Garnet drifted off into a troubled sleep where bed-sheet ropes slid through fumbling fingers, and railing posts snapped like toothpicks, and the prying eyes of Bain Carson—no, no, perhaps they were Drew's, she couldn't be sure—bore into her mind, laughing at her, making her feel inadequate in more ways than one.

Bain moved through the darkened upstairs hallway lighting the gas jets of the wall sconces as he went. Reaching the lamp next to the door of the room where Garnet was staying, he paused, his thoughts riveting on the woman behind the barrier. After only a slight hesitation, he lifted his fist and knocked softly. He just wanted to see her, confirm she was still there.

His summons received no answer. He knocked again, and this time he placed his ear against the wood slab, listening. Silence. Fear leaped into his throat. She had to be in her room as there was no way for her to escape short of leaping over the veranda balustrade. Having spent the day in his study, which was directly below her room, he'd had a clear line of vision of both the outside gardens and the downstairs central staircase. He would have seen her if she'd tried to escape. Besides, there was Choie Seem, who was hindered by her bound feet. Garnet wasn't going anywhere without her companion, of that much he was positive, and with the girl, she wasn't likely to get far.

He dropped his hand to curl about the doorknob. Turning it, he felt like a burglar in his own house, invading places he shouldn't, but he had to make sure.

The bedroom was as dusky as the view beyond the window, the curtains still thrown open allowing silvery moonbeams to slash almost magically into the room to highlight a corner. In the darkness he could barely make out the two figures lying side by side on the bed, fully dressed, their shoes still on, their fingers entwined in a gesture of friendship and trust.

His first instinct was to awaken them, ask them if they were hungry and would like to have a dinner tray sent up, but spying the untouched tray of cold food on the dressing table, he decided to leave them alone, and resisted even the urge to unlace their shoes, fearing it might rouse them. It would be best for all if they rested until morning. The journey was long, the road dusty and full of bumps. Besides, how much trouble could they get into asleep?

Moving silently across the lavender rug, he pulled the drapes closed and picked up the food tray. Then he stopped, staring down at Garnet, so beautiful in sleep, almost as beautiful as in the throes of passion, and he felt his loins tighten in response to his imaginings. Again he considered removing her shoes and loosening her stays, but knew better than to touch her. Such actions would never remain innocent, not for very long. His desire for her grew with every ragged breath he drew.

Spinning away, he crossed the room in determined steps. He had sworn he would leave her alone, and by damn, that is what he'd do even if self-denial killed him.

And it just might. His body seemed unwilling to listen to the logic of his mind. He wanted Garnet Sinclair, and the more he denied himself, the stronger the need grew, until it was almost physical pain.

Out of the room and down the hallway he traveled, clutching the tray in his strong hands until his knuckles turned white.

Things would be different once they reached Rancho Carmelo. There they would be in his domain, a place where Drew had never ventured, at least not for many years, not since the death of Nattie's mother. At the ranch Drew's demise was not common knowledge, as he'd felt it unwise to tell Nattie. Such information might well be his sister's undoing. In fact the only one who might know was Mae Ching. Even then, he wasn't sure the child had understood what had taken place that eventful afternoon aboard the *China Jewel*.

Yes, once he reached the ranch, he could shed the final skins of deception and leave them here in Monterey, confident that no one would mention his brother's name again.

* * *

Garnet awoke, with a strange feeling that an unwanted presence had invaded the room. She blinked in the darkness. It was cut only by a thin stream of moonlight pouring through a tiny slit in the curtain and bouncing across the top of the dressing table on the far wall. When the door clicked softly shut, she jumped, jarred into full awakeness.

The first thing to register was that the long-awaited cloak of night had arrived. She sat up, taking her hand from Choie Seem's grip. It was time to make good their escape.

The second thing she noticed was the absence of the tray Ana had brought them earlier. Apparently the girl had entered and removed it, she surmised, forcing her tripping heart to slow down. There was no reason for anyone to be suspicious; at the most the servant might wonder why the food was untouched.

Choie Seem stirred on her own accord, and without a word rose, the sound of her shuffling feet so loud even on the carpeting that Garnet was sure someone below would hear and decide to investigate. When the girl threw open the curtain and looked back expectantly, the moonlight giving her dark hair a silver halo, Garnet finally moved, scooting across the coverlet and reaching under the bed to remove their makeshift rope. There was no more time to contemplate the possibility of failure. They had to move now.

As a final precaution, she tiptoed to the door, cracked it open enough to view the length and breadth of the hallway, and found it empty, the gaslights lit and dimmed to tiny flames meant only to aid someone to move safely down the corridor, nothing more. The silence was complete except for the sighing hisses from the flames, and each doorway she checked revealed no evidence of light coming from the room beyond.

Drew was on the ship, the servants most likely retired by now to their downstairs quarters or to the kitchens on the other side of the house. And Bain? Well, she would just have to take the chance that he was asleep as well behind one of the half-dozen sealed bedrooms.

Closing the door, she considered propping a chair against the handle to keep anyone from entering and discovering their absence. Spying the library chair in one corner, she dragged it forward and managed to wedge it under the handle. Dusting her hands, she stood back to view her handiwork. It would stop someone at least for a few moments.

Joining Choie Seem at the window, she threw up the sash and tossed the sheets out first before crawling through the cramped opening. Then she reached back to assist the other girl over the ledge.

In silence she moved toward one of the posts she'd selected earlier and dropped the coil of sheeting at its base. Wrapping one end about the sturdy beam, she reached out to test and make sure it was strong enough and wouldn't snap like the ones in her nightmares. Thick and solid beneath her fingers, it was completely reliable. Pulling the rope along, she moved to the next post, the one easily viewed from Drew's unoccupied room. She turned, studied the curtained window, and felt confident no one would see them. She wrapped the sheet about it twice, leaving a dangling tail in which she knotted a loop. Then she signaled to Choie Seem to join her.

She helped the girl over the banister, silently instructing her to hang on to the post as she knelt placing one small, deformed foot into the sling Garnet had made for just that purpose. Then showing Choie Seem how to hang on with both hands to the rope once she had the other end, Garnet smiled and gave the girl a quick, reassuring hug.

Choie Seem's eyes, glistening in the newly risen moonlight, were mournful, but trusting.

Garnet crossed to the other post, at the base of

162

which the rope was coiled. Sitting down on the rough planking floor, she braced one foot on the bottom rail and grabbed the rope, wrapping it about her upper torso and around one wrist, hoping to gain as much leverage as possible by doing so.

The silence crackled between them, ominous and foreboding. This was the only way, Garnet assured herself, and it would work. Nodding her head as a signal, she pushed with her feet and leaned back into the sheet rope. Choie Seem released the post which she'd been hugging, and to Garnet's relief hung suspended in the air, twirling slightly from side to side.

The strain against Garnet's back was deadly, and she knew tomorrow would find her sore, but concentrating only on allowing the rope to slip slowly across her back and over her wrist, she inched the sheets through her fingers.

Exhilaration coursed through her. The plan was working. In no time at all they would both be safely on the ground and on their way to the dock. Finally, on their way home to China.

Having dismissed a grumbling Rosita to take the untouched tray to the kitchens for disposal, Bain smiled to himself, remembering how the little Spanish servant had let it be known in no uncertain terms what she thought of perfectly good food going to waste. Once he was alone in the downstairs corridor, the smile faded, to be replaced by a deep frown when he pictured the woman he'd left undisturbed on the bed upstairs. Then he wrenched his thoughts to other things. There were household accounts that needed a final going-over, as well as Drew's accounts, and if the truth be known, he supposed the shipping accounts should also be checked one last time before they headed inland. It

163

might be awhile before he returned to town.

With a sigh, he headed toward the study, and with the aid of the moonlight pouring through the window navigated his way to his desk. Reaching to light the oil lamp on its broad, neat surface, he changed his mind, and instead moved toward the window, almost as if the magic of the moonbeams beckoned to him.

He glanced out over the secluded garden surrounded by an adobe privacy wall. To his right he heard a strange rustling, and his suspicions aroused, he twisted his neck trying to see beyond the veranda, but the overhanging balcony blocked his view. What would be making such a strange scrapping noise against the side of the building? He stepped forward, and considered investigating further.

Then a light breeze stirred the single date palm near the corner of the house, and he relaxed. That damn old tree always was noisy, like chalk on a slate. Before they departed he would have to leave instructions for the gardener to trim the fronds away from the balcony.

Turning to present his back to the window, he crossed over to the desk to jot down a reminder to see to the tree the first thing in the morning. As he wrote his note on a piece of blank paper, his limbs were attacked with a sudden jolt of weariness that dragged a sigh from deep inside him. He'd had his fill of monotonous tasks for the day. Having gone over those damnable books all afternoon, he was in no frame of mind to delve into them again. What he needed was a good night's rest before the long trip to Rancho Carmelo. He just prayed carnal images of the woman across the hall from him would leave him alone long enough to get it.

Ignoring the guilty stabs of responsibility, he swept from the study and closed the door behind him. As he crossed to the stairway, a strange feeling that all was not as it should be permeated to the very marrow of his bones. How strange. The feeling must simply be the result of his uncustomary lack of desire to bury his nose in accounting books. But before heading up the stairs to his bedroom, he decided to check the kitchens. There he found the fires properly banked and the areas empty and tidied as usual. He shook his broad shoulders to eliminate the unrest that was settled there. The servants had already retired. Nothing was out of order, he convinced himself.

Without further hesitation, he returned to the corridor and took the stairs two at time. At the doorway across the hall from his brother's room, he stopped, glancing at Garnet's door next to Drew's. He considered checking on her again, then reconsidered as a tightness in his groin warned him to do so would be a mistake. If he gazed upon her sleeping form again, he would never be able to resist touching. And if he touched her . . .

He opened the door to his own room and closed it behind his back before his resolve weakened. By damn, he was man enough to leave the lady alone. Then he shut his eyes and pressed his back to the barrier. The forbidden beckoned like the apple in the Garden of Eden. More like a sweet plum, ripe and juicy, and itching to be plucked and tasted. He swallowed, moistening his dry lips with the tip of his tongue. Dear God, he had never experienced such a terrible longing in his entire life.

Pushing away from the door, he stripped the checkered shirt from his torso with rough, almost violent movements and tossed it in the chair in the corner. His boots soon followed, slamming into the wall beside the chair. His britches were next, and standing in his socks and tight knee-length underwear, with the forgotten kerchief still knotted about his neck, he reached for the brown coverlet on the bed and gave it a vicious jerk.

Staring down at the bare mattress beneath, he blinked in surprise to find no sheets. The two pillows still were encased in their covers. But no sheets!

"What the hell is going on?" he mumbled. Why would Constanza strip his bed and forget to recover it? Then his eyes narrowed. What if it wasn't Constanza? What if . . . ?

What in the hell would Garnet want with his sheets? Forgetting his unseemly state of dress, he rushed to the door and threw it open, and with determined strides crossed the hallway to her door. He tried the knob, and when it wouldn't turn, obviously jammed by some obstacle, he knew immediately she was up to something. Something he wouldn't like.

He barged toward Drew's room and flung himself through the doorway, noting the hastily stripped bed in there as well, the strange sounds he'd heard earlier from his study coming back to haunt him. Racing to the window, he jerked open the drapes and saw the trailing sheets hanging over the balustrade.

"God damn it," he cursed, throwing up the sash, knowing in his heart he was probably too late. God knows how, but Garnet and the crippled girl had managed to escape.

Crawling through the window, he couldn't believe what he saw. The most proper Miss Sinclair was squatting on the veranda floor, almost lying, the knotted sheets slung about her body, her face contorted with concentrated pain as she slowly allowed the makeshift rope to inch forward. No doubt on the other end he would find Choie Seem. And no doubt Miss Sinclair was so intent on her work, she had not noticed him slip through the window.

In stocking feet he edged forward, and wrapping his wrist in the sheet, leaned his weight into it, until he had control of the descending rope. Her back still

166

to him, Garnet released a whimper of relief assuming her burden had at last hit bottom. She swayed her body forward, taking several deep breaths to ease her exhaustion.

Then her eyes swept up and discovered him standing there, and a shriek whistled passed her parted lips. "You. What are you doing here?"

"Putting a stop to your most unseemly actions, ma'am," he drawled.

Her beautiful jade-green eyes traveled the length of him with a languid sweep. A spurt of laughter he'd not anticipated bubbled from her throat. "You're a bit unseemly yourself, Mr. Carson," she declared, averting her eyes, but her amusement continued to pierce him like poison darts tipped with humiliation.

He looked down, realized he was dressed in socks and underwear, with a bright red kerchief about his throat, and an embarrassed growl ripped from the depths of his powerful chest. She was laughing at him, and he didn't find her reaction one bit funny.

Flattening his mouth, he swiped at her like a maddened bear trying to rake her in, but she darted back out of his reach, the still-intact smugness on her face serving to stoke the flames of his irritation higher. Easing up from the rope, he swung again and heard Choie Seem's scream of panic when her rope lurched downward.

In the most awkward of positions, he spun to confront the task at hand. "Help me get her back up," he ordered, glaring at the just-out-of-reach Garnet Sinclair.

She shook her head in denial, an impish bow to her lips as she began edging toward the open window of her room.

"By God, I'll drop her if you take one more step," he threatened.

Her eyes sparkled. "No, you won't. Not the

scrupulous Bain Carson. Now, if you were your brother, I would take your threats much more to heart."

For a flash of a moment he considered showing her just how much she'd misjudged him, to prove to her there was plenty of Drew's brutishness in him as well, but he glanced over the banister, saw the frightened, pleading eyes of the helpless Oriental girl clinging to the bed sheets, and knew he didn't have it in him to do something so terrible. Yet to reel her back up would take too much time, and Garnet might take advantage of the situation to make good her escape. Therefore, his only alternative was to lower the girl to the ground, then deal with the overly confident Miss Sinclair.

In seconds he lowered Choie Seem to the ground below, and when he was satisfied she was free of the sling and standing on her own, he shouted down at her, "Stay put, and damn it, don't you dare move."

The girl nodded with undisguised fear at the sound of his commanding voice, most likely concerned as much for her mistress as herself. And rightly so. He had full intention of dealing firmly with Garnet.

Bain spun to find Garnet ducking through the raised window of her bedroom. Releasing the rope, he chased after her, bending to squeeze through the narrow opening. In the darkness of the room, his eyes took a moment to adjust. Then he spied her, struggling at the door to unwedge the chair she'd propped under the knob.

"Now we'll see just what you take to heart, lady," he mouthed under his breath, recalling her taunting words out on the balcony. In three long strides he was behind her, his arm clamping about the well-remembered slenderness of her waist. He dragged her backwards against the hard plane of his bare chest, and his stomach lurched at the feel of her soft,

168

rounded breast flattened against his arm, her enticing buttocks pressing against his loins. His breathing grew loud and raspy, noticeable even to himself. The way she stiffened in his arms, he knew she was as acutely aware of him as he was of her.

"Take your hands off me," she squealed, digging her nails into his arm in an attempt to brush him away. She squirmed, her round bottom wiggling against his groin.

What he dreaded would happen did. His manhood swelled against the valley of her buttocks as if those parts of their anatomies that touched had been especially designed for such a perfect fit. "I don't think my hands are the problem," he growled against her ear.

As if sensing that her struggle only made matters worse, she stilled, yet he could feel her quiver as she tried to shrink away from his closeness and his arousal.

"What do you plan to do?" Her whispered fear coated with anticipation didn't go unnoticed.

If it were Drew that held her, he knew what she'd expect him to do, and if he were Drew he knew he wouldn't disappoint her, but Drew was gone, no longer a part of this tangled relationship.

Taking a deep, ragged breath, he circled his other arm about her, clamping down her wrist where her fingers still dug into the flesh of his forearm. Releasing the claim on her waist with reluctance, he stepped back, the circle of his fingers as steely as a handcuff as he held her at arm's length.

"I know what I *should* do, Miss Sinclair," he replied, his voice much steadier than he expected it to be considering the aroused condition of his body. "You deserve a beating for taking such a risk with your friend's safety. If you had dropped her, chances are she would have broken her damn fool neck."

"I had the situation under complete control until

169

you interfered. You will remove your hand from me immediately," she ordered, her chin notching noticeably.

Oddly enough, he had to admire her strength of conviction. Most *men* he knew could benefit by taking lessons from her in determination and self-confidence—in knowing how and when to bluff and get away with it. She was bluffing; he could tell by the way she twisted and tugged against the pressure of his fingers on her wrist.

He released her, an overtly polite smile curling his lips as he conceded her demands. Stepping toward her, he allowed his expression to widen as she visibly shrank against the door at her back. His hands rose and were placed on the oak slab on either side of her head—making him a wall, a barrier of strength and power that encompassed her. Tilting his face, he moved so close, her warm, sweet breath raked his face. "I don't think you understand, ma'am. The only thing under control here is my temper." *And if you're lucky, my desire,* he added mentally. "It would be best not to try me further." *Best for both of us.*

He watched her throat convulse in response, her tongue dart out and swipe at her dry lips, leaving behind a moisture that made his own mouth go dry. He noticed the spark of defiance ignite in her jade-green eyes, felt the air stir as her hands were lifted and placed against his chest, which rose and fell with the same determined rhythm as hers.

"Do you expect a royal commendation for your efforts, Mr. Carson? Because, if you do, you are mistaken. Her Royal Majesty, Queen Victoria, would find you sadly wanting." She looked him up and down. "In more ways than one."

The spell broken, he clamped his jaws tight. "Royal opinions don't hold much water here, ma'am, especially from a horse-faced, crepe-hung, half-cracked old biddy who has nothing better to do than try to tell people how they should live their lives. You might say, in Vicky's own immortal words, 'We are not pleased.'"

He knew the moment she stiffened he had struck a sensitive cord in this very Victorian Englishwoman. A pang of regret pierced him. He straightened, pulling back from her, his hands dropping to his sides. What in the hell was wrong with him? There was no excuse for him acting this way. He'd baited her and, she'd baited him, like two roosters at a cock fight, circling, circling, looking for a vulnerable spot to attack.

But damn it. His hands curled into fists at his sides. The way she flaunted defiance, it made him itch to strike back. His gaze slid down the contours of her desirable body. The way her bosom thrust forward when she puffed in puritanical pride—like now—his palms burned to reach out and caress her warm, pliant flesh. Knowing her as intimately as he did was hell in itself. Denial of what he felt was rightly his only became that much more difficult.

"The Queen of England is hardly deserving of your vulgar American gibe. As one of her loyal subjects I find it and you most offensive." She spoke with a quiet dignity that stung worse than if she had shouted at him.

This wasn't going at all the way he'd planned it. Garnet Sinclair was suppose to discover and admire his good qualities, not see him in the same light as Drew. Damn it to hell, where had he gone wrong?

In bewildered frustration, he clamped his hand about her waist and hauled her close. "Then that's something you'll just have to learn to live with."

He scooped her up and carried her squirming out into the hallway. Her fists pummeled his bare shoulders, the side of his face, anywhere she could reach as she screeched her indignation. In the corridor stood the servants, dressed for bed. Apparently they had heard the racket and had rushed upstairs to investigate. Their mouths gaped opened at the sight of their near-naked master carrying the protesting *señorita* from her bedroom.

"Go get the other girl and bring her back upstairs," he ordered, annoyed at the intrusion yet acutely aware of what the domestic help must be thinking.

They swayed like young willow trees in the face of a strong wind. Not one of the three females moved or seemed willing to.

"Well, do as I say," he said, spurring them with his harshness.

"Where is she?" stuttered Constanza, finally coming unglued from her spot on the floor.

"Down in the garden." Without further explanation he crossed the corridor and charged into his bedroom. Spying the unmade bed, he whipped back around. "And damn it, I want sheets on this bed immediately."

The saucer-sized stares of the servants took in their master's uncharacteristic nastiness in silence, but when he slammed the door closed against their amazement, he could hear the sounds of scurrying on the other side of the door.

"Be not hasty in thy spirit to be angry: for anger resteth in the bosom of fools."

"What?" His hooded gaze dipped to the woman he clutched to his chest as if he feared that if he let her go she would vanish.

She give him a haughty, superior look. "Ecclesiastes 8:9," she supplied smugly.

Here they stood on the threshold of his bedroom, him in his underwear and a red bandana, and she quoted the Bible at him like some black-coated tent revivalist. Well he knew a few verses too.

"The one without sin, let him—or her," he added meaningfully, "cast the first stone."

Her head pulled back as if surprised to find he could spout Biblical verses with the best of them.

"It's in there somewhere, but I'm not sure where," he finished with a lazy, yet challenging drawl.

"Yes it is. John 8:7. The exact quote is, 'He that is without sin among you, let him first cast a stone.'" Her gaze softened as if he had stroked some very personal memory for her. "Point well taken, Mr. Carson." She lowered her chin, subdued.

Staring down at her, he found her concession much more potent than any verbal riposte she could have concocted. Noting the sad turn of her mouth, he wondered just what she was thinking in that pretty head of hers. Was it of some other man?

The idea startled him and set his heart to hammering in his chest. Another man besides Drew? That was one problem he'd never anticipated.

"Yes, well," he muttered, "I suppose I could stand to take my own advice as well."

A hesitant knock on the door broke the gentled mood in the room. Constanza entered upon command, and without saying a word, she quickly made up the bed. Her dark Spanish eyes slid speculatively to Bain time and again, as if wanting to know just what he planned to do with the *señorita*. The servant gave him one last, long look before scooting out the door and closing it behind her with a click.

He glanced down at Garnet and read the same burning question in her jade-green eyes. Hell, just what was he going to do with her? He knew what he would like to do with her, but no. That was totally out of the question. But the one thing he knew he couldn't do was let her out of his sight the rest of the night.

Turning, he dropped her on the bed. "Don't you move," he ordered. He reached out, without once taking his eyes off her, retrieved his hastily discarded denims and checkered shirt, and put them on. As he

173

fumbled with the buttons on the fly of his pants, he saw her eyes dart down once, then skitter away.

When he lay down beside her, she tensed. And when he threw his arm across her body and pinned her to the mattress, she gasped.

He reached up and turned off the light over the bed. In the darkness he could hear her rapid breathing, feel the rabbit-like thumping of her heart against his arm.

"Sleep, damn it," he snapped. "We've got a long day ahead of us tomorrow."

And one hell of a long night, his tortured body assured him as the agony of desire ripped through him like a flash of heat lightning on a hot summer night.

Garnet lay in the crook of Bain Carson's arm, dismayed at the way her body tingled and her heart slammed into her rib cage as if a sledgehammer resided there. But worst of all was the disappointment echoing the heartbeats. He was going to do nothing, and though she didn't want to admit it, especially to herself, she had wanted him to . . . to . . .

To at least kiss her. Would it be the same as kissing Drew?

Dear God in Heaven, just what was she thinking? Good women never had such lurid fantasies comparing one man's caresses to another. Good women fell in love with and desired only one man in their lives. Good women never experienced carnal desire at all, and if they did, they didn't succumbed to their baser side before they were married.

Let's face it, Garnet old girl, you're not a good woman. You failed miserably when God finally put you to the test. She looked upwards toward the ceiling and the heavens beyond. *Forgive me, Lord. I*

174

won't disappoint You again, she vowed.

She was not attracted to Bain Carson. She squeezed her eyes closed trying to forget he held her intimately. It was just that he looked so much like Drew. But Drew was wrong for her as well, she sternly chided herself. She wasn't enamored with him either. At least, not anymore.

But lying there in the dark on a bed with the arm of Bain Carson draped across her middle, she had to take a deep breath to force her heartbeat to slow down. *I am not tempted by him. I am not,* she chanted over and over in her mind. But regardless of her affirmation, sleep wouldn't come, and the forbidden images of his sensuously curved mouth tasting hers refused to scatter even before the disapproval of God.

Chapter Ten

Bain lifted his hand and knocked on the closed door of the room where Choie Seem had spent the night. A beam of first morning light pooled in the corridor not far from where he stood, warm and alive with the freshness of a new day. A day that held promise in the wake of the long, sleepless night, at least for him. He dreaded facing the Oriental girl, the way she always stared at him, as if she knew more than she should, making him feel a bit uncomfortable when he was around her. Nonetheless, she had to be faced and made to understand that she must cooperate with him. When they left for Rancho Carmelo today, it was important she go willingly. Give Garnet a good example to follow. Within moments the door swung open, revealing her dark, sagacious eyes.

He shook his shoulders to throw off the strange sensations that mantled him whenever he was in Choie Seem's presence. This was ridiculous. Her perception might be keen, but she was just a child and he a man. There was no way he would allow her to take charge.

"Yes?" she asked, her soul-searching gaze penetrating to the very center of his consciousness.

"We must talk."

Her eyes slid down the length of him as if she sought answers in the way he held himself, in the pointed, shiny tips of his cowboy boots, his silver spurs that jingled whenever he shifted his weight, then her gaze darted back up, taking in the cut of his Western clothing, the way his throat convulsed under her scrutiny. "Tell me, Sir Dragon, to which head do I speak?"

Bain's insides jerked in surprise, yet he smoothed his expression into a blankness, revealing nothing of his inner turmoil. He knew of what she spoke. The dragon she had described to him—to Drew—aboard the *China Jewel*. With the ease of an ancient soothsayer, she'd seen through his ploy, but her suspicions—and that was all they could be—had to be based on mere speculation. She could have no proof that Bain and Drew were one in the same.

"We have many kinds of beasts here in California, li'l lady," he drawled lazily, hoping to throw her off by appearing confused by her words, "wolves, bobcats, and even grizzly bears—but dragons?" He scratched his head as if deep in thought. "Couldn't say there are any of those about."

They stared at each other for what seemed like eternity.

"Though the dragon isn't obvious to most, I can assure you I see him clearly." Her mouth lifted at the corners in a knowing smile.

Bain swallowed the acknowledgment that strained for release. He cleared his throat and forced his mind to think levelly. It was better not to admit to the truth as he didn't know how far he could trust this girl, though some sixth sense told him that, oddly enough, Choie Seem was on his side. "I came to tell you Miss Sinclair is safe."

"I never questioned her safety for a moment."

His eyes narrowed. How could this slip of a girl be so sure? There were times during the night when he

178

had doubted his own ability to restrain himself. "We'll be leaving soon to head inland. I want you both ready to go within an hour." Glancing at the girl's most unsuitable attire, the black sahm she'd worn at the barracoon, he sighed, aware she was much too tiny for the clothing in the trunk. "I'll have one of the servants bring you around something more appropriate for the road."

Her eyes lit up like the flame of one of the wall sconces behind her head, revealing a glimpse of the young girl within her. "Something pretty and gay?"

"Something pretty and gay," he assured her with a nod of his head. So Choie Seem was human after all and had a streak of vanity. Smiling to himself, he turned to go.

"Mr. Carson."

He pivoted back around to face her.

"I know not what game you play or why, but know this. Garnet Sinclair is a dragon-slayer, as was her father and his ancestors for many generations before him. If I were you I would be concerned for my own safety. She will smite you with her sword of righteousness if given the chance."

The side of his mouth quirked as he tilted his head in amusement at the girl's keen sense of reality. "Tell me something, Choie Seem, is Garnet aware of how wise beyond your years you are?"

She returned his smile, a bit of caginess revealed in her expression. "Like so many of the Christians who come to our ancient country with good intentions, Mr. Carson, she was not ready for the Truth. I feel through you she will learn what life is all about. She is good—kind and giving. No God, not hers nor mine, could ignore her inner beauty. That is why we love her so much."

He eyed her warily. Just who did Choie Seem mean by "we"? The people in China? Or did she include him among those who love Garnet?

179

A strange feeling rushed into the void that was his heart. Did he wish to be included? Confusion bombarded the secure sanctuary he'd built about himself and maintained for so long. He wanted Garnet Sinclair, there was no question of that. She was the caliber of woman who could fit into his life—strong, capable, yet ever so feminine—and leave no residue of guilt in his mind. Garnet Sinclair was not a woman to weaken before adversity or the harsh elements of living in an untamed land. But wanting and loving were two different things.

Weren't they? At least in the sense he meant them? Hell, he didn't know the answer. Exasperated, he brushed away the battle raging within him. "I'm sure Miss Sinclair doesn't lack for admirers," he mumbled.

"But none so important as you."

He turned his back to shield his heart from further examination. It didn't seem right that someone else could fathom what was hidden there before he could. He needed time to think and room to breathe, both of which he would find at Rancho Carmelo.

Garnet's lurid dreams were such that when she woke at daybreak to find Bain bending over her so close his breath brushed her cheek, she reddened beneath his scrutiny. Dragging her eyes away, she feared he would read the desire she tried so hard to ignore, a battle she was surely losing.

"It's time to get up, Miss Sinclair." His smile was brilliant, his gray eyes bright. Apparently he'd had no trouble sleeping last night, although it had taken her hours to finally do so. Bain Carson was more of a gentleman than she was a lady, and the realization didn't set well with her. Not at all.

"Choie Seem is waiting for you across the hall to help you get ready. And by the way, Miss Sinclair, I have taken the liberty of having your window temporarily nailed shut, and have posted a guard in front of your door. Breakfast will be in thirty minutes, and we leave for Rancho Carmelo within the hour, so I suggest you spend your time getting ready to go, not thinking up new ways to get into trouble.'' He stepped toward the door and held it open, expectantly.

Her lashes fluttering, her mouth tipped open to protest; then she snapped it shut. What choice did she have except to get up and follow him? At least for the moment.

From across the room she took in the long line of his sleek yet powerful body. She found herself seeking differences between Bain Carson and his brother—some subtle physical contrast. Except for the way Bain spoke and the undercurrent of civility lacking in Drew, they were the same. God help her, they were exactly the same if her memory served her right. Again thoughts of what it would be like to be kissed by this man invaded her mind. Just as quickly as they'd come, she sent the images packing. She was attracted to Bain only because he reminded her so much of Drew. Nothing more.

Rising from the bed, stiff and sore from holding herself as far from him as she could through the long night, she marched across the room with as much dignity as she could muster, considering her hair was in a shambled disarray and her dress looked as if she'd slept in it, which indeed she had.

"I'm not hungry," she declared, brushing by him, trying to ignore the electric sparks showering her insides merely from his manly smell and the light touch of his shirtfront on her arm.

He shrugged his wide shoulders under that clean, crisp, checkered shirt. "That's up to you, ma'am, but after ten grueling hours on the road, I think you'll regret such a hasty decision. The sumptuous table of

181

Rancho Carmelo is a long way from here."

She refused to give him the satisfaction of an answer even when he clamped his strong fingers about her arm and escorted her to her own threshold across the hallway. With a perverse sense of satisfaction she shut the door in his face as he began to speak. Smiling to herself, she spun, and just as Bain had promised, she discovered Choie Seem rushing toward her.

They hugged. After the escape fiasco the night before, Garnet was glad to see her friend looking so refreshed. Apparently Choie Seem had had no trouble sleeping either. With a sigh, she squeezed the girl again.

"We must hurry and get you ready to go, *Sse Mo*," the girl urged. "Men will be here soon to remove your trunk."

Noticing the girl was no longer dressed in the black sahm she'd worn since they'd left San Francisco, Garnet stared long and hard. Instead Choie Seem wore a simple skirt and cotton blouse of Spanish flavor. She looked exotic—and feminine—and very pretty with her long, dark hair loose about her slim shoulders, and not the least little bit unhappy with the fact that they'd failed to escape in the night.

"I'm not going anywhere," Garnet declared stubbornly.

"Of course, *Sse Mo*, but at least you'll want to change into something fresh. The servants even brought you up a bath." The girl pointed to a partitioned corner of the room. "It would be a shame for all that warm water to go to waste."

Garnet stepped forward, glanced around the embroidered screen, saw the whorls of steam drifting up from the bathwater, and smelled the soothing scent of lavender. Yes, it would be a shame for something so heavenly to go to waste.

She would take advantage of the bath and change her clothing for the sake of propriety, but that was all she would do. She still refused to eat, and there was no way Bain Carson would force her to go with him to his ruddy ranch. What if Drew should return and find her gone into the unknown wilds with his brother? What would he think?

But what was she thinking? Drew had deserted her without a qualm, leaving her in his brother's care. It would serve him right to find her gone. Then a strange sensation consumed her. What if Drew planned to never return?

In her mind she knew that would be the best thing, but in her heart . . .

She stripped off her wrinkled gown and underclothing and sank into the bath, a groan of pure delight surging up from the deep well inside of her. She could stay here forever, warm and secure in a haven of her own making, but just as quickly as the bubble of peace had formed about her, it burst.

"Please hurry, *Sse Mo*," Choie Seem called out as she banged about the room beyond Garnet's view, "before the *v-v-vaquer-os* come."

She mulled over the word that had issued from the girl's mouth so strangely and tried to make sense of it. Sitting up, she strained unsuccessfully to see around the screen. "The what?"

Choie Seem peeked around the partition, her face etched with concern. "I'm not sure what they are, but the way Ana described them, big and frightening . . . They must be something awful."

"Oh-h-h. You mean the cowboys," Garnet explained, finally making sense of the awkwardly spoken Spanish.

Choie Seem's expression remained perplexed. Though she spoke English very well, she was not familiar with American slang. And when it came to Spanish . . . No wonder she was confused.

Groping for a word to explain to the girl what a *vaquero* was, Garnet rose and began drying herself with the large, fluffy towel the girl provided for her. "*Vaquero*," she pronounced slowly in her best teacher's voice. She glanced at Choie Seem, waiting for the girl to repeat after her.

"*V-va-que-ro*," Choie Seem dutifully chirped, doing her best to parrot the syllables that were most unnatural to her Chinese tongue.

After several tries, Garnet was satisfied with her student's pronunciation. "A *vaquero*, a cowboy, is merely a male servant who works with the livestock," she explained, donning her underclothing and slipping into yet another of the dresses from the trunk, this time a lilac silk affair with plenty of lace and frills. She turned her back to allow the girl to button her up. When the fasteners were secured, she pivoted to face her student and smoothed down the big rosette bows on the front of the bodice. "I see we have work to do, Choie Seem. It's time you learned your Spanish."

Her busy hands stilled. A rush of adrenaline boiled up inside her like long-suppressed steam. It was good to be teaching again. This was what she'd been missing for so long in her life, since that unspeakable day at her father's mission. She needed to be needed, to serve a purpose, to be doing for others.

Sitting determinedly on the chaise, she drew Choie Seem down beside her. "I will teach you just like I used to do."

A fist sounded upon the door. With a sigh, Garnet lifted her head in response.

"The *vaqueros*," Choie Seem announced in a respectful whisper, the residue of fear still evident in her voice.

Garnet patted the girl's small hands. "There's nothing for you to be afraid of as we're not going anywhere, Choie Seem. Don't you worry." Rising

184

from her seat, she crossed the room to answer the summons, determined to send whoever was there away.

Ready to deal with servants, even if they were big, strapping *vaqueros*, she was not prepared to face Bain Carson. Her heart set up an instant clatter against her ribs the moment she saw him.

His gaze roved over her, his brow lifting inquisitively beneath his wide-brimmed felt hat when he noted the bustle and the excessive lace on her lilac-colored gown.

"May I suggest, ma'am, you change into something simpler, more comfortable for the road?"

"You may suggest whatever you please, Mr. Carson," she replied, battling the urge to tuck tail and run, "but I have no intention of going anywhere—at least not with you," she reiterated, folding her hands in front of her and unconsciously planting her feet. If this were Drew she'd defied so openly, she would find herself bodily lifted and carried down the stairs. What Bain Carson's reaction would be, she couldn't be sure, not unless she pushed him beyond endurance as she had last night. And that she would not do unless she was forced to.

He stared, his eyes raking her until her insides quaked with fear and something else she refused to acknowledge, yet his stance remained relaxed as he braced himself in the door frame, filling it completely. The jingle of his spurs cut into the silence. "Yes, you are," he said in a low, yet authoritative, voice. "The debt, Miss Sinclair? Have you forgotten what you owe my brother?"

She puffed up with indignation, feeling the pressure of helplessness building, building. God, she was tired of hearing about that bloody debt. It was not her intention that she and Choie Seem become like the other women the Carson brothers had forced to go to this Rancho Carmelo. She would not willingly subject them to such a depraved existence. "I know what you plan to do, Mr. Carson. I know all about the other women you hold hostage." She gathered Choie Seem to her heart and held her in the protective circle of her arms.

Bain pushed back his hat from his face, amusement illuminating his smoky gray eyes, which were surrounded by laugh crinkles. Did Drew have those same lines? She honestly couldn't remember, though she strained to conjure him up in her mind's eye.

"Tell me, ma'am, just what is it you've heard?" he asked in that lazy drawl she'd come to associate with the easy-natured Carson brother.

"I know you hold someone named Nattie at your ranch, as well as another Oriental woman whom the servants claim has never been allowed to return to Monterey," she gushed. "What kind of monster are you, sir?"

"You have it all wrong, ma'am," he answered ever so politely. "Nattie is my little sister, and she comes to town quite often considering her youth. And as for Mae Ching . . ." He paused as if he wished to gage her reaction. "She's my niece."

"So what does that make me, your long-lost cousin?" she snapped, not believing his pat explanation, not for one moment.

"I suppose we could say that, if that's what you want," he readily agreed as if he thought she strove to protect her reputation. "Or perhaps we should say I've hired you as the governess for the girls."

"A governess?"

Their gazes met, his calm, reeking of sympathy, yet full of unsuppressed pain that she had goaded him for no apparent reason. She caught her breath deep in her lungs, surprised at his unexpected reaction. She had a reason, a good reason for acting so belligerent, didn't she? She was being held against her will when all she wanted was to go home, to be rid of the conflicting emotions that had laid siege to her heart from the moment she'd set eyes on Drew Carson that fateful night at the barracoon.

She lifted her chin, unwilling to admit even to herself that she might be in the wrong, but guilt for her most unchristian thoughts and deeds curdled like soured milk in the pit of her stomach.

How could she accuse Bain Carson of being reprehensible when from the moment she'd met him yesterday he'd simply asked that she uphold the bargain she'd made with Drew—no matter that she'd made it under duress. The debt might not be binding in her eyes, but Bain had every right to demand repayment based on what his brother most likely had told him. Drew was the culprit here, not his twin. Look at how Bain had treated her with the utmost respect last night. He could have just as easily throttled her or worse for trying to escape. Instead he had maintained his honor—and hers—through the long hours, even when she yearned for something more.

She couldn't say the same for Drew, as she remembered only too well how he had treated her their last time together.

A rush of confusion shot through her like a flint-tipped arrow. She darted a glance at Bain, saw the open honesty on his face so like Drew's yet so different, and knew she battled the wrong person. If he had wanted to harm her, to conquer her, he could have easily done so in the privacy of his room during the night. No one would have been the wiser, or if they had been, they would have never attempted to stop the master of the house from doing as he pleased.

All of a sudden her fight to remain in Monterey was of little importance. With time she could show Bain the error of his thinking and convince him that the right thing to do would be to send her on her way. And if nothing else, she knew with all of her heart that *Bain* Carson would strive to do the right thing no matter what.

She allowed her mouth to soften, a shy smile to bow her lips. "Very well, Mr. Carson, we can claim I'm the governess." If only that were true. But wasn't it? She did have Choie Seem to instruct in Spanish. And who could tell? Perhaps she *would* find more students in the Carson household.

Before she could explore the possibility further, Bain signaled to a couple of men waiting in the hallway. They entered, their spurs jingling as they walked to where the trunk sat, apparently packed and locked by Choie Seem when Garnet had been otherwise occupied.

She glanced at her student, saw the look of mute awe on her youthful face as one of the men, young and almost what she would call pretty, tipped his *sombrero* in the girl's direction and muttered a polite "ma'am."

"Vaquero?" the girl mouthed, her lashes batting in an unconscious display of femininity.

Garnet nodded confirmation as the man respectfully dragged his eyes away from the exotic picture Choie Seem made dressed in the Spanish skirt and blouse, and with the help of his *compadre* hoisted and carried the clothing trunk out of the door.

"Will *he* be going with us?" the girl inquired, her mouth close to Garnet's ear, her dark, exotic eyes refusing to release the cowboy.

Garnet felt a surge of motherly amazement at her friend's sudden interest in a young man. "Most likely, but please, don't stare so," she whispered back. "It's most unladylike."

"Miss Sinclair, if you're ready," Bain said, offering his crooked arm in assistance. His insistence was not to be denied.

Garnet swung to face him and paused, studying him with a critical eye. Yes, she decided, noting his gallantry and politeness, she could trust Bain Carson.

"*Sse Mo*," said a quiet voice in her left ear.

Her gaze flicked to Choie Seem, whose face was covered by a radiant smile. "What?" Garnet murmured, still watching Bain, aware only that he was looking back at her with the same intensity.

"You're staring," the girl informed her.

Red crept up Garnet's neck and flushed her face. Jerking her eyes away, she took his arm and followed his lead through the corridor, down the steps, and out the front door into the dusty streets of Monterey.

If she bided her time, she could make Bain see things her way. *Patience is a virtue. Patience* is *a virtue*, she recited over and over in her mind. Realizing it was about the only virtue she had left, she was determined to see to it that her forbearance remained intact.

Leading Garnet toward the buckboard stationed in the street before the house, Bain couldn't help the feeling of elation that threatened to burst from his chest. He had seen the transformation on her lovely face, a miracle if ever he'd witnessed one. The moment she had finally recognized and acknowledged the difference between himself and Drew had been a moment of triumph. At last, she was willing to trust him. That had been the highest hurdle for him to conquer. If she trusted him, with time she could grow to care for him, the real Bain Carson, the man who spent his time creating beauty, not destroying it the way Drew had spent the thirty years of his life doing.

He couldn't wait to show Garnet Rancho Carmelo. He would share the beauty with her, the beds of asparagus he had painstakingly planted side by side with the peons, burying the spiderlike root systems

189

he'd had shipped from England in trenches to precisely the right depth. The beautiful lacelike growth sprinkled with red berries was a frothy wonder in itself. Then there were the artichokes, row after row of the tall, thistly plants whose unopened buds were the culinary delight of kings and queens. He had salvaged a few precious root cuttings from the gardens gone wild in the abandoned mission. Now he had a field of them that was quite impressive.

And the fruit trees. He closed his eyes and imagined the precisely patterned layout of the orchards that no matter which way you looked formed perfect rows. Seeing them dripping with ripened plums, pears, peaches, and cherries, he would gladly play Adam to her Eve and pick the sweetest fruits for her delight. Eden. Yes, Eden, and it would be theirs to share.

Reaching the buckboard, Bain turned and handed Garnet up into the seat, then took the Oriental girl's arm and settled her next to beautiful Miss Sinclair. He was aware that when he joined them from the other side his hip would rest next to hers, their shoulders brushing. By the way she pressed close to Choie Seem, he sensed she was thinking the same thoughts.

"Señorita, señorita." Constanza rushed from the front door, cutting through the mounted *vaqueros,* a parasol, one of Nattie's, under her arm. Reaching the side of the wagon, she poked it handle-first toward Garnet. "To shade your fair *tez de la cara.* You can get *quemadura del sol,* sunburn, even this time of year."

Garnet's smile was gracious, truly the expression a *patrona* bestows upon a beloved *servidora.*

"Gracias." She shoved the runner up the wooden shaft and tilted the open parasol over her head.

What a delightful picture she made, sitting in the seat of the buckboard, the lace of the sunshade as she spun it in her fingers without thinking compliment-ing the frills on her bodice. Now he was glad she'd refused to change into something more practical. He smiled to himself. The very proper Miss Sinclair. Perhaps that was what intrigued him most about her. Because he knew only too well that beneath that prim exterior lay a woman of fiery passion. A passion he wanted all for himself.

He dragged his eyes away. The last thing he needed to think about was her passionate nature. It was hard enough to keep his hands off her without imagining her. . . .

Damn it, he was doing it again, picturing her in ways he was better off not thinking about.

Moving away from his position below her, he crossed in front of the team, checking harnesses and bridles as was his habit before beginning a trip. On the far horse he tightened a breast collar, adjusting the leather against the warm flesh of the animal's broad chest. Feeling eyes upon him, he glanced up to find Garnet watching him, her back straight, her free hand resting palm-up in her lap, the jaunty twisting of the parasol coming to an abrupt halt. He deciphered the message radiating from her gaze, a message she was probably not even aware she sent him. Safe, secure, confident she would come to no harm with him beside her.

He hoped to God he could live up to her expectations.

Clearing his throat, he walked to the driver's side of the buckboard and mounted, the springs sagging as he pulled his weight up. Although Garnet stiffened, her bottom slid perceptibly his way on the seat, and when he settled beside her they touched hip to knee.

Igniting fire shot through him like molten lava. Her tongue darted out, moistening her sculptured lips; then she scooted away, the heat apparently scorching her as thoroughly as it did him.

"Sorry," they mumbled in unison, their eyes meeting and parting like the swooping swallows that congregated in the old mission bell tower.

Clicking his tongue and snapping the reins over the backs of the horses, he was only too glad to have to concentrate on keeping the team in line as they rolled through the dusty streets of the city heading toward the Carmel Valley Road, the three mounted cowboys riding alongside as escort. The team snorted, sensing the long journey before them; the wagon wheels squeaked as they jaunted over stones and ruts; Bain's thoughts returned to the woman beside him.

Garnet Sinclair. Garnet Sinclair. She was worse than an obsession, more fatal than an addiction, and far more wonderful than unearthing one of the many pots of pirate's gold alleged to be buried throughout the Monterey Peninsula. A China jewel worth more than a treasure chest of precious gems.

His gaze slid to study her finely chiseled profile, her high forehead, the prominent cheekbones denoting her intelligence. She stared directly ahead, her spine as straight as an arrow, an indication of her strength of will. The imagine of a schoolmarm, yet with her jutting, full breasts nothing at all like the educators of his youth. "Tell me, Miss Sinclair, are you a good teacher?"

Her head whipped about, surprise creasing the perfect arch of her brows. Her jade-green eyes darkened. "Depends on what you define as good, Mr. Carson. I don't teach to the tune of a hickory stick as I believe my students should learn more than the three R's. They should be shown what life has to offer them and to make the best of their circumstances, male or female." She stiffened as if she expected him to ridicule her unorthodox beliefs.

Instead he smiled. "That's good, Miss Sinclair. I

192

MORE PASSION AND ADVENTURE AWAIT... YOUR TRIP TO A BIG ADVENTUROUS WORLD BEGINS WHEN YOU ACCEPT YOUR FIRST 4 NOVELS ABSOLUTELY *FREE* (AN $18.00 VALUE)

Accept your Free gift and start to experience more of the passion and adventure you like in a historical romance novel. Each Zebra novel is filled with proud men, spirited women and tempetuous love that you'll remember long after you turn the last page.

Zebra Historical Romances are the finest novels of their kind. They are written by authors who really know how to weave tales of romance and adventure in the historical settings you love. You'll feel like you've actually gone back in time with the thrilling stories that each Zebra novel offers.

GET YOUR FREE GIFT WITH THE START OF YOUR HOME SUBSCRIPTION

Our readers tell us that these books sell out very fast in book stores and often they miss the newest titles. So Zebra has made arrangements for you to receive the four newest novels published each month.

You'll be guaranteed that you'll never miss a title, and home delivery is so convenient. And to show you just how easy it is to get Zebra Historical Romances, we'll send you your first 4 books absolutely FREE! Our gift to you just for trying our home subscription service.

BIG SAVINGS AND FREE HOME DELIVERY

Each month, you'll receive the four newest titles as soon as they are published. You'll probably receive them even before the bookstores do. What's more, you may preview these exciting novels free for 10 days. If you like them as much as we think you will, just pay the low preferred subscriber's price of just $3.75 each. *You'll save $3.00 each month off the publisher's price.* AND, your savings are even greater because there are never any shipping, handling or other hidden charges—FREE Home Delivery. Of course you can return any shipment within 10 days for full credit, no questions asked. There is no minimum number of books you must buy.

4 FREE BOOKS

TO GET YOUR 4 FREE BOOKS WORTH $18.00 — MAIL IN THE FREE BOOK CERTIFICATE T O D A Y

Fill in the Free Book Certificate below, and we'll send your FREE BOOKS to you as soon as we receive it.

If the certificate is missing below, write to: Zebra Home Subscription Service, Inc., P.O. Box 5214, 120 Brighton Road, Clifton, New Jersey 07015-5214.

FREE BOOK CERTIFICATE

4 FREE BOOKS

ZEBRA HOME SUBSCRIPTION SERVICE, INC.

YES! Please start my subscription to Zebra Historical Romances and send me my first 4 books absolutely FREE. I understand that each month I may preview four new Zebra Historical Romances free for 10 days. If I'm not satisfied with them, I may return the four books within 10 days and owe nothing. Otherwise, I will pay the low preferred subscriber's price of just $3.75 each; a total of $15.00, *a savings off the publisher's price of $3.00.* I may return any shipment and I may cancel this subscription at any time. There is no obligation to buy any shipment and there are no shipping, handling or other hidden charges. Regardless of what I decide, the four free books are mine to keep.

NAME

ADDRESS _____ APT _____

CITY _____ STATE ____ ZIP ____

TELEPHONE ( )

SIGNATURE _____ (if under 18, parent or guardian must sign)

Terms, offer and prices subject to change without notice. Subscription subject to acceptance by Zebra Books. Zebra Books reserves the right to reject any order or cancel any subscription.   ZBMS02

like that." He could picture the frightened, lonely Mae Ching responding to this woman. And Nattie. Ah, sweet, wild Nattie. Perhaps someone like Garnet, gentle and loving, could make her predestined future a little easier to bear.

He flicked the reins over the backs of the team, urging them a little faster as they bounced and jostled out of the city following El Camino Real, the old royal road that had been there since the Spanish missionaries had settled the California coastline.

Garnet Sinclair had come into their lives most unexpectedly, but she would be good, damn good for his entire family. Before long she would come to realize they would be good for her too. He glanced at her one last time. Then she would love them, love them all, and become a permanent member of Rancho Carmelo.

Chapter Eleven

Several hours later, her spine as ramrod straight as when they'd begun the long, arduous trip to Rancho Carmelo, Garnet's backside screamed for an end to the bone-jarring punishment meted out by the wagon seat beneath her. Her arms ached, one from holding up the parasol over her head to shade her fair complexion from the unrelenting sun that was hot even though it was October, the other from bracing herself against the hard, wooden slab she sat upon. If she had to suffer one more bump or wheel rut in the road, her muscles would surely refuse to function. What she wouldn't give to toss down the sunshade and throw her arms about the man beside her and beg him to bring her torture to a end, even for just a few moments.

But no. She would never do something so weak. Not again. Her gaze slid to the tall, relaxed figure to her left. She'd already made the mistake of allowing her vulnerabilities to peek through with this man's brother. And look what she'd gotten for her trouble. Unceremoniously dumped as if she'd had no more worth than an old, battered suitcase. She highly suspected Bain Carson, for all of his polite manners, wouldn't be much different. Even if he displayed a gallant front, inside he would laugh at her if she showed signs of weakening.

Tearing her eyes from his masculinity, she glanced at Choie Seem on her other side. At the beginning of the trip the Oriental girl had quickly refused her offer to share the sunshade, instead pulling up the brightly colored shawl from her shoulders and draping it about her head in such a way that it shaded her face and neck. The girl, her shoulders slightly rounded and relaxed as she rolled with the motion of the buckboard, looked like a pretty Spanish peasant until she turned those beautifully angled eyes in one's direction. Then she was an exotic vision. An opinion the young *vaquero* shared with Garnet, as he was making a point of riding as close to the right side of the wagon as he could.

Garnet wished she'd had such foresight to think to bring such a head covering, and wondered if she would look as appealing as Choie Seem did at the moment. But that was a stupid thought. What did she care how she looked anymore? She had no one to look pretty for. Her beautiful dress was wilted and covered with a thick layer of brown road dust. Another dress to meet ruination because of one of the Carson brothers.

She straightened her slipping spine and righted the drooping parasol, clutching the seat with her free hand so tightly her knuckles whitened. Seeing the back of one of the horses dip as it crossed through a pothole—yet another one—she clung to her perch, prepared to be thrown forward as the wheel followed suit.

As braced as she was when the wagon bottomed out, to her horror she felt herself slipping. Hang the bloody parasol! She didn't bother to watch as it flew from her fingers. Angling, she closed her eyes and clutched whatever her fingers found beside her. The thought of tumbling from the seat set her heart to racing. Bain Carson would laugh, really laugh at her if she landed at his feet, a tangle of limbs and petticoats.

She clung with the tenaciousness of a bulldog—nothing would make her turn loose. Nothing. Squeezing the solid, yet pliable bolster, she couldn't remember a cushion being on the seat beside her. Thank God that it was there. Yet strangely enough, this pillow seemed anchored to the bench as if . . .

Snapping her eyes open, she glanced up into the gray gaze of Bain Carson. His eyes were anything but laughing. They bore into her with the intensity of a lobo wolf on the prowl in mating season. She dropped a look at her grip and found her fingers curled about his thick, solid thigh, high above his knee, nearly to his groin, the back of one hand brushing against the crotch seam of his tight Levi's.

"Oh, I . . ." Red-faced, she snapped back her hands. As the wagon lurched forward on its way, she felt her precarious position slip.

Without a word, he slid his hand under her forearm and pulled her up on the seat, anchoring her against his solid length as if she were a rag doll, light and boneless, totally incapable of supporting herself. She struggled; he squeezed.

"Be still," he ordered.

Holding the reins in one hand, he turned the team to the right off the road toward a crumbling stucco building.

"What are you doing?" she demanded in a choking whisper, remembering only too well her hand pressing against his manliness moments before. Had he misinterpreted her clumsy attempt at self-rescue as a blatant sexual advance? Surely he didn't think she had . . . touched him on purpose. And with all of the witnesses around he wouldn't dare try to . . . to . . . or would he? "There's no need to stop."

"I think there is." He pulled the snorting horses to a halt beneath a grove of laurel trees, wrapped the reins about the brake handle, and turned to face her on the seat. "I have watched you all morning, Miss Sinclair, so prim and proper."

God, she wasn't even aware he had looked at her once during the entire trip.

"I thought for sure any moment your spine would snap in two beneath the torture you forced it to suffer." His hand slid up her back in emphasis.

"I don't think you have a right to . . ."

"Relax, ma'am," he drawled, at last the amusement brimming in his eyes as if she were a little bantam rooster puffed to face a much larger foe. "I'm not gonna bite ya."

Before she could reply, he released her and jumped down from the wagon, forcing her to clutch the seat to keep from sliding off as it sprang back into place. Then he turned and offered her a hand down.

At first she considered rejecting his assistance, in fact refusing to get down at all, but when Choie Seem bent to speak to her gallant *vaquero*, apparently eager to alight and stretch her legs, Garnet placed her fingers in Bain's and scooted forward, allowing him to clasp her about the waist and swing her to the ground. Her hands resting on his broad shoulders, their gazes met, but she quickly pulled hers away, still embarrassed that she'd touched him so intimately earlier, even if it was by mistake. She had touched no man that way, not even Drew, with whom she'd done things. . . .

She blushed, remembering only too well what those things were. Unbidden thoughts rushed in. What would it be like to kiss Bain, to . . . ?

Glancing up guiltily, she read a similar curiosity in his smoky gray eyes. No, his look was more a starving man's hunger. His hands were still on her waist, hers on his shoulders, and for a moment she thought he would sate her mental desire, and she found herself unable or unwilling to move, to see if he would make an overture. Then she would refuse him, she vowed smugly to herself.

To her disappointment he released her, and stepped back and around her, motioning to the rest of the escort to dismount.

The spell broken, Garnet surfaced, her emotions sucking to pull her back down like a drowning swimmer. Disappointed that he had had the strength to resist her, she found herself watching him with resentment as he turned to help Choie Seem down and gallantly retrieved the girl's shawl when it slipped from her shoulders as she stood talking to Bain and the young cowboy.

She would have said no to him. She would have, Garnet assured herself. She was not the kind of woman who found two different men appealing at the same time, no matter how much they looked alike.

Yet as Bain continued to ignore her and speak easily with Choie Seem, the resentment blossomed into full-blown envy that he couldn't be as comfortable with her. It was because of her relationship with Drew. That was it. He found her undeserving of his attention and affection.

Her thoughts came to an abrupt halt. His affection? But she didn't want his af-f-fection. Her only attraction to Bain Carson was the fact that he reminded her so much of Drew. That was all.

She forced her attention away from the congenial picture the cowboy, Bain, and Choie Seem made, and began to explore her surroundings. The abandoned building was old, very old, and in a state of disrepair. Cutting around a corner of an abode wall, she found herself beneath a crumbling tower and dome where one of twin arches still held a massive bell. A bell tower?

"Why, this is an old Spanish mission," she said aloud, her amazement obvious in her voice.

"Basilica San Carlos Borromeo del Rio Carmelo to be exact," Bain supplied, so close behind her she jumped. Apparently he had followed her. "It was beautiful once, the pride of the Franciscan padres, but long ago the Spanish governor sucked the poor priests dry and they couldn't afford to maintain it. The gardens, the orchards, the vineyards—all of it was deserted. Now you'll find the owls and ground squirrels have taken it over, and cattle have stomped the grapevines to nothing." He sighed. "I would like to see it restored one day, but I don't know if that dream will be possible in my lifetime."

Garnet glanced up, not sure whether to believe his show of sentiment or not. Sincerity radiated from his gaze as he looked out over the ruins. Bain Carson might remind her of Drew in looks, but in personality—they were as different as night and day.

"So you named your ranch after the mission?" she asked.

"Actually my father did that, but I made the naming have meaning. I managed to save cuttings and graftings from the fruit orchards and vegetable gardens and take them to the ranch. I think Father Sarria, the mission's founder, would be pleased with my efforts."

"I'm sure the good padre would be," she replied softly, honestly meaning what she said.

"Come," he stated, touching her arm and pointing toward the grove of laurel trees where the wagon was parked, Choie Seem standing patiently beside one wheel. "I don't know about you, but I'm hungry. Rosita packed us lunch."

Hungry? She was starving, having stubbornly refused to eat that morning before they'd departed Monterey. She followed him willingly as he led the way back to the buckboard.

There he pulled a large wicker basket out from under the seat and placed it on the ground beside his feet. Then he retrieved a colorful blanket, which he spread under the shade of the trees, which amazingly still clung to their riotously autumn-painted leaves.

Without thinking about what she was doing, Garnet picked up the amazingly heavy food hamper and placed it beside the blanket. Kneeling, she began unpacking its contents. Tantalizing smells escaped as she unrolled woven checkered cloths filled with all kinds of taste-tempting delicacies. There was a tin of deviled eggs smothered in a cheesy cream sauce. In another was a pot of *frijoles* still warm from refrying, and another of shredded chicken and chilies and tomatoes. Finally there was a round of yellow cheese, a butter crock filled with snow-white sour cream, and a pan of soft tortillas. The mouth-watering aromas filling her senses, Garnet sat back on her heels, unsure how she should serve the strange array of food.

"Here, let me show you." Bain joined her on the blanket, taking the pan of tortillas from her hands. The warmth of his fingers on hers heated her blood, and she willingly allowed him to take the platter.

"A spoon, please," he requested, putting out his hand as a surgeon might in an operating room.

Stupidly she stared at his fingers, still rocketed by the searing sensations his touch stirred in her.

"In the basket behind you," he added patiently.

"Oh, yes, a spoon." She twisted about to reach into the hamper. Discovering the utensil at the bottom of the basket, she swung back around, presenting it to him. She found him whittling away slivers from the round of cheese with a pocketknife. Taking a thin slice between his thumb and the blade, he popped the piece of cheese in his mouth, then turned, presenting her with a bite in the same fashion.

She opened her lips, accepting his offering. The cheese's tangy flavor was distinct, different from the Swiss and French cheeses she was accustomed to.

"Monterey Jack. It's good, isn't it?" he commented, slipping another piece into his mouth.

She nodded, chewing. "Another credit to Rancho Carmelo, no doubt."

Taking up a tortilla in the flat of his hand, he began spooning beans, chicken, and sour cream into its depths. "To tell the truth, yes and no. Actually, it's an old family recipe of our neighbors at Rancho Los Laureles. Doña Juana made it first many years ago, and our cook at the ranch is a distant cousin of hers and knows the recipe, which she refuses to divulge to me. She's the one who named it Monterey Jack. It seems Doña Juana always placed a heavy jack atop the pressboards of the kegs she made her cheese in." He set the filled tortilla on a cloth, folding and rolling it several times. Then he handed her the finished product. *"Burrito,"* he announced, and started making another one.

Garnet took a bite. It was definitely Spanish in flavor, though she'd never had anything to compare with it in Spain, and she decided she liked this *burrito*. "Another local concoction?" she asked, taking another bite.

Bain laughed, the sound rich and melodic. "Not at all. The Mexican peasants have been making their version for years. Kind of like your English invention of the sandwich. Everybody has his own variation." He handed Choie Seem the second filled tortilla, and quickly made more for the *vaqueros*, who eagerly accepted their lunch. Then he began one for himself.

Soon they were all eating, the men lounging against trees and wagon wheels, Garnet and Choie Seem demurely kneeling on the edge of the blanket, Bain cross-legged between them wolfing down his meal and alternately wiping the sour cream from the corners of his mouth like a hungry little boy. Discovering a jug of cool white wine, Garnet poured them all a mugful and passed the mugs around amid murmurs of *"gracias"* from the men. She smiled when she noticed the young cowboy edge as close to Choie Seem as he dared without seeming improper and attempt to engage her in a limited conversation in broken English.

There beneath the laurel trees on a carpet of multi-colored leaves, protected from the wind by the old Spanish mission, munching on *burritos*, Garnet was happy, innocently so. But how could that be possible? she asked herself with amazement. She had been callously used by one brother and was the prisoner of the other; no matter that there were no chains to bind her, getting away was still impossible. And at the moment she wasn't sure she wanted to escape even if she had the opportunity.

Finishing up the last of her food, she licked her fingers clean, then wiped them dry on one of the cloths she found in the basket.

"Would you like more?"

She glanced up to find Bain staring at her. More food? No. She shook her head in refusal. But something more from him? Yes.

What she needed was an explanation. Why did he insist she go with him to Rancho Carmelo? His motives were more than his brother's ludicrous claim of a debt owed. From what she'd seen of Bain, he was sensitive enough to realize no man demanded something so unreasonable from a lady. Did Drew hold something over him as well? Of course. That was the only explanation that made sense. Bain was a victim as much as she was.

Such reasoning should have made her feel closer to Bain, knowing they shared a common enemy, but oddly enough, it had the opposite effect on her. She found herself comparing him to Drew, a man who would never allow himself to get into a situation where someone else had control. Instead of making Bain seem more attractive, it made him appear weaker. And though she despised Drew for what he did to his brother, she admired his strength of will and found it strangely exciting.

Shocked by the disappointment coursing through her, she tore her eyes from Bain's pointed stare. What was wrong with her? This was not at all the response she should be having under the circumstances.

"Garnet."

Reluctantly she looked back at the man who'd spoken her name so gently. In that moment she realized he had sensed her comparison between him and his brother, and had been just as surprised by her finding him lacking as she'd been.

"It's time we were on our way." Unfolding himself, he rose, motioned to his men, and moved toward the wagon, leaving the women to clean up after the meal.

Garnet tackled the task with relish. Anything to take her mind off this aspect of her personality she'd never know existed and didn't wish to confront. Choie Seem handed her the empty pots and pans, and she packed them back in the hamper with an unnecessary show of force.

"*Sse Mo?*"

Garnet slammed the lid down on the basket and turned to face the Oriental girl. "What?"

"Is everything all right?"

"Yes, of course," she replied, standing and picking up the basket. But it wasn't. God knows, nothing was right anymore.

Bain forced himself not to use unnecessary roughness as he adjusted a loose belly strap on one of the horses. She had been comparing him to Drew and had found him lacking.

He took a deep breath and let it out slowly. Why were women all the same? For as long as he could remember they had found Drew's flamboyance and brutishness more attractive than his own quieter nature. Somehow he had expected Garnet Sinclair to be different from the others.

From the corner of his eye he saw her trudging toward the buckboard toting the hamper and the blanket. His first instinct was to go after her and relieve her of her burden. Instead he held himself in check, issued a pointed stare at one of the men when he moved forward to help, and waited for her to reach the wagon. Taking the basket when she handed it to him, without a word he swung it up behind the seat and dropped the blanket atop it. He could sense she was miffed at his lack of gallantry.

What did she want from him? Hell, what did he expect from her? He realized he didn't have an immediate answer to either question.

Maintaining his silence, he assisted the women into the wagon only because Garnet stood beside the front wheel expectantly. She murmured a clipped "thank you," and he replied with an unenthusiastic "you're welcome," neither looking at the other.

As soon as he was settled on the seat beside her, he flicked the reins against the horses' rumps and set them at a trot once they were back on the road. Perversely he enjoyed watching Garnet attempt to maintain her decorum as she floundered on the seat beside him, trying to hang on as well as hold up that damned parasol, which now sported one broken rib, making it sit ridiculously cockeyed.

Give it up, Garnet.

As if his thoughts had penetrated her thick, protective wall of pride, her shoulder slumped, and she closed the sunshade, defeated, not caring that soon her clear, delicate skin would turn the color of the bandana knotted at his throat. She clung to the seat with both hands, concentrating only on maintaining her precarious balance.

205

Her complete surrender set off an avalanche of guilt in his conscience. He slowed the team to a mere clip-clop pace, twisted, and reached behind the seat to pluck up the large square of cloth Rosita had used as a cover on the food hamper. Then clamping the reins between his knees, he draped the cloth over her once-coiffured hair and across her rounded shoulders, pulling it forward to shade her face—even the tip of her finely shaped nose.

How pretty she looked beneath the blue and white checkered makeshift scarf, her jade-colored eyes looking even greener in contrast. His jewel, his little China jewel. The desire to gather her to his heart and tell her he would take care of her always—assure her there was no Drew to stand between them, that he would soon have answers regarding her father and students—burned a path from his heart to his tongue. Yet he knew it was best he kept his silence. What if he found out something terrible had happened to her family? Would he want her to know the truth? Or would her ignorance be better? As for Drew, she would never believe him, not now, not after all that had passed between them. She would have to exorcise Drew's demonic presence on her own. Otherwise it would be meaningless—for both of them. *Patience,* he reminded himself. With time this was one battle he would win—if he only gave her, as well as himself, time. Good did conquer evil; he had to believe that, or else he wouldn't be the man he was.

"Thank you," she chirped in a sincere whisper, her hand reaching up to tuck a wayward curl beneath the head covering.

"You're welcome," he replied with a gentle smile, meaning what he said as well.

Taking up the reins, he clicked to the team, careful to keep them at a brisk but even walk.

Two hours later they crested the mountain path

that opened up into the Carmel Valley. Poised at the top, he brought the horses to a halt, giving them all a chance to rest and take in the lush view. Emerald-green fields dotted with ancient, twisted oaks spread out before them. To the right the Rio Carmelo cut through the canyon, its banks lined with drooping willows, the golden heights of the Santa Lucias Mountains a backdrop to it all. He wished it were spring. Then the fields and banks would be carpeted with pink buttercups, crimson shooting stars, golden poppies, and deep blue lupine. The gateway to the Garden of Eden, and Bain was ever so proud of it.

The women sat silently staring, sharing his awe. The fact that Garnet saw the beauty of his home made Bain's heart swell with hope. She would love Rancho Carmelo, and with time she would learn to love him too.

Flicking the reins, he started the team and wagon down the dusty, winding road. Within a couple of hours they would be home. He was eager to see Nattie, and more than anything to witness the joy on Mae Ching's drawn little face when at last she had someone who could understand her, talk to her, and take her to a motherly bosom and assure her all was well. Even if Garnet was able to find fault with him, she would never be able to resist Mae Ching. The child would bind her to Rancho Carmelo more securely than any jailer's chains could.

Bain smiled to himself. Garnet's generous heart would be her own undoing. If he were a gambling man, he'd be more than willing to "let it all ride" on such a sure bet.

Chapter Twelve

The buckboard took a bend in the road, and there it was. Rancho Carmelo. Garnet knew it by the perfect symmetry of the house, outbuildings, and surrounding trees. They were exactly the way Bain would want them. To the left of the main house a vineyard snaked its way up a rise, down into a small dip, and back up another hill, perfectly aligned, each plant appearing as if it had been hand-pruned to await the first signs of spring. She took a sidelong glance at Bain, wondering if indeed he had had a personal hand in the grooming of the grapevines.

To confirm her suspicions that they had at last reached their destination, one of the team gave a loud whinny of greeting, which was answered by a lone, spotted horse grazing atop a rise in a pasture that ran along side the road. The massive animal trotted forward, his neck arched, his tail held high—not that Garnet could be sure the animal was a stallion from that distance, but something in the way it carried itself, so proud, so virile, made her think it could be nothing else. Once the great beast reached the fencing, he paced himself to the team and riders, but his strides had a lot more spring to them, his head bobbing up and down as he snorted.

"Be off with you, you big show-off," Bain responded with a snort of his own.

As if the stallion understood, he lowered his great head and bucked, then took off at a dead run toward the barn, where he knew by instinct the arriving party would head.

"He's beautiful," Garnet's voice warbled with fascination. "I've never seen anything like him. What kind of horse is he?"

"The Nez Percé Indians call his type Appaloosa after the Palouse River. Quixote will be the grand sire of a great breed of horses one day."

Don Quixote de la Mancha. The idealistic hero in Cervantes' novel. *Mancha* meaning "spot." How appropriate. She smiled her appreciation of his play on words. "I'm sure he will be if that's what you want."

He brought the wagon and team to a stop before the great doors of the barn, the escort riders milling around them to find a spot to dismount and tie off their mounts. Twisting in his seat, Bain studied her, his eyes drifting slowly down her figure. *That's not all I want*, his hungry gaze seemed to say.

Dragging her eyes away, she concentrated on the cowboy who stepped forward and began unharnessing the wagon horses. Why did Bain have to look at her that way? It reminded her so much of Drew.

A feminine squeal and the crunch of running boots in the gravel of the drive brought her head around. Racing toward them was a girl no more than fourteen or fifteen, her long hair flying like a dark banner behind her. Shocked to see a young woman wearing tight jeans and a checkered shirt, her breasts unrestrained by corset or even a chemise under her clothing, Garnet turned to watch the girl cross in front of the wagon and throw herself bodily into Bain's arms.

"Bain, Bain," she shrieked, her enthusiasm as contagious as a yawn.

"Nattie. Nattie, girl," he replied, swinging her about before gently settling her back on her feet.

So this wild creature was his little sister.

"Oh, Bain, you were gone so-o-o long this time," Nattie complained.

Gone so long? Garnet mused. Why, she'd assumed Bain had been in Monterey only a few days. The girl spoke as if he'd been absent from the ranch for weeks.

"What did you bring me from town?" the girl continued, her slim hands dipping into the pockets of his shirt and jacket. Much as she, Garnet, used to do with her father. A spark of longing ignited and her eyes misted.

"Ah, Nattie, you're spoiled rotten. What makes you think I have something for you?" he teased.

Nattie pouted dramatically, yet her eyes—the same shade of gray as her brother's—watched him reach into the buckboard under the seat and remove a gaily wrapped package.

"It's so big," Nattie squealed, snatching the present from his hands. "Oh, thank you, thank you," she cried, turning to rush toward the house, the big blue ribbon already untied and trailing on the ground.

"Nattie, wait," Bain called. He held another, smaller gift out toward her.

The girl turned.

"For Mae Ching. Will you give it to her for me?"

Nattie smiled, and in that instant Garnet could see the likeness between her and her brother. "Why don't you give it to her yourself?" She pointed toward the veranda of the main house across the expanse of the drive.

There in the shadows, Garnet could make out a small form squatting beside an oversized terra-cotta flowerpot as if attempting to hide, a dark head peeping around the corner every now and then.

Bain straightened as if in utter awe of the child's

presence. "Mae Ching," he called softly. "For you." Then he stepped forward as if approaching a wild animal he feared would bolt away.

Garnet watched as the little girl scooted back into the shadows as Bain neared the house.

Seeing no sign of the child, he sighed, set the prettily wrapped package on the veranda, and edged backwards.

Something made Garnet step forward and join Bain. *"Liwu, ti ni,"* she said in a clear, yet gentle voice, picking up the package and stepping up onto the porch. "Mae Ching, a present for you," she repeated in Chinese, kneeling down and waiting patiently.

At last her vigilance was rewarded. The girl peeked around a wooden post, her youthful curiosity taking charge.

"Ti wo?" Her dark, almond-shaped eyes looked skeptical, as if she were unable to believe the gift was for her.

Remembering Bain had told her this child was his niece, she pointed toward him and nodded her head. *"Ti ni.* From your *bofu*—your uncle."

The child glanced at Bain, a tiny frown marring her features. *"Fahn Quai,"* she announced with a shake of her head. "He stole my father's spirit."

Garnet's gaze moved to Bain, then back to Mae Ching. "Oh, no, dear, not white devil, your *bofu.*" Stole her father's spirit? She tried to make sense of the little girl's words. Then it dawned on her. The only person who could be this child's father was Drew. Mae Ching was confused because they looked alike.

Her breath caught in her lungs as she acknowledged that Drew had sired a child. How could he so callously ignore the child? He had not even bothered to come see his own daughter while in port.

Mae Ching studied Bain, as if unsure whether to believe Garnet or not. *"Bofu,"* she mouthed, took the package from Garnet's hands, and dipped a respectful bow at Bain. Then her eyes lit on something behind Garnet. *"Yun Mo?"* she asked.

Garnet looked over her shoulder to find Choie Seem silently observing the exchange from the bottom of the stairs. "No, Mae Ching, she is not your mother." This poor child. How confused she must be, not even sure who her mother was.

"Are *you* my mother?" she questioned further, her gaze hopeful, pleading. Garnet yearned to answer her with a yes.

"Sse Mo," Choie Seem answered, stepping forward and placing an arm around Garnet's shoulders. "So much more than a mother."

"Sse Mo," the child repeated, seeming satisfied. Then flashing Bain a brilliant smile, she bowed to him again. *"Xiexie nin,* thank you, *bofu."* She skipped away hugging her box.

Bain watched her go. "You're a miracle worker, Miss Sinclair. I'm not sure what you said to her, or what she said to me, but that is the first time she's smiled since I brought her here."

"Bofu means uncle. I think you will find she will call you that from now on."

"Bofu, bofu," he repeated. "It does have a nice ring to it, doesn't it?" He studied her, and she felt he had more he wished to say, but instead he moved to the front door. "You both must be tired. I'll see to your rooms."

Disappointed that he had withdrawn and changed the subject so abruptly, Garnet followed. Questions burned her tongue demanding answers. Answers only he could supply regarding Mae Ching. But she held her silence, at least for now.

He led them into the main salon of the house, which was long, narrow, and low, very Spanish, making Bain appear even taller than he was as his head was barely a foot below the ceiling. The

213

furniture was just as dark, massive and old, yet beautiful in its antiquity. Just ahead were a pair of French doors that opened out into a large courtyard. She could see a three-tiered fountain rising out of a reflecting pool, an array of aquatic plants decorating its base.

"This way," he said, heading toward the doors.

Once through them Garnet found herself in a virtual fairyland. The house was like a fortress, completely surrounding the courtyard. Each room had a door leading out into it, a covered portico all the way around the interior completing the picture. Potted plants were everywhere: orchids, bromeliads, ferns, and vines, many of which she couldn't name. Graceful wooden benches, chairs, and tables were strategically placed in the shade and in the sun to please any mood. The fountain trickled, the sound restful, completing the perfection of the scene.

"Why, Bain," she exclaimed, spinning around to take it all in, her barriers lowered enough to use his given name without thinking about it. "This is as fine as any villa I've ever seen. How did you manage to gather all of these wonderful specimens?" She knew only too well how exotic many of them were. Her father was an avid botanist and always brought home his own specimens from every trip. He had a glasshouse full of plants that didn't do justice to what surrounded her now.

He shrugged off her praise as if it embarrassed him, and paused to inspect the leaves of one multi-colored orchid growing on a large slab of bark.

How out of place the tall, well-proportioned man appeared, tending his flowers with an expert hand. Her father was reed-thin, wore spectacles on occasion, the image of a horticulturist.

Was it Bain's stature, his bearing, that made this all seem so wrong for him? Or was it merely because she had known Drew first that made his brother's ways seem out of character to her? She had only known men like her father, would have willingly accepted the suit of a gentle man, would have probably married one eventually and have been content—before she'd met and made love to Drew. And a man like Bain—well, he would have set her heart to racing once, before Drew. How did she purge Drew's essence from her soul and regain her innocence, not only in her body but in her mind?

If only she could take it all back. But no. She would never give up knowing the wonder and ecstasy she'd experienced in Drew's arms. She glanced around the beautiful villa. Not even for all of this! The temptations of the flesh held her firmly in their claws refusing to release her, even if it seemed in her own best interest.

"This way," Bain said, breaking into her musing. He crossed the courtyard and stepped onto the portico to the right, passing several doors, some opened, some closed, revealing bedrooms, sitting rooms, finally storage rooms. Then they came to a roomy, well-ventilated kitchen near the rear.

Pulling large loaves of bread out of the oven, as apparently today was baking day, was the cook Bain had spoken of on the trip. She turned at his approach, a steaming loaf pan in her hands that caused beads of sweat to form on her brows. She gave him a huge smile befitting her size, her teeth as yellow as the cheese she was famous for making. "Ah, *Señor* Bain. You have picked a good day to return home." She lifted the pan of bread toward him for a sniff. "Fresh leavened bread for dinner." She angled her wide, flat nose and pointed it toward a corner, where a little Spanish girl worked a churn, up and down, up and down. "And sweet, fresh butter as well."

"Ah, Inez, you will make a *gordo hombre* of me yet."

215

"*Sí*. Then there will be more of you to love—like me."

Bain stepped out of the doorway, revealing Garnet to the obese servant. The woman spied her, looked her up and down, then grinned, revealing those yellow teeth of hers. "But perhaps you don't need me to love, hey?"

Garnet reddened; Bain cleared his throat; the woman laughed out loud, the only one to enjoy her bawdy joke.

"Inez, *Señorita* Sinclair and her companion need accommodations. Could you please see rooms are made ready for them?"

The round little woman frowned, set her loaf of bread on a large chopping block, and dusted her flour-coated hands on her apron before plopping them on her wide hips. "Two rooms?"

He nodded.

"Then we will have to use the *Señora* Carson's chambers," she warned.

Bain frowned. "Then so be it. I will settle the *señoritas* in the courtyard until the rooms are ready. They've had a long trip. Serve them something to quench their thirst while they wait," he ordered, his tone of voice suggesting he wasn't pleased with what the serving woman had said.

Soon Garnet found herself seated in a padded chair at a wrought-iron table drinking a tall glass of *sangria*, watching Bain's retreating back moving toward the front salon. She glanced at Choie Seem, who was wandering about the courtyard aimlessly sipping at her own glass of fruited wine. Realizing she didn't want Bain to leave, not just yet, she sat up in her chair and leaned forward. She had questions that needed answers, and if he left she had no idea when she might have a private moment again to ask them.

"Bain?" she called.

Instantly he stopped and turned to face her.

"I know you must be anxious to see to . . . your ranch, but please, couldn't you give me a few moments?" she asked, swallowing hard, fearing he would say no, fearing more he would say yes and she would be obligated to him.

"A few moments, Miss Sinclair? I imagine I could spare a couple of minutes." He cocked his head in curiosity and returned to where she sat, staring down at her as if saying, "Well?"

He looked so formidable, his arms crossed over his broad chest. Garnet's eyes groped around, seeking Choie Seem to reassure herself she wasn't alone with him. The Chinese girl was clear across the courtyard, studying a massive staghorn fern large enough to easily grace the head of a giant moose. Garnet's gaze darted back to Bain. "I was wanting to ask you some question regarding Mae Ching."

Apparently she'd struck a sensitive cord. He slid into the chair opposite hers, his expression serious and expectant.

"It's obvious she doesn't speak English," said Garnet.

"Not a word."

She took a sip of her *sangria*, then settled her glass back on the table. She wanted to know how that could be if Drew was her father, but instead she asked, "Would you mind if I spent time with her? Teaching her, I mean?" she explained quickly. Her heart slammed against her rib cage as she studied his face, on which not a single emotion was revealed.

"I see no problem with you instructing Mae Ching, if it amuses you," he replied. For a moment she caught a glimpse of pure, raw excitement on his features, and she remembered how pleased he had been earlier when the child had at last spoken to him. Why was he being so careful to protect his feelings from her?

217

"It's what I do best, you know," she countered, trying to sound as unaffected as he did.

His gaze drifted down to her lips watching her form each word as she spoke. They grew dry under his intense scrutiny, and the need to moisten them with her tongue overwhelmed her, but she held the impulse in check. She didn't dare make such a suggestive move—not with the way he was looking at her. Soon her own gaze focused on his mouth, a strange fascination filling her. When at last he began speaking, she couldn't tear her eyes away.

"I believe your rooms are ready," he informed her, glancing up once at something over her shoulder.

He could have been spouting words of love to her if her reaction was any indication. Her heart began to hum like the plucked strings of a guitar, vibrating all the way down through her body, making her keenly aware of her womanly parts. She pushed her glass away and rose, eager now to be away.

He stood with her. "Let me show you the way." Before she could protest, he took her arm and led her across the patio. His fingers on her skin burned like camphor upon an open sore, creating an anticipation of the relief soon to follow if only he would continue caressing her.

This was crazy. This man held no attraction for her; he was not Drew. Yet with the feel of his hand on her arm, her emotions contradicted her mind, denied the truth. It was as if Drew held her, led her forward, and she knew she was powerless to resist him. How could her wretched body be such a traitor?

At the door to her room he paused and pushed open the barrier. The darkened chamber was cooler than the outside air, still warm with the afternoon sun. She shivered when the chilled air caressed her. Or was it—God help her—a reaction to Bain's touch? She couldn't be sure. Turning her head away to avoid looking directly at him, she noticed in the corner a

218

brazier had been lit to heat up the enclosure. Oh, why didn't it hurry up and do its job?

Bain leaned her against the door frame, his free hand moving up to slide along her other arm as if he were attempting to warm her. "Why don't you rest until supper?" he suggested.

Closing her eyes, she nodded and pressed her spine against the doorjamb, unwilling to look at him, afraid yet yearning for him to move closer—to kiss her. It was wrong, this desire she had to experience his caress, yet at the moment she couldn't remember why it was so. She suspected his kiss would be gentle, nothing like Drew's. Perhaps it was the allure of the untried that held her enraptured at the moment—it couldn't be more than that.

Yet when his lips grazed hers she was shocked by their firmness. Gentle at first, as she'd predicted, soon he was hungrily feasting upon her mouth, his tongue probing the sealed seam of her lips. She was taken aback by his insistent gesture, somehow thinking such intimacy was special between her and Drew. But how foolish. They were not the first and only couple to make love, but she stubbornly struggled to retain her illusion that they were. Her lips parted and Bain explored, a man seeking to quench his thirst at a familiar well. On its own accord her tongue coiled about his, and she knew instinctively the dance it would do.

But how was that possible? She'd never kissed Bain before now. Was there nothing unique in the art of making love? She found such a discovery disappointing, yet she couldn't ignore the thrill racing through her like quicksilver to every nerve of her body. There was no denying the physical desire Bain stirred within her so easily, so like Drew in the way he touched her, kissed her.

Abruptly he pulled away, leaving her feeling exposed and vulnerable. Her lashes parted to discover the naked desire turning his gaze to a smoky gray—just as Drew's had done time and again. Placing his hands on her arms, he set her away, into the chilled room, and stepped back. Regret radiated from his gaze. For what reason? Because he'd kissed her or because he didn't do more? She couldn't be sure.

"Inez will ring the dinner bell when the meal is ready." He spun around and moved swiftly away from her. To her chagrin he didn't look back, not even once.

Bain tossed his suitcase on the bed and unlatched the straps. He knew this was bound to happen—eventually. He'd kissed her and now he wanted her. It was as if a spring flood had been unleashed inside him, the waters of desire cresting the dam he'd so carefully constructed, spilling forth unchecked.

Too soon, damn it. He had wanted the still-fresh images of Drew to have time to fade before pressing his suit. But now he was no better than a lovesick lad—all he could think of was the curve of her lips, the flare of her hips, the feel of her hand resting lightly on his shoulders.

Groaning his despair, he flung the lid up on the bag and glared at the clothing Constanza had so carefully folded and placed inside it before leaving Monterey. His breath caught and hung in his chest. If he were a man who believed in heaven and hell, in Satan's ability to place temptation before a man, he would swear that God was testing him now.

On top of his clothing was Drew's black leather coat, the same jacket he had instructed Constanza to get rid of. Yet there it lay on top of his possessions, folded with care, taunting him, daring him to take advantage of the situation.

Would Garnet accept the presence of Drew, or

would it only serve to alert her to the deception he played on her? He stood there staring at the coat for several minutes before he slammed the lid back down on the suitcase and turned his back on it.

Forgetting his purpose for being there, to change into something more suitable for dinner, he hurried from his bedroom, through the courtyard, without stopping to tend to his precious "specimens" as she'd called them. He headed out an unobtrusive side exit that led to the stableyard, stopping in the storage room where Inez kept bags of apples, potatoes, and onions. Crossing the grounds, he spied the big Appaloosa. Just as he'd suspected, Quixote was hanging out near the mare pens.

Bain gave a loud whistle. The stallion perked up his ears and blew, his head bobbing in recognition. Charging the fence, the horse met Bain with eagerness, his velvety nose nuzzling the fist closed about the apple.

"You old charlatan. Is it me you welcome or only what I bring you?" Laughing, Bain opened his hand and pressed the apple into the horse's seeking lips.

Quixote chewed, his big, intelligent eyes closed in what Bain surmised was ecstasy. The moment he was finished he nosed Bain's other hand and then his pockets. Finding them empty, he turned and moseyed back to his station near the mare pen. He looked back once, as if sending regrets for choosing his desire over his master.

"Can't say I blame you, old friend." Bain leaned against the fence and lifted one booted foot and propped it on a rail. "Women have a way of taking precedence over everything else, don't they?" He thought again of that damn coat lying in his suitcase, so accessible, so easy a solution to his own discomfort.

Brushing the temptation away, he strolled from the corrals and crossed to the gardens where the artichoke and asparagus beds had been cultivated and mulched for the winter months. Dropping to one knee, he scooped up a handful of dark, rich soil, brought it to his nose to analyze, then allowed it to filter through his fingers. He was pleased with the work that had been done in his absence. Next season's harvest would be abundant if all went as he'd planned.

A small frown creased his brows. But then nothing of late had gone as he'd planned. He had not planned for Drew to extract a deathbed promise from him. Nor had he planned to rescue two women from the cesspool of San Francisco's Chinatown and then to fall madly in love with one of them. Damn it, he'd never planned to deceive her, but deceive her he had, and now he was caught in his own web of lies and illusion, a victim of his lack of planning as much as she was.

Suddenly Bain was tired of being led around by the nose by fate. No longer did he have an irresponsible brother whose every deed he had to counteract. There was only himself now, Bain Carson, only his own mistakes to be concerned with. God knows, he'd made as many as Drew had during his short life, the difference being he'd never done anything to hurt someone else intentionally—at least not yet.

The arrival of a certain proper little English miss into his life had made that all different. There was nothing he wouldn't do, nothing, to get what he wanted. And what he wanted, body and soul, was Miss Garnet Sinclair. Perhaps the only real difference between himself and Drew was that until now there had never been anything he had truly desired enough to go after with a vengeance.

With the clanking of the dinner bell ringing in his ears, Bain turned and marched determinedly back toward the house, toward the one thing he wanted even more than honor or self-respect.

Chapter Thirteen

Garnet crossed the courtyard from the dining room, weaving her way along the pathway between groups of plants and garden furniture lit by occasional lanterns. In the darkness she listened to the settling coos of doves, and in the distance she heard the "whoo-whoo" of an awakening owl. All around her the cloying smell of flowers enveloped her, their sweet scents made stronger by the night-time. She reached the closed door of her room and paused, looking back over her shoulder, and spied Choie Seem crossing the patio to the other side of the house. Poised at their respective doorways, they smiled and waved a greeting before stepping into their quarters.

Once inside, the door closed firmly behind her back, Garnet issued a sigh of relief. All through the evening meal Bain had watched her in silence, his gray eyes, hawklike, never leaving her except for brief moments when Inez arrived with another course or Nattie attempted to capture his attention. Finally even the girl had given up trying to distract her older brother, and Garnet had breathed a little easier when at last she could excuse herself without seeming rude.

Bain had risen with her, and she'd feared he intended to escort her to her chambers, but Choie

Seem had conveniently stood and announced she would walk with her, squelching any ideas Bain might have harbored of being alone with her. Stoically he'd sat back down and given them a brief nod of dismissal from his table, but his eyes had never left her as she departed the dining room.

His kiss earlier in the day had unnerved her completely, had left her aching for more—much more. She was not about to tempt fate by being alone with Bain Carson, at least not tonight. She had given herself to Drew, and Drew exclusively. Right or wrong, she wouldn't turn to another man because her lover had deserted her without a thought for her feelings. That would make her no better than the strumpets that roamed the streets of London, or Beijing, or San Francisco for that matter.

She crossed to the only light source in the room, the brazier that glowed red and hot. Locating the bucket of coal next to it, she picked up several chunks with the tongs provided and added them to the burning embers. Rubbing her hands together over the heat, she warmed her palms, then turned to make ready for bed.

A good night's rest was all she needed to clear her brain of these idiotic notions that she was attracted to Bain. Tomorrow the situation would look different. There was Mae Ching to instruct.

And then there was Nattie. Though she'd not talked to Bain about enlightening the impetuous girl in the proper ways of becoming a lady, surely he wouldn't object. Soon Nattie would reach a marriageable age—he wouldn't want her to be wild and untamed as she was now. He would want the best for her. And to learn manners was advantageous for any young lady of good reputation and family.

Confident her reasoning was sound, and with a sense of order giving her direction, she hummed as she unbuckled the brown and gold ribbon belt of the dinner gown she wore, releasing the green grosgrain overskirt. Carefully sliding her arms free of the wide split sleeves, which left her dressed in an underbodice and skirt, she turned to hang the outer garment in the armoire.

She paused at the click of heels out in the courtyard passing near her door. Moving to the window, she lifted the heavy brocade curtain, watching through the batiste as Bain crossed the patio and disappeared into rooms just a couple of doors down from hers. His head bowed, he looked deep in thought, or perhaps overcome by defeat. What disturbed him so? Had their shared kiss unnerved him as completely as it had her? Was it guilt because he coveted his brother's inamorata that lowered his head?

The patio empty, she dropped the curtain and returned to her toilette. Stripping off the underbodice and skirt, she quickly hung them up, then peeled off her petticoats, bustle, and corset. Draping them over an armchair in one corner, she sat down at the lace-encased dressing table in only her camisole and drawers as the bedroom was now warm from the heat of the brazier.

Releasing the ash-blonde curls of her coiffure one at a time, she brushed them smooth to cascade freely down her back. She lowered her lashes, remembering how Drew's fingers combing through her tresses felt, and conjured up his image in her mind's eye.

Foolish girl, she chided herself. *Drew's not coming back, so forget him.* But forgetting was not that easy with a walking, breathing replica there every day to remind her of his existence. As if in a dream, she rose and moved to the washstand. Untying the ribbons of her camisole, she took up the moistened cloth and began mindlessly washing circles on her body until it glowed from her ministrations. Her skin still tingling from the roughness of the washcloth, she slipped into her nightgown, a fresh one from the chest Drew had given her. As she began buttoning it up from the bottom, she again thought she heard the shuffle of boots outside her door.

Her fingers stilled on the fastener just above her navel. This time the sounds were closer and coming nearer. Was Bain out wandering in his courtyard? More likely it was merely a servant blowing out the lanterns for the night, she reasoned.

Convincing herself there was nothing to be concerned about, she turned away and reached up for the next button on her gown. Her hand paused in midair as she swore the footsteps were definitely moving toward her door. Her heart began hammering against her ribs. The urge to run to the bed and bury herself under the covers ballooned within her chest. But that was foolish. Only silly, frightened children reacted in such a manner.

Grasping for the next button, she discovered it missing. She looked down, and to her dismay the remaining fasteners were gone, apparently ripped from the gown many washings before, as there was nary a sign of thread holes where they would have been attached. She should change, but then, what did it matter? The room was quite warm, and the open collar felt good on her bare throat and collarbone, where beads of sweat were popping up like pearls.

She stood stock-still waiting for the footsteps to resume, but there was only silence. Perhaps she should investigate, but no matter how many times she told herself there was nothing to be afraid of, she couldn't bring herself to move to the window and peek outside. What if someone was on the other side staring back at her? It was a foolish, age-old fear of a Peeping Tom, but no amount of self-chiding could make her go to the window. If it was a servant, they were too well trained to intrude, and if it was Bain, he was much too polite to do more than stand there. Who else would it be at this isolated ranch at such a late hour? There was no reason for her to concern herself even though the door had no security lock.

She crawled into the bed, the covers turned back invitingly by a servant before she'd returned from dinner, and she lay in the semi-darkness, listening, straining. To her relief there was only silence, except for the tinkling of the patio fountain.

Awhile later, her heart resuming its normal beating, she flipped over on the bed, pulling the coverlet over her shoulder, and nestled down to fall asleep.

Cre-e-eak!

The turning of her door handle brought her straight up into a sitting position, the covers clutched at her throat where her pulse leaped against her knuckles. The brazier had burned low, the light it produced so dim she couldn't see the outline of the door or latch.

"Who's there?" she called in a strained voice.

The door flung open, revealing a broad-shouldered silhouette outlined by a glowing lantern behind it in the courtyard. The apparition's legs were spread wide apart in a stance that reminded her of . . .

"What do you want?" Her voice was a near-whisper lowered by fear.

"Why, *pequeña joya*, what would a man want at this time of night in a lady's boudoir?"

"Drew?" How was it possible that he was here?

Closing the door behind him, he stepped farther into the room, the dim light reflecting off his face and on the glossiness of his familiar leather jacket. For a brief moment she marveled at how much he looked like his brother, uncannily so; except for his mannerisms she couldn't for the life of her tell them apart.

"Where did you come from?"

His familiar laughter boomed, filling the room, making it seem small in comparison to his strong-willed personality. "My mother's womb, most likely," he bantered, crossing the space between them in long, confident strides.

Without thought she dropped the covers, her arms reaching out to welcome him. His gaze dropped to the gap in the front of her nightgown, his hungry appreciation only too evident as he devoured her with his eyes.

"I had to have you one last time," he mumbled, dropping to one knee on the bed beside her.

There was no prelude, no permission asked or granted, no further questions or answers regarding his unexpected appearance in her room or at the ranch so far away from his ship that should have sailed long before now. Their arms snaked about each other, possessively, their fingers touching, exploring.

The moment Drew's lips claimed hers, she opened her mouth, only too willing to meet his tongue more than halfway. The tip grazed his teeth, and the thrill of something new and exciting coursed through her. Soon he enticed her deeper into his mouth, and then she was dipping into unknown territory, a sense that she was setting the pace turning her nether regions into liquid fire. He lay back, allowing her to drape on top of him, giving over the reins of domination because it pleased him—at least for the moment. But she knew the minute he wanted to regain control he would. Realizing her time was limited, she grew even bolder.

Her hands slid into his open jacket, releasing the buttons of his shirt until her fingers could thread through the mat of soft hair on his chest, tipping the tiny nodules of flesh buried within the downy whorls. His nipples sprang to life beneath her touch, and soon her hand was traveling lower.

"Easy, woman," he growled, encircling her wrists with his strong fingers, and just as she'd predicted, he mastered the situation, rolling her to her back beneath him. "I hadn't anticipated such eagerness. I thought for sure you'd be angry with me for leaving you in Monterey without warning."

"I am angry with you," she replied in a clipped tone, but at the moment her desire overrode her ire. The way he smiled down at her, as if he found her willingness to forget amusing, brought her irritation rushing to the surface. She tried to raise her hands and push him away, but he held them pinned over her head to the bed. She struggled; he laughed and buried his face in the soft contour of her cleavage exposed by the missing buttons, his mouth nuzzling at the soft mounds.

"And not just because you've treated me so abominably," she seethed behind her ineffectualness and the electric shock bolting through her. "How could you be so neglectful of your own family?"

She felt his fingers tighten on her wrists with a seriousness she had not expected.

"Just what are you talking about?" he demanded. "Just what do you know of my family?"

"I know that Mae Ching is your daughter, and you've not even bothered to visit her while in port." Breathing hard, again she tried to twist away, but he pinioned her down against the mattress. Suddenly she was aware of his groin grinding against her hip. It was as if he found her resistance much more stimulating than her eager compliance.

His eyes glistened with humor at her obvious discomfort. "Tell me, little Miss Busybody, how do you know what I've done or not done?"

She squirmed, twisting her face away from his as he leaned closer to her. "I know. I just know," she replied, at that moment hating him and hating herself for finding his brutishness so exciting. "Let go of me, Drew." She choked, still struggling to escape.

229

"Not on your life," he growled, forcing her knees apart so he could sensuously mold every contour of his hard body to her softer one. Then he took the knob of her defiant chin between his teeth and nipped her playfully. "But then you really don't want me to, do you?"

No, I don't, damn you, she agreed mentally, but she refused to voice her disgrace as she continued her resistance. She did love the way he took charge, the way he was so confident of himself. A man. A glorious man—one who took her breath away. Yet why, why couldn't he have a little of his brother's sensitivities?

Her senseless struggling ceased like an earth-shattering quake that left the world atremble in its aftermath. Lying there beneath Drew as his mouth moved from her chin to her ear in such an exciting way, she found herself unable to stop comparing brother to brother. If only she were a sculptress who could take a little from both and mold the perfect man to suit her needs. Strong and in charge, yet giving and kind, a passionate lover who took the time to find the beauty in the world about him. Could all of those characteristics exist within one man, or was she being much too idealistic?

His probing tongue dipped into the shell of her ear, drawing her down into a whirlpool of sensations. She couldn't deny that when Drew was making love to her he was all the things she wanted and more. Sighing, she allowed the eddies to suck her deeper, deeper into a timeless world of perfection.

His fingers trailed a path down her bare arms, leaving streams of gooseflesh in their wake. Then they moved to the front of her gown, releasing each button in their turn until he reached the last one at a point just above her Venus mound. Brushing aside the fabric, he pushed himself up so he knelt between her open thighs. In the red glow from the brazier she saw his eyes take in the inviting display she made before him, her stomach rising and falling as she breathed, her breasts moving provocatively, the open gown plunging to that point just above the thatch of golden down that covered her womanhood.

He raised his hand and paused, his fingers hovering just above one breast as if he were unsure where to touch her first. She arched her back, the hardened nipple nudging the underside of his hand, which closed about the rounded globe. Stroking the quivering flesh, he brought his fingers to a peak about the nipple; then they trailed down again until her breast refilled his hand.

She groaned her delight as he rubbed the sensitive center of his palm against the hardened nodule, round and round until sparks ignited deep in her belly. Then he stroked again, sending her senses soaring skyward.

Scooping her up, he lifted her and set her on her knees before him. Like praying hands they meshed, her bare breasts rubbing against the soft fur of his chest. He leaned over her, and she bent like a willow, moving with him until her arched back offered up her bosom to willing sacrifice. The brush of his hair under her chin and along her collarbone was soft as down as he drew the nipple into his mouth. Sucking ever so gently as if he was aware of the fine thread of sensation connecting that part of her to the cord of her being, he set her body humming. Taking the nipple deep into his mouth, he circled it with his tongue, swirling, swirling until she thought she would explode with sheer pleasure. Clutching his face between her hands, she threw back her head, allowing him to do with her what he willed, confident that whatever he did would be wondrous. She would follow, willingly, to the ends of the earth and into an abyss of Hell's fire if that was where he led her, if only he would love her.

His face lifted, and the warmth of his mouth was replaced by the cool night air. Then his hands, which had been bracing her back, moved around to cradle her breasts and lift them up and together until the nipples were like twin buttons side by side. Again he lowered his head, taking one between his lips, then moving to take the other, back and forth, until it was merely his tongue lapping at her flesh. Her hands moved up to his shoulders to brace herself, to keep from crumbling like old adobe beneath the heat of his worshipping mouth.

"Oh, Drew," she whispered, her trembling fingers clutching him until they hurt.

He released her bosom and laid her back against the mattress. The gown gapped open at the top and gathered about her waist at the bottom, concealing nothing, serving only as a further enticement. He stood, quickly stripped off his jacket and shirt; the strain of his flexing muscles as he proceeded were outlined in the glow from the embers, making him appear as if he were made of marble, hard and glistening—a physical paragon.

Catching her watching him, he paused, that infectious grin of his curling his mouth as he studied her as well. "We were made for each other, you know."

She didn't reply. She didn't have to. The answer was clearly etched in the way she admired his naked torso. His fingers reached for the buttons on his waistband. As if a magnet sent its magic force her way, she rose. Kneeling on the edge of the bed, she pushed his hands away to unfasten his trousers for herself. Pushing the coarse fabric down from his hips, she released his manhood, proud and confident as the man. Fascinated, she circled him with her finger and slowly slid her hand down his rigid staff. She felt his entire body stiffen, so she raised her hand and stroked again.

This time he couldn't suppress the groan that rumbled in his chest and rolled from his lips as her hand lifted to caress him a third time. His fingers encircled hers, and together they moved over his aroused flesh.

"Enough," he moaned, stilling her hand in his powerful grip. "Or it will end here and now, and that would be a shame for both of us."

Stripping off the remainder of his clothing, he reached out and hooked her gown, pulling it off her shoulders and allowing it to pool about her knees. He encircled her slender nakedness in his arms and drew her close, searing her with a kiss so passionate she merely hung in his arms as he plundered her mouth. His hand explored, tipping her breasts, which were still hard and rosy from his caresses, down her belly, and lower, to her secret well of fulfillment. His fingers dipped inside her, stroking, creating sensations much as she must have for him moments before. She buckled, her knees refusing to support her, so he held her up with one muscled arm, his kiss deepening, his fingers within her moving faster.

He lifted his mouth, but his hand never lost a beat. "Give me your hand," he whispered in her ear.

Mindless to obey, she lifted her hand to his mouth.

Gently he sucked on her fingers. "No, love. Here." He rubbed against her nodule of sex, sending her mind spinning. From somewhere a note of discord clashed with the music of love he created.

"Where?" she asked, unable to believe she'd understood him right.

His hand moved up and combed through the pelt between her legs. "Here," he repeated.

She swallowed, hard, the pounding of her heart making it an almost impossible task. Hesitantly she took her fingers from his mouth and eased them to rest against her own stomach.

He reached up and grasped her hand, guiding it down to that place she'd never openly acknowledged, much less touched. Gently he placed her hand between her thighs and directed her movement.

To caress herself so was shocking, unacceptable, even though the pleasure was as intense as ever. She jerked her hand away and gasped. "No, Drew. I don't want to go blind."

He threw his head back and laughed. "Oh, God, what stuffy old nanny told you that?"

"It's true. To touch yourself there will make you go blind. I know."

"Have you ever done it before now?" He cocked a curious eyebrow at her.

"No," she retorted indignantly. "Of course not."

"Then how do you know you'll go blind?" He gave her a devilish look.

"Because. When I was little, Jonathan Inglenook lost his sight. Everyone said it was because he'd touched himself . . . there."

"If that were true, love, every man on earth would be groping about in darkness."

"Did you?" she queried.

He chuckled. "My brother and I . . . Well, you don't need to know what my brother and I did as kids, but the answer to your question is yes, I have. And I don't have any trouble seeing, at least not yet."

Sweet, gentle Bain doing something so unacceptable. Drew yes, but Bain? She found that impossible to believe. "Well, then," she countered, unwilling to concede Drew might be right, "it's different for women."

"No, it's not." He took her hand and slid it back downward, but she balled it in resistance. "I bet you don't even know what your body is like—down there."

"I know what I need to know."

"Do you, Garnet? Do you know how perfectly

you're molded to accommodate me? How warm, and tight, and exciting?'' He placed his own hand at her crux to demonstrate what he meant.

Still she refused to relent.

Gently he laid her back on the bed and urged her knees to part. Only after a moment's hesitation did she do as he wanted. His hand kept on fondling her, driving her wild with want. "Do you know," he continued, grazing the button of her passion with the tip of his finger, "that here you're most like me? A few simple strokes"—he demonstrated—"can bring you to the edge."

God in Heaven, he was right, it did. She swayed there on the crest of fulfillment, knowing in seconds he'd send her tumbling over the brink. "Show me, Garnet, what you like, and I'll give it to you," he cajoled.

Giving in to her need, she covered his hand with her own and guided his touch, orchestrating the release her body cried out for. Plummeting through timeless pleasure, she felt his mouth upon her ear whispering, "Oh, yes, Garnet, yes. You're more woman than any man could pray for."

Then he was upon her, entering her, lock and key—a perfect match—the contours of his body releasing the mechanism within hers to begin the climbing process all over again. His hips rose and fell with a slow precision that was calculated to draw out every drop of sensation her body could give her, an almost tortuous process that made her hips rise to meet his if only to speed it up.

His groin forged against hers, he paused, quivering with a need as strong as hers.

"Easy, Garnet," he purred, his mouth capturing hers in a slow, probing kiss.

He began once more, inching within her, circling, round and round until he filled her completely; then he pulled back and descended again. Like climbing a winding staircase to the top of a tower, each measured thrust forced her one step closer to the apex. She matched his rhythm, savoring the pleasure created by his expert lovemaking, until there was nothing for her except his driving force, the play of his muscles flexing beneath her hands, his rasping breath fanning her face and neck.

And his words of encouragement. "Yes, *pequeña joya*, yes."

At last she was there, at the brink, teetering, straining to take the plunge, yet he continued his deliberate teasing, fanning the waves of sensation that almost sent her over the edge, only to pull her back at the last possible moment until she thought she couldn't take it anymore.

"Please, Drew, please," she begged, grasping his taut buttocks in urgency.

With the whipping force of a hurricane, he complied, plunging, filling her, driving her over the brink into the spiraling whirlwind of fulfillment. Sobbing out her pleasure, she gripped his backside harder, and felt him stiffen with his own release. Then he joined her in that swirling funnel until, wrapped in each other's arms, they plummeted back to reality.

A thin trickle of sweat dripped from his chin and rolled down her cheek like an unbidden tear. Her heart still pounded, and she could feel his above hers battering against his chest. So near, yet so far away, impossible to grasp. Her eyes were closed, and she dared not open them, wanting to cling to the shared oneness for as long as she could.

Then he dropped down on her, crushing her beneath his weight, but she didn't care, if only she could hold on to this precious moment for a lifetime, cling to the giving side of his nature.

His arms released her, reached behind his neck, and uncoiled her clinging limbs. With a sigh of contentment, he clasped her hand and kissed her knuckles one at a time. He rolled away, the only parts of them still touching their entwined fingers.

Reluctantly she lifted her lashes, noting the brazier had burned low, a residue of chill reinfesting the darkened room and invading her questing heart. In the thin red light remaining, she turned her head to look at him—hoping for a miracle.

"Drew?"

He gave no indication he had heard her. Was he sleeping?

Not wanting to fall asleep herself only to awaken later and find him gone, she raised up and twisted over him, running her tongue over his bare shoulder. "Drew?" she whispered huskily.

His eyelids fluttered and parted, his gaze flicking over her nakedness with the swiftness of a darting swallow. "Go to sleep, Garnet."

"No. I have to know. When are you leaving?" Not "Are you leaving?" There was no question in her heart that he would go—eventually.

"It doesn't matter." He closed his eyes, patting his bare shoulder in invitation. "Here. Come here, *pequeña joya*," he murmured.

In silence she waited. She would not be brushed off so easily.

Finally he opened his eyes and stared up at her. "Let it go, Garnet."

"No. Tell me. When are you leaving?"

Releasing a sigh, he propped himself up on one elbow and angled to face her. "Soon," he answered evasively.

"Tomorrow? The next day? When?" she demanded.

He raised his hand and ran his fingers through the ash-blonde silkiness of her hair. "The sooner the better for you, don't you see that?"

Tossing her head, she shook off his condescending

caress and reasoning. "All I see is that you take what you want, and then you leave, until the next time you're . . . in need."

"Seems to me, honey, you come out all right in the deal," he retorted, dropping all pretense of civility. "Your needs, as you call them, are well taken care of." He trailed a finger along one bare breast.

Remembering the things she'd done to please him, to please herself, she blushed. All of a sudden her nakedness felt wrong, and she fumbled with the covers, drawing them up over her. Why did their lovemaking always end this way? In anger and degradation? This wasn't what she wanted, but somehow her actions, her demands, had been the catalyst this time. Her intention to force his hand seemed only to have pushed him away instead of making him commit to her. Swallowing the acid comment that threatened to spill from her lips, she brushed away his hand and moved to vacate the bed—to escape the look he gave her as if she were no better than some . . . whore he had every right to do with as he pleased.

He reached out to stop her. This time she slapped his hand, wanting no part of him, of herself, of what she'd done with him. Standing, she whirled, the sheet she'd taken with her tucked under her arms and chin. "When it comes to you, Drew Carson, I don't have any needs. Not anymore. So don't come to me the next time."

He soldered his lips and lowered his hand, placing it behind his head as he rolled to his back. "Don't worry, Garnet. As far as you and I are concerned, I've already decided there won't be a next time."

It took a few seconds for the meaning of his words to sink in. He'd made up his mind long before now to jilt her. She blinked, took a step backward.

She wanted to scream her indignation, her refusal to accept what he dared to do to her. She needed to cry in frustration as she knew better than to have expected better treatment from him. Instead she pressed her lips together and pointed toward the door. "Get out, Drew," she hissed.

Sprawled in all his glorious nudity, his hand clasped behind his head, he looked at her as if she'd lost her mind.

Spinning when he made no move to obey, she gathered up his clothing, not caring that some of her own were scooped up as well in her haste, and tossed them at him. One of her silk stockings cascaded along the side of his head. She would have liked to take it and wrap it around his throat and . . .

"I said get out."

Without hurrying, he slid to the edge of the bed and pulled on his pants, sorted his shirt and coat from her things, and stood, taking the time to button up the fasteners in the front. He moved toward her, and she stumbled backward. Taking the stocking, he draped it across one of her bare shoulders, then he clucked her under the chin.

"It's been good, Garnet." One corner of his mouth lifted in a lopsided grin. "Perhaps you'd have more luck with my brother. You two have my blessing. I think you'll find Bain can fill your needs better than I ever could." He laughed and spun away, moving to the door in long, untroubled strides.

Turning, he winked at her. "By the way, love, the slate is clean. Tonight you more than satisfied the debt between us." He slipped out the door and closed it softly behind him.

Her heart an empty well, she blinked away the tears that burned the back of her throat, threatening to drown the pride that had held her tongue. Damn him! As always, he'd showed no remorse for his callous ways, nor did he bother to say good-bye.

Chapter Fourteen

The next morning, Garnet donned the most severe dress she owned, a black crepe that was better suited to wear to a funeral than to the dining table. Staring at her reflection in the mirror of the dressing table, she grabbed up her long, blonde tresses and pulled them back into a tight, unattractive chignon at the nape of her neck. She studied her features, hoping to find repentance etched in them. Instead she saw only the flaws of her features, her slightly pinched nose, her chin that jutted too much to be pretty, her eyes too large for her face, all accented by the starkness she'd subjected it to.

Vanity, she scolded herself, tossing down the hairpins she held in her hand in self-disgust. Was there no sin which she hadn't committed? Frustrated by her lack of discipline, she turned away from the condemnation written across her mirror image.

This was what Drew Carson had done to her. He with his carnal knowledge and impassioned promises had seduced her, both mind and body, then left her to wallow in a cesspool of sin. Redemption would be of her own making, and atone she would.

And if Drew Carson thought the debt was settled between them, he had another thing coming. There was no way she was going to allow him to get away with . . .

Vengefulness, she chided. She straightened her shoulders. She would not succumb to its siren's call as well. She was better than that. *Turn the other cheek. Turn the other cheek,* she could hear her father's gentle voice urging. Damn it all, that was hard to do.

But she would take his advice to heart no matter how difficult it was.

Outside she heard the clanging of Inez's bell. She lifted her head. Breakfast would be served soon. A new day begun—one that she would make productive.

Her first order of business was to see if Drew had made good his word. As far as he was concerned the debt was paid, but had he taken the time before leaving to inform his brother?

She knew in her heart Bain would realize how she had gone about settling the account, but no matter what he thought of her, facing him couldn't be avoided, not if she wanted to establish her freedom. Once done, she would simply work out an arrangement with him—a legitimate one. She would tutor Mae Ching for a limited time in exchange for passage home for both herself and Choie Seem. Bain Carson was a reasonable man. He would find such an agreement acceptable.

Walking out the door, her head held high, even though the punishing hairpins scraping her scalp pulled harder, she crossed the courtyard with purposeful strides. Yes, she could face Bain.

Then her steps faltered. What if Drew was still here? What if she was forced to confront *him* across the breakfast table?

Thoughts of returning to the safety of her rooms scurried across her resolve like frightened little mice seeking winter shelter. No. If Drew was here, then all the better. She would see to it he made the situation

242

perfectly clear to his brother that she owed him nothing further—not even the time of day. As she marched forward, the power of right on her side lightened her steps.

From his window Bain watched her parade across the courtyard like some lady evangelist marching off to save the sinners of the world, her black dress as stiff as her rigidly held spine. Dropping the curtain back in place, he seriously considered skipping breakfast altogether and heading directly to do his morning rounds and chores.

As tempting as the idea was, he was more of a man than that. And after last night, he deserved having to face her righteous wrath.

Last night. He turned from the window to finish knotting the scarf about his throat and gather up his vest and hat. Images of Garnet in his arms, loving him, giving him all she had to offer, then giving more, did nothing to cool the heat burning in his loins. The things he had said to her when they had parted had come out all wrong. His intentions had been gallant, but the words he had chosen had been far from it. He had only meant to release her from the unfair claim he had upon her, release her and rid himself of this alter ego that seemed to have a hold on him, refusing to let him go.

That wasn't quite true. *He* had refused to allow the charade to come to an end. At first his masquerade had been for a good reason, but last night—he could make no such excuses for his actions. He had deliberately taken advantage of her innocent faith that no one would stoop so low to get what they wanted from another.

He was not so self-deceived as to deny he'd enjoyed every minute, every caress he'd shared with her, and had he to do the events of the night over, he doubted he would do anything different. Desire was a powerful opponent to righteousness. It made the best of men calculating and manipulative.

He straightened, picked up his hat, and dusted it across his knee. No matter how clumsy his attempt, he had made a stab to right the wrongs he'd committed. Drew was gone, buried, not only in his mind but hopefully in hers as well. The morning consequences must be faced.

Stepping out of his quarters unobserved, he watched her pause before the dining room door as if gathering up her courage to proceed.

"Good morning, Miss Sinclair," he called from across the patio, the tinkling of the fountain a perfect accompaniment to the cheerful, innocent tone he put in his voice.

Garnet turned, worry marring her perfect features, still undeniably beautiful though she had apparently done everything in her power to conceal her attractiveness.

He sauntered toward her, smiling. "Hope you slept well last night."

"Mr. Carson." She nodded, but didn't acknowledge his inquiry. Instead her frown deepened, her lovely mouth puckering in old-maidish disapproval of his joviality.

"Lovely morning." He raised his hand, indicating that she should precede him to the table. How inane he sounded, but he was doing his best to shield her from embarrassment. If he showed any signs of knowledge of how she'd spent her evening, it would only make the situation that much more difficult—at least for her. He sincerely wished to spare her.

She glanced down at his gentlemanly gesture with suspicion, then accepted his offer, stepping forward with a barely perceptible tip to her chin.

"I think you'll find Inez makes wonderful *heuvos rancheros*." Reaching the table he pulled out a chair

244

midway up, offering it to her.

Which she accepted, allowing him to push her closer to the table. "Inez is indeed a wonder at the stove." She folded her hands primly in her lap and stared straight ahead, but he could feel her eyes appraising him and his mood as he turned his back and strode to his own chair at the head of the table.

As he sat and busied himself with spreading open his napkin, he heard her clear her throat. He looked up.

"Mr. Carson, are you aware of your brother's arrival last night?"

He raised a brow as if surprised. "Drew here?" He shrugged. "It's been known to happen on occasion."

"Then you haven't spoken with him." She leaned forward in expectation.

How best to answer her? Just what was she fishing for? He stared and started to open his mouth. Fortunately Nattie and Choie Seem joined them, the girls engrossed in animated conversation as they crossed the sunlit flagstones and entered the flung-open doors of the dining room.

"Good morning," they said in unison, moving to occupy the empty seats between the two adults. Choie Seem gave Garnet a curious glance and turned to Bain in silence, requesting an explanation of her companion's unusual garb.

He gave her an innocent look.

But Choie Seem apparently knew that he somehow had to be involved, and she scowled at him.

The only one not aware of the tension was Nattie. Sweet Nattie. Her unbound hair cascaded down her back, her softening curves concealed beneath a checkered shirt and jeans. Still giggling as young girls do, she began. "Did you know, Bain, that Choie Seem and I are almost the same age?" Her slate-gray eyes danced with excitement, and Bain couldn't help but feel happy for her.

"Then the two of you must have much to talk about."

"Oh, yes," she continued breathlessly. "Choie Seem was telling me all about what life is like in China—the rituals—the beautiful clothing—the—"

"You know, Nattie," Garnet's voice interrupted, a ring of teacherlike authority lacing her words. "In any proper society—even here in America—the same things exist."

Bain riveted her with a glare. What was the woman doing? What right did she have filling his sister's head with a bunch of Victorian nonsense?

"What do you mean?" Nattie asked, her interest piqued.

"Why, in China the ritual of tea is a daily affair. But ladies everywhere meet socially at tea, to exchange pleasantries and current events."

"They do?"

Garnet smiled. "Of course. Later, if you would like, I could show you. I'm sure Choie Seem could join us."

"Oh, yes," Nattie replied, clapping her hands with enthusiasm. "Won't that be fun, Bain? We're going to have a tea party."

"I suppose," he mumbled. "But you haven't forgotten the prize mare that's due to foal, have you? I need you to keep an eye on her for me like you promised you would."

Nattie's face fell. "Of course, Bain. I won't let you down."

"I certainly can't see how taking an hour or two later in the afternoon could interfere with her chores, Mr. Carson. I sincerely doubt the animal will choose that precise time to deliver. And if she does, we can simply postpone our tea by a few hours." Garnet's jade-green eyes challenged him to deny her reasoning.

Damn it! He didn't like her interference. This was

246

not what he had planned for Nattie, sipping tea with a bunch of old gossips, but the three of them looked at him, Nattie pleading, Choie Seem only curious, and Garnet, damn her, daring him to find fault with her scheme. There was nothing he could do but agree—today. But tomorrow Miss Sinclair would not manipulate him so easily.

"Very well." Tight-lipped, he nodded.

Inez bustled into the room and served the meal, the eggs as delicious as he'd predicted they would be. Nattie chattered on, telling the Oriental girl about the mare and how important her foal was to the ranch. As soon as the girls abandoned their plates Bain pushed his back as well.

"Why don't you show Choie Seem around, Nattie?"

"Would you like that?" she asked her newfound friend.

The Oriental girl nodded.

Then Nattie turned to Garnet. "And you, Miss Sinclair, would you care to come too?"

"Miss Sinclair and I have some things to discuss," Bain announced before Garnet could accept. "You two girls run along now."

They scampered out like two young squirrels, Nattie patiently waiting for Choie Seem to join her in her slower, miniature steps. "Tell me again, why did your parents bind your feet?"

After the girls were gone, Garnet carefully folded her napkin and placed it beside her plate. "It's wonderful the girls have discovered each other, don't you think?" She gave Bain a pointed look.

"I don't want you filling Nattie's head with nonsense, Miss Sinclair." He refused to beat around the bush. When it came to his sister's welfare, nothing or no one was going to ruin his carefully decided plans.

As if the force of his words had shoved her, Garnet

247

sat back. "I don't think teaching a budding young girl the social amenities is nonsense, sir. I think perhaps you're being a bit—"

"I don't care what you do or don't think, ma'am. Nattie is my responsibility, and only I know what's best for her."

He was surprised to see her clamp her lips together without uttering another protest. How unlike Garnet to squelch her natural desire to defend her own opinions.

"Mr. Carson, I do not wish to argue with you. I only made my offer to Nattie thinking you would want her to learn how to become a woman. You must realize she is on the verge of growing up. I only meant to . . . offer my help. In fact, that is what I wanted to talk to you about."

"You offering me your help?"

She nodded. "You see," she explained, "your brother, Drew, came to . . . visit me last night, and we managed to work out . . . an amiable agreement between us. He released me from the debt he'd placed upon me, and, you see . . . I have every desire to return home."

An amiable agreement, was it? How eloquent she made last night sound. *Ah, Garnet, love, there is nothing amiable about the fire you make burn within me, and I have no desire to allow you to leave me—ever.* "I see. But what proof do I have that what you say is true?"

She studied him for several moments as if seeking to assure him of her honesty. "I have no proof, only my word. I had hoped Drew might have spoken to you."

"I'm afraid not." He saw her shoulders slump forward, and his heart twisted in sympathy. God, he didn't want to lose her, but he didn't want her miserable either. "Let's say that what you've told me is true. Just how did you plan to pay for passage . . .

248

home." Damn it all, he had to make her start visualizing Rancho Carmelo as home.

"I thought I might work out an arrangement with you."

His eyes narrowed. "What kind of arrangement?" Perhaps she'd taken his ill-given advice to heart after all. Was she offering herself to him?

"I feel my services as a tutor for Mae Ching, to teach her sufficient English in order to communicate, is a fair exchange for passage for myself and Choie Seem. I'm an excellent instructress, Mr. Carson. I don't think you'll find my abilities lacking."

She was a superb teacher, and he found nothing about her lacking. She had taught him to see himself for what he really was—no saint by any means. The turn of his thoughts made him frown.

Noting his look, she hurried on. "And I thought perhaps I could help Nattie with her social graces as part of the bargain, or perhaps . . ." She groped for that something that would please him, make him agree to her terms.

"How long do you think it would take you to teach Mae Ching English?"

Her brows knitted in connection. "She seems a bright child. Three months, maybe four." She looked at him to gauge his reaction. "But I am willing to stay until the job is completed."

Four months, maybe more. That would give him plenty of time to put his own plans into action. "All right, Miss Sinclair, with one more stipulation. I want you to teach me Chinese."

"Teach you?" She blinked in surprise.

"How hard can that be?" he asked, irked to think she might find such a task impossible. "I'm bright too, you know."

"Chinese is a very difficult language to learn," she replied, choosing her words of excuse carefully. "It took me several years to master it."

"That's my offer, ma'am. Take it or leave it." He could see she was not pleased with the prospect of spending the hours with him necessary to uphold her end of the bargain they were about to strike, but he needed that time with her to teach her what he wanted her to learn—that Rancho Carmelo was home. He would not back down, not even to the frustration he read in her jade-green eyes.

"Very well, I agree," she finally conceded.

"Until the job is done?" he reiterated to make sure he had that loophole to keep her there should he need it.

"Until it's done." She extended her hand to finalize the bargain.

The moment he clasped her fingers the need to bring them to his lips and kiss each one with slow deliberation made his heart do flip-flops within the prison of his rib cage. Instead he gave their silky lengths a quick squeeze and dropped her hand, the desire racing through his veins like quicksilver.

"And Nattie?" she inquired. "Is she to be a part of this bargain as well?"

"Leave her be, Garnet," he ordered. "I have my reasons, and I expect you to honor them."

A flash of resistance crossed her face, but then it was gone. He could fathom her reaction; it was understandable for her as a woman to want to help another woman, but for Nattie's sake he had to make sure Garnet did nothing about her natural instincts.

Tucking the hand he had held moments before into the folds of her gown, she rose. "Then I imagine if I ever wish to get home I should get started right away. Could you please tell me which room is Mae Ching's?"

Wordlessly he pointed across the courtyard to a door not far from her own.

"Thank you." She turned toward the exit.

"Miss Sinclair."

She looked back at him.

"I will be free this afternoon for my first lesson."

She stiffened. "Very well, Mr. Carson. After tea—if that mare of yours doesn't decide to foal."

That damnable tea she'd promised Nattie! Well, he had agreed, but he hadn't promised to stay away. "After tea."

She continued toward the door.

"Miss Sinclair," he called to her again.

This time she turned, impatience evident on her stark features.

"May I suggest you change into something less formidable and do something different with your hair? The way you look now you will probably scare the child half out of her wits."

She tossed her head, but he caught a glimpse of the fire in her eyes before she spun away. Once she'd sped from the dining room, he chuckled to himself. The teacher had a thing or two to learn herself. He had every intention of seeing to her instruction, personally.

The sting of Bain's criticism nipping at her heels, Garnet sped across the courtyard. Passing by the fountain pool, she couldn't help but to pause for a moment to stare at her reflection. As much as she hated to admit it, he had a good point. She *did* look like some of the old biddies she remembered from her childhood who had latched on to her father when he took a parish assignment—the ones who were always looking to catch the new vicar making a mistake. When she was a little girl, the way they had looked had frightened her. She could clearly remember stationing herself behind her father's pants legs in the churchyard, watching them cackle and gossip behind the protection of their cupped gloves.

Perhaps Bain was right. It was very important that Mae Ching trust her, not run away from her in apprehension. The poor thing was frightened enough already.

Returning to her room, she noticed a servant had already been there to straighten the bed and tidy up her mess, and had taken the time to empty her clothing trunk of its contents, putting away shoes and undergarments and hanging each item in the massive wardrobe in the corner.

Throwing open the doors she stared at the dresses crammed into it—more than could have been in the trunk. Many of the things were simple, skirts and blouses, walking or riding costumes meant to wear around a ranch. She ran her hand along the line of multi-colored outfits. Where had they come from? Consolation gifts from Drew? Or perhaps offers of bribery from her host? Whoever had seen to them had anticipated her staying awhile.

She took out a flared, wool plaid skirt with an emerald green blouse to match, admiring the way the two were so well suited to each other. Well, "whoever" had good, practical taste—these clothes were nothing like the ones she'd brought with her from the ship.

A few minutes later, dressed in the green skirt and blouse, her hair swept back softly from her face, she made her way to Mae Ching's door. She knocked, wondering whom she would find taking care of the child as there was apparently no one at the ranch who could converse with her.

The woman who answered was so gentle of face and actions that Garnet liked her right away.

"*Señorita,*" the woman said, stepping back respectfully to allow Garnet to enter.

"I have come to teach the *niña,*" she informed the servant, glancing about the darkened room, void of toys or playthings of any nature meant to please a little girl. She frowned, wondering what Mae Ching did with all of her time.

Then she saw her, sitting cross-legged in a corner playing with a pile of buttons and bobbins, threading them one at a time on a piece of string.

"Mae Ching," she called softly.

The child looked up from her busy play, and spying Garnet, she scrambled to her feet. Skipping toward her, her arms raised, the girl paused just before she reached her and dipped in a formal bow. "*Sse Mo,*" she said with proper Oriental respect.

Garnet bowed in return, then she couldn't help herself. She knelt against the cool tiles of the floor and opened her arms. Mae Ching didn't hesitate. She flung herself into their waiting invitation, only too eager for affection.

Looking over the child's thin shoulder, Garnet glanced up at the servant. There were tears in the little woman's eyes. "I'm so glad you've come, *señorita.*"

"How did you ever manage to talk to her, to make her understand what you needed from her?"

"Aiee, at times it wasn't easy, but we managed. We would act out what we wanted." She did a little pantomime of taking a bath.

Mae Ching looked up and began laughing at the little woman's antics. "*Xizao,*" she announced.

Garnet squeezed her. "Yes, that's right," she replied in Chinese, nodding. "Take a bath." Then she switched to English. "Bath," she said slowly. "Ba-a-a-th."

Mae Ching's serious, dark eyes watched her mouth as she spoke. Carefully the child formed the unfamiliar sounds on her little mouth. "Ba-a-a-th," she mimicked.

Garnet smiled her pleasure. "Very good. Now we will start with the basics." She settled on the floor beside her newest student, confident that within the few hours before teatime she would make the serving woman's job a bit easier and a lot less exhausting.

Slapping his Stetson against his knee to knock off as much dust as he could, Bain studied the tea party taking place around one of the wrought-iron tables in the courtyard. There they were, the female influences in his life—Garnet, Choie Seem, Nattie, and Mae Ching—each a responsibility acquired, not sought. He'd asked for none of them, yet now that they were there, he didn't want to lose any of them. They were laughing. No, giggling and chattering at the same time better described what they were doing—even Garnet, her beautiful face sparkling with delight at something Nattie was apparently telling her.

Ah, Nattie. His heart lurched painfully as her heart-shaped face—so like her mother's—tilted toward Garnet, absorbing every gesture the woman made. Garnet had managed to find her a proper dress. Though it sagged a little in a few places, especially the bodice, the day gown transformed his little sister into a beautiful, young woman. It didn't seem fair that she had so little to take for granted. Tea socials and womanhood should be hers without asking. But he did what he had to do—for her sake.

He stood there a while longer—just watching. Like one of those lovely pastel paintings he'd seen once in an art gallery, the women reminded him of delicate confections. They continued the tea party unaware they were being observed. Garnet lifted the pot and poured the last of its contents into empty cups. Then Nattie glanced up and spied him in the shadows.

"Bain," she trilled, forgetting how she was dressed, and leaped to her feet. As she tried to move toward him, she stumbled in her high-heeled shoes on the

254

long hem of her dress, and had to catch the table to keep from falling. One of the fragile teacups tipped over and spilled its dark liquid over the white tablecloth, blotting the gaiety.

As much as he wanted to rush forward and encourage the girl not to be upset and to try again, he held his ground, forcing his face to reveal none of the brotherly protectiveness coursing through him. He returned his hat to his head, fingered the brim in an insolent salute, and directed his comment toward Garnet. "Looks like your tea's about over, ma'am."

Busy mopping up the mess with the linen napkin from her lap, Garnet paused long enough to glare at him, condemning his insensitivity toward his sister. She turned to Nattie, who had sat back down sobbing. "Not to worry, dear," she soothed. "It can happen to the best of us. What you must learn is how to handle the situation graciously."

But there was no consoling Nattie. Garnet rose, but Bain grasped her shoulder and sat her back down, allowing Choie Seem to take his sister by the arm and lead her away still crying.

When Garnet at last looked at him, he thought she intended to scratch his eyes out. "How could you be so cruel?"

If only she knew how hard it had been for him. But it was best Nattie not be too enthralled with womanly things. Let her stick to her horses and Levi's. "I told you to let Nattie be. You've had your tea. Now that will be the last of it."

"You know, Mr. Carson, no matter how hard you try, you can't keep Nattie from growing up."

They glared, each unwilling to allow the other to win. The staring contest would have continued indefinitely if Mae Ching had not reminded them of her presence.

"Go-o-od af-el-noon, Un-cal Bain."

Startled by the child's staccato attempt to greet

him, Bain tore his gaze from Garnet's and looked down at his niece in amazement.

"Good afternoon, Mae Ching," he replied.

She grinned at him. He glanced at Garnet, who was smiling too.

"I told you she was a bright child."

He wanted to hug this wonderful woman, to pick her up and swirl her about to show his gratitude. Instead he offered her what he hoped appeared as a begrudging smile. "I do believe it's time for my lesson now. Let's see if you're inclined to teach me as eagerly."

"Eagerness on my part has nothing to do with it, sir. It takes a bright pupil, like Mae Ching, to learn."

There she went again—trying to insinuate that he wasn't capable of learning. Well, he would show her a thing or two. "How do I tell her congratulations on learning so fast?"

"*Gongxi*," she offered after a brief hesitation.

"*Gongxi*, Mae Ching," he said as well as he could, and bowed in a courtly manner to the child.

Mae Ching giggled, and he glanced up to see that Garnet was laughing too. "Did I say something funny?" he demanded, wondering if perhaps she'd played a cruel trick on him.

"Not really. It's just that in Chinese your tone and inflection can change the meaning of what you're saying. You said you were going to attack her."

He frowned. How could any language be so complicated?

"I told you Chinese wasn't easy to learn."

"Then I guess we'd best get started, hadn't we?" he insisted. He wouldn't allow a language to get the best of him.

Once the woman in charge of Mae Ching's care led the little girl away, he grasped Garnet by the arm and steered her from the table through the courtyard to the side exit.

"Where are you taking me?"

"I thought perhaps you would like to see something of the ranch." In the familiar surroundings of his land he would be in charge. "You can begin by teaching me the names of things I work with everyday."

"I think we should begin with basics, Mr. Carson." She came to a halt, refusing to take another step. "There are four tones used when speaking Chinese," she explained in her best teacher's voice. "First you need to master them before—"

"Miss Sinclair," he interrupted, adjusting his hat to sit lower on his forehead, "in my opinion you think too damn much."

"That, Mr. Carson, is what you are paying me to do. A teacher that doesn't think isn't much of a teacher," she proclaimed.

"Believe me, ma'am, some things to be learned aren't done so with logic. Sometimes you just have to 'do.'" He led her away from the house toward the stables. "Nature isn't logical. No amount of thinking will make it rain when there's a drought. And no amount of thinking will reposition a foal presented breech."

She didn't reply, but the grudging agreement in her eyes said more than words.

Once they reached the stables, he turned to her, feeling a bit guilty for being so unreasonable. "Very well, Miss Sinclair. We'll begin with the basics," he consented. "But why not make the schoolroom as pleasant as possible? Can you ride?"

"If you mean horses, well enough, but what has that to do with a schoolroom?"

"There's a grassy bank beside the river not far from here. As a boy I used to go there with my books to study. Very conducive to learning. And thinking," he added with a smile meant to console as well as sway her.

"Very well, Mr. Carson. I'll go with you." She lifted a pointing finger in his face and shook it. "But I warn you there will be no 'doing' in my classroom."

He raised his hands in defense. "Just thinking. Yes, ma'am," he agreed. He smiled to himself. Little did she realize he was "doing" already. Before long the magic of Rancho Carmelo would take her in its grasp and seduce her before she had a chance to think about it.

Chapter Fifteen

Sitting in the deep-seated, Spanish sidesaddle, Garnet reined the Appaloosa mare along the winding path. But no matter which way she attempted to steer her, she had no doubt the horse would follow wherever Quixote led.

She had been surprised to see how gentle the solidly muscled stallion was. All of her life she'd been told stud horses were unmanageable, something to be leery of. But Quixote had acted like the most docile of creatures with Bain. His soft velvet nose had poked into each of Bain's pockets like a child seeking sweetmeats. And when Bain had slipped a small lump of sugar into her hand, Garnet had been delighted to find that Quixote frisked her with his muzzle without hesitation until he located the booty tucked in the folds of her skirt. Carefully taking the sweet between his expressive lips, he had nuzzled her empty hand demanding affection.

"He's a shameless beggar," Bain had told her laughingly as he placed a leather halter on Quixote's head and led him into the stables.

Once the horse was saddled, the stallion had shown the manners of a gentleman, yet his spirit and power were evident in the way he lifted his feet and tossed his head as Bain reined him down the path.

Reaching a rise, Bain halted and waited for Garnet to draw abreast of him. Below in the valley the Rio Carmelo lumbered along its streambed like a big, sleepy bear. Drooping willows, hunched like napping old men, trailed their woody fingers in the water. Lush grass that stayed green the year round rolled in waves as a breeze caressed it.

Garnet couldn't help but find it all beautiful—breathtakingly so. Leaning forward, she stroked the silky neck of her mount murmuring words of encouragement.

Quixote whinnied and pawed the ground anxious to continue on their way. The mare's ears, which had been turned back to catch Garnet's words, rotated forward, her head bobbing her agreement.

"He needs a good run," Bain announced, tightening his hand on the reins to hold the horse in check. "Do you *think* you can keep up?"

"I *know* I can," Garnet replied, leaning forward and giving the mare her head.

The race was lost before it ever started. Quixote outpaced the mare with ease, but the feel of the wind snatching at her hair and pulling it from its pins, the smooth gait of the horse beneath her brought color to Garnet's cheeks and freed her heart from the society-made boundaries she'd placed around it.

When he reached the riverbank, Bain turned his mount, his face open and full of life. For the moment Garnet forgot just who he was. Bain—Drew—they became one in her mind—the tall, handsome male she raced toward, the man of her dreams. Exuberance bubbling forth, she fell into his arms as he slowed her mare using Quixote's solid body as a breakwater.

"Easy, woman," he said in a satiny voice that brought memories flooding back. Drew had said that same thing to her in times of passion in exactly the same way. The warm, muscled arm wrapped about her seemed so familiar, yet . . .

The merged images divided. This wasn't Drew that held her so intimately but his brother.

Garnet straightened, fumbling to gather up the reins of her horse, her face flushing red with confusion and embarrassment. "I'm sorry, I should have not let her get away," she mumbled, meaning her heart as well as her mount. Her hand moved up attempting to bring order to her disheveled hair. How had she managed to let things get so out of hand?

Bain released her without hesitation, but she saw the flash of desire in his gaze before he urged Quixote to again take the lead in somber silence.

He worked his way toward a knoll between two willows. There he dismounted, allowing the reins to trail along the ground. Then he turned to help Garnet down from her saddle.

If it were possible to dismount without his assistance, she would have refused him. But she was not that good an equestrian, and it was a long way down to the ground. She didn't relish the idea of falling and making the situation worse. His large hands circled her waist and swung her down as if she weighed no more than a feather. The moment her feet touched solid earth she placed her hands on his, a signal for him to let go. Instead he clung, his gray gaze gone smoky just as Drew's did whenever desire filled him.

Her head thrown back, she felt her throat convulse as she swallowed. "You can let go now," she whispered.

As if pulled from a trance, he reluctantly lowered his hands. "Of course," he replied, and turned back to his horse.

Releasing cinches, he unsaddled Quixote, placing the gear over a low branch. Then he slipped the bit from between Quixote's teeth and turned him loose with a sound whack on his rump. "He won't go

261

far," he explained, and turned his attention to the mare.

Once the two horses were grazing their way through the lush, virgin grasses, he spun to face her. There was nothing left to remind her of Drew, and for the moment she doubted her sanity. Bain's countenance was smooth—the man in control.

What had made her imagine that he was his brother? Drew would have never allowed such a potent moment to pass. Self-control was a trait he'd never displayed. He would have simply scooped her up in his arms and made love to her then and there without hesitation.

A most unladylike thrill rushed through her, and she frantically redirected her thoughts to something safer and definitely more acceptable. Yet she was sorry the bubble of fantasy had to be burst as quickly as it had formed.

"All right, Miss Sinclair, I'm ready to learn," he said, taking her by the arm and leading her toward a rocky outcrop. He settled her on a ledge that overlooked the river and sat down in front of her, his hands draped across his knees—waiting.

As if he expected to learn it all in one afternoon.

Garnet tried to get as comfortable as possible, and cleared her throat as she organized her thoughts. He would be very lucky today if he succeeded in mastering the tones. "All right, Mr. Carson," she challenged, "we'll begin with the sounds."

Bain watched her lovely mouth form each consonant sound and, without thinking too much about it, repeated each one after her. When she came to the *r*, he stumbled over the strange sound, and he had to keep himself from smiling when she scolded him for not paying the proper attention.

"Say it again, Mr. Carson." She repeated the sound

and waited.

Taking his time, he screwed up his mouth and made the appropriate sound, then looked up grinning like a schoolboy.

"Very good. Now I want you to practice that at least fifty times before you go to bed tonight," she instructed.

"Yes, ma'am," he said still grinning. Homework. Already. He wanted to ask her if she would tuck him in tonight to make sure he completed the assignment.

Finishing up the consonant sounds, she turned to the vowel sounds, going through them slowly to make sure he said them correctly.

Hell, this was almost fun. The urge to tell her how lovely he thought she was made him fidget.

"Now, we will learn the tones," she stated, lifting her hand and tucking the thumb against the palm. Noting his inability to keep still, she frowned at him and cleared her throat. "Now for the tones," she began again as soon as he quit fidgeting. "There are four of them. The first is called the 'upper even tone.'" She dropped all except one finger. "That's because it is spoken high but the voice neither raises or falls," she quoted as if reading from a textbook. Then she made an *a* sound using this first tone.

When she paused and looked at him, he did his best to mimic her.

Apparently satisfied, she continued. "Now the second tone." She raised another finger. "It begins with the voice lower, then rises as high as the first."

Again she demonstrated and he repeated.

"The third begins by dropping your voice, then you draw it out as you raise it." Another finger joined the others.

This was more difficult, but he managed to emulate her example rather well.

"The fourth." She lifted the last finger. "Your

263

voice falls from high to low, like this." Making the sound, almost musical, she lowered her hand.

Once he'd completed that task, she raised her hand once more. "All right, Mr. Carson. Number one." Again her finger popped up.

He made the sound. And they continued down the line saying each one over and over until he had them memorized.

The sense of accomplishment that engulfed him was nothing compared with the rush of pride he felt for Garnet. She was so beautiful, even in her schoolmarm primness. He could well understand how schoolboys became infatuated with their teachers, especially if they looked like Garnet. He wanted to reach out and touch her, to run a finger over her finely carved lips, wanted to lean forward and kiss them to silence. Instead he looked over her shoulder at the lowering sun and sighed. "It's getting late. We should be heading home."

Garnet glanced about as if surprised to discover so much time had lapsed. That was good. That meant she'd enjoyed herself as much as he had.

"Oh, my, you're right," she exclaimed and stood, brushing at the wrinkles in her skirt—one of the skirts he'd had put in her room.

It pleased him to no end to see her wearing it. He wondered if she suspected the gifts were from him— or did she credit them to Drew? The thought sparked a flash of resentment.

Pushing up from the rock, he turned and gave a sharp whistle. Several hundred yards away, Quixote lifted his head and responded with a friendly nicker. "Come on, old man," Bain growled, still angry with the situation he'd created, "it's time to get going."

With slow deliberation the horses came toward him. Noting the tender way the mare placed her left front hoof, he moved forward to investigate, grumbling to himself because something else had gone wrong. Bending, he touched her leg below her knee, and the horse instantly lifted her foot for inspection.

Wedged in her hoof was a stone, and in his mind a plan began to formulate.

He looked at Garnet and pointed toward Quixote's gear still hanging on the low branch. "In the saddlebags is a hoof pick. Would you get it for me?"

He could see the confusion on her face, and it satisfied him to realize that in some subjects he knew more than she did. "A little L-shaped tool." He crooked his finger to demonstrate. Smiling to himself, he waited. Perhaps he could use that knowledge to his best advantage.

She fumbled in the leather pouches until she located the item. "This?" she said, turning in his direction.

He nodded, took the pick from her hand, and carefully dug into the mare's hoof until he finally dislodged the stone. Noting the reddish bruise marks on the sole and sidewall, he carefully set her foot back down, satisfied what he planned was not complete fabrication.

"Well, it looks like this mare can't be ridden for a while." He tipped his hat back and handed her the pick.

"Wh-what does that mean?" she asked as she skirted around him as if to take a look for herself.

"That means, Miss Sinclair, we'll have to double up on Quixote—unless you plan on walking."

For a moment he saw her seriously consider doing just that—walking back to the ranch. "But what if we take it slow, couldn't she carry me the distance?"

No doubt the horse could make it without causing undue damage, but he was not about to pass up such a good excuse to hold Garnet's womanly curves in his arms again. "'Fraid not, ma'am," he replied, eyeing her boldly. Noting the look of dismay on her face, he wondered if she found him so distasteful. Or was it, perhaps, she found the idea too much to her liking?

Was the proper Miss Sinclair at last beginning to thaw? Feeling a grin starting to part his lips, he wiped all expression from his face and set about saddling Quixote, trying to look as serious and concerned as Garnet did.

As soon as he was ready he mounted, slipped his foot out of the stirrup, and bent low, offering her a hand up.

She eyed it suspiciously, then glanced over at the hilly terrain between the river and the ranch. With a sigh, she gave him her hand and slid her foot into the empty stirrup.

He swung her up, stationing her in front of him, his arm braced behind her back to keep her from falling off. "You ready, ma'am?"

"I suppose, as ready as I'll ever be."

Quixote responded to his knee pressure and took off at a trot, covering the ground in his long, easy strides. The mare followed without coaxing, moving —much to Bain's dismay—as if nothing was wrong with her foot. To keep Garnet from noticing, he engaged her in conversation, taking a different route so as to show her more of Rancho Carmelo and to give himself a chance to hold her as long as possible. Ambling down a road between rows of dormant grapevines, he told her of his future plans.

"I have joined with several of the neighbors to expand the winery." At the top of a crest he pointed at a structure half completed. "Next year we should be able to increase our production twofold for each of us." He switched the reins to his other hand, savoring the feel of her breasts brushing against his arm.

Riding along the ridge, the curve of her hip pressing intimately between his thighs, images of what he would like to do to her here and now, atop Quixote, set his pulse to racing.

If it were Drew that held her so, she would

266

willingly melt against him, but because he was Bain . . .

Damn this deception he'd created and now was powerless to end. He was like a spider caught in its own web. He wanted her, and there was no reason why he shouldn't have her—except that she didn't want him, not the man he really was.

Kneeing Quixote, he urged him to go faster, and willingly the stallion took off, running a race against the thundering of Bain's heart.

Garnet uttered not a sound, not even when he wrapped his free arm about her tiny waist. She clung to him as if she feared for her life. But once they reached the confines of the stable and he reluctantly let her slide to the ground, she looked up at him, her cheeks flushed with what he wished to be excitement but knew was discontent.

"I think tomorrow, Mr. Carson, we should confine our lessons to the house." Then she walked away, her head held high, her spine stiff with pride.

"Yes, ma'am," he answered, smiling to himself as he watched her hips sway in unconscious provocation. At least she'd agreed there would be another lesson. He would just have to come up with a private spot closer to the house.

Trying hard to forget the feel of the strong arm about her, Garnet rushed from the stables into the open yard. She took a cleansing breath of fresh air— air that didn't do much to eliminate the rush of excitement brewing in that area just below her belly. It smelt of manly things—leather and horses . . . and a whiff of cigar smoke.

She heard what she thought was laughter—male and female. Cocking her head, she listened and caught the sound again. Lifting her skirts, she followed the trailing noises and smell.

Behind the bunkhouse she saw them. Choie Seem, so demure and ladylike, and Nattie, a wild, little pony who tossed her mane of dark hair and flirted outrageously with the circle of ranch hands that crowded around the two girls.

Garnet couldn't fault the men—not really, even though she wanted to. They were only responding to Nattie's lack of discipline. And though she didn't blame them, she wasn't about to let these ruffians take advantage of such innocence. Putting on her best teacher's face, she marched forward. The minute the cowboys spied her, they stepped back, jerked their hats from their heads, and muttered sporadic "ma'ams." She recognized one man in particular, the young *vaquero* who had accompanied them from Monterey—the one who had shown Choie Seem attention.

Shooting the men a look of disapproval, she gathered up the two girls and herded them toward the house. "It's time to go in," she insisted.

"But we were having fun," Nattie declared, balking like a spoiled child—which in Garnet's opinion was exactly what she was, lovable but spoiled.

Garnet stared at Choie Seem, and was satisfied to see guilt etched on her pixielike features. The Oriental girl should know how unseemly such actions were. Garnet had taught her better manners.

"Nevertheless we will go in now," Garnet insisted.

"But why?" Nattie demanded.

How could the girl be so naive? Taking a deep breath, Garnet started to speak, then remembered Bain's warning that she leave his little sister alone. But how could she look the other way and allow this child to act so improperly?

"Because, Nattie dear, to flaunt oneself before the male of our species is asking for trouble."

"But why? They seemed to take no offense." The

girl's gray eyes, so like her brothers', narrowed. "In fact, I think they were having a good time too," she declared.

"Nattie." Garnet turned and grasped the girl's slim shoulders in her hands. She wanted to shake her; instead she squeezed gently. "There are just some things a young woman like yourself just doesn't do, especially with young men."

"But they're my friends," she cried in desperation as if Garnet was attempting to take something precious away from her. "Have been since I can remember." Her eyes pleaded for understanding.

Oh, Bain Carson, how could you be such a fool? Can't you see what is taking place right under your nose?

"Look, Nattie, I want to explain it all to you, but your brother has forbidden me."

The girl frowned as if she didn't believe Bain would do something so unfair. "Then I'll ask him."

"I think that is a wonderful idea, child." A damn good idea. She would love to see Bain Carson's handsome face when his sister asked him why she couldn't keep company with his male employees— his woman-starved *vaqueros*. Would he be so quick to defend his reasoning regarding the girl's sorely lacking education? She sincerely doubted it.

Watching the girl race toward the house, she smiled smugly to herself. Perhaps now Mr. Know-it-all Carson would be forced to allow her to take Nattie in hand and teach her how to become the lady she should be. Then the smile faded. What right did she have teaching social morals to anyone? She who had succumbed to the honeyed words of a man in exactly the way she feared for Nattie.

"I'm sorry, *Sse Mo*."

Garnet glanced to the side to see Choie Seem's shame-faced look. "As well you should be. You know better." *God knows, I should know better too, but that didn't stop me.*

"I know, but Mateo is so handsome, and so gallant. I find it hard to resist. . . ."

"Is that your young *vaquero?*"

"*Sí. Es un hermoso hombre, no?*" Choie Seem said with very little hesitation.

Garnet tilted back her head and laughed. "Ah, *sí, muchacha,* very handsome indeed. Someone has been teaching you." Then she grew serious. "I hope they've only taught you Spanish, nothing more. Please, Choie Seem, be very careful. Young men spout silky words without much thought to the future. Don't fall victim to his hastily spoken promises," she warned as they entered the courtyard.

"Not to worry, *Sse Mo.* You have taught me well. Perhaps better than you taught yourself." Giving her a kindly smile, the Oriental girl veered off in the direction of her own room.

Garnet watched her go, her self-confidence shaken to the core. She only wished there had been someone there to remind her that she tread a dangerous path before it had become too late to turn back.

Bain could tell by the way Nattie stood there, her little fists propped on her hips, her eyes questioning him, that sometime between sunrise and sunset she had begun the dreaded process of growing up on him.

"Why, Bain? Why would you tell her not to talk to me?"

Bain dropped back in his leather chair and witnessed the protective dam he'd so carefully constructed about the girl come tumbling down around him.

"You have to understand, Nattie. Miss Sinclair has some funny notions about how we should act, which are fine where she comes from. But here, at Rancho Carmelo, we can do things our own way."

"But she made it sound like I was doing something wrong. I was just talking to Mateo and Raimundo and some of the other hands. She said there were some things young ladies don't do with young men. Is talking to them one of those things?"

His eyes narrowed as he wondered just what had taken place behind the bunkhouse. Nattie made it all sound so innocent, but men were men. By damn it, he'd bullwhip any of the *vaqueros* that dared to lay a hand on his sister. She was just a child!

Then he looked again and saw the swell of her budding breasts clearly outlined beneath her cambric shirt, and the way her hips curved in the tight jeans she wore.

Ah, hell, Nattie. Why couldn't you just stay a child? How much simpler it would be for all of us.

"Talking's not wrong, honey, but perhaps you should confine your conversations to—"

"No!" She stamped her foot in anger the same way her mother had so long ago. "You can't make me, not unless you tell me why," she demanded, her chin notching with determination. "Not unless you let *Garnet* explain. She's everybody's teacher, even yours. I want her to teach me too." She threw out her bottom lip in a pout.

Guilt assaulted him. He didn't want Nattie to know why, but most of all he didn't want her unhappy. For too many years he'd shielded her from the truth. Hell, he wouldn't be in the bind he was in now with Miss Garnet Sinclair if it wasn't for the fact he'd been trying to protect his sister—doing what he had to in order to keep Drew quiet—making promises and deals to stop the son of a bitch from carrying out his constant threat to destroy the protective shell he'd so painstakingly constructed for their sister. If Nattie ever found out the circumstances of her mother's death, it could push her over the edge. Merely growing up could possibly do the same. It was a risk he did everything in his power to avoid. But watching the displeasure twist her lovely features into a frown was not what he wanted either. It was important to him that his little sister have whatever it took to make her happy. The choice was not a simple one to make. Nattie was not one to give up easily.

"Okay, honey," he said consolingly, thinking to resolve the situation by tackling it from a different angle. "I'll talk to Miss Sinclair."

An instant smile of victory bowed her lips, and she rewarded him with a quick peck on the cheek. "Thanks, Bain. I knew you would understand."

He sighed. He didn't really understand, but how could he make things go back to the way they were yesterday? How could he explain his sudden change of heart to Garnet? The urge to fabricate an elaborate story to convince her to do what he wanted began taking shape in his mind. No, damn it. He was tired of the lies, whether for a good reason or not. How could he take back the terrible deception he'd already played on her without losing her completely? Watching Nattie spin about, he cursed the fact that he seemed destined to always deceive those he loved. Why? Why couldn't he run his personal life with the efficiency with which he ran the ranch?

He didn't have answers to any of those questions— at least not ones to his liking.

As Nattie skipped out, her long, dark hair flying behind her, he stood. Might as well get it over with. For Nattie's sake he'd swallow his pride and ask Garnet to take over the girl's education, but he'd make sure she taught Nattie only enough to satisfy her current curiosity.

The knock on her door caught Garnet by surprise. After the harrowing experience this afternoon, she'd returned to her room to rest. Not that she'd needed

272

rest, but what she'd needed was time alone to sort out her confusing feelings. From the moment she'd spied Drew in the crowd at the barracoon her life—her very moral fiber—had been turned topsy-turvy. And like a leaf caught in a maelstrom, she had been carried away by circumstances that were beyond her realm of experience. Choie Seem was right. She hadn't then followed, and still didn't follow, her own dictates, which made her a hypocrite of the worst kind.

God help her, but her father—bless his soul— would disown her if he knew what she had resorted to in order to save her own wretched skin. And Choie Seem's, she reminded herself. Her original bargain with Drew had been made in order to rescue the girl from a life worse than death.

The knock sounded again. "Miss Sinclair?"

Bain Carson's voice—so like Drew's yet so different—could not be ignored. He was her employer, at least for the moment.

She rose from the bed and crossed to the door. Cautiously she cracked open the barrier, and saw him standing there, his hands buried in the front pockets of his jeans. "Yes, Mr. Carson, what do you want? I was resting." She tried to sound as firm and in charge as she could.

"I want to hear what you have to say about the incident today outside the bunkhouse."

That fiery desire to protect innocence—both her own and the girl's—flared within her. "I owe you no explanations, sir. The girl needed to be taken to task. I could do nothing less." She tried to slam the door— the subject closed—but Bain's boot planted on the threshold, no doubt on purpose, stopped her.

"Well, your damned interference has caused repercussions that you know nothing about, and probably care less about." Bain forced the door open, and it crashed against the wall of her room.

The fact that Bain had openly cursed her made her

blood boil. What right did he have to assume what she felt or to question her actions or instincts as a woman? "You know nothing of repercussions, sir," she choked. "Not that you can blame Nattie, for God bless her, she doesn't know any better because some fool thinks to keep her in the Dark Ages." She faced him with the strength of right on her side. "She was flaunting herself outrageously, stirring up those young men in ways she couldn't begin to understand. She even had Choie Seem involved in her antics. I was *not* going to stand by and watch, no matter what you demanded."

"She was simply talking to them, madam." He bent low, challenging her to contradict his words. Nose to nose they stood, the heat of their convictions sawing in and out, neither willing to give in.

"I don't call what she was doing merely talking." Her fists curled, her own unbound hair flying provocatively about her face and shoulders, Garnet refused to be cowed by a stubborn oaf who refused to see the truth.

To her surprise his mouth ground down against hers, trapping her righteous breath between them. Possessive, probing, and completely out of bounds.

But worse. She felt her body and lips yearning to respond.

No! Damn it!

Placing both of her fists on his heaving chest, she shoved him away—or rather, she shoved herself away as his solid body didn't budge. Placing the back of her hand against her open mouth, she wiped the temptation and taste of Bain Carson from her lips. "I am not a ball to be volleyed back and forth between you and your brother. You have shared many things in your lives," she cried, remembering only too well Drew's alluding to such terrible, dark secrets, "but I will not be one of them. Stay away from me, Bain Carson." Putting her weight against the door she again tried to slam it shut. She didn't care if she broke his damn foot.

But she couldn't make his foot go away by wishing. And though she could tell by the pinched look on his face she was hurting him, he refused to move until he'd had his say. "Don't worry, Miss Sinclair, I'm not accustomed to taking my brother's leavings. But you and I—we do have a bargain, and you will uphold your end of it. You will continue your instructions with Mae Ching. And since you refuse to see to my education, you're to help Nattie understand the ways of men and women."

"Nattie? You want me to teach her? But . . ."

"I want it understood there will be no romantic nonsense filling her head—just facts. I want her taught manners and morals and nothing else. Understood?"

She nodded, unable to believe he was giving her what she wanted, a chance to mold Nattie into a loving, caring woman. And as for romantic nonsense. She notched her chin with conviction. As far as she was concerned it was nonexistent.

Chapter Sixteen

January 1871

Garnet looked up from the weekly progress report she was writing and glanced inquiringly at Mae Ching as the girl came to a stuttering halt. "Evening," she supplied, completing the trailing sentence the child had begun.

"Yes, *Sse Mo.* I look for-ward to this ee-ven-ing," she said dutifully in English. Then she looked up, her mouth puckered with a question. "But what if I do not look forward to it?" she asked in Chinese.

"It doesn't matter," Garnet replied in kind. "When you accept an invitation to dinner, you say you look forward to it regardless."

"Oh." The little girl tilted her head, apparently still not satisfied. "Then it is proper to lie in Engleesh?"

"No, Mae Ching. Of course not. It is never acceptable to lie in any language, but sometimes we say polite things to make others feel comfortable."

The child's perplexity turned into a frown of confusion, making Garnet stop and think about what she'd just told her student. Social graces did seem contrary to the laws of God sometimes, but now was not the time to explain the complicated reasoning of polite society.

"Now," Garnet began, changing the subject. "How do you ask for . . . ?" She thought for a moment, trying to come up with something to challenge Mae Ching's budding knowledge of English. *"Jian."*

The child frowned. *"Jian? Jian?"*

Garnet could see the girl's mind churning, grasping for the answer.

Then Mae Ching looked up smiling. "I be velly pleased . . . to . . . take a piece of paper."

"To have, not take," Garnet corrected, more than pleased herself at Mae Ching's progress even if it wasn't perfect.

"To have a piece of paper," she repeated.

"Very good," Garnet praised.

And it was. In less than three months Mae Ching had mastered enough English to easily make herself understood. Garnet quickly jotted down her observation in the progress report propped on the table before her. Once a week she gave a detailed account of both Mae Ching's and Nattie's lessons to Bain. Actually, she laid the review on his desk in his office when he was away from the house.

Never once had he questioned her or her reports, but she knew that he read them, as quite often the girls would comment to her that Bain had made specific inquiries about what they had learned that week.

Otherwise she'd never seen him or heard reference to his presence since that day so long ago when he had brutally, and out of character, kissed her. He had kept his promise to leave her alone, a demand she had never intended to mean total abstention on his part.

Nevertheless, that was how he had taken it. He never took meals when she did, and the only physical evidence she had that he was still there at the ranch was when occasionally she saw him in the stable yard working with the mares and Quixote. And though she wanted to approach him, those times were somehow inappropriate. How did one talk to a man who was busy with the act of . . . breeding? Even if it was only livestock.

Just the day before, she had sat in one of the bentwood rockers on the front veranda, watching him lead the huge stallion into the breeding yard and secure him with restraints. Quixote had metamorphosed from the gentle beggar who still searched her pockets whenever she visited him for lumps of sugar into a wild-eyed, snorting stud. The only one who'd seemed capable of handling him was Bain, and the *vaqueros* were only too willing to let the *patrón* take charge. They were frightened of the stallion, she had sensed that fact even from that distance. Frightened and rightly so.

Quixote had reared up, pawing the air with his powerful hooves. Garnet had planted her fist into her mouth in fear when Bain refused to back away. Instead he'd held his ground and using gentle force, persuaded the stud to wait clamly as the selected mare was brought to him. Once the breeding process began, Garnet had turned away, unwilling to engage in voyeurism even if the act was between two horses. But the ranch hands were not so self-conscious, and had stood around watching and commenting until the mating was completed. Apparently Bain had done the same, though she didn't watch long enough to be sure. And though she knew observation was a necessary part of breeding livestock, all she could think of were the comments Drew had made the last time they had been together—men had no such compulsion to modesty, at least not the Carson men.

"*Sse Mo?*" The chair before her scraped the flagstones of the courtyard in impatience.

She looked up from the words she'd been writing that had blurred before her eyes as she'd lost herself in

279

thought. Then she glanced down at the pin watch attached to the bodice of her blouse, and looked back up at the wiggling child. "Lesson over, Mae Ching. I want you to think about the difference between take and give and have."

The little girl nodded and scampered from her chair, eager to get away. But before she left, she threw her arms about Garnet's neck in a genuine show of affection. Knowing her student wouldn't give the lesson another thought until tomorrow, Garnet hugged the tiny body in return, unable to find it in herself to begrudge the child anything.

Not with the day as beautiful as it was.

January was the customary rainy season in the valley, but today the sun was shining, and though there was a crispness to the tangy air, it was warm sitting in the solar-splashed courtyard.

As much as she hated to admit it, she had fallen in love with Rancho Carmelo, but who could blame her? The weather was all one could ask for, rarely cold. In fact she could only remember one night that the servants had gone about the courtyard covering the ferns and orchids with oilskin tarpaulins to protect them from a possible frost. Then there had been several days of rain, but even those hadn't been so undesirable, for the leaves of all the plants were shiny and clean from the washing. Of all the places she had lived, she found the wild, somewhat uncivilized coastal hills and valleys of California the most memorable. Yes, she could easily stay here for the rest of her life—if things were different—if the man she loved called it home—if . . .

She sighed, and closed the cover to the journal in which she wrote. There were just too many ifs to allow herself to be drawn to this place or the people who called it home. Drew was never coming back, and even if he did, there was little likelihood of him becoming attached to either the ranch or herself.

Besides, she needed to find out the fate of her father and the children at the mission school. And then there was Choie Seem. She had to be returned to her family. And . . . and . . .

She groped about, searching for as many reasons as she could think of to make herself set into motion the necessary steps to leave such a paradise. To go home to her own life. But all of the logic in the world didn't help. China, her father, the children seemed so far away now, so unimportant. But that was wrong. She couldn't feel that way. Her family, her responsibilities couldn't be ignored.

It was with appalled guilt that she reopened the writing journal and set about finishing up her report, stating clearly that she had completed the services which she'd been hired to perform for both Mae Ching and Nattie. Her final statement requested an interview to make arrangements for passage for both herself and Choie Seem to China at the soonest possible date. Then she signed it and dated it in the English fashion, the day before the month.

Tearing the page out and folding it quickly before she had a chance to change her mind, she rose and walked across the courtyard to the door of Bain's office. Knowing he was elsewhere, she stepped into the cool, dark depths of the room to deliver her missive.

Normally she would place the report on the desk and depart as quickly as she'd come in order to avoid a possible encounter with Bain, but today the uncustomary disorder on the smooth, flat surface caught her attention.

Against the tiny voice that urged her to retreat and respect the privacy of others, she moved closer and ran her fingertips over the leather bindings of the stack of books piled high on the desk. Volumes on psychology and psychiatry, one an account of Franz Mesmer. She had heard of his reported work on

281

healing the sick by using the method he called mesmerism. Interesting. Why would Bain be reading such unusual texts?

But the one that completely baffled her was a book by a man named Sir Francis Galton, *Hereditary Genius*. She remembered hearing about the book. It stated that man obtained his abilities and disadvantages from his lineage, and told how selective parenting could improve mankind. How odd. The only sense she could make of Bain's interest in Sir Francis's theory was the development of his Appaloosas. She closed the book with a resounding thud. Of course, that was what this strange research was all about. Bain's attempt to create a new breed of sturdy, dependable horses, nothing more.

Then she dropped her report on the desk and stepped away, her curiosity assuaged, but nonetheless she felt the need to excuse her actions. Just healthy interest in the written word. Besides, she'd not bothered any of his personal papers, just looked through the books. She assured herself she'd done nothing wrong by doing so.

Departing the office through the row of glassed French doors, she hurried to her own rooms. It was time to consider selecting the clothing she would take with her—only what she truly needed, nothing more, for deep in her heart she acknowledged that everything she'd worn had been supplied by one or the other of the Carson brothers and still belonged to them.

Soon she would be returning to her own kind, her loved ones. And though she felt a pang of regret, she knew it was best this way. It was better she leave before she found herself unable to do so. There was no future for her at Rancho Carmelo, and at the moment her future was all she had to cling to.

* * *

Scraping the mud from his boots, Bain paused in the doorway of his office and glanced about. Instantly he knew she had been there. Sweeping the top of the desk with his eyes, he spied the weekly report she'd left for him. The mud forgotten, he hurried forward eager to read it. Not that what she had to say was so important, but the fact she'd written it, held it in her hands, made it all the more precious to him.

Reaching across the surface, he claimed his prize. Quickly he skimmed the pages and felt his heart sink with dread. She was asking to leave. And though he knew the time was nearing, he'd hoped to keep her here until spring. Who could resist the beauty and riotous color of the valley in springtime?

Well, he would just have to think of another way to hold on to her. Perhaps he could make her believe there would be no passage available until March or April. Yes, that was what he would do. Stall for time by telling her he was making the arrangements as quickly as possible. A lie, another deception, another reason to despise himself, but unavoidable as far as he could see.

"Perdóne, Señor Bain."

He glanced up to find one of the servants standing in the open doorway.

"This message came for you earlier this morning."

Bain accepted the letter and tore it open. Once he read it, he smiled to himself much like a gambler who had just pulled an ace out of the hole. Enoch Sharp was back, and the man had the information regarding Garnet's past he'd sent him to China to find out. Maybe things weren't as bad as he'd figured, and he could make her request work in his favor. He would meet with Garnet and agree to her terms, then head to Monterey in hopes his first mate had the answers he needed to make her change her mind about leaving.

"Find *Señorita* Sinclair. Tell her I have a few

moments to spare now, if she wishes to speak with me," Bain instructed the woman.

The servant hurried away to do his bidding, and Bain settled in his chair, turning his attention to the stack of books before him and the possible insight and solutions they might offer regarding Nattie. As much as he hated to admit it, he was becoming dependent upon the undaunted Miss Sinclair and the way she had of making the ranch feel like a family unit. He had never seen his sister so happy, so full of life. Maybe he worried about nothing—all these years of frantically trying to protect her. Perhaps all she needed was what Garnet offered her, the understanding and concern of another woman. He couldn't afford to lose Garnet now, but just how far was he willing to go to keep her there, he just wasn't sure.

The expeditious summons from Bain came unexpectedly. Garnet abandoned her packing and checked her hair in the mirror before following the servant from the room. It had been many weeks since they had met face to face, and for reasons she couldn't fathom she found it important to look her best. Professionalism, she told herself. What teacher wanted to be interviewed unless she was neat and tidy and projected an unblemished image?

Reaching the office door she'd left less than an hour before, she could see him sitting at his desk, his nose buried in one of the many reference books she'd looked through earlier. He looked up when she knocked, and she couldn't help but notice the smugness around his mouth as if he knew something she didn't.

"Miss Sinclair, do come in."

Her spine straight, her arms held stiffly at her sides, she slipped through the French doors to stand before his desk.

He looked her up and down twice before he spoke. "Won't you be seated?"

She obliged, settling in a chair opposite him and perched on the very edge, her hands folded in her lap. She waited. Since she was the employee, it was only proper that he begin the conversation.

"I've read over your report, and as usual I find it thorough."

She accepted his compliment as if it were fact. As indeed it was. No one had ever faulted her for being less than exhaustive when it came to teaching.

"I note here you recommend a private girls' school for Nattie."

He was beating about the issue, but she would indulge him. She smiled. "I believe my report explained my conclusion. Nattie is an intelligent . . . inventive, young woman. In my opinion she knows her manners. She just needs the influence of other girls her age to reinforce the importance of abiding by the social graces."

Bain smiled, almost cockily, as if he were pleased with his sister's "inventiveness." "I see," he replied. Then his fingers tapped at the edge of the paper. "Here you say Mae Ching is competent in English."

She nodded.

"I don't agree. I find she quite often stumbles over many words."

"Perhaps, but she knows them." At last he'd broached the issue at hand. She found his angle of approach most interesting, but she was not going to be intimidated. "With practice she will master them, and with exposure to everyday English here at the ranch, she could excel beyond even my expectations."

"With time."

"Yes, Mr. Carson, with time and patience."

"As I recall, Miss Sinclair, the agreement you made

with me was to continue until the job was done."

She knew what he was attempting to do, call her hand on a technicality. "My work here is complete, sir. You have no right to say otherwise. Mae Ching—and Nattie for that fact—are no longer in need of instruction. What they require is a loving, but firm hand to guide them. Only family can give them that—not a hired teacher. I suggest, sir, you spend more time with them yourself."

His shoulders tensed, and for a moment she thought she'd gone too far. Would he renege on their verbal agreement? Her pulse pounded with apprehension. There was very little she could do if he chose that course of action. Everything depended on his adherence to his gentleman's code of honor. Had she misjudged him? Would he refuse to let her go? But why? She meant nothing to him. Heart trapped in her throat, she waited for his decision.

"I think, Miss Sinclair, you are right. Loved ones do make the best instructors. I will be going to Monterey at the end of the week. At that time I will make the necessary arrangements for your departure."

He had conceded to her wishes, yet in the process he'd managed to insult her. His barb about teachers had not gone unnoticed, but she ignored it nonetheless. What she found hard to ignore was the intense look he gave her. If she had to give his expression a name, it was somewhere between desperation and disappointment. But why did her leaving affect him so?

"Thank you, Mr. Carson." She stood, attempting to bring the interview to an end, but his smoky gray eyes refused to release her.

He circled the desk, and to her utter amazement and shock, he took her hand, oh, so gently, and held it between his much larger ones. "Garnet, I have one request I wish you would grant me."

She tilted back her head to look at him towering above her. "Gr-r-ant you? I-i-if I can."

"Call me Bain. Just once I would like to hear you call me by *my* given name."

She tugged at her hand, but he refused to release it. "Bain," she whispered, and surprisingly, the name tasted sweet upon her lips.

As swift as the night wind Bain urged his mount a little faster. Monterey was only a few hours away, as was the dawn. He couldn't wait until the end of the week to find out what Enoch Sharp had to report. He had to know now if Garnet had a life and family to return to. If not, he felt no compulsion to release her right away. In fact it would be for her own good if he delayed her leaving as long as possible.

But if her father was still alive and looking for her, not even with all of the terrible things he'd done to deceive her could he bring himself to deny her what was rightly hers.

Common decency demanded that he wish only for the best, her father's life to have been spared, but, oh, God, what he really wanted was to discover she had no one to return to—no one who cared except himself. He could then offer her a place at Rancho Carmelo, a respectable place, not just as a teacher, but as a companion to both Nattie and Mae Ching.

In one aspect Garnet was right. Both girls were in dire need of a loving, but firm hand to guide them. For him the loving came easy, but he didn't have the heart to be the disciplinarian his sister and niece needed. Besides, Garnet had shown him they all needed a woman's influence, including himself. Without a doubt they needed the very proper, the very beautiful, the very loving Miss Garnet Sinclair. He as much as if not more than the others.

As the sun began to crest the mountains behind

him, Bain reached the edge of town and paused. In the harbor he saw her, proud and sleek, the *China Jewel.*

"My China jewel," he whispered to himself, clinging to the hope that Garnet would one day come to know him for who he really was. "I love her, damn it." He patted the neck of his horse as it turned its ears back to catch what he was saying. "God give me the time, and I can teach her to love me too."

With each word Enoch Sharp spoke Bain sank deeper into despondency.

"I talked to Reverend Sinclair. He was eager for word of his daughter, and I was as vague as I dared to be, sir. Told him I'd only seen the girl on one occasion and that she was in the good hands of a friend of mine." The side of the first mate's mouth lifted in a knowing smile. Then he continued before Bain could react. "He asked—no, he pleaded with me—to instruct you to see that she goes home to the family in England." He pulled out a knotted handkerchief and spilled its contents on the table between them.

Bain's gaze followed the sailor's actions. Money. Not a lot, but enough to pay Garnet's passage. He said nothing, but his insides twisted in guilt.

"I swear, sir, it was all the old man had, and he gave it to me in trust without once questionin' my scruples. Said to assure Miss Garnet the children are all fine, but since the incident at the mission the village has refused to send them back to the school. Then he muttered somethin' about how God was callin' him to Siam, otherwise he would come after her himself. He was a strange one, sir, a bit on the absentminded side, and seemed perfectly confident that I would see to his daughter's welfare." From the same pocket from which he had taken the knotted linen, he removed a sealed letter and placed it beside the open handkerchief.

Bain frowned to himself and picked up the letter. It was addressed to Garnet. Her father did sound a bit odd, and apparently believed in the adage that God provided. But would the old man be so willing to see it in that light if he knew how Enoch's "friend" had taken advantage of his innocent daughter? If it were his own child, Bain knew he would drop whatever he was doing, sacrifice everything, to come to her rescue.

"Thank you, Enoch. You provided much more than I could have hoped for," he stated with a sour twist to his lips.

"Aye, sir." The seasoned sailor studied Bain for a long moment. "So tell me, how is the little miss?"

"Eager to return home."

"Ah, I see. Sorry, sir. Thought for sure by now you would have married her, seein' as how you went to so much trouble to . . ." The first mate looked away, uncertain if he should finish his statement.

Trouble to what? To seduce her? Enoch was right. He *had* gone to a hell of a lot of trouble just to stand by now and watch her leave without doing everything he could to stop her, knowing in all likelihood that once she was gone, he'd never see her again.

The only one who had a sailor's chance in hell of making her reconsider her course of action was Drew. Damn him—which was probably where the bastard was at the moment, in hell, thoroughly enjoying watching his "virtuous" brother succumb to the deception one more time. And though he hated what he'd become, Bain couldn't stop the thrill of anticipation and excitement that coursed through him when he thought of donning his brother's personality and immersing himself in the masquerade.

Standing, he scooped up the money, returned it to the linen cloth, and tied it in a neat knot. "Thank you, Mr. Sharp. You're to remain in harbor and await my orders.''

As soon as the man departed, Bain tossed the money and the letter into his saddlebags on the table, and uttered a string of curses that would have made the real Drew laugh with glee. If Reverend Sinclair thought God provided, the foolish old man had not seen the extent Lucifer would go to to counteract the divine order.

Chapter Seventeen

In the quiet of the courtyard, Garnet sat beneath the spread of a giant staghorn fern contemplating the pearl-like sheen of the January moon. There was a ring about it, unearthly and ominous, yet she couldn't quite remember just what such a phenomenon meant. Danger? A storm brewing? Or the warning of deception to come? Whatever it foretold, she found herself wishing to return to the safety of her room as quickly as possible.

Rising from the stone bench that had suddenly grown cold beneath her, she hurried across the patio. An eddy of wind danced over the flagstones, catching a pile of leaves and whirling them to life. Then it caught the edge of her nightdress, making it billow like a rain-ladened tulip. She shivered and pulled the Spanish lace shawl tighter about the shoulders of her night wrapper, wishing desperately she had her father there to put his arms about her and assure her she'd made the right decision. The moments she'd spent with Bain yesterday had made her come to realize just how much he—not his damnable brother—meant to her.

Drew had been exciting, had fulfilled forbidden fantasies of a secret lover, but he'd offered little else. In the morning sun, he would pale next to his twin, who was a man of his word, truly strong, and compassionate. A man who deserved the love and loyalty of a woman.

But it was apparent that Bain cared nothing for her. How could he? He had to be only too aware of the relationship between herself and Drew.

For once in her life she knew irrevocable shame, and with all of her heart she regretted her mistakes, wishing desperately she could have back the events of the last few months so she could act differently. If only she'd met Bain first, there might have been a chance for them. But now . . . She lowered her head and continued on her way. It was best she leave immediately.

A layer of clouds drifted over the late night moon, and darkness engulfed the unlit courtyard. Ignoring the siren's call of the tinkling water, she skirted around the fountain and trudged toward her quarters.

"Garnet."

Though the speaker was masked by the darkness, she came to a halt, her heart bleating a faint protest like a lamb lost in a storm. She didn't need to see him to know who was there. Drew. She could tell by the confident way he said her name. Oh, why, why did *he* have to return now? Perhaps if she pretended she'd not heard him he'd allow her to pass.

Taking a deep breath, she moved forward determined to continue on her way.

A hand, warm and demanding, snaked out and grasped her upper arm. "Damn it, Garnet. Don't think to ignore me."

She turned, and in that moment the moon sailed from its cloud bank illuminating his face—so devastatingly handsome and sensuous—so damned desirable.

"You said it was over, Drew. What more do you want from me?" But she knew the answer without thinking. He wanted to slake his thirst for her, a craving she shared with him—this terrible need to immerse herself in his smell, his taste, his touch, to listen to and believe the promises his body made but his heart never kept.

Tears crowded the back of her throat, and though she ached to swallow them, she discovered she couldn't. But worse, she found it impossible to pull away when he circled her shoulders with his strong arms, brushing the shawl from her grasp.

Her heart, which had been so timid minutes before, began to thunder with excitement, with a need that couldn't be denied. She leaned back, searching his face, looking for something with which to assuage the burden of guilt that hung heavy on her heart. If only this were Bain who held her so.

The potency of her thought became trapped between them as his mouth claimed hers, seduced her senses, tamed the reluctance pounding in her veins.

Let it be Bain, her soul cried, and she closed her eyes allowing, no, encouraging the imagery to take shape in her mind. Bain laughingly sharing a day by the river. Bain attempting to conquer the complexity of Chinese, grinning back at her like a schoolboy. Bain racing across the hills atop Quixote, master of his own world, a world she found she wanted to be a part of. Bain cradling her to his heart as they galloped back to the ranch, one man, one woman.

His mouth softened as if he'd read her desire, and he pulled back, the kiss lingering before their lips parted. God help her, perhaps it was only her mind's trickery trying to ease her conscience, but it very well could be Bain who stared back at her, his gaze caressing, his heart open to her perusal.

Her hands, which had been splayed across his chest, in a show of resistance, moved upward to curl about his neck. With one finger she traced the arch of his upper lip, still moist from their intimacy.

Without taking his eyes from hers he drew the wondering appendage into his mouth, sucking gently.

"Sweet Garnet," he murmured. "I could no more resist you than a child could a stick of candy." Then his hands captured her face, and he took her mouth once more, greedily plundering. His tongue swept away the last of her hesitation, and soon she found herself pressed against him most wantonly, her own tongue darting, teasing, undaunted when he encouraged her to take the lead. Like a fine-honed rapier he parried her thrusts, then unexpectedly retreated, drawing her weapon deep into his mouth, entwining it with his own to create a sensuous coming together that left her only too willing to surrender.

Dominance was ambrosia, a gift from the pagan gods that left her wanting more, craving so much more, as a nomad lost in a desert of desire where there was only this one man, the oasis from which she could slake her thirst. Nothing, not social dictates nor Victorian morals, would stand in her way. She realized how alike they were, both striving to sate themselves from the carnal well, regardless of the consequences.

That was when she realized she could try to fool herself, but the truth was Drew held her, not Bain. And the blossoming feelings she had for one could be sated, if only momentarily, in the arms of the other. The truth was she and Drew were well matched, each there for self-gratification, and neither deserved better than they got.

So what difference did it make if she made love to him one last time? Damnation awaited the sinner whether he strayed from the path once or eternally.

His fingers picked at the sash that held together the waist of her wrapper, hers tore at the buttons of his fine linen shirt. The belt dropped to the flagstones, and one of his buttons hit it, ricocheted, and bounced across the courtyard, rolling into a crack, forever lost and forgotten.

The thin lace of her nightdress bodice was like nothing, the warmth of his hands penetrated its thinness, sending waves of desire that telegraphed through her body with lightning speed. Her own hands discovered the whorls of chest hair beneath his shirt, soft yet manly, exciting as she combed her fingers through its mass to discover the jutting hardness of his aroused nipples.

"You're a temptress and an angel all rolled in one, Garnet Sinclair," he growled, taking the lobe of her ear between his teeth, then licking the place he'd nipped to demonstrate what he meant. "No matter how hard I try, I can't get enough of you."

"And you, sir, are a smooth-talking flimflammer. Tomorrow you will sail away and forget all about me." She took a deep breath, inhaling the aromatic scent of him.

"What if I told you I planned to stay awhile?"

Her heart somersaulted and came to a skidding halt, fear gripping her insides. "To stay? Here at the ranch? But, but why? You don't like it here." What would Bain do if his brother decided to remain? Would he care? Did *she* care?

"I've heard you're leaving. If I stay, will you?"

She leaned back in the circle of his arms and studied his hooded gray eyes. For one fleeting moment she wondered if the Carson twins—so alike as they were—had played some cruel trick on her. Was this Drew that held her or Bain? Were the two of them working together to keep from upholding their end of the bargain? Her eyes narrowed. Bain's bargain, she reminded herself. She raised her hands and attempted to push his arms away, needing a moment to think, to sort out the suspicions crowding her brain. "My mind cannot be changed," she declared.

Whoever he was, he refused to release her. It had to be Drew, as Bain would never be so presumptuous. She swallowed in confusion. Or would he? Damn it, she didn't like this feeling of paranoia. She would find out just what was going on.

She raised her foot and brought the heel crashing down upon his instep. His arms slackened in surprise, and in the second that he was off guard, she lurched away. If in truth this was Bain before her, she would show him she could not be so easily deceived.

Before she could voice her protest, he snatched her back, pulling her hard against his solid length, his leg pressed between her thighs in emphasis. "Everything is changeable, Garnet." He gently rubbed against her in that familiar way that drove her wild. "Even mountains can be moved and seas parted given the right circumstances."

She tried to dislodge his leg from between hers, but he held her firmly, one hand cupping her backside to make sure she felt the full impact of his caress. "Only God can perform such miracles," she choked, digging her fingernails into his bare chest. Though she felt him flinch, he didn't release her, and he never lost his rhythm.

"Perhaps, *pequeña joya*, but I believe it has more to do with know-how than heavenly phenomena." He gripped her buttocks harder, displaying the knowledge he prided himself in.

And his expertise couldn't be ignored, nor the fact that this was definitely Drew that held her. Drew, who knew just what to do to make her abandon her social morals. Drew, damn him, and she was helpless to resist him.

He bent and locked his arm behind her knees, sweeping her up against his bared chest. The look of triumph on his face was undeniable. Her long, ash-blonde hair trailing over his sleeve, she looked up into his eyes, utterly lost in their gray depths. Only when he carried her through the courtyard toward the outside did she glance away.

"Where are you taking me?" She had thought he would go to her bedroom.

He smiled down at her, his gaze glistening like some lusty desert sheik from a storybook tale of virtuous women kidnapped under star-filled Arabian nights. "We go for a ride, my love," he purred in a deep, seductive voice.

The thrill of imagination sparked every nerve in her body. It wasn't hard at all for her to envision him as some caftan-clad Bedouin out to seduce and enslave the woman of his dreams, to take her on some madcap race over shifting sand dunes to his rug-lined tent beneath a palm tree.

Ah, Drew. It was always like the first time with him—the excitement never waned. This was the side of his personality she found so hard to give up—the something she suspected Bain lacked. She wrapped her arms about his neck, a willing player in the wildly provocative fantasy he so skillfully weaved.

He carried her to the stables, and just as she'd surmised, a horse stood bridled just beyond the great doors of the barn. However, she was a bit surprised to see that it was Quixote, Bain's prized stallion. As they approached, the great spotted beast snorted, most likely irritated to be disturbed from his sleep.

"Perhaps, Drew, we shouldn't take Quixote," she suggested, not sure how familiar he might be with the Appaloosa. "If he's not used to you, he can be quite difficult to handle at times." She remembered only too well the way the powerful animal had reared even with Bain, the master he knew and loved. If Drew was not as experienced a horseman, he might not be able to control the situation.

"You let me worry about handling things, woman," he retorted with a confident laugh that suggested he found either her concern amusing or the challenge to his liking. Before she could protest further, he swung her up onto the horse's broad, bare back.

Quixote danced in place, his regal head bobbing his dissatisfaction. Garnet clung to the stallion's long, dark mane. Then, much to her surprise, Drew swung up behind her with graceful ease and took the reins in his hands. Immediately the animal quieted.

"I had no idea you knew so much about horses." Draped in the circle of his arms she looked up at him with new respect. She had assumed he spent all of his time at sea and knew nothing of landlocked life.

"There are many things you don't know about me, Garnet." He grinned, and his eyes danced with untold secrets. "But there are other things you do know about me only too well." He took her face between the fingers of his free hand and angled it in his direction. Then he kissed her, potent and sweet. Her arm curled about his neck, and as Quixote started forward she was rocked so gently in the secure cradle of her lover's arms.

Out through the paddocks the horse took them, mostly moving at a slow, languid pace. The moon escaped the cover of clouds, and bright as a street lamp it illuminated the landscape around them, creating strange black and white silhouettes. Drew's fingers found the laces of her nightgown, and once they were a distance from the corrals and the bunkhouse, he untied one shoulder, his hand slipping beneath the bodice to cup the swell of her breast.

The fabric slid downward, and unconsciously Garnet trapped the satiny folds against her bosom, her hand covering Drew's where it encircled her womanly flesh.

But he peeled away the clothing and her resistance with little more than a smile and a tug. "There's no one here but you and me. I want to see you, revel in the alabaster glow of your beauty in the magic of the moonlight."

The side of the gown dripped down revealing the round globe. He feasted on both with his eyes and his hand. Then he sought the other tie, and soon the nightgown was heaped about her waist, the wrapper gone as well and draped across the horse.

The January air was cool and crisp, but the warmth of his desire brought heat to her skin. His hand cupped and kneaded and adored until her breasts stood proud and hard.

At some point Quixote came to a standstill, his muscled neck arched and strong, patiently awaiting direction from his riders. Secure in the circle of Drew's arms, she didn't protest as he urged her to swing about to straddle the stallion's withers facing him.

With the warm solidness of the horse beneath her, she lay back against the crest of his neck. The strands of his mane caressed her spine, Drew's hands stroked her naked flesh, and soon she was arching upward wanting more.

Drew covered one beckoning breast with his mouth, sucking gently, nuzzling the rock-hard nipple until the tightness within her belly cried for release. Taking his head between her palms, she directed him to the other peak, which he worshipped with equal zeal. Then his hand was upon the core of her need, rubbing, caressing, carrying her toward the apex. Nothing existed for her except the man whose maestro touch created melody from her body like a bow drawn across the strings of a violin.

Then it seemed as if the world dropped out from beneath her, and she screamed, sure that she was falling. Drew's arm caught her, and laughing, he pulled her up against his chest.

"Guess I should've known a horse is no different

than a ship. A good captain never turns loose of the wheel."

Garnet glanced behind her back to discover that the Earth had not disappeared as she thought, merely that Quixote had grown bored and lowered his head to nibble at the grass, the reins trailing along the ground. "And a rider never turns loose of the reins," she offered, pointing her finger at him in mock anger, then joining in his merriment.

"And a gentleman never leaves a lady in the lurch." He nuzzled her ear and nipped the tender lobe.

"Drew," she squealed in protest, balling her fist.

Before she could retaliate, he slid to the ground and scooped her from her perch aboard Quixote. The stallion looked up and snorted as if disgusted with their antics, and moved off to graze once Drew slipped the bridle from his head.

Drew lay her gently down on a mattress of thick grass, and pressed himself intimately between her thighs.

"Now, it seems to me there's some unfinished business between us. Something about a lady in the lurch, if I recall." He kissed her neck, skimmed over to the sensitive spot below her ear, and trailed a line of fire along her collarbone to the knob of her shoulder. Taking in a deep breath, she sighed, closed her eyes, and turned her head, only too willing to take up where they'd left off before they'd been interrupted.

The sweet smell of crushed grass encompassed her, mingling with the manly scents that hung about Drew like a halo—so familiar, intoxicating. The sounds he made as he tasted and caressed her were an aphrodisiac all in themselves, but combined with the lonesome call of a nighthawk in the distance, a cricket serenade, and the contented blowing of the grazing horse several yards, they were heavenly, sounds she would never forget for as long as she lived.

Her lashes parted, and her gaze focused on the moon, a great silver lantern overhead, a stage light skimming the world beneath it looking for a drama to center upon. Naked and beautiful as any great master's sculpture, Drew was just such a perfect spectacle, one she couldn't tear her eyes away from.

Yes, tonight would be a keepsake. One of those wonderful remembrances a woman pressed between the pages of a book, and took out every now and then just to look at and recall the events so very precious. Every woman had them, but none so rare as the memories of one's first love.

Watching him as he made love to her, she felt a heaviness invade her heart. How could she bring herself to leave him when he was doing everything in his power to keep her there? But was he really? Once she agreed to his wishes wouldn't he then go on about his business, slipping in and out of her life from the side wings whenever the desire possessed him? And how could she face Bain each day, torn in her feelings between these two men, so alike, yet so completely different?

Her many questions went unanswered as Drew pulled her back into his world of unsated sensual delights. His mouth explored her shivering flesh, drawing the bowstrings within her tighter and tighter until she thought they would surely snap in two. Lying totally open to him, she whimpered her dismay, pleading with her every move, her hips undulating, her fingers digging into the soft ground beneath her, her back arching upward.

When at last he filled her, she cried out her relief and pleasure. The nighthawk took wing in the nearby underbrush from the startling noise she made, its harsh call of fear setting off a chain of reactions. The crickets stilled, and the horse moved off snorting.

And Drew. He praised her. "Yes, love, yes. Tell me how good it feels," he encouraged. "Tell me there is nothing more wonderful than these moments between us."

God help her, she did what he asked, not only with her words but with the way she rose up to meet his thrusting hips, time and again until the waves of fulfillment crashed over her, nearly drowning her in the swirling undertow that enveloped her.

And when at last she surfaced, her lungs dragging at the cool night air, her heart thundering in her ears, Drew spoke again.

"Tell me, my sweet China jewel, that you'll stay. For me. For the pleasure I give to you."

As if the sensual sea had cast her upon the beach, naked, lost, and near death, she caught a rising sob, trapping it in her throat. There was only one answer she could give him, although it broke her heart to say it.

"I'm sorry, Drew. I can't. Not for you or anyone else. It's not fair to you, or me, or to . . . to . . ." She clamped her lips tight. She had nearly said Bain.

"To whom, Garnet? Who else figures into this?" He shook her by the shoulders.

She saw his anger transform into realization. Then his expression melted into something that resembled horror. "Just what does my . . . brother mean to you?" Pain was evident in his voice.

As much as she wanted to suppress her feelings, they came tumbling out on their own. "Oh, Drew, how can I explain? There are things about him . . . his gentleness, his kindness, his honesty and integrity. They mean a lot to me."

"Are you saying those traits in a man are more important to you than what we share?" His voice choked on emotion.

Were they? If she told him the truth, in essence she was selecting one brother over the other. And she was not choosing the one who lay naked against her, his turbulent gray eyes unwilling to let it go. She swallowed hard, a feeling of self-condemnation rising like bile in her throat.

He shook her again, none too gently this time, demanding an answer. "Is that what you're saying to me? That you want nothing to do with a man who is not kind and gentle and goddamn honest?"

She knew her head was nodding, but she couldn't stop it, though God knows, she tried desperately. Then the words came tumbling out. "Yes, Drew, yes, damn it. That's exactly what I'm telling you."

The cold night air whipped over her. She looked up. Drew was standing, slowly buttoning up his pants. "Get up, Garnet," he ordered as he jerked on his shirt, his voice as cold as the sudden wind that blew across the meadow. "I think you're right. It's best we both go our separate ways as soon as possible."

Shivering as much with the cold as with fear and self-loathing, she rose. She groped in the tall grass for her nightgown and wrapper, and discovered them in a heap damp and wrinkled from where Quixote had stepped on them. Still shaking with humiliation, she donned them, and soon tears were silently coursing down her cheeks.

If Drew saw them, he said nothing, just gathered up the stallion, mounted, and reached out his hand to help her up. This time he placed her behind him, and she had no choice except to grasp him about the waist as he set the horse in motion.

As they rode across the open fields Garnet realized she had gotten what she'd wanted for so long. She would be leaving Rancho Carmelo, no matter what. But now she wasn't so sure going home would make her happy. Yes, she missed her father, needed to find out what had happened to him and the children, but the thought of never seeing Bain again now that she had finally acknowledged her feelings for him left a hollowness in her heart.

Once they reached the ranch, Drew dropped her off at the front porch. She slid to the ground and holding her wrapper tight against her chest, she watched him rein Quixote toward the stables and disappear into the barn.

Without regret she turned away from Drew and looked longingly at the darkened *hacienda*. Bain was there. How could she have disregarded his qualities for so long? How could she have even considered choosing Drew over him? It was true Drew had rescued her from the barracoon. But hadn't he made his motives only too clear from the beginning?

It had been Bain who had truly helped her with no ulterior motives. As she ran up the front steps she came to the decision to confront Bain, to reconfirm for herself that she'd made the right choice. She owed him and herself at least that much. Yes, the first thing in the morning, when Drew went his separate way, as she had no doubt he would, she would find Bain. He had asked her to stay for the children's sake, and if he were willing to help her discover the fate of her father and the mission, she would remain. For as long as he so desired.

It took all of her will power to go sedately to her own rooms instead of racing to Bain's door. But impulsiveness was a thing of the past, gone with her desire to be swept off her feet by a domineering man like Drew. Bain deserved all that he gave: kindness, gentleness, and above all else honesty and integrity.

She smiled to herself. All she could think of was how pleased her father would be to discover how well her situation was turning out. *God provided*, he would say. *Did you expect anything less, daughter?*

He had no right to be angry with anyone but

himself. In fact, he had gotten exactly what he'd striven to achieve. Bain told himself that over and over, and yet he couldn't help feeling cheated. He had worked so hard to make Garnet turn to him, Bain, but now that she had, he couldn't give her the things she found most important—honesty and integrity.

He laughed, but it wasn't a pleasant sound. Honesty. Damn it. Before Garnet had come into his life he would have never questioned his probity, but would have simply taken it for granted.

But from the moment of that first deception, he'd been no longer the man he'd prided himself in being. No longer Bain, the redeemer, the good, but a man who had faced true temptation and had failed miserably. And by succumbing, he had lost the one thing he had hoped to gain. Garnet Sinclair.

He turned and finished placing the last of his clothing in his valise and closed the lid, strapping the buckles in place.

For one brief moment he considered confronting her now with the truth, but what purpose would that serve? He couldn't expect her to understand or forgive him. And facing her now with the facts of his deception would only serve to embarrass and enrage her, as well it should.

Garnet had deserved better than he had given her. Better than he could ever give her. He'd be damned if she'd be beguiled into accepting less than a man with the honesty and integrity she found so important.

Taking up the letter and money from her father that Enoch Sharp had given him earlier, Bain turned and slid them into a leather pouch in which he'd already placed her passage home, along with a ticket for Choie Seem back to China. They had made a bargain and he would keep it. She had more than earned their fare by teaching Mae Ching and Nattie. The money her father had sent was hers to do with as she willed once back in England.

His hand fingered the pocketed letter, and temptation flared once more in spite of his resolution, planting the fertile seeds of doubt in his mind. Perhaps he should familiarize himself with what the Reverend had written to her, if only to assure himself she would be going home, not attempting to return to China with Choie Seem or to follow her father to his next mission. No, if Reverend Sinclair wrote she was to go to England, which is what he'd assumed by his conversation with his first mate, then he couldn't doubt for a moment that the proper Miss Sinclair would follow her father's instructions regardless of her personal feelings.

Opening the missive was something Drew would do, not Bain. He released his grip on the envelope and quickly fastened the pouch with the leather strap that wound about it. He was through with making such mistakes. By damn, he'd learned his lesson even if it was the hard way.

Snatching up his bag, he swung it over his shoulder and marched out of his room. Then he walked to Inez's quarters near the kitchens and deposited the pouch into the cook's outstretched hand with instructions to give it to the *señorita* at the morning meal. By then he would be gone, most likely in Monterey and aboard his ship on his way to San Francisco. He had decided earlier the ranch could run itself for a while in the capable hands of his foreman. He needed time to make sure Garnet was safely on her way home, out of his reach, no longer a temptation to be touched, to be caressed—yes, damn it, he had to admit, even to be loved.

Though love had not been part of the original bargain struck between them, he would have gladly sacrificed all he owned to hear those three words—I love you—from her lips just once. But he knew such was never to be.

Chapter Eighteen

Garnet hurried toward Bain's office hoping to catch him there. It was early, the sun barely risen, but she had to find him now, before her courage failed her.

What would she say to him? God knows, she had rehearsed a million different ways to express her feelings during the night, but none had sounded quite right. Therefore she would rely on the moment to provide her with the proper words.

"Oh, God, please, don't fail me now," she whispered as her feet flew across the cold flagstones still damp with the morning dew.

Reaching the doors of Bain's office, she came to a halt. Usually they were open when she passed them each morning on her way to breakfast, but today they were closed. Her fingers touched one of the latches, and when she pushed it she was surprised to find it locked.

Alarm pounded against her temples. Her hand snapped away as if scalded. Where was Bain? Then the rational side of her mind took charge. It was early—that was the only reason the doors were locked. She stepped closer and bent at the waist, using her hand as a shade to peer through the glass panes. The desk was tidied, more than usual, but again she explained the unusual by the earliness of the hour. Bain simply had not risen yet.

The image of Bain asleep made Garnet smile. She tried to picture how he must look in his bed. Was he one of those people who lay on his back with symmetry? The pillow aligned perfectly, the covers folded neatly, arms pinioning them against his solid frame? Or was he the kind of sleeper who bunched the pillow beneath his head, his arms, legs, and covers sprawled in total disarray?

When Bain was involved, she found both ways appealing. Then it struck her. She'd never once wondered about Drew's personal habits.

She sobered. Sleeping manners were not what was at question here. She had to find Bain. Discovering she had walked toward his bedroom, she nodded at the serving woman who came out of his door with a bundle of linen under her arm.

"The *señor* is up?" she questioned.

"*Sí, señorita.* Arisen and gone already," the woman replied, gathering up the trailing sheets and hurrying toward the laundry at the rear of the *hacienda.*

Gone? But where would he go so early? Garnet asked herself, again the fear drumming against the sides of her head. *Where else but the stables,* she answered, chiding herself for being a silly goose. She gathered up her skirts and hurried back across the courtyard to the arch-covered exit. Urgency pressed her, but she didn't understand why. No matter what he was doing—even breeding his horses—she would talk with him then and there.

As she stepped from the protection of the *hacienda* a chilly, unfriendly wind whipped at the fringe of her shawl, the same one she'd worn last night. But now, even with the sun spreading its warmth across the fields, she shivered, as much with apprehension of at last coming face to face with Bain as with the cold.

Dear Lord, what would she say to him? What would he say to her?

She came to a halt just outside the stable doors. The wide barriers were thrown open, and a finger of morning light painted a square of brightness in the entryway. From the depths of the building she could hear the frantic, angry neighing of a horse. The crack of a whip followed so closely she gasped in surprise.

"Behave yourself, *diablo loco.*"

She rounded the corner and saw a group of *vaqueros* struggling to subdue a rearing Quixote. Sweaty froth darkened his powerful chest outlining the ropes around his neck.

Expecting Bain to step forward at any moment and take control of the great, snorting beast, she watched in silent awe. Was this the same gentle animal upon whose back Drew had made love to her last night? She found it hard to believe.

Quixote reared again, pulling against the many lariats looped about his powerful neck. He managed to lift one man clearly off the ground and slam him against the wall of the stall in which he was trapped.

The crash was deafening. On its wake came the whizzing snap of the whip.

"No," Garnet cried, unable to believe that such cruelty was needed to control the stallion. All she could see was the gentle, devoted pet that followed her about seeking treats. She stumbled forward, grasping the rising arm of the man wielding the whip. "Can't you see he's only frightened?"

The *vaquero* stared at her as if she'd lost her senses. "Frightened?" He laughed. "Quixote is merely showing his dislike for us. *Señor* Bain put that devil in a stall last night after riding him and then left us to return him to his pasture this morning."

"It wasn't Bain who put him in there, it was Drew," she informed him, feeling a ridiculous need to protect Bain from this man's anger.

The cowboy cocked his head and gave her a patronizing look. "*Señor* Drew? Not likely, *señorita*." He snorted his disbelief. "Quixote would have never allowed it." Turning back to the task at hand, he dismissed her and her information as erroneous.

A strange feeling sprouted in the pit of her stomach. "What do you mean, the horse would never allow it?" She clutched his arm, demanding an explanation. "He was docile and gentle as a lamb last night with Drew."

The man sighed and angled her way, resigned to the fact he would have to answer her before he could continue his work. "You must be mistaken, *señorita*. The only person who can control this unruly beast, much less ride him, is *Señor* Bain. Anyone else Quixote would surely kill, even you."

Before she could scoff at his ridiculous warning, the man pushed her aside—and just in time. Quixote's hooves flayed the air, coming down inches from where she had been standing. Then, as if he had made his point, the stallion began moving forward. The men sidled with him, shouting and pulling, cajoling him into the pasture. Once he was released, the horse raced away snorting his disfavor, his tail lifted high in pride, not once looking back at Garnet—his friend, or so she had thought.

She swallowed hard and watched him go feeling betrayed. Only Bain could ride him? At last what the man had been saying to her penetrated the haze of disbelief. If what the cowboy had said was true . . .

That could mean just one thing. Last night she had been with *Bain*. Bain, who had stroked and ignited her willing flesh. Bain, who had been familiar with her body as if he'd made love to her before.

The world about her seemed to go black. She struggled to block the logical conclusion of her discovery. Had Bain tricked her and deceived her . . .

310

since . . . oh, God, since that first time together aboard the *China Jewel?* But why would he do something so devious?

She felt the sharp pain of the stones beneath her thin soled shoes as she ran, but it was nothing compared with the agony ripping apart her soul. How could he have made such a fool of her?

Had he found it so amusing watching her agonize with her conscience over . . . ? Drew and Bain? Were they in truth the same man? If so, which side of his personality was the real man, the rogue or the gentleman? The more she thought about it, the more she found they had much in common other than their looks. Only she saw Drew. Everyone else acted as if he didn't exist, servant and family alike.

Was Bain now laughing at her for being so easily duped? A sickening feeling spawned in the pit of her stomach and matured. As he had made love to her, hearing her call out her pleasure to a nonexistent person, had he in some twisted way received satisfaction?

Her lungs near to bursting, she slowed. Stumbling, she barely caught herself before she fell; the tears were so thick in her eyes she had trouble seeing where she placed her feet. Soon she was sobbing, her breath coming in great gulps, her heart shattering into a million pieces.

What kind of a monster had she fallen helplessly in love with? She sagged wearily on the porch steps and buried her face in her open palms, unable to accept that anyone could be so cruel.

The two distinct personalities meshed in her mind. Drew and Bain. She loved him, yet she hated him with all of her heart. Then the image divided, leaving confusion.

Her head lifted and she swiped at the tears. Was she merely jumping to an unfounded conclusion? Perhaps the *vaquero* was mistaken. Bain and Drew

311

looked exactly alike. If she could confuse them, wouldn't the stallion also be unable to tell them apart? Bain deserved an opportunity to explain. Yes. Yes. She would gladly give him that chance.

Rising, she straightened her gown and brushed back an ash-blonde curl that had escaped her hairpins. If Bain was not in his office, his rooms, or the stables, where would she find him? As she marched through the door into the front room the answer she received was not encouraging. Nowhere.

"Risen and gone," the maid had said. "Left us," the ranch hand had stated. Like a judge's gavel lifting and striking home, his flight condemned him. An innocent man wouldn't run away. Bain Carson had used her and deserted her, and the sinking feeling in the pit of her stomach told her he wouldn't be back, would never bother to explain or apologize.

But the answers she wanted were still within her grasp. Vividly she recalled her first meeting with Mae Ching. The child had insisted that Bain was not her uncle, merely that he had stolen the spirit of her father. The little girl knew more about this situation, the truth was in her innocent statement, and Garnet was determined to get to the bottom of this unsavory mystery.

From a distance she could hear laughter, youthful, unbridled enjoyment. Nattie, the child-woman that she was, apparently was making faces with her food, much to the delight of Choie Seem and Mae Ching. Unsupervised, except for Inez, who would never interfere unless one of the girls was in trouble, Nattie grew bold in her antics, flipping a piece of bacon into the air from a balanced fork. They all laughed when it dropped on the floor.

Watching them made Garnet feel old, much older than twenty-one. She cleared her throat, making her

312

presence known, and had to suppress a chuckle as the girls scrambled to resume decorum in the dining room.

"*Sse Mo*," Choie Seem choked, draping her forgotten napkin across her lap and trying to appear as if nothing out of the ordinary had taken place.

Nattie looked up, her expression the one of the cat who had stolen the cream, and snatched up her fork, pretending to eat.

Only Mae Ching—dear, sweet Mae Ching—made no pretense to cover up what had been going on. "You should see the trick that Nattie can do," she warbled.

"Ssh," both of the older girls hissed, and only then did the child grow quiet.

"Nattie is full of tricks," Garnet replied, settling in her customary chair and taking up her napkin. She shot the older girls a look of disapproval.

Inez bustled in. Spying Garnet, she rolled her eyes. "Ah, *señorita*, I am glad you are here. The *niñas*, they are a handful. Too much for an old woman like me." Quickly she served Garnet a plate and started to leave. Then as an afterthought, she reached into the deep pocket of her apron and brought out a leather pouch. "For you," she announced, placing it beside Garnet's hand.

Garnet glanced at the offering, a feeling akin to fear mushrooming in her middle. The pouch was from Bain, of that she was sure. Her breakfast forgotten, she unlaced the leather thong and reached into the pouch's depths. There she discovered passage for both her and Choie Seem, the Oriental girl's to China and hers . . . to England.

England? But she wanted to go back to China, find her father, learn the fate of her students left in the hidey-hole in the rectory. She groped in the pouch once more and discovered a folded letter. Her heart quickened. From Bain. Who else would write to her?

She tore open the sealed envelope, and to her shock she discovered a neat stack of money and her father's handwriting, his familiar scrawl almost illegible. She smiled. *Dear Father. Always in such a hurry.*

Her smile faded when she read what he had to say.

Go home to England? But she wanted to be with him. She read on. At least the children were all safe and had thought the whole ordeal an exciting adventure. The people of the village had not been so easily soothed, and now the Church was sending him to Siam. She wanted to be with him, she could help him in so many ways. Didn't he miss her as much as she missed him?

She dropped her hands, still holding the letter, into her lap. Home to England. No matter what her personal feelings, she would do what her father instructed, but she couldn't help feeling betrayed, not only by her father, but by Bain as well.

Bain. Had he nothing to say to her? She felt into the pouch once more and came up empty-handed. No. Apparently he felt he owed her no explanation.

"Sse Mo?"

She glanced at Choie Seem, noting the worried look on the Oriental girl's face. Smiling, she waved the letter. "Good news, Choie Seem. This letter is from my father."

The girl sat up straight, eager for news.

"All is well, the children fine, and this . . ." Garnet waved the tickets in the air. "You're going home, back to your family."

Expecting the girl to be overwrought with joy, Garnet couldn't believe when she frowned instead and shook her head. "Oh, no. I want to stay here."

"Stay here?" The tickets, so precious, dropped from Garnet's fingers, forgotten. "But why?"

"It's Mateo. He's asked me to marry him."

Garnet's mouth dropped open. Marriage? Oddly enough, all she could think of was the childish way

314

Choie Seem had acted moments before. She was too young to consider a husband and the responsibilities that came with one. But looking at the girl's earnest face, Garnet realized there would be no changing her mind. Perhaps she *was* being too protective. In China girls Choie Seem's age married all the time. But Choie Seem was her friend—the thought of leaving her behind . . .

Then Garnet remembered. She was leaving her companion behind anyway as she was going home to England. "Very well, Choie Seem." She tried hard to look pleased. "Are you sure you know what you're doing?" she couldn't help asking.

"I know," she replied with a great rush of enthusiasm. "Mateo says that *Señor* Bain has promised to build houses for any of the *vaqueros* who take a wife and settle permanently on the *rancho*. Just think, *Sse Mo*, my very own house."

Garnet could well understand the girl's excitement. In China, especially in small villages like the one Choie Seem came from, many generations of a family might live in one small dwelling. To have one's very own home was a luxury reserved for the very rich. She leaned forward, cupped her friend's hand with her own, and gave it a squeeze. "I'm happy for you, Choie Seem. Truly I am."

The Oriental girl rose out of her chair and moved to stand beside Garnet. Without hesitation Garnet stood to meet her, and they hugged, the silent communication between them strong and undeniable.

"Oh, Garnet, I shall miss you so," the girl at last sobbed, calling her by her given name for the very first time Garnet could remember.

"And I you," she choked in a voice already wrought with emotion from the discovery of Bain's possible deception.

Choie Seem leaned back and gave her a puzzled

look. "Are you sure *you* wish to leave Rancho Carmelo?"

"I must," she whispered. "There are things you don't understand." She cleared her throat, forcing her tone to resume normalcy. "There are things I don't understand. Besides"—she curved her lips into a smile—"my returning to England is my father's wish. It would be wrong to disobey him."

Choie Seem frowned. "Yes, I suppose, but what about . . . Captain Carson?" She searched Garnet's face for signs of her true feelings.

Which Garnet hid behind propriety. She had a sneaking suspicion Choie Seem knew what was going on. Lifting her chin, she asked. "Do you mean Drew or Bain? Or is there a difference."

"Why . . . why," the girl stumbled, apparently unsure how to respond.

"Of course there is a difference," came a confident reply.

They both turned to look at Nattie, who was staring at them in consternation.

"Drew and Bain are twins," she went on to explain. "But we rarely see Drew, he's at sea a lot—doesn't care much for the ranch."

Garnet glanced at Choie Seem, who gave her a perplexed shrug. "Tell me, Nattie, when was the last time you saw your brother Drew?" Garnet asked.

The girl paused to think, one slim finger poised on her bottom lip. "Well. It's been quite a while. I'd say over a year ago. I was in Monterey the day he arrived in port, and he told me he had a very important secret to tell me." She frowned, the perfect arch of her brows coming together. "I remember Bain gave him a nasty look. Then they spoke off to the side, and Drew left before he got a chance to tell me his important news."

"That wasn't the last time my father was here."

They all turned to face Mae Ching.

"When did you last see him?" Garnet asked in a

quiet, unexcited voice though her heart beating frantically against her rib cage.

"Why just a few months ago when he brought me here to America."

"And you haven't seen him since?" With bated breath Garnet waited for a negative reply.

"How could he come back? He died."

Garnet had expected any answer but that one. She glanced at Choie Seem, who shook her head, then she turned her attention to Nattie.

The poor girl had gone pale with shock. Her lips trembled, and her head wobbled back and forth in denial. "No. That's not true. Bain would have told me." She looked to Garnet. "Please, tell me that's not true."

Garnet's heart, which was crying out its own refusal to accept, went out to Nattie. Apparently Bain had deceived his sister as well. Why? Why would he do that? "Mae Ching, are you sure?"

The little girl nodded. "Oh, yes, *Sse Mo*," she insisted. "The cabin velly dark. When Uncle Bain came in I not see his face, but Father hurt velly bad and yelling. Uncle Bain yelling too. I not understand what they say, but Mae Ching velly frightened, so I hide in the shadows." She looked around at the intense faces and struggled on in her imperfect English. "I know when Father die, Uncle Bain began to cry, then he turn and I see his face. All I could think was that he steal my father's spirit. I scream. I call him a white devil." The little girl's voice cracked with emotion unexpressed until now. "I remember the last thing I see when he carry me away from my father's cabin. Father's unseeing eyes staring back at me." She sobbed and buried her face into her tiny hands. "He die."

If what Mae Ching said was the truth, then Drew had been dead long before she met him in San Francisco. Pushing her feelings of anger and confusion aside, she gave her attention to Mae Ching and Nattie, both of whom were sobbing pitifully. She so wanted to comfort them, but what could she say? Soothing words to one might only cause the other to grow even more upset. Silently she held the two girls allowing them to weep.

Soon the wails quieted into sniffs.

"Don't worry," Garnet said, gently stroking the dark hair of both girls. "I plan to find out the truth from Bain."

Nattie lifted her head, her eyes so like her brother's narrowing with determination. "Yes. We'll find Bain and make him tell us the truth." She stood and made a move toward his office.

"Nattie, he's not there."

The girl spun about. "Then where is he?"

"I'm not sure. I've looked everywhere for him this morning, and from what I can gather he's left the ranch."

Her little chin notched, and Garnet's heart lurched in understanding. The girl reminded her of herself when faced with adversity. Once Nattie grew up she would be a very capable young woman.

"Then we'll just have to figure out where he's gone," Nattie announced. She turned and marched across the courtyard toward Bain's rooms.

Garnet followed, as did Mae Ching and Choie Seem. She had an uneasy feeling about Nattie. "How do you figure to do that?"

"It's easy. I've a system that never fails."

Soon they were in front of his door. Without hesitation Nattie pushed it open and entered the sanctity of his bedroom. On the threshold Garnet paused, but couldn't help glancing around. Bain's room. She'd never been in there. "Nattie, this isn't seemly."

The girl spun about, indignation on her face. "So?

318

Why not, if he's lied to me?"

Garnet wanted to say two wrongs don't make a right, but she sensed Nattie held the key to figuring out how to track down her brother. Right or wrong, it was imperative to find him. "What is this system of yours, Nattie?" she questioned with a sigh of resignation.

The girl began opening drawers and wardrobe doors. "By how much he takes I know how long he'll be gone. Hm-m-m." She thumbed through the few clothes she found there. "And by what he takes where he's going." She pivoted and glanced at the others, a shrewd, mischievous twist to her features. "That way I can decide what kind of a gift I can expect from him when he gets back." Without a qualm she continued her obviously experienced snooping.

"Well, what did you decide?" Garnet demanded at last. She sounded more anxious than she'd intended, but she couldn't help it. She wouldn't rest easy until she'd confronted Bain.

"A very long time, and I would say . . . San Francisco." Nattie grinned triumphantly.

"How can you be so sure?" Skepticism rang in Garnet's voice.

The girl's smile widened, and she pointed at the nearly empty wardrobe. "He took his fancy clothes. He only does that when he goes to San Francisco."

San Francisco. Such a long way. With a shiver of apprehension, Garnet recalled only too clearly the fateful events of her arrival in America. Returning to that cesspool was the last thing she wanted to do, yet go back she would. But how?

Then she remembered the tickets in the leather pouch, and it seemed to her she'd seen passage from Monterey to the city. She hurried from the bedroom to the dining room, discovering the pouch she'd abandoned in her chair. Delving into the deep

319

pocket, she found what she was looking for. Passage from Monterey to San Francisco—ten days from now.

"Damn!" The cuss word slipped out before she could stop it. Guiltily she glanced over her shoulder to find she had an audience.

"What's wrong?" Nattie asked, unruffled by her outburst.

"My passage to San Francisco isn't until the end of next week. If I wait that long, Bain might be gone, but I'm not sure how to get there any quicker."

"That's easy," Nattie replied. "The stagecoach comes through the valley once a week every Thursday. That's tomorrow. We can catch it at Rancho Los Coches. In San Jose we can get on the train to the city."

"How do you know so much, Nattie?" Though she was pleased to receive the information, Garnet felt the need to express concern.

The girl shrugged. "I just know. In case I ever decide to run away."

"Oh, Nattie." Garnet wanted to applaud the very same "inventiveness" she'd attempted to squelch in the child not so long ago. She started to smile, then remembered exactly what the girl had said and frowned instead. *"We* can catch the stage?"

Nattie nodded ever so confident.

"Nattie, this is something I must do alone."

The girl's nod rotated into a shake of refusal. "No. I have a right to confront Bain too."

"Look, Nattie, you have every right, once he comes home."

"He won't be coming home soon. I've got to know about Drew. I can't wait months. That's forever."

Waiting wasn't easy when one was young. Garnet could testify to that only too well. How many times had she said the same thing to her own father when he had suggested she stay behind while he went on his next assignment? But take Nattie with her? She ust wasn't sure.

"Garnet, if you go without me, I'll only follow," the girl warned. "You can't stop me. Besides, I know how to locate Bain in San Francisco, you don't."

"Tell me, Nattie," she demanded, not doubting for a moment the girl had her ways of knowing.

"Not unless you take me with you." Nattie's knob of a chin jutted.

Garnet's lifted also. They stood staring at each other. Realizing the girl was as determined as she was, Garnet took a deep, frustrated breath. Nattie was right. How would she ever locate Bain in a big city like San Francisco without so much as a clue as to where to start? A thorough search could take days, even weeks, time she couldn't spare. "All right, Nattie. We'll go together."

The girl squealed her delight.

"But," Garnet said, "you must remember your manners and that I am in charge. Do you understand?"

"Oh, yes, Garnet. You're in charge. I'll get ready to go." She raced away before Garnet could give her any further instructions.

"May I go too?"

Mae Ching's request was one Garnet fully expected. She knelt down beside the little girl whom over the months she'd grown incredibly fond of. Her china-doll face was streaked with the remnants of her tears. Garnet brushed at them with the sleeve of her dress. "No, Mae Ching. I'm sorry."

"When will you be back?" the child asked, her face radiating trust.

Garnet couldn't lie to her, and didn't have the heart to tell her the truth. She glanced at Choie Seem as she groped for the right words to say, and found her throat choked tighter when she saw the mist in the young Oriental woman's eyes. A vision of Choie

321

Seem married and having children filled her mind. A sputter of tear-induced laughter erupted from her mouth when she found there was no right way to tell Mae Ching good-bye.

"Come, Mae Ching. Until *Sse Mo* returns we'll have each other. Don't worry," Choie Seem said in a voice husky with emotion. "I'll take good care of her."

She nodded, unable to speak, confident that the time she'd spent teaching the young woman had not been wasted. Choie Seem would make an excellent protector, and eventually a mother. Clutching Mae Ching to her heart, Garnet wanted more than anything to be able to tell the child she'd be back. Oh, God, how she wished she could come back. But that wasn't possible. Not now.

She rose, giving the little girl one last squeeze.

"And don't worry, *Sse Mo*," Choie Seem assured her with the authority of a mature woman as she gathered Mae Ching to her side, "I'll ask Mateo to arrange an escort for you to the stage."

How she yearned to ask Choie Seem to watch out for Bain's domain, and Bain as well, should he return to Rancho Carmelo. Instead she forced a smile to her lips and replied woman to woman. "Thank you, Choie Seem. I would appreciate that very much."

Chapter Nineteen

The rolling rhythm of the train worked its magic on Garnet. Her eyes grew heavy, though in truth she wasn't tired. Her chin drifted toward her chest. As her head nodded, the clickity-click of the wheels against the rails became the voice of her father.

"Gar-r-net."

She raced toward him, amazed to find herself a little girl again. Reaching him, she encircled his familiar waist, burying her face against his great coat.

"Oh, Father. I pray to God each night I will hurry up and get grown so we can be together always."

The Reverend Sinclair gathered her closely, urging her little hands to explore the depths of his deep pockets. To Garnet's delight her fingers discovered three pieces of taffy. Father always brought her surprises. Carefully she unwrapped one piece and slipped it into her mouth, chewing slowly to enjoy every morsel of her treat. The others she clutched in her fist—for later. "Oh, Father, I asked God to . . ."

His finger pressed against her taffy-tainted lips. "Careful, daughter, what you ask of God. He always listens and answers our prayers."

Peering up at his wise, loving face, she demanded, "But isn't that what we want him to do? Give us what we wish for?"

"Are you so sure about that? Sometimes we ask for things that aren't good for us—like growing up before we are ready."

"I don't care, Father." She nestled against his coat aware she left a sticky taffy stain. Her father saw it too, and ignored it. But then that wasn't unusual. He rarely scolded her, merely tried to show her the error of her ways with gentle guidance. "I want to always be with you, and I do want to grow up now. I do," she assured him.

"Ah, Garnet girl. Growing up isn't the answer to all of our problems. Just remember what I said. Be careful of what you ask of God, you just might receive it."

"Receive it. Receive it. Receive it."

Whoo-a-whoo.

Garnet's head jerked up, and she was aware she was on the train from San Jose to San Francisco, no longer sheltered from reality by her father's comforting presence. The wheels squealed as brakes were pressed against them, and the locomotive began to slow down, a great lumbering beast of iron and steel.

"Are we there yet?" she sleepily asked a wide-eyed Nattie, at the moment glad to have the girl's company.

Nattie nodded, her eyes glued to the scene taking place beyond the window by which she sat. Garnet leaned forward to look too. What she saw wasn't pleasing. People were everywhere, pressing, shoving, some even shouting. Then they would roll out of sight to be replaced by more. She wasn't so sure anymore she wanted to tackle the heartless city that stretched out before her. Maybe she should just send Nattie home, take her passage to England tucked in her reticule, and forget all about Bain and Drew and the real man who was somewhere between the two.

The whistle blew one last time, followed by the

whoosh of steam from the stationary wheels. As she remembered the dream she'd just had, her father's final warning, one he'd given her over and over for as long as she could remember, still echoed in her mind.

"Be careful what you ask of God, you just might receive it."

At last his prophecy made perfect sense. She had repeatedly wished for a man who possessed certain aspects of Drew's and Bain's personalities. Well, she was relatively certain she had gotten what she'd asked for. Now that she had it, this perfect man she'd conjured, she wasn't sure how to react. But regardless, she had to face him, face God's granting of her unthought-out prayers.

The other passengers in the car stood and began crowding out of the train. Garnet waited for them to clear, though Nattie repeatedly asked her what she was waiting for.

"Patience is a virtue," she replied. God, how she sounded like her father spouting Biblical verse. She glanced at Nattie, saw her eager anticipation. Was that how she used to be not so long ago? Impetuous, anxious to meet the world head on?

When at last she stood and walked down the aisle to the exit, she wished with all of her heart she could simply turn around and sit back down. Since that was not an option, she continued on. Reaching the steps, she descended them slowly, one at a time, as if at the bottom awaited her doom.

The smells and noise of the city assaulted her. After spending all that time in the quiet cleanliness of Rancho Carmelo, the stench of city sewer and station yard, intermingled with the unpleasant racket of the trains and people, grated on her senses.

Only a few yards away a group of young Oriental girls were being held in check by several grotesquely large Chinamen. She knew immediately they were slave girls being forced to go where they didn't wish to go. She could hear the singsongy voice of the slavemonger ordering them to move ahead and board the train. She tried to see him, but he was hidden behind his henchmen. Images of her own experience at the hands of men like these filled her mind. How vividly she remembered the faces staring at her with lust and greed, and the gray-eyed American who had risked his life to rescue her.

Glancing about the train yard, she found it hard to believe the citizens of San Francisco could be so callous. Not one person seemed to notice the women or care about their predicament. Not one! What she wouldn't give to be able to help them. Seriously considering rushing forward and making a scene to give the girls a chance to escape, Garnet paused. Nattie bumped into her back, and she realized she had more than herself to think about. Her desire to help victimized women would have to wait. But she wouldn't forget them. Some day . . .

She turned to speak to Nattie. Steam poured from the mighty engine, and the whistle blew a warning to passengers boarding to hurry. Over the hullabaloo she practically had to shout to get the girl's attention. "Where to now?"

Nattie glanced about, her gaze taking in everything. "We have to find. . . ."

The train whistle blew so loud and close Garnet couldn't hear her. "What?"

"The hotel."

"Which one?" she shouted back.

"The Grand. Bain always stays at the Grand."

"Are you sure?" Before Nattie answered, Garnet knew she would be.

The girl nodded.

Garnet didn't question her further. An uneasy feeling cloaked her and crept down her spine. She just wanted to get out of the station as quickly as she could. "Come on. We'll find a cab to take us." The fare was no problem. She had the money her father had sent to her.

Once out in the street, the task of locating a carriage was harder than she'd anticipated. There were several in sight, but the passengers that had departed the train before them had already engaged their services. There was nothing to do except wait until the crowd dispersed and the vehicles returned to take on more fares.

Patience is a virtue, she reminded herself, but she couldn't eliminate the strange need to get out of the train station as quickly as possible. It was almost as if someone watched her every move. But that was ridiculous. It was just all those wide-open spaces back at the ranch and the image of those poor girls being forced to board the train that left her feeling so hemmed in, nothing more.

Time inched by slowly; the crowd began dispersing in small groups, some on foot, some in cabs, others with friends and family in private vehicles. Soon she and Nattie were standing alone. Across the thoroughfare and down a ways she saw a street sign proclaiming they were on Third. She considered asking directions to the Grand Hotel and walking, but there were the bags to consider. She didn't want to leave them at the station unattended.

Then in the distance she saw an approaching carriage. She straightened and lifted her hand to flag the driver down. The man smiled and acknowledged her, and reined the horse toward where she and Nattie stood.

Relief swathed her. It was dusk, and she'd not relished the idea of standing on the streets at night.

The vehicle stopped at the curb, and the driver jumped down from the dickey and came around to where she stood.

"Yes, ma'am. Where can I take you?"

"The Grand Hotel." She noticed the man hadn't

doffed his hat, but she put his lack of physical manners—he'd spoken to her most politely—down to city breeding. "We have baggage in the station."

He nodded. "Why don't you hop aboard. You ladies can sit and rest on the inside while I round up your luggage."

Garnet was only too willing to take him up on his offer. When he opened the carriage door, she allowed Nattie to step inside first, then followed, accepting the cabbie's hand in assistance.

In the dark interior she joined Nattie on the seat, concentrating on arranging her skirts. "I can't tell you how glad I am this carriage came along when it did," she said to a strangely quiet Nattie. "To be quite frank, I was beginning to feel a little uneasy there in the station. Don't ask me why, but . . ."

"Garnet?"

The uncertainty in Nattie's voice brought her nervous chatter to a halt. She glanced up, and her gaze fell on the unexpected occupant on the opposite seat of the carriage. The slanted Oriental eyes were familiar.

"Oh," she gasped, her breath catching on a rush of fear.

"At last, we meet, White Lotus. When I saw you step from the train, I couldn't believe my good fortune." The singsong of the Chinaman's voice made her shiver.

She could never forget the man's long, unpleasant face and his cold, unnerving stare. He had been standing beside Drew the day she'd been forced to undress at the barracoon. Then he had pulled out an evil-looking knife and threatened to take his revenge. Garnet tried to swallow the painful lump in her throat. She could tell by the way his gaze slid over her, he thought the time ripe to collect his due.

She inched her hand along the seat, groping for Nattie's. Once she found the girl's icy, trembling fingers, she squeezed them, trying to convey her urgent message. Without turning her head she studied the view outside the carriage window. As far as she could see all was clear.

"You are more beautiful than I remember. Captain Carson must have treated you velly well, better than most of his . . . women." He leaned forward as if to touch her, and the repulsion of his gesture set her in motion.

Grasping the door handle, she threw her weight against it. The barrier flew open, and clutching Nattie, she tumbled out of the carriage. The fact that the Oriental sat calmly in his seat making no effort to stop her alarmed her. But whatever his reason, she didn't stop to think about it. She and Nattie had to get out of there.

Since the carriage steps had been pushed underneath, Garnet fell to her knees in the street. The unprepared Nattie landed on top of her, the heel of her traveling shoe coming down hard on Garnet's bare fingers. But she was not about to be daunted by mere pain. Scrambling to her feet, she grabbed Nattie with her good hand and began to run.

Right into the solid wall of the Chinaman's henchmen.

She screamed when her hands were twisted behind her back. Swinging her feet in an attempt to kick her assailant, she found she might as well be striking out at tree trunks. The man who held her didn't even issue a single grunt of discomfort. She glanced to the side, hoping beyond reason that Nattie might have gotten away. The girl was putting up a more than fair tussle, unfettered by any social mandates. Though she was held firmly, her teeth were buried in the forearm of her captor. The man yelped, and swinging back one great paw, he whacked the girl on the side of the head. Nattie clung, refusing to let go, and the henchman swung again.

"No," Garnet screamed, fearing the man would kill her companion if he struck her again. She squirmed against the pain in her own shoulder in an attempt to escape until she could take no more. "No, Nattie," she groaned, her knees collapsing in surrender.

Like a loyal collie, the girl unclamped her jaws and looked to Garnet for further instructions. She could only offer a helpless but hopeful stare in return. She might be bested for the moment, but she was not defeated.

Dragged back toward the carriage, Garnet noted the driver standing off to one side. She gave him a pleading look, hoping to find assistance there, but he glanced away, refusing to acknowledge her plea. Her captor bound her hands behind her back and lifted her bodily into the vehicle, tossing her unceremoniously inside.

There the Chinaman waited for her, his mouth curled in an unpleasant smile, one she recognized as dangerous. "I find your disobedience velly unsatisfying, White Lotus. If you continue resisting I will have to beat you."

Nattie was shoved into the interior, her hands bound, her eyes wide with fear. "Garnet, who are these men?"

The Oriental's attention swung to the girl. His eyes narrowed, assessing. "Velly young. Velly marketable." He turned to Garnet. "But not near as desirable as you, my *zhenpin*."

"I am not your treasure," she declared in Chinese, her chin tilting noticeably.

He laughed. "Ah, so. Li Fung forget the morsel speaks the true language. Tell me, White Lotus, has the captain grown tired of you and cast you into the streets so soon?"

The carriage lurched forward, and crowded in one corner of the cab Garnet debated her best answer.

"Captain Carson will be looking for me when we don't show up."

"We?" he asked, his shrewd mind missing nothing. "Who might your companion be?"

Should she tell him who Nattie was, or was it better to conceal the girl's identity? She decided the Carson name might serve as protection. "She is Captain Carson's little sister."

Fung swung his attention to Nattie, showing interest.

"And if you are smart, you will not harm her. Not unless you wish to anger Captain Carson."

"Garnet," the girl whispered, the terror of not knowing what was being said evident in her voice, "what is he saying about me?"

She gave Nattie a look meant to comfort and silence at the same time, and returned her attention to their adversary.

"Captain Carson does not scare me," the Chinaman boasted in an imperial tone. "I can make many *yuan* on the sale of this girl."

"Then you know nothing of the captain's powerful brother," Garnet snapped right back, hoping to bluff him.

"Brother? What brother?"

"His tong is very respected in Monterey. If you should harm his sister his men will hunt you down in revenge." She spoke a language she knew this highbinder understood. She prayed he believed her story.

Apparently he did, as he straightened and grew silent as if thinking out his next steps. The carriage continued on its way, the occupants of the inside swaying in unison to its rhythm. Li Fung studied her, dissected her, looking for signs of weakness.

Garnet made it a point to show not a flicker of fear, though her insides quivered like boiled gelatin.

The interior of the carriage moved in and out of

331

shadow as the vehicle traveled down gaslit streets. In the darkness Garnet could hear her own heart hammering away as she wondered what her abductor was thinking. Then a finger of light would find its way inside, illuminating the Chinaman's face. In those precious moments she could read his indecision. Was there a chance he might reconsider and let them go?

When at last the carriage came to a stop, Garnet glanced outside. They were somewhere in the twisting, narrowing streets of Chinatown as she could smell the sharp odor of fried fish and incense.

She swallowed down the feelings of helplessness and terror that left her cold and hollow. "If you are wise, Li Fung, you will heed my warning," she said, hoping her boastful lies might have made him unsure.

"If you are wise, White Lotus," he countered, leaning so close she could smell onions on his breath, "you will do what I tell you. Your concern for the girl is commendable." He glanced at Nattie, then reached out one long-nailed hand and caressed her arm. "If in truth you want no harm to come to her, then you will heed my every wish." His thin, cruel lips curled upward.

Her skin crawled with revulsion, but she didn't dare pull away. By the leering gleam in his eyes she knew exactly what he would demand of her.

The carriage door opened. At Li Fung's insistence, she allowed one of the henchmen who had apparently followed the vehicle on foot to help her down. She turned, expecting Nattie to follow. Instead Li Fung joined her, then two of his men climbed into the carriage.

"Garnet!" Nattie's frightened scream echoed in the darkness and was muffled.

"Dear God, Nattie!" She tried to return to the carriage, which was beginning to move away.

The stinging slap of Li Fung's hand against her cheek momentarily stunned her, long enough for the carriage to get out of range. "Silence, I say," his singsongy voice demanded.

Pain puddled in Garnet's jade-green eyes as they followed the vehicle rattling down the street. The cabbie looked back once, and for a moment she thought she saw a spark of compassion in his gaze, but then he turned away.

Compassion? Not likely. She choked on her own skepticism, unable to stop the sob of frustration that erupted from her chest. There was no compassion in this world. Only the fanciful delusions of a foolish woman who should know better than to look for heroes where none existed.

Chapter Twenty

Stepping up to the lobby counter, Bain waited for the man in front of him to complete his business with the desk clerk. With all of the details of his cargo arranged, he was anxious to check out and return to the *China Jewel*. Trying not to show his impatience with the crudely dressed fellow who seemed out of place in the Grand Hotel foyer, he found himself eavesdropping on what the man was saying.

"Are ya sure there ain't no Drew Carson stayin' here?"

"I'm quite positive, sir," the clerk answered without a blink of an eye though his mouth puckered in distaste. He glanced at Bain over his wire-rimmed glasses seeking approval.

Hearing his brother's name, Bain straightened. He studied the inquiring man's back. What would this person want with his brother? He held his tongue, deciding chances were there were a lot of people in San Francisco who would like to get their hands on Drew.

When Bain didn't respond, the clerk dismissed the man and his questions as trivial by turning his attention to the paying guest who had been made to wait. "Yes, sir. How can I be of service?" Bain noted that the hotel employee carefully avoided using his name.

"Room one-twelve. I would like to check out." He continued to watch the shabbily dressed man as he shuffled by, muttering.

"I coulda swore she said the Grand Hotel."

Something about the stranger struck Bain as not the type his brother would have kept company with. Besides, Drew always stayed at the Palace. Why would anyone come looking for him here at the Grand?

"Will that be cash, Mr. Carson, or shall we send you your usual bill?" the clerk inquired now that the other man was out of hearing range.

"Hm-m-m? What?" Bain turned back to the clerk. "Cash," he replied, reaching into his jacket pocket for his money.

"I'm sorry about that, sir." The clerk angled his thumb toward the stranger, who disappeared through the front door. "That man's a local cabbie. I figured if you'd wished to pursue his inquiry you would have spoken up."

"Yes, of course. Did he say anything else?" Bain couldn't help but ask.

"Not really. Asked for a Drew Carson. Mentioned something about a lady needing his help."

"A lady?" The oddest feeling that he had just allowed something important to slip through his fingers caught in his throat. The urge to find out what the cabbie wanted overrode his common sense. "The bill? How much?"

"Well, let's see." The clerk shuffled several papers. "I need to add up. . . ."

"Just guess." Bain shoved a wad of bills toward the man.

"But, sir, I must. . . ."

"If there's any left over send it to my Monterey address." Bain turned, gathered up his valise, and rushed toward the door through which the cabbie

ad left moments before, the image of the confused
otel clerk holding out the excessive amount of
honey the last thing he saw of the Grand Hotel.

"But, sir."

By then Bain was in the street, checking out every
arriage for hire, looking for the stranger. Damn, if
he man had managed to get away before he could
alk to him . . .

Then he spied the driver he sought mounting the
tand of his vehicle.

"Wait, cabbie," Bain shouted, waving his hand in
he air.

The man turned, looked him over. "Sorry, sir, I'm
ff duty. I'm—"

"I know. I heard you ask for Drew Carson."
Standing on the sidewalk staring up at the man, Bain
began to have second thoughts about his impulsive
ictions, but he'd gone this far; he might as well find
but what the man wanted. "Could you please tell me
vhy you are looking for him?"

"Are you him?" the cabbie asked, his own
suspicions rising to the surface.

Bain debated for only a moment. "No. But I'm his
prother," he confessed.

"Then why didn't you speak up before?"

"To be quite frank, people who are usually
looking for Drew are not out to make a friendly
call." He smiled crookedly. "But something about
you . . ."

"You trust me?" the cabbie asked.

"No, not really. You intrigued me, that's all."

The cabbie stared at him, looked up the street in
front of his carriage, then twisted to look behind him.
"Get inside, sir. We'll take a little ride, and we can
talk through the trapdoor."

Bain could sense the man's uneasiness, and he
considered turning down the request. "There's a lady
involved?" he demanded.

337

"Yes, sir, a pretty, little yella-haired gal and her dark-haired friend. They're in a peck of trouble."

With a resigned sigh, Bain crawled into the carriage. If this was another one of Drew's women . . . By damn, he was not going to get involved again. He had his own troubles with a "pretty, little yella-haired gal."

His heart snagged in his chest. Garnet? But that was impossible. She was at Rancho Carmelo waiting to go home. She wouldn't be in San Francisco—not yet.

The carriage took off and the trapdoor snapped open. Bain looked up, but couldn't make out the face of the cabbie. They moved along in silence for awhile, each waiting for the other to begin.

"You know Li Fung, the highbinder?" the cabbie finally asked.

"I know him," Bain replied, remembering well their one and only encounter. He had no desire to cross swords with the Chinaman again.

"The yella-haired gal and her friend got off the train. Fung made arrangements to pick them up—in my carriage. I owe him money, so I do what he says and don't ask no questions."

"So?" Bain still couldn't see a reason to show concern. Not yet. There were plenty of blonde women who might be getting off a train in a city as large as San Francisco.

"So this little gal didn't want to go with him. Seemed real upset. He called her White Lotus, and they spoke of your brother. Does that mean anything to you?"

A sickening feeling balled in the pit of his stomach. Garnet and Choie Seem. It had to be them. "More than you can imagine." Bain leaned forward and stuck his head out the window to convey his urgency. "Quickly, take me to where you dropped them off."

338

The driver kept his horse at an even pace. "Only a fool would try to go into Chinatown after Fung alone."

"A fool or a desperate man," Bain retorted. "Damn it, man, I don't have any choice."

"You wouldn't make it through the front door of his gaming house. Besides Fung would be after me in a moment. He'd recognize my cab. No, sir. I'm not gonna take that kind of risk, not even for a pretty, little yella-haired gal."

"Then by God," he roared his anger, "take me as close as you dare and give me directions the rest of the way."

Still no reaction.

Bain slammed his fist against the window ledge in frustration. What would make this man take an interest? His eyes narrowed, and his mouth flattened against his teeth. "There's money in it for you. Perhaps enough to pay off the Chinaman."

The clip-clop of the old nag that pulled the carriage sped up. Bain sat back in the seat and tried to compose himself, but the wheels in his mind raced ahead, much faster than the carriage. Damn it, he could run quicker than this, but he knew he needed the cover the cab afforded him and the time to work out a feasible plan.

Reaching across the seat into his valise, he took out a revolver, checked the bullet chambers to make sure the gun was fully loaded, and spun the cylinder.

He cast his gaze out the window, watching the buildings and citizenry of San Francisco slide by. How did Li Fung know of Garnet's arrival so quickly? The answer was only too obvious. The Chinaman had spies everywhere, knew everything that happened in his domain practically before it happened.

His eyes caught the image of a uniformed man on horseback. Perhaps there were untapped resources he'd overlooked—like the police. Leaning forward, he rapped on the ceiling to attract the driver's attention. "Whoa there," he ordered. "I want to get out for a moment." As soon as the carriage stopped, he scrambled out of the interior and approached the officer. The cabbie was right, trying to rescue Garnet on his own was foolish. He smiled up at the mounted policeman, hoping to have found a sympathetic ear.

Perhaps he wasn't alone after all.

Through the winding maze she trod, almost as if she were in a trance, yet Garnet was sharply aware of everything around her.

Above her she could hear the sounds coming from the mah-jongg parlor, where men lost their earnings at crooked gaming tables, or else to the prostitutes strategically stationed about the rooms to make sure no customer left the establishment with money in his pockets. As she passed the rooms of assignation, she could hear the prostitutes earning another day of life the only way open to these women, by selling their poor, battered bodies.

She stumbled and placed a palm against the wall beside her, and was appalled by the grease and filth she touched. Then a hand grasped her silk-encased arm, reminding her of her own fate, and forced her to move along.

The sickening sweet smell of opium hit her like a living, breathing wall. Led past an open door, she could see them, the men and women whose existences were controlled by the demon drug, surrounded by the hazy smoke of their addiction. Their moans were a blend of pleasure and defeat, lives trapped and destroyed by the product of an innocent-looking flower. Hell's irony. How could God allow such pain and horror?

But then God had deserted her as well, and left her

o make choices she had no desire to make.

Steered toward a closed door, she knew the end was near. Li Fung in all his glorious degradation waited for her. She knew the Oriental passion for servitude, knew she would do whatever she must to hopefully save Nattie, and knew that afterward she would crave only to die in order to avoid the continuous reliving of Hell.

The henchmen who held her halted, and one lifted his hand to knock. After a short, respectful pause he turned the knob and opened the door.

The room was dark, except for a small halo of light coming from a lantern on one wall. The smell of incense and opium wafted toward her, curling their evil tendrils about her in such a way she found it hard to breathe.

"Ah, at last. My White Lotus."

Pressed forward, she saw Li Fung at last, sitting cross-legged on a thin pallet hung with a richness of silks and brocades worth a small fortune. He was naked, his thin chest hairless and gleaming with oil, his . . . his preparedness to receive her proudly displayed between his spread thighs.

Garnet swallowed so hard it hurt. How could any man be so repulsive, yet so confident?

"Do come in, my *zhenpin.*"

Though his endearment sickened her, she said nothing. She didn't dare. Not until her guards pushed her forward did she move, then when they shoved her to her knees, she bowed her head, and found herself praying for deliverance, knowing in her heart her plea was in vain. God might hear her, but she feared his answer might come too late. Who was there to send to rescue her? No one. But she could do her best to see Nattie unharmed.

"Go," he ordered his men. His tone of voice suggested he was eager for the night of entertainment to begin.

Once they were alone, Garnet lifted her chin, but avoided looking directly at the Oriental, knowing if she did she would see him again in all his glorious lust. But filled with a martyr's zeal to commit self-sacrifice to save the innocent, she demanded in a loud voice, "Where is Nattie?"

His face transformed from repulsive to frightening at her show of courage, but Garnet held her ground feeling like Joan of Arc as the flame licked at the hem of her gown. Concern for Nattie's safety overrode her fears.

"The girl is where she is . . . protected," he replied. He showed his yellow teeth in what appeared to be a smile, but Garnet knew better. "You would not want her here, would you? Only working girls stay here."

Backed against a wall with no way to escape, she shook her head, comprehending that he looked upon her as merely a "working girl." How she performed her job determined not only her own right to live but Nattie's as well. A long, potent silence prevailed, one in which she prepared for the inevitable.

At last the Chinaman spoke. "Come here."

She slid one foot beneath her to rise.

"No, on your hands and knees you crawl. Show me the respect I am due."

Garnet lowered her foot and dropped to all fours and began inching forward.

"Lower, bitch. Your head must never be above mine."

Humiliation pooled on her lashes, but she did as she was told. From somewhere deep in her soul she heard her father's strong, lyrical voice singing, giving her courage.

"We shall gather at the ri-ver. The beautiful, the beautiful ri-i-ver."

A revolting hand slid over her hip and cupped her backside, fondling. At that moment her courage and her convictions failed her. Disgust gathered at the back of her throat, and she thought for sure she would retch. When Li Fung's fingers probed beneath the loose silk sahm, her entire body convulsed. She pulled away and slapped at the invading appendage. There was no way she would simply allow this man such freedoms without putting up a fight. God forgive her, but she was no martyr to sing hymns while he violated her.

Pushing up, she tried to stand, but Li Fung was swifter and rose first, twisting his fingers in her long, unbound hair. For his size his strength was amazing, and he shoved her back down on her knees before him. His dark gaze glistened with excitement and challenge, and she knew at that moment that he wanted her to resist, as it would serve to heighten his enjoyment.

She struck out at his vulnerable nakedness. He anticipated her attack and easily dodged her fist, jerking her head around and slapping her across the face. Then he waited for her next move. Like the mad dog he was, saliva gathered in the corner of his mouth, his lips opening to pant with excitement.

Her head ringing with the force of his punishment, her mind refused to function. Then as it cleared, she saw the glint of light reflect from the blade of the knife he held in his hand.

"You try my patience, bitch," Fung announced, wielding the weapon with an expert hand so close to her left cheek she could feel the wind from its movement.

She closed her eyes knowing the moment to be strong upon her. Could she do it? *Oh God, give me courage*, she pleaded inwardly.

The door to the room flew open. "You try more than my patience, you son of a bitch," declared a voice more welcome than had God Himself spoken.

Fung swung about to confront the new challenge, tossing Garnet down on the pallet as if she were a worthless rag.

That's when she saw him. Bain. The gentle unpretentious rancher standing in the door frame exposed, without a single means to defend himself as far as she could tell. But he was there to save her, and she completely lost her heart to him at that moment. Oh, God, please, she didn't want to lose him as well.

She gathered up her courage and her strength and leaped upon the unsuspecting Chinaman's back. "He has a knife," she screamed, willing to forfeit her own safety for the man she irrevocably loved.

The Oriental spun like a wounded bear, throwing her off balance and into the path of the knife. The cold blade pressed against her heart, and she welcomed it if only her sacrifice would save Bain.

"Let her go, Fung," Bain demanded, but the Oriental only laughed and raised his hand to plunge.

Garnet closed her eyes and prepared to die.

Then a shot rang out, and Fung's grip relaxed, the knife falling away and thumping against the floor. The Chinaman slumped forward against her back and slid downward, his slack body landing with a crash over his weapon. He was dead from a bullet between his slanted, sightless eyes.

Garnet looked up and saw the smoking gun in Bain's hand. Peering up into his face, she recognized the other side of his personality. Confident, sure, in charge of the situation, in direct contrast to the man she had just attempted to save. She recognized Drew. And she knew at that moment she loved this aspect of his personality as surely as the gentler side.

"Oh, Bain," she cried, throwing herself against his chest.

His arm curled about her automatically as she wept, mostly from relief that the terrible ordeal was over.

A swarm of uniformed officers filled the room, but the only presence that mattered to Garnet was Bain's.

She clung to him unashamedly, savoring the feel of his strong, solid arm about her.

"It's all right, Garnet," he soothed, his fingers brushing through her ash-blonde curls. "Hush now, *pequeña joya*. It's all over."

Garnet smiled to herself, knowing her suspicions correct. Only Drew called her that, never Bain. Then her smile turned into a frown. It wasn't over. There was Nattie.

"No, Bain." She backed up. "We still have to find—"

"I know. Not to worry. I know where they are keeping Choie Seem."

"Choie Seem?" she asked, her face blank. "Why she's still at the ranch."

"Then who was with you on the train?"

"Nattie," she whispered.

The stark fear on his face twisted her heart. "God Almighty, how could you have brought Nattie with you?" He gripped her shoulders so hard, she had to bite her tongue to keep from crying out. "Who gave you the right? She'll never survive such a terrible experience." He jerked her arm and dragged her over Li Fung's body and into the hallway, calling to the accompanying officer to follow him.

"I'm sorry, Bain." She clawed at his fingers where they dug into her flesh. "I would have never let her come if you hadn't—"

"If I hadn't what?" he demanded, releasing her so suddenly she almost fell against him.

"If you hadn't lied to her—and to me," she hissed. "Why didn't you tell her Drew was dead? Why didn't you tell *me* instead of allowing me to believe . . . believe there were two of you?"

His face contorted with self-condemnation. He looked longingly at her; then his expression hardened, and he offered her no explanation. "I won't lie to you now, damn it. If I don't get to Nattie soon, there will be no need to explain anything to her." He gripped her hand and led her down the hallway.

She would allow her accusations to ride for the moment, but as soon as they found Nattie, she wouldn't be so lenient.

Minutes later they were out in the street. Police were everywhere. She looked about blinking, unable to believe that all this hullabaloo was for her sake. The officers were rounding up the dead highbinder's henchmen, but no one paid much attention to the frightened Oriental women who were clustered off to one side.

"Why doesn't someone help them?" Garnet demanded as Bain steered her toward a group of officers standing near a carriage.

One of the policemen escorting them shook his head. "We tried, ma'am, but most of them refused to come with us. Those who do come probably won't tell us anything. Then before you know it, they'll be back on the streets. But then there's no place else for them to go. Nobody wants them."

As she looked back at the abandoned slave girls, Garnet's sense of Christian duty was aroused. There were so many like them who needed help—needed *her* help. She sighed in frustration. Right now Nattie had to be found, but she would remember these women as she had shared too much with them to ever forget.

She glanced toward the carriage they approached, and she recognized the driver—the same one who had been instrumental in bringing her here in the first place. He smiled sheepishly at her, and she returned a look of gratitude, her faith in human goodness somewhat restored. She could well imagine what he had risked to help her.

Bain gripped her arm as if he thought she might attempt to run away. She lifted the flowing hem of her sahm, prepared to enter the carriage, but to her surprise Bain handed her over to one of the uniformed men. "Escort her to the Grand Hotel and stay there with her."

"Bain," she cried out, tugging at the restraining hand on her arm with no results. "Let me go with you," she pleaded. "Nattie needs—"

"You've done enough for my sister already," he said, cutting her off with a vengeance. Then he dismissed her with a blank look and turned to her escort. "Don't let her out of your sight for a moment, or you'll be damned sorry."

"Yes, sir," the officer replied.

"Bain," she shrilled as he walked away, his shoulders straight. There was no regret or shame in Bain Carson. "Don't you walk away from me."

He didn't slow down, nor did he look back.

"Damn you," she railed, frustrated by her inability to do more. "Hate doesn't begin to describe what I feel for you," she shouted, but her words deflected off him as if he'd never heard her.

Accompanied by an officer Bain entered the carriage, which sped away. A contingent of mounted officers followed, the pounding of their horse's hooves ringing loudly on the pavement. Not sure where they were going, if they would find Nattie, or when Bain would be back, Garnet kept her gaze pinned on the vehicle until it rounded a corner and disappeared.

"Bain," she whispered, the fight and inner fire flickering in the wake of her fears. Her emotions were as tattered as one of the last autumn leaves tenaciously clinging to the tree, shredded by wind and rain, love and anger. Yes, he had saved her, that she couldn't deny, yet he had lied to her, taken advantage of her, then deserted her, all time and again. And now he'd wrongly accused her of harming Nattie, when in truth it was his *own* fault that his sister had come to the city. She had thrown herself into his arms seeking

347

solace and . . . his returned love, only to encounter his insensitive allegations and his refusal to see reason.

"Come on, miss, we'd better go along now," the policeman said.

Garnet lifted her chin with angry pride. Yes, she would go—for now. But she wasn't through with Bain Carson, not by a long shot. Her heart painfully skipped a beat. Unless he decided he had had enough of her.

Perched on the edge of the damask-covered sofa in the auspicious lobby of the Grand Hotel, Garnet nervously toyed with the crisp lace of her new kid gloves. In fact her entire outfit was new, purchased with the money her father had sent her. No longer would she wear the charity of Bain Carson. Nor would she accept his arrangements with the hotel to pay her bill. She was quite capable of taking care of herself, thank you.

But she was nervous just the same.

It had been two days since the night of her rescue, two long, uninformative days. All she had learned from the officer who had guarded her was that Nattie had been located in the private home of a Chinese family, and she had been taken to a hospital.

Was she injured? He hadn't known. Where was Bain? He hadn't known that either.

Then the messenger had arrived with the letter, most properly composed. Bain requested she meet him in the lobby this afternoon. What he would say to her? She had no idea. What she would say to him? She couldn't be sure.

When at last she saw him coming down the lobby stairs, her heart beat so rapidly in her throat that she couldn't swallow, much less conjure up the anger on which she'd thrived the last two days. He wore his "fancy clothes," as Nattie had labeled them, doe-brown dress jacket with matching pants, a waistcoat of a lighter tan, the collar of his cream-colored shirt starched against his neck—very proper, right down to the bowler grasped in his strong, brown fingers.

"Miss Sinclair," he said in a voice as stiff as his collar. His gaze slid over her newly purchased percale walking dress with approval, then he returned his gray-eyed inspection to her face. "I appreciate your agreeing to meet with me today."

She dipped her chin, and consciously had to keep her eyes staring straight ahead and her hands curled sedately in her lap. "I did not mind at all." What did he want to say to her?

"The purpose of this meeting is twofold." He remained standing before her.

"Please, Mr. Carson, won't you sit down?"

At her polite request he selected the wing chair next to the sofa. "Thank you," he said, clearing his throat as he settled in his seat.

"As you were saying, Mr. Carson?" She waited for him to continue.

This was all wrong. She should be telling him how she felt, the terrible turmoil she was going through, her need to share her confusion with him. Why had he deceived her so?

"As I was saying, the reason I asked for this meeting is twofold. First, to make sure you have your ticket for the ship and all is in order for your departure on Wednesday."

She nodded. Yes, she had everything. Her reticule had been intact—tickets, money, personal items— along with her clothing, which the police had found at the gaming house.

"Good."

She leaned forward in anticipation. Would he ask her to stay? Would she stay if he asked her? Her heart fluttered its answer. Yes, oh, yes.

349

"Then I'll see to it you have an escort from the hotel to the docks—for your safety."

She sat back, a feeling of abandonment piercing her fragile heart. "Thank you, Mr. Carson. Your considerate gesture is appreciated." She hid her disappointment very well, if she had to say so herself.

He looked at her for one long moment, as if trying to decipher her true feelings. "The other thing I wanted to tell you was that I don't blame you for Nattie's condition."

"Condition? Has she been injured?" She sprang forward like a cat.

"No, not physically. But . . ." He paused.

"Please, don't you think I have a right to know? I"—she hunted for just the right way to express her feelings without giving herself completely away—"care for your little sister deeply."

He smiled ever so sadly. "Yes, she cares for you too. When I found her . . ." Again he cleared his throat. "When I found her," he repeated in a stronger voice, "her first concern was for you."

"How is she? May I see her?" Garnet gushed before she could stop herself.

"No, I'm afraid not."

It wasn't right that he denied her one last chance to see the girl. She opened her mouth to say as much, then she shut it when he began to speak.

"You see, she is under the strict care of a . . . special physician. A doctor of psychiatry. I tried so long to protect her, but apparently that was the wrong thing to do. I am responsible for her present condition, Miss Sinclair. Not you—me."

Bain, her heart cried inwardly, wanting to reach out and take him by the hand. He was hurting so badly. "If I had only made her stay at the ranch . . ."

"No, Garnet. Her condition was only a matter of time. You see, her mother, my stepmother, had to be put away by the time she was twenty. Nattie never

350

knew her, never knew what horrible inheritance she had to look forward to. Doctor Rhengard said if I had only told her, prepared her, she might have been able to control . . . control . . ."

He stood, his face a gaunt mask of concealed emotions. "I'll be going now." He lifted his hand to her. "Miss Sinclair."

Not knowing what else to do, she placed her smaller fingers in his much larger ones, reveling in the remembered strength of his grasp. "Put your troubles in God's hand, Mr. Carson. He will provide."

"No, ma'am. I disagree. I believe God helps those who help themselves." He shook her hand, dropped it, and turned away. Before she could react, he walked toward the front door of the hotel.

He was leaving. She blinked in disbelief. All of the valid reasons she had for being angry with him—his deception, his callous treatment—melted like butter beneath the heat of her love.

"Bain!" Her call rang through the foyer, causing people to look at her appalled at her most improper outburst.

He stopped and squared his shoulders. For a moment she thought he would simply continue on his way without acknowledging her cry. Then he turned, his face a readable slate of sadness and determination. "Let me go, Garnet. Can't you see I'm not the proper man for you?"

She stood there, heart pounding, straining, bursting in two. She could see nothing, her eyes were awash with a flood of hot tears. When at last she blinked them away and found her voice to protest, he was gone, the foyer empty of his presence, her heart shattered like precious Dresden china into a thousand irreparable pieces.

Her mind was made up. He *was* right. She *would* let him go. The proper thing to do was to go home.

Chapter Twenty-One

April 1871
Gloucestershire, England

Garnet gathered the lace shawl about her shoulders. The English spring, even in the southern part of the country, did more to chill the bones than the worst of the California winter.

Stepping into the humid warmth of her father's glasshouse, she took a deep breath of remembrance. Though the botanical specimens weren't as magnificent, they were as close as she could come—to Bain.

Bain. Like a dowdy old maid she pined for love encountered and lost. Well, she was officially a spinster, wasn't she. Yesterday she had turned the ripe old age of twenty-two and marriage was not in her plans for the future. How long before the village children began to call her "crazy ol' Miss Sinclair"? She vowed then and there never to turn into one of those babbling old women whose every sentence began with the name of the man who had forsaken her. Bain this. Bain that.

At least not openly. What she did in the privacy of her mind was no one else's business.

"Garnet. Gar-r-r-net." She could hear Aunt Tilda's lilting shrill calling her from the back porch of

353

the cottage. Glancing about the building, she seriously considered hiding behind the soil bin to keep the older woman from finding her. But that would only put off the inevitable. Instead, she gathered up one of her aunt's favorite begonias, covered it with a burlap sack to protect it from the nip in the outside air during the short walk from the glasshouse to the cottage, and tucked her alibi for not being in the house under her arm. Then with a sigh of regret, she moved to the door and left the one place she felt completely alone and at ease.

"Coming, Aunt Tilda," she replied, knowing full well what waited for her within.

Once in the kitchens, she stationed the flowerpot on the table and threw off her shawl.

"He's here," her aunt told her, her faded blue eyes lighting on the fragile pink blossoms. "Oh, how beautiful." She plucked at a few shriveled leaves, removing them, then turned the pot this way and that seeking the best angle.

"Who's here?" Garnet asked, knowing full well whom her aunt meant.

"Why, the Squire, of course. Who else were you expecting?" She looked at Garnet out of the corner of her eyes before continuing her inspection of the begonia.

"Did you tell him I was indisposed?" Garnet moved to the dry sink and rolled up her sleeves.

"I told him that yesterday and the day before. I think, Garnet, you need be polite enough to at least receive your callers."

I don't want callers, she snipped inwardly. *Especially the Squire Trevelyan.* "I suppose," she conceded, dipping her dirt-caked hands in the pail of water and drying them on the bit of toweling hanging beside it for that purpose.

"He's in the front parlor."

"Oh, Aunt Tilda, you shouldn't've shown him

such deference."

"When a man of the Squire's stature comes to call, he deserves the best."

"Such stature," Garnet mumbled under her breath, "deserves a chair large enough to support it."

"What, dear?"

"Nothing, Aunt Tilda." Rolling down her sleeves, she ambled toward the front room that her aunt rarely used except on special occasions.

From the doorway she saw him, his large frame overfilling the delicate wicker settee her aunt set such pride in.

"Squire?"

His head swiveled from his contemplation of the mantel, the sofa groaning as he rose. "Ah, Miss Sinclair," he brayed, fumbling to lodge his monocle in his left eye. He reached out one beefy hand, but Garnet ignored it, settling in the chair farthest from him. If the Squire noticed her affront, he showed no outward sign. He sat back down, grinning without malice at her.

"Squire," she acknowledged. "To what do I owe this pleasure?" Vividly she remembered Mae Ching questioning her about protocol that demanded politeness where none was meant. She would have much rather asked him to get his fat bottom out of Aunt Tilda's favorite chair.

Taking a neatly folded handkerchief from one pocket of his coat, the Squire mopped at the sweat popping out on his ruddy face like beads escaping from their strand and bouncing across a floor. "I think you know why I'm here, Miss Sinclair." He looked at her like a hopeful puppy wanting only a pat on the head.

"Squire Trevelyan," she sighed. "I am very flattered by your offer, but I've told you, I have no desire to get married."

"Miss Sinclair, have you considered what benefits

matrimony would provide for you?"

She had heard them numerous times, from him, from Aunt Tilda, from the neighbor woman, from the rector as well.

"We've been through all of this before, sir. Why do you persist?"

"I think, Miss Sinclair, you'll find today is different." He grinned like a jackass as if he knew something she didn't.

Well, nothing he could say would change her mind, but she knew from experience no matter how she protested he would not be stopped from offering his rhetorical arguments again. "Squire, please." She raised her hands hoping beyond reason he might take the hint—this time.

He reached into his other pocket and pulled out a letter, waving it at her as if it held the magic potion capable of making her reconsider her position. "From your father. Would you care to read it?"

"Father?" Garnet couldn't help but sit up and take notice. Since that letter she'd received from him through Bain, she'd not heard a single word from him. There was even talk among the folk that he had been lost in the jungles of Siam. "What a shame," they whispered when they thought she couldn't hear. "She's been through so much, and now to lose her father too."

"They" had no earthly idea just what she had been through, and she was not about to enlighten them. Nor would she accept a proposal from a man she felt nothing for in order to squelch the gossip-mongers.

But read a letter from her father—she would do that gladly. She reached out to accept the unsealed envelope, her fingers shaking with excitement and relief. Her father was alive.

She didn't care if the Squire witnessed her eagerness. Let him gloat that he had been the one to bring her the good news. Her eyes quickly scanned

356

the familiar scrawl—addressed to the vexatious man sitting across from her.

"In case you might wonder, I've been trying to track the Reverend down for several months. His diocese sent out a search party—at my expense, I might tell you. With them they carried a letter from me addressing the situation here, and my solution."

His words skipped over her brain like flat stones skimming across the still waters of a pond, never once sinking in—not until her father suggested in a separate note to her to accept the Squire's offer of marriage if she wished to continue her missionary calling. "With the protection of a husband, and the Squire has expressed a willingness to accompany you, I would welcome you with open arms. Otherwise, daughter, I insist you stay home. Missionary work isn't proper for an unmarried female. I know that now, and I should have never given in to you in the first place. Look at the disaster that resulted.

"However, should you choose to refuse the Squire's most generous offer, I will keep my disappointment to myself, and you can rest assured that as soon as this assignment is completed, I'll join you. It shouldn't be more than a year or two."

Or three, Father. The pages of the letter drifted like autumn leaves to her lap. Her father return? Not likely. He was always saying each assignment was his last.

Garnet dug deep within her soul. For too long she'd been floating along, unwilling to acknowledge that—wanted or not—she had an entire life ahead of her. *Let's face it, old girl,* she chided herself, *no amount of dreaming and pining will make Bain Carson a part of your plans.* All she had left to build a future on was her teaching and missionary work.

She glanced up at the Squire's triumphant face. But marry him . . . ?

Refolding the letter, she stuffed it into its envelope,

handing it back to Trevelyan.

"Does this mean you'll accept my sincere offer, Miss Sinclair?"

"No, Master Trevelyan, it only means I'll think about it."

He snatched up her empty hand and pressed it fervently to his wet lips. "You won't be sorry. I'll make you happy. You'll have whatever you wish, I promise."

Gently she extracted her fingers from his. No one could possibly give her what she wanted, for all she desired was Bain Carson. But in all consciousness she would never agree to marry Trevelyan unless in her heart she could convince herself to accept him without regrets—without looking back. "Please, Squire."

"I understand perfectly, Miss Sinclair." He smiled confidently and stood. "I'll return at the end of the week for your answer. Does that give you long enough?"

She nodded, her eyes cast down, knowing she would talk to Aunt Tilda this evening, and her decision would be made by morning. The end of the week. *Pray God, bring time to a standstill. Let it remain Tuesday forever.*

The fare was simple as usual. Aunt Tilda chatty—as always. Garnet pushed her food around with her fork, listening, yet not really hearing anything the older woman had to say.

"The Squire seemed in fine form when he left this afternoon. Did your visit go well?" Aunt Tilda asked hopefully.

Garnet sighed, knowing the time came to talk about what was on her mind. "Well enough. He brought news of Father. He's alive and well and buried in his work deep in the jungles of Siam."

"Oh, Garnet, I'm so glad and relieved to know he is well." Tilda lowered her fork and reached out with sincerity, grasping Garnet's cold hand with her warm one. Then noting Garnet's solemn face, she asked, "Aren't you happy to hear from your father?"

"Of course, Aunt Tilda. It's just . . . just . . ."

"Just what, dear?"

"The Squire asked me again to marry him," she confessed.

"And did you accept?" Tilda resumed her eating, her question as matter-of-fact as if she was confident of a negative answer.

"I didn't refuse."

"Oh, child, this is wonderful." Her aunt's fork clattered against her plate, and she rose to her feet. "Your father will be so pleased to learn—"

"No, Aunt Tilda, I haven't made up my mind." Still toying with her food, Garnet hesitated to open up her heart to her aunt. Then her need to know how the older woman felt overrode her uncertainty. "Is it wrong to marry a man you don't love?" she blurted out.

"Ah, so that's what is troubling you so." Tilda resumed her seat and recaptured Garnet's icy fingers. "You know, dear, there is no right or wrong when it comes to the whys of marriage as long as you are honest with the man and with yourself. I married your Uncle Gerrod for love, and it was a good marriage. But when he died I accepted Lawrence for different reasons."

"Not love?"

"Not in the sense I think you mean it. Lawrence took good care of me, and I respected him as my spouse. That marriage was satisfying too, in a different way. What you have to decide is what you want out of the union. Then you must let the Squire know as well."

"But how can I in all consciousness take the

wedding vows: love, honor, and obey? I don't love him.''

"Just remember love can come in many guises besides romantic. Can you not at least harbor a soft spot for such a gentle man?"

She did feel a certain amount of compassion for the Squire. But was that enough?

Tilda squeezed her hand with confidence. "You're a level-headed girl. I'm sure you'll do what God deems proper."

Proper? Ah, yes, there was that damnable word that staked a total claim to her life. She was tired of always worrying about what others would think. How could a society condone a marriage for all of the wrong reasons, yet frown upon the natural passion between two people in love?

But what was important was what she thought about herself. Her own conscience told her that it was wrong to continue to yearn for a man who didn't want her. God wouldn't want her to waste her life regretting the many mistakes she'd made so far. He would want her to continue His work regardless. And the only way she could do that, it seemed, was to be properly married.

Her aunt was right. As long as she was honest with Trevelyan she did nothing wrong.

"I'll accept him," she said in a low, raspy whisper.

"Good gracious, dear, this is wonderful." Tilda leaped to her feet, her dinner forgotten for the rest of the evening. "When do you wish the nuptials to take place?"

"As soon as possible." Before she had a chance to change her mind, she added to herself.

"There's so much to do." Tilda's stubby hand splayed against her forehead. "My goodness, this will be the event of the season. Everyone in the shire will want to come. This will take months of planning. And there's the bishop to contact." Even though the

360

older woman complained, Garnet could tell she couldn't wait to get started.

"I don't want to prolong this for months," Garnet warned.

"Then weeks. At least give me a few weeks."

"Three weeks."

"Four, dear. You must give me at least four. There are the banns to be posted still and then—"

"All right, Aunt Tilda," she conceded. "Four weeks." She smiled, getting caught up in the older woman's exuberance. It was exciting if she didn't stop to think about whom she was marrying. When she did . . .

She couldn't have picked an easier man to get along with, she rationalized, trying to erase the beefy image of the Squire from her mind. Trevelyan would never deny her anything, most likely would agree with her every opinion. What more could an upstanding Victorian woman wish for than a husband who gave her an unusual amount of free rein?

Turning to the window to watch the waning sun slide beneath the windbreak of budding beech trees, she shook her head. Nothing, damn it. The passion she had shared with Bain had been anything but decent, he had said as much himself—he was not the proper man for her. He had been the one to send her away, hadn't he? she reminded herself.

In her heart she finally accepted that Bain would not come sweeping down from the heavens, and she could not go to him. Her only course of action was to marry the Squire Trevelyan and spend the rest of her days satisfied with serving those who needed her— just as she had planned before Bain Carson had waltzed into her ill-prepared life.

She moved away from the window, and as she did, the sun spread its dying rays across the sky, then disappeared. As it vanished, the vibrant golden ball claimed the tattered remnants of her youthful blush and innocence. Never again, she vowed, would she be any man's fool.

Halfway around the world, Bain stood on the quarterdeck of the *China Jewel* waiting for that same sun to peek over the eastern horizon. Hunched in his oilskin coat, he dreamed of warm California nights wrapped in the arms of Garnet Sinclair. His one regret. He had never made love to her as himself. Never heard her cry out *his* name in gratification.

All he could hear was her calling to him that last day in San Francisco, reaching out to him. Fool that he was, he had walked away—just as he had turned his back on anything that made him take a delving inner look at himself and see the real Bain Carson. Unless he found the shining knight of his illusions he didn't want to look, didn't want to face the fact that there was a negative side to his nature, a side Garnet Sinclair had plucked out of him with very little effort.

It was not love that made him act so irrationally, but the lack of it, he'd convinced himself long ago. Had he truly loved Garnet, he would have never deceived or hurt her the way he had.

But perhaps this gut-wrenching reckoning served a purpose after all. He *had* come to terms with his brother's failings, realizing that he himself was not all good, and Drew was not all bad either. Just like himself, his twin had struggled to make the best of life the only way he knew how. Unfortunately Drew had gambled and lost, not only love but his life as well.

Bain figured he should count himself lucky. He had walked away still breathing, given a second chance to learn from his errors, to recognize his strengths and weaknesses and not lose sight of himself—not to make the same mistakes again.

Oh, God, if only he had the chance to do it all over, he would welcome the opportunity.

"Garnet," he mumbled, willing to forfeit all this hard-earned inner knowledge to be able to relive those final moments together.

This time he wouldn't walk away. Damn the social standards that had said he must. Damn himself for not following his heart. Damn the seas that divided them.

He straightened. Damn his own stupidity! He had once told her God helps those to help themselves, but until now he'd never listened to his own sound philosophy.

If he wanted Garnet Sinclair, then by God, it was up to him to go and get her.

Chapter Twenty-Two

May 14, 1871

A more beautiful day for a wedding couldn't have existed. The apple and pear trees were in full bloom, and sprays of the pale pink and snow-white blossoms decorated the chapel of St. Michael's. Her aunt had even woven a sprig of the fragile pink blossoms into Garnet's ash-blonde hair.

"You look radiant," Tilda murmured, adjusting the Valenciennes lace veil that fell over Garnet's slim, satin-covered shoulders clear to the floor to compliment the long satin train of her dress. She was ever so careful not to step on the yards of material, as she didn't dare ruin such a beautiful dress. She had spent every penny she had in order to see to it her clothes befitted her new station as the Squire's wife.

The cream color of her wedding gown suited Garnet well, bringing out the yellow highlights in her hair. She had insisted on the off-white shade, though her aunt had tried to dissuade her from her decision. But she had taken the older woman's advice to heart. Honesty. She was no blushing virgin, and she had not withheld such vital information from her future husband. Though it had been painful for both of them, she had sat the Squire down and told him everything.

Well, almost everything. She had not revealed that love for Bain Carson still lingered in the deepest recesses of her heart, but she could tell by his expression he had guessed as much.

Squire Trevelyan was a good man—the best, Garnet convinced herself. He had stoically accepted her confession and assured her it didn't matter to him—not one bit. She would make him a good wife, she swore venomously. She would!

"It's such a shame your father couldn't have been here to give you away." Tilda's clucking tongue and shaking head intruded into Garnet's thoughts. "But your cousin Lawrence does look dashing, doesn't he?"

Tilda's obvious pride in her son from a loveless marriage touched Garnet deeply. Perhaps in time she would have children to fill the aching void in her heart. Little ones to love and hold in her empty arms. *Enough of this, Garnet Sinclair. There will be no regrets, remember?* "Yes, he cuts quite a figure, Aunt Tilda," she agreed, trying without success to bring discipline to her roving thoughts. *I wonder what the Squire would say if I named my firstborn Bain instead of after his father.*

Charles. Her groom's given name seemed unnatural to her tongue. Always she called him Squire, or Master Trevelyan, and she assumed she would go on calling him that just as he always called her Miss Sinclair. Once they were married she imagined he would address her as Mistress Trevelyan—even in the bedroom.

A most sobering thought. But no one else seemed to find such formality between husband and wife that unusual. It was the norm in polite society. Yet she couldn't picture Bain calling her Mrs. Carson as he stripped her of her clothing and . . .

Garnet paled. Why couldn't she exorcise the

366

damnable American from her life?

"Garnet, dear, are you all right?"

Tilda's concerned face focused before her.

"Of course, just last-minute butterflies, that's all," Garnet assured her. Oh God, was she making a big mistake? She glanced at her aunt. After all the work the woman had done, she didn't have the heart to tell her she wanted to call the whole affair off. She couldn't hurt Aunt Tilda so.

Her gaze slid to the mantel clock. Two hours. Only two more hours, and she would no longer be her own person but the wife of a man she didn't love.

The *China Jewel* slipped into the Gloucester harbor without fanfare. From his customary place on the quarterdeck Bain glanced around the port, surprised.

"Damn," he muttered. "The city's bigger than I imagined." It wouldn't be easy to locate Garnet, not easy at all. But he'd come this far, he wasn't going to turn back now, not until he found her, faced her, and told her how he felt.

How many churches could there be? he wondered. Somewhere in one of them, somebody had to know of Garnet Sinclair. He would just have to start looking.

The moment the lines were secured and the ship anchored at the pier, Bain rushed forward eager to begin his quest.

"What do you want us to do, Captain?"

He turned to his first mate and waved an impatient hand. "Take leave, but you tell the men the first one caught in a brawl will be left behind. Understood?"

"Aye, sir." Enoch grinned. "You won't be catchin' us, sir."

Bain figured by tomorrow half his crew would be in the hands of local magistrates, and he would have to bail them out. He sighed. Such was the fate of all ship captains, one reason he cared so little for the life at sea—but it had been a better alternative than remaining at the ranch, where memories and smells of Garnet lingered. Well, at least he would know exactly where to find his men, which is more than he could say of locating Garnet.

Once he left the docking area, oddly enough he found the streets empty. Few carriages or pedestrians moved about. Perhaps today was some British holiday he knew nothing about. He strolled on a few more blocks until he came to the district crowded with hostelries and liveries. Walking into the first one that looked decent and clean, the New Inn, he inquired after a room and directions to a church.

"A church, gov'ner? Which one?"

Bain shrugged, and the proprietor gave him a strange look as if to say, "Crazy Yank," but he took Bain's money and gave him a key and mumbled directions to St. Michael's.

As Bain turned to go, the man spoke again. "But you won't be wantin' to go there today."

"Why not, today some kind of holiday?"

"Better than a 'oliday. The Squire Trevelyan be gittin' married there today. I'd be there meself if my clerk 'adn't taken ill last night. But if you're into a little sightseein', gov'ner, you can't do better than St. Michael's Cathedral."

Bain frowned. A wedding of the local gentry. Maybe that was why the streets were so empty. "I'm not sightseeing, sir. In fact, I'm looking for a church maybe not so auspicious as a cathedral." Somehow he pictured Garnet in a more pastoral environment. "Someplace simpler, where one might locate a missionary's daughter," Bain explained.

"Funny you should mention a missionary's daughter. It seems the Squire be marryin' one. A right pretty one at that. Reverend Sinclair's daughter, though 'e not be 'ere to give her away."

368

"Garnet?" Bain blinked with surprise. Of all the difficulties he'd foreseen he'd never considered she might be getting married. Disbelief and alarm pounded like steel-shod horses hooves in his head. "How soon's the wedding?" *Please don't say it's already in progress.*

The innkeeper took out his pocket watch and flipped the top open to stare at the timepiece. He was so painstakingly slow Bain wanted to reach out and shake him. "Noon, gov'ner, less than an hour the ceremony should begin," the man finally announced with a closing click of the watch lid.

A sigh of immediate relief coursed through Bain. "How fast can I get to the cathedral?" he demanded.

"By carriage, say 'alf an hour, by foot an hour if y'er quick about it. And seein' 'ow little traffic there is, you might make it."

"Then call me a carriage."

"Sorry, gov. Ain't no carriages to be 'ad in all of Gloucester, not today. They've all be 'ired out for the weddin'."

"Damn." Bain turned, determined to run the entire way if he had to.

"But I 'ave got one 'orse 'ose mate is down. 'E's a high-stepper, mind you, but you can 'ave 'im if you can ride."

"I can ride," Bain assured him, angling toward the door.

"Tell O'Mallay I said you can 'ave the bobtail 'ackney."

Bain tore out of the inn and down the steps, racing toward the stables in the back. What would he do if he didn't get there in time? Jesus! What would he do if he did? Pictures of a dashing Englishman having swept Garnet off her feet and down the aisle refused to be dislodged from his active imagination. What if Garnet didn't want him? What if she didn't even remember who he was?

369

How could she forget? They had shared too much. Too much for him to turn his back now. At the very least, he had to learn what the future held for her.

O'Mallay turned out to be a crotchety old Irishman who found Bain's brisk manners not to his liking. Not at all. "The bobtail, ya say?" His bushy brows furled. "Think I better check with Master Hanson to be sure."

Bain grabbed the old groom by the collar and yanked him back around. "Get the horse, or I'll get him for myself."

"All right, gov. No need to get rude about it." Mumbling protests to himself, the hostler brought out a compact chestnut. Speaking softly, he bridled the horse with a complicated headstall that had two sets of reins.

Bain frowned. The gear was nothing like he had ever seen before, but that was not about to stop him.

However, when the old man tossed a bit of leather that Bain assumed was supposed to be a saddle upon the animal's broad back, he knew he wasn't about to tackle such a strange riding apparatus. He was in too much of a hurry.

"Move aside, old man." He jerked the saddle from the horse and tossed it to the side. Then he leaped upon the animal's bare back and gathered the reins in one hand as he was accustomed to doing. The horse refused to turn.

"Two hands, Yank," the groom said with a snicker. "This ain't no Wild West pony, ya know." He grabbed the reins on each side of the horse's head to demonstrate.

"Two hands," Bain muttered, still wondering why in the hell there were four reins. But who was he to question English logic, even though it had no rhyme or reason that he could see?

Yet to the horse it must have made sense, for they took off down the street, Bain feeling like a fool atop the high-stepping hackney.

Soon enough he found the rhythm, and recalling the innkeeper's directions, he rounded a corner, reciting over and over in his mind every turn he must make. There was no time for mistakes. He didn't dare take the wrong street.

What he didn't know was what he would do once he reached the church. Somehow he had to convince Garnet to change her mind about marrying this Squire of hers. He glanced down at the rough jeans and checkered shirt he wore. What a bumpkin he would look next to the debonair Englishman. But still he rode on, pushing such uncertainties from his mind. There was only his gut-wrenching love for Garnet Sinclair that mattered to him any longer.

To his relief he began to notice carriages parked along the street curbs. Around a last curve—and there it was. St. Michael's, swathed in age-old splendor from the stone steps leading up to the massive oak doors to the soaring, spiral-topped bell towers several stories above. A crowd packed the stairway from doors to street. Apparently there was not room enough inside for all of the spectators. Bain brought the horse to a rearing halt to assess the situation.

In the distance he caught the peals of an ancient clock. He counted twelve strokes. Then he heard the first chords of the wedding march being struck on the cathedral organ. On foot he wouldn't get within a hundred yards of the door. Damn it, he couldn't stop a wedding if he couldn't make himself heard.

There was only one thing he could do. Clamping his jaws together in resolution, he dug his heels into the tender belly of his mount. "Come on, boy. Even Englishmen aren't fool enough to stand in the path of a determined horse." Then he shouted, "Make way, I'm coming through."

Amidst protests and gasps of shock a passage cleared as Bain worked the balking high-stepper up

371

tread and riser to the church doors—one step at a time. The horse slipped once, but Bain pushed on, refusing to allow the animal its head.

God forgive him. He was about to break every rule of protocol he'd ever believed in. Even his brother, Drew, would have had second thoughts before doing what he planned to do.

Behind the safety of her Valenciennes lace veil, Garnet hid her fears and doubts. She smiled at Cousin Lawrence as he led her the last few steps to the altar and placed her kid-gloved hand in the Squire's. Then he moved to sit beside his mother, careful not to step on Garnet's long satin train. As soon as her cousin was seated, she turned her attention to her groom.

Trevelyan beamed at her, squeezed her stiff fingers, and whispered reassuringly, "Not to worry, Miss Sinclair. You are a vision."

Garnet smiled wanly, but found she couldn't look at the Squire. Instead she stared at her fingers entwined in his. A sob caught in her throat and hung there like a chicken bone refusing to be dislodged. *Oh, God, please let me get through this without bringing shame to me and my family*, she pleaded. Beneath her skirts her legs trembled and twitched, wanting to turn and escape while there was still time. Trevelyan's grip tightened, preventing her from following through.

Run, her feet directed.

I dare not, her conscience debated. *What would Aunt Tilda do? And the bishop?* Her gaze climbed to the clergyman opening his prayer book to begin the ceremony. Having a change of heart was bad enough, but doing something about it was unthinkable.

As if on cue the bishop, come especially to Gloucester to preside over the Squire's nuptials,

372

cleared his throat and began intoning the familiar ritual.

The cold ball of apprehension grew a hundredfold in her middle. *I can't do this.* Turning to the only avenue open to her, Garnet closed her eyes and prayed for divine intervention. *Please, don't make me go through with this.*

"Make way, I said!"

She heard the shout from the street below, and turned her head to dart a look over her shoulder. Though several of the seated guests were craning to see what the commotion was, she could make out nothing. The Squire squeezed her hand, reminding her that protocol demanded that she focus her attention on the ceremony, not the vulgar goings-on in the street.

The bishop droned on, but the familiar words that should have been so important, ones she had heard her father recite many times during her life, were mere mutterings that made no sense to her.

Yet the sounds coming from outside were crystal clear. A woman's squealing protest. The snorting response of a horse. A clear curse from a very proper English gentleman. An audible gasp from the crowd behind her. Yet the bishop continued, and propriety forced her to show no outward reaction to what was taking place behind them.

"If anyone can show just cause why this man and this woman should not be joined in holy matrimony, speak now or forever hold your peace."

The response? Garnet could swear she caught the resounding clatter of shod hooves in the vestibule leading into the central nave of the church.

"Continue, your lordship," the Squire hissed, beads of perspiration popping out on his round face.

Garnet glanced at her intended and saw the anxiety in his monocled gaze. He had heard the hoofbeats too, and feared them. Rebellion welled inside of her. Why was it so important to pretend nothing out of the ordinary was going on when apparently it was?

"No," she protested so loudly, the murmuring audience silenced.

She pulled her trapped hand from Trevelyan's. Even if she was to be denied her happiness all for the sake of propriety, she was not to be denied her curiosity. Spinning about, she carelessly trod upon her long train, ignoring the footprint she left. Through the lace of her veil, she saw a flash of prancing horseflesh moving toward her, down the aisle she had trod moments before on her cousin's arm. Her gaze moved upward, and caught the blue of jeans and a familiar checkered shirt.

Bain? With shaking fingers she tossed the veil back revealing her face. Had God truly answered her prayers? Then seeing him sitting atop his horse in the middle of the cathedral, she remembered her father's age-old warning to be careful of what she asked of God. Was this what she really wanted? Was she willing to break all the rules of society for the love of a man?

"Garnet."

Both the Squire and Bain called her name at the same time. She glanced back at Trevelyan, who represented all that society said she should be, and saw the pain in his gentle gaze. The Squire had been nothing but kind and caring, wanting only to give her whatever her heart desired. If she hurt him she must be willing to sacrifice a basic part of herself— the proper part. But if she didn't . . .

Her head swiveled and she found Bain. Proud and tall, with a touch of arrogance, he straddled that horse as if he had every right to be there in St. Michael's cathedral. He made no move toward her, just sat there waiting for her to make up her mind. Vividly she recalled the deception, the pain he had

374

caused her, but she couldn't deny she loved him—all of him, the good with the bad.

Then her gaze slid to the spectators. They watched her with eager anticipation, straining forward, also waiting for her to make her decision. To choose between her heart and everything she'd been taught since childhood about right and wrong.

The proper thing to do, of course, was to turn back to the Squire and go through with her promise to marry him. But was that the right choice—right for her? If she chose love, she would have to forget what the dictates of society demanded of her.

She stood there in indecision. Then she saw her aunt sitting in the audience in her seat on the front row. *Follow your heart, child,* her gentle blue gaze urged, and Garnet knew what she must do.

Her breath rushing in and out, she tore her gaze from Bain to look back at Trevelyan. "I'm sorry, Charles," she mouthed.

And though it pained him, the gallant Englishman shrugged and waved her on. With a sad smile he moved toward the side door.

Kicking at the yards of satin that trailed her every move, she rushed toward Bain, knowing that the bridge of propriety crumbled in the wake of her footsteps. There was no turning back now. Yet strangely enough, for the first time in her life she felt freed, and she couldn't stop the bubble of joy that burst from her throat.

"Bain," she cried, throwing out her arms as she picked up speed.

Urging his mount forward with his knees, Bain approached her too. Halfway down the aisle they met, Garnet reaching for him. He bent, scooped her up in front of him, dropping her in the familiar crook of his arms. Her train draped across the horse and trailed several feet on the floor. She reached down and wound its length about her arm in total disregard of good manners.

Then a belated shyness engulfed her. "What do we do now?" she asked in a breathlessly small, uncertain voice.

"Now?" Bain's deep, melodic laughter rolled over her. "What do you suggest?"

"I *am* dressed for a wedding," she hinted.

"I would say so, and dressed to the gills." He placed a loving kiss on the ash-blonde curls peeking out from the rim of the veil.

"It would be such a shame to let this gown and"— her arm made a wide sweep—"and all these witnesses go to waste."

"My ever-so-proper Miss Sinclair, are you by chance asking me to marry you?" One brow lifted in mock disbelief.

The horse pranced, turning its rump toward a heavyset woman sitting on the aisle. Garnet couldn't suppress a spurt of laughter as the most proper woman scrambled over the man sitting next to her before the animal did something most improper. It seemed she was no different than anyone else. Everyone had their price for breaking the rules of polite society.

"Yes, I suppose I am."

"Then, ma'am," he drawled in that lazy way she found so endearing, "I'll just have to accept." He tapped the horse with his heels and sent it moving forward, toward the altar and the bishop who stood there, his mouth agape, in utter shock.

All Garnet could think was that she had gone down the aisle in a most unique way, and most of all she had no regrets. This would be a day she would remember for all eternity.

Once they reached the chancel rail, Bain dismounted and helped Garnet down to stand beside him. "I think, sir, you were about to perform a wedding," Bain informed the still slack-mouthed clergyman.

"Yes, well, I suppose." His face was beet red, and probably for the first time in his clerical life he was at a loss for words.

"Then I suggest you continue."

The bishop stammered a protest, then he snapped his jaws shut when he saw the authoritative look on Bain's face.

"If anyone sees reasons why *this* man and this woman shouldn't be joined in holy matrimony, speak now or forever hold your peace."

An unearthly silence reverberated about the church. Garnet suspected everyone, including the bishop, expected the Squire to step forward, but she had seen him leave, knew he had no intention of interfering. God bless him. She hoped that someday he found a woman truly worthy of his kind nature.

The sound of Bain's resonant "I do" caught her attention. Then the bishop was asking her if she promised to love, honor, and obey.

"I do. Truly, I do," she replied emphatically, looking up at Bain's smiling face.

Before the bishop could pronounce them man and wife, Bain's lips captured hers in a searing kiss. "I love you, Garnet. Only God knows how much," he vowed against the soft contours of her eager mouth.

"And I love you. All of you. The rakehell and the redeemer. The bad as much as the good. Don't you ever change on me, you hear?"

"Not likely. I think I've thoroughly enjoyed myself today."

The bishop harrumphed at them, and they both looked up at the interruption. "If you're quite through," the man said.

They both nodded.

"Then I suspect I best pronounce you man and

wife as fast as I can. I suppose there is no need for me to say you can kiss the bride.''

''No, sir,'' Bain said, again kissing her swift and hard. Then he swept her up and deposited her on the back of the hackney, and pulled himself up behind her. As he urged the horse back down the aisle and down the steps, Garnet heard the many diversified comments. From ''how romantic'' to ''how vulgar'' she welcomed them all. Yes, it was romantic and it was vulgar by these people's humdrum standards, but it was uniquely Bain. And she was proud to claim he had done it all for her.

Once they reached the streets, he set the horse to high-stepping. An hour later they stopped in front of an inn. From the entrance emerged a puffing innkeeper, his hands raised in an urgent signal to stop.

''You don't plan on ridin' that 'orse into me common room, do ya?''

Healthy laughter erupted from Bain. ''News travels fast in Londontown,'' he said as if reciting a children's ditty.

''Aye, and in Gloucester as well, gov'ner,'' the innkeeper added with a nervous laugh.

Bain jumped down, gathered Garnet into his arms, and swung her down. ''I tell you what, Mr. Hanson. I'll make you a Yankee deal.''

The man looked at him in utter confusion. ''A deal?''

''Yes. I won't ride that horse into your inn if you'll see to it that my wife and I have three solid days uninterrupted.''

Garnet blushed at his blatant insinuations.

The innkeeper snickered in delight. ''Aye, gov'ner, you're on. In fact, since I'm sure the locals will fill me tavern in hopes of catchin' a glimpse of the newlyweds, I'll even throw in the Royal suite as part

378

of the bargain."

Without further adieu Bain carried her over the hreshold and up the stairs to the grandest room in he inn. Garnet hardly expected that royalty would choose to stay there, but to her it was grandiose, truly he haven for a princess.

Once inside, Bain slammed the door shut with his foot and dropped the key on the floor forgotten. However, he lay her gently on bed, her long train spilling over the windowpane coverlet and across the floor.

"My wife," he said almost as if it were a miracle.

"Does that please you, my love?" Garnet asked shyly, blushing from the intensity of his stare.

"How could it not?" he replied, taking up her hand and pressing it against his lips. "You are so kind and caring and beautiful. Everyone misses you back home, you know."

Home? She closed her eyes and conjured up a picture of Rancho Carmelo. Her heart swelled with joy. They were her family now, each and every one of them.

And she hadn't forgotten the sad, lonely faces of the Chinese girls she had seen in San Francisco. She was going back there now. She could fulfill her desire to help the slaves of Chinatown escape their cruel masters. She looked at Bain from the corner of her eyes, and wondered what his reaction would be to her plans. In her heart she knew he would support her in every way that he could. He was that kind of a man. "I miss all of them too, terribly. How are they?"

"Well, Mae Ching is talking up a storm now. It's impossible to keep her mouth closed long enough to reply. And the words she uses." He rolled his eyes. "Mr. Webster could hire her as a consultant."

Garnet laughed. "I told you with practice and love she would do well. And what of Choie Seem?" She leaned forward eager to learn how her friend had fared.

"Married, you know. The latest report is that she and Mateo are expecting their first child."

"Choie Seem, having a baby?" Garnet clapped and squealed with delight. Then she brought her hands down into her lap and tempered her joy. "And Nattie?" she asked quietly.

A long silence prevailed.

Then at last Bain spoke. "Doing much better. The doctors sent her home recently." He looked down at her, and she could read the hope residing in his gray eyes. "They think with time she can fully recover, but she needs you, Garnet—just as I need you."

"Oh, Bain," she cried, holding out her empty arms to him.

Gladly he filled them, pulling her body against his own with such an intensity she thought for sure he would never let her go. When at last he released her, it was to reach down and remove the wedding veil from her hair. Lifting a handful of her ash-blonde tresses, he buried his face in their silky warmth. Taking a deep breath, he moaned, the sound one of intense relief.

Then he kissed her. Gentle, sweet, and, oh, so achingly potent.

This was Bain she was kissing. Bain. As if someone had released her heart with a long-lost key, she reveled in the freedom of his love.

Her arms curled about his neck, her fingers toying with the thick waves of dark, sun-kissed hair that lapped at her hand, warm and silky.

His hand discovered the tiny clasps on the back of her gown, and his fingers tore at them as if he couldn't unfasten them fast enough.

She touched his arm in gentle chiding. "We have three uninterrupted days, remember?"

He growled deep in his throat. "I know, but I don't want to waste one moment of them with something as extraneous as clothing."

She giggled. "Do you plan for us to stay naked for three whole days?"

"And what's wrong with that?" he demanded. "After what we've done so far today, it doesn't sound all that bad." He stripped the gown from her shoulders, revealing the virgin lace of her corset cover. He frowned, reaching out to trace the gentle swells of her breast above the eyelets. "Would it really bother you to be naked with me for three days?"

"Oh, no," she cried. And to show him how sincere she was, she scrambled from the bed, allowed the gown to drop to the floor, and began removing the rest of her clothing.

Sprawled on the bed, he watched her, fascinated as she slowly unveiled, inch by tortuous inch, her lush, womanly body.

"Garnet," he said in a quiet whisper when she stood before him unabashed. He moved to stand next to her, and took her in his arms with such care she might have been made of the finest Dresden china. "Pequeña joya," he declared, taking her breasts into his hands.

How warm his flesh was cupping hers. How exciting his thumbs brushing against the rosy buds that sprang to life merely from his touch. Bending her backward, he took one of the hardened nodules into his mouth, sucking and lapping until the coil of desire in the very core of her felt as if it would surely burst.

Her knees willingly collapsed when his hand touched the back of them, lifting her up long enough to return her to the bed. Their marriage bed. Where she and *Bain* would be truly united for the first time, man and woman, husband and wife, virgin in their hearts until this moment.

At last she understood his eagerness to do away with clothing. She ripped at the buttons of his shirt, the fasteners of his pants, and he never reminded her that she had been the one to speak of patience earlier. Placing her on her knees on the bed before him, he just stood quietly as she stripped him of his worldly assets until there was only their bodies to adore.

She kissed him reverently in the hollow of his breastbone, then moved lower to taste the dip of his navel, and found the more she discovered of him the more aroused she became. In awe she flicked her tongue over his manhood, and felt him tremble just as she had done earlier when he had feasted upon her womanly flesh.

With a groan he took her by the shoulders and guided her away. "I think you were right, love. No need to rush. We have three glorious days."

He lay her on her back and joined her on the bed. Pulling her to his side, he took a lock of her hair and curled it about his finger. "Shall we see who has the most patience?"

She heard the challenge in his voice and gladly took up the gauntlet. "No question about it, Bain. I do."

"How can you be so sure?" He chuckled, the devilment in his eyes sparkling. "Let's say . . . the one with the least amount of self-control has to wait on the winner hand and foot for twenty-four hours."

Remembering how easily aroused he had been, she smiled back confidently with a challenge of her own. "I'll win, you know. Let's make it forty-eight hours." She stretched out her hand to seal the bet.

He gladly accepted her hand and brought it to his mouth, slowly sucking on each finger until she began to tremble. "Want to call the bet off?"

She gathered together her scattered senses and leaned forward, taking her tongue and dipping it

nto his ear. Goose bumps gathered on his arm
eneath her fingers. "Do you want to call it off?"

"No way!" Grabbing her by the waist he forced her
o her back. First he trailed a finger between her
reasts, then settled on one nipple, kneading,
troking, igniting the fire within her with his expert
ouch. She gasped.

But she could do that too. She felt his nipple
arden against her palm as she mimicked his
novements.

Then his hand moved lower, tracing the swell of
er belly, and lower, dipping into her womanly
lepths. Like a moth lured by the flickering light she
elt herself growing weaker, wanting nothing more
han to give in to his challenge.

Instead she slid her hand down his lean stomach to
ncircle his manly flesh. Slowly she stroked, fighting
er own feeling of drowning in the lush pool of
lesire. At first he seemed insensitive, much stronger-
villed than she, then he groaned, his free hand
noving down to direct her movements. Then just as
he was sure she would win, waves of need washed
ver her, pulling her down like eddies into a
vhirling vortex of desire.

"Oh, Bain," she breathed, unable to resist his touch
nother moment. Her hand moved around his body
o clutch at the firm muscles of his hips. She wanted
nim, now . . . now.

Then he was filling her, driving her before him up
oward the cliff of fulfillment one tortuous step at a
ime. When at last she hung over the edge, she took
he plunge, no longer caring if she won or lost their
bet, needing only to know the wonder of his
ovemaking.

Floating. Floating. Expanding. Shattering with
he sparks of a million pinpoints of light. Then a
eeling of utter bliss engulfed her.

Seconds later—or had it been hours?—she felt his

moist lips against her ear. "Garnet?"

"Did I lose?" she murmured against the column of his strong neck.

His chuckle was warm against her throat. "Lose? I think not, my beautiful China jewel. As long as we have each other, we will always come up winners."